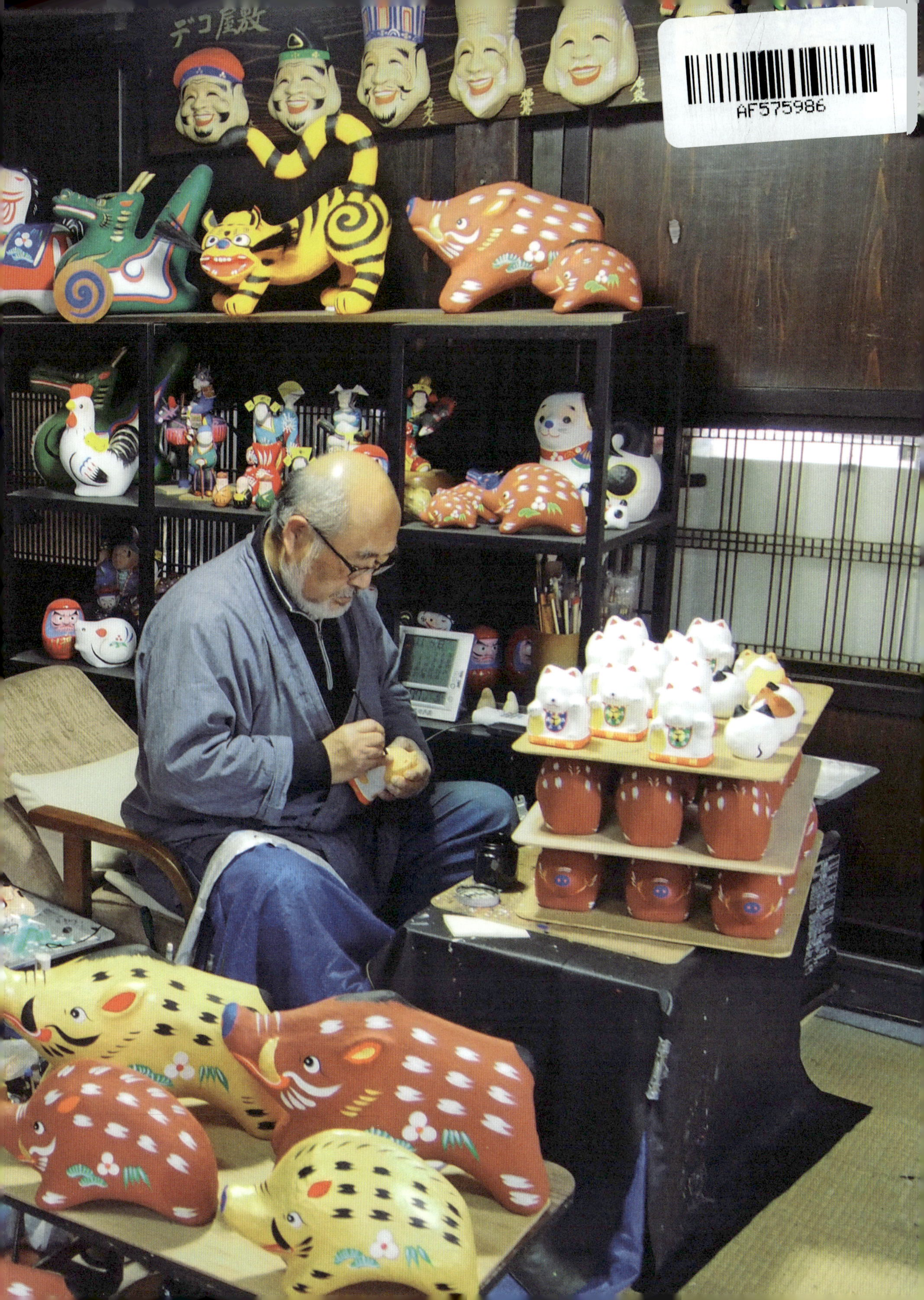
デコ屋敷

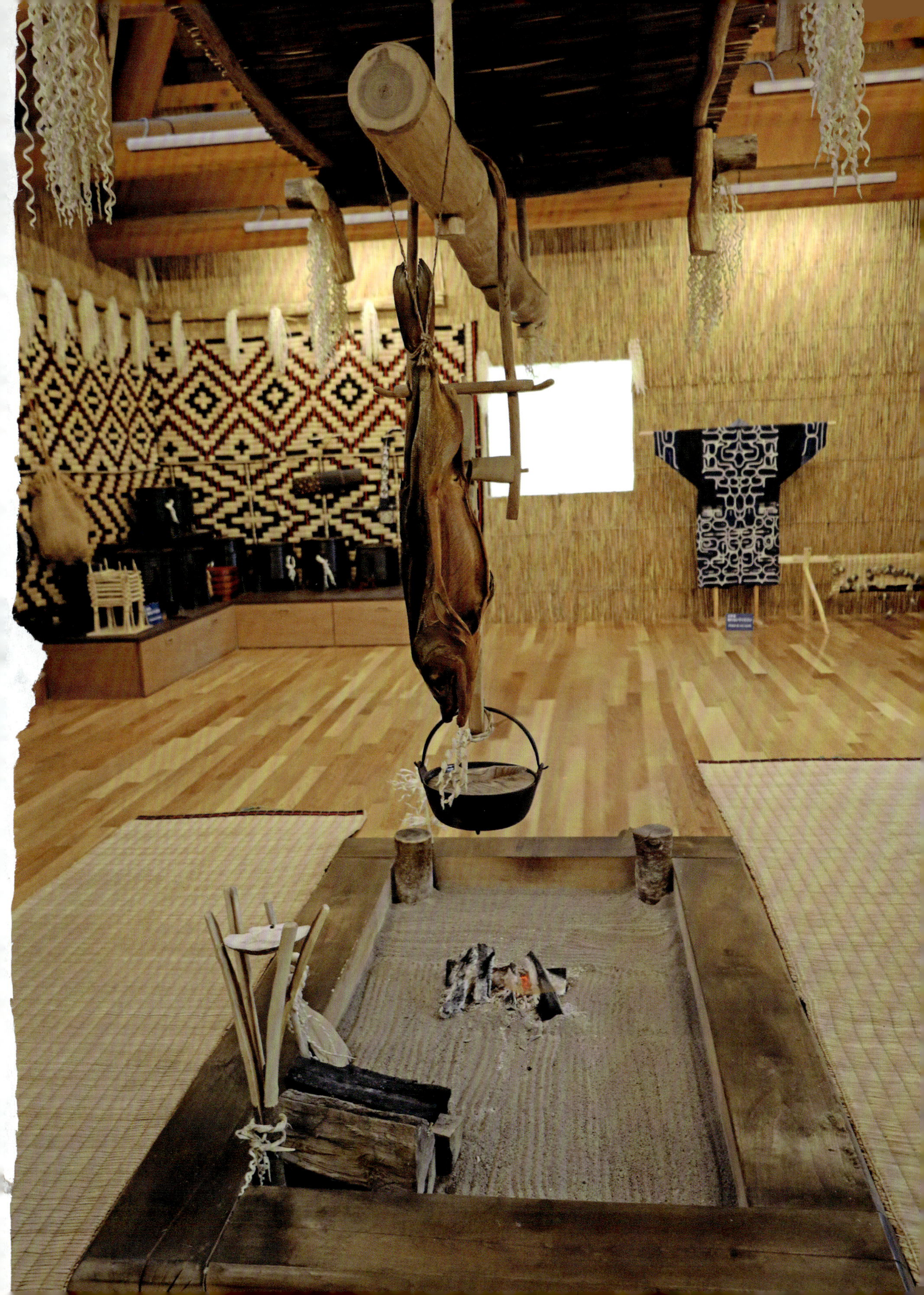

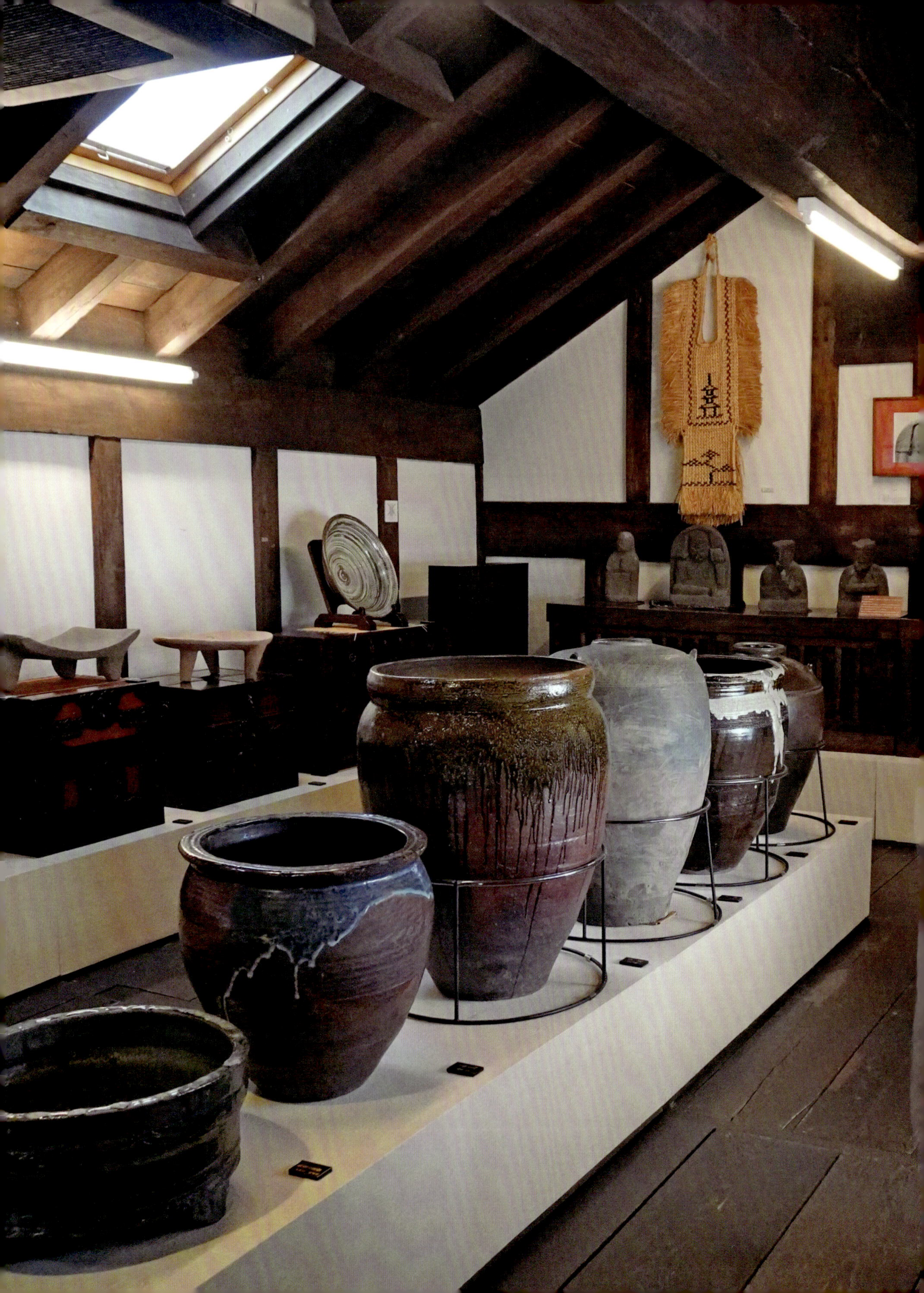

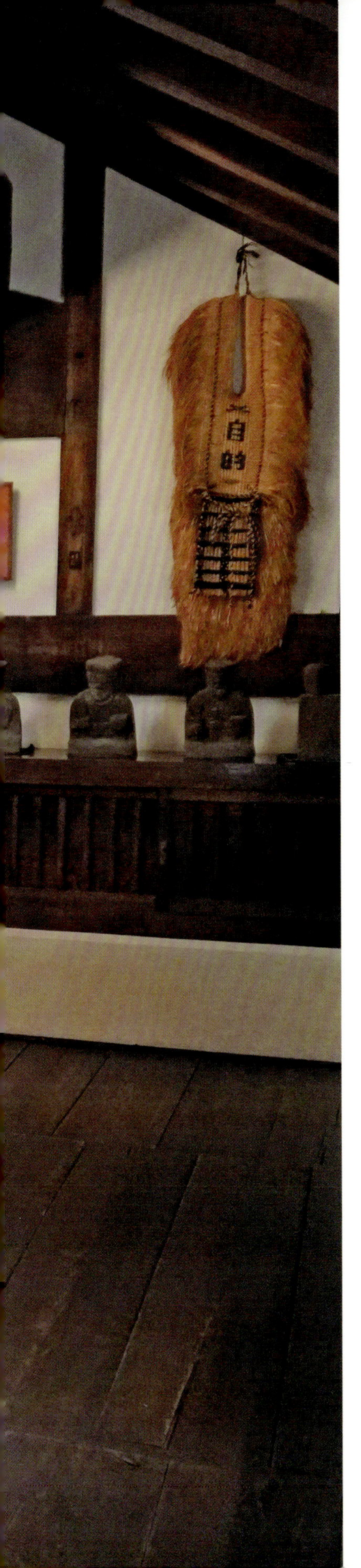

JAPANESE MINGEI FOLK CRAFTS

An Illustrated Guide to the Folk Arts and Artisans of Japan

MANAMI OKAZAKI

TUTTLE Publishing

Tokyo | Rutland, Vermont | Singapore

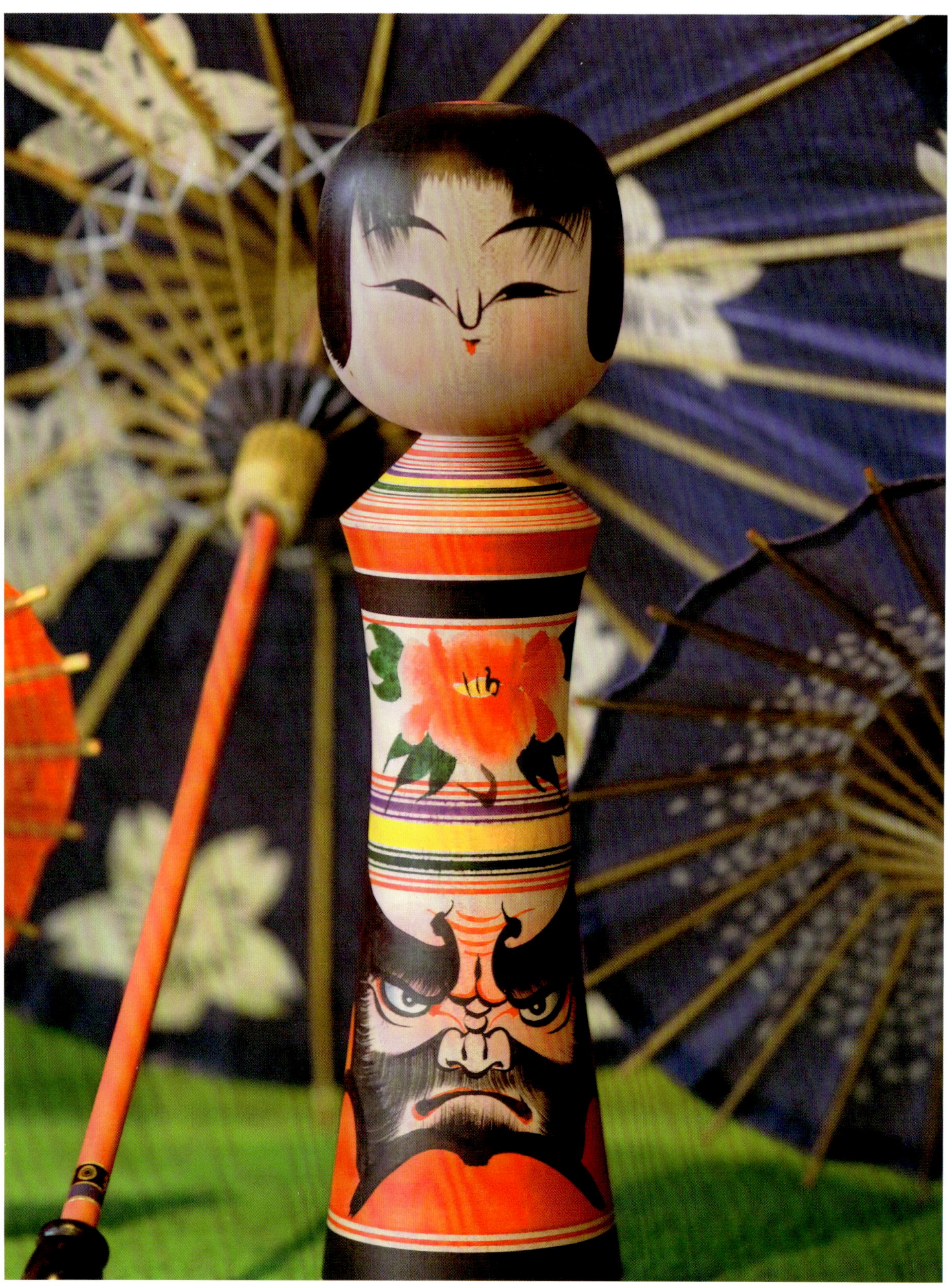

Contents

Folk Crafts to Calm the Soul

Folk crafts are practical items made by artisans and imbued with a simple and rustic aesthetic that is calming to the soul. Fans of folk craft are attracted to the beauty of the mundane and even though folk-craft pieces are made with utility in mind, they reflect modern and minimalist design sensibilities that espouse a restrained, understated beauty. Compared to commercial items that are made in bulk in a factory setting, folk crafts are made with skilled hands. They signify an artisanal life characterized by perseverance, dedication and a reverence for the process rather than just the product. As such, the narrative and backstory reflected in the work has a beauty in itself. Unlike industrial production where the process might be exploitative in nature, folk craft is seen to represent honest, humble labor.

Historically, there is a close relationship between folk craft and nature. From the ancient pottery kilns of Tachikui in Hyogo Prefecture, to the clay folk dolls of Yonezawa and the kokeshi doll artisans of Naruko Onsen in the Tohoku region, folk crafts tend to be made with materials that are locally accessible. Places that are famous for pottery flourished where they did due to the particular qualities of the local soil. Carvers of the *otaka poppo* talismanic hawks featured on page 132 use wood from the *koshiabura* tree that grows locally in Yamagata Prefecture. Folk crafts that make use of hemp (see page 40) grown in Tochigi Prefecture have existed for over four hundred years. So it can be said that the aesthetic characteristics of a particular folk craft are determined by the materials they are made from, which are connected to the surrounding environment and climate.

Many folk crafts made in the northern regions of Japan are traditionally produced by farmers, so there is also an intrinsic link between agriculture, seasonality and folk crafts. Prefectures such as Aomori, Akita and Yamagata are blanketed under several feet of snow every year, when farmers are forced to rest. Many use this farming downtime to work on crafts such as papier-mâché dolls, reinforcement stitching—a type of embroidery used to strengthen cloth—and woodworking. Yuji Sakai, the warazaiku straw craft artisan featured on page 144, explains: "In the past, all rice farmers were also straw artisans. If you were born into a farm and you couldn't do warazaiku you couldn't make rice bales either. In the past being a rice farmer equated to also being a warazaiku artisan."

Folk craft is also related to the customs of a locality. Folk toys are talismanic and often served as protective amulets. Before Western medicine was the norm and healthcare was subsidized, talismans were used to protect from bad health and other evils. There were good-luck charms to ask for wealth, happiness and love. The iconic and ubiquitous *maneki-neko* beckoning cats that flourished from the seventeenth century onward are thought to attract luck in the form of customers and business prosperity as well as to protect against calamities. Other cat talismans were used by farming homesteads as replacements for real cats, as a symbolic way to repel mice.

The notion of *mingei* (which literally means

Facing page Historically there is a close relationship between folk craft and nature. Traditional maiwai fishermen's coats are decorated with celebratory motifs and presented to fishermen when there has been a good catch.

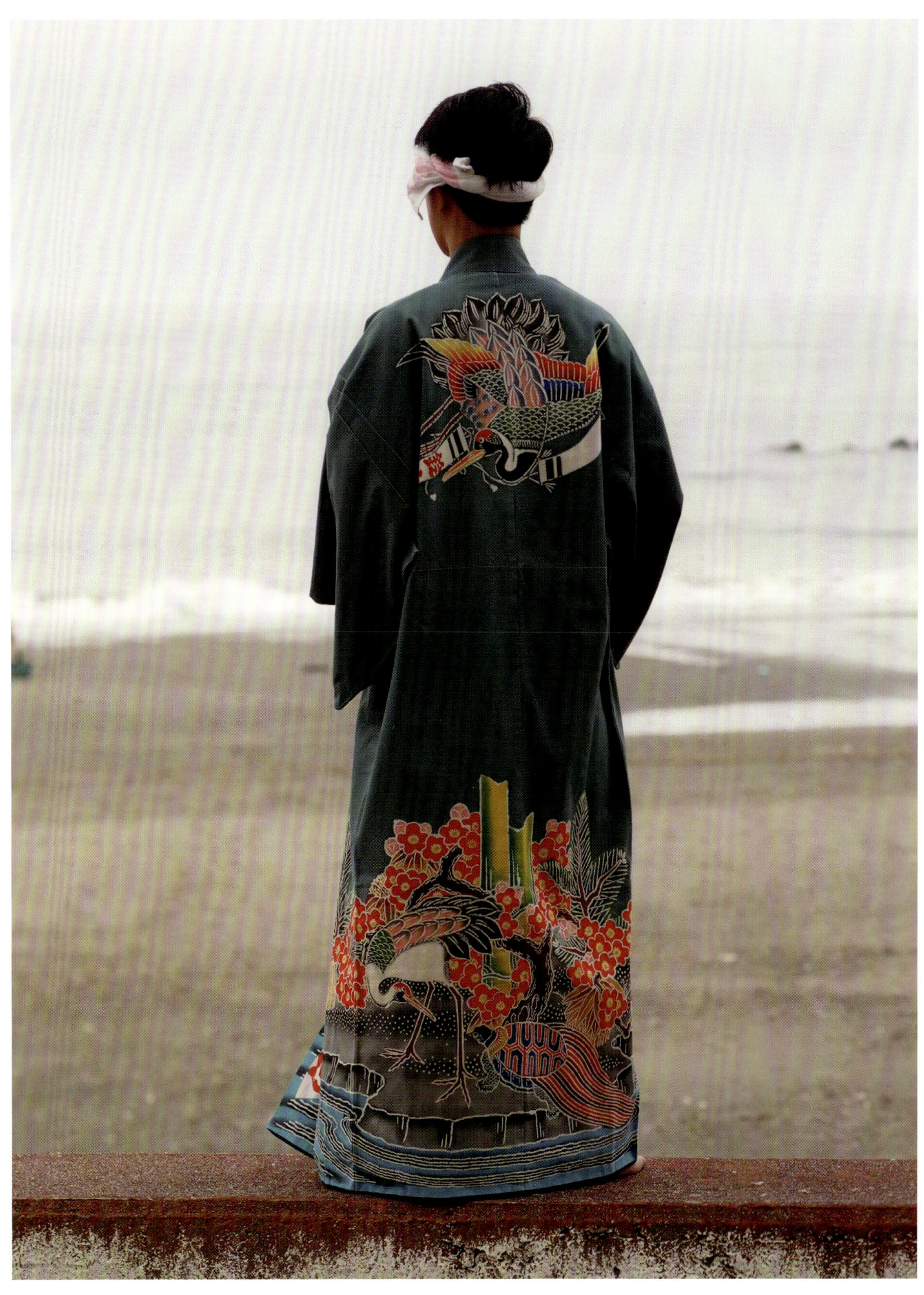

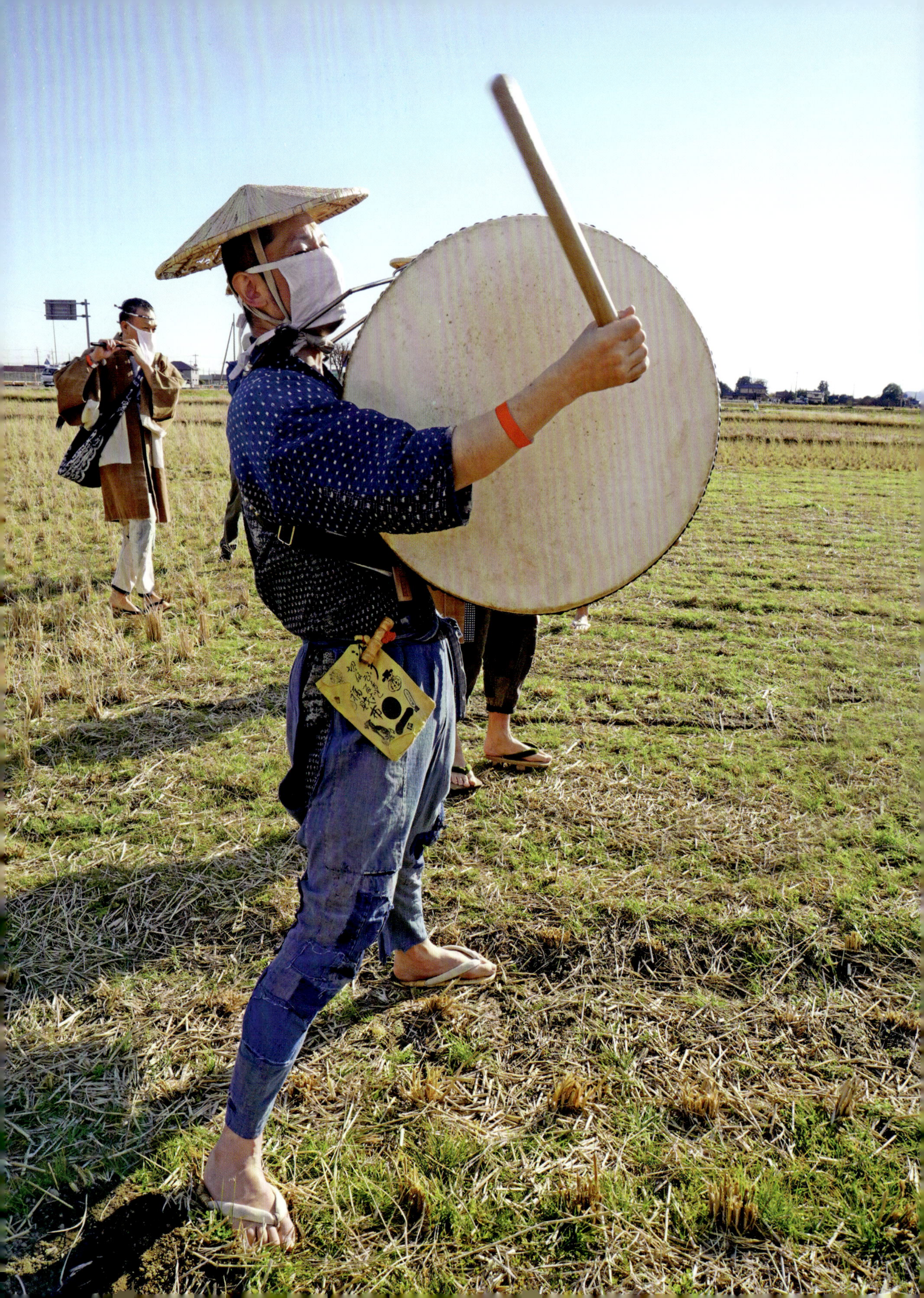

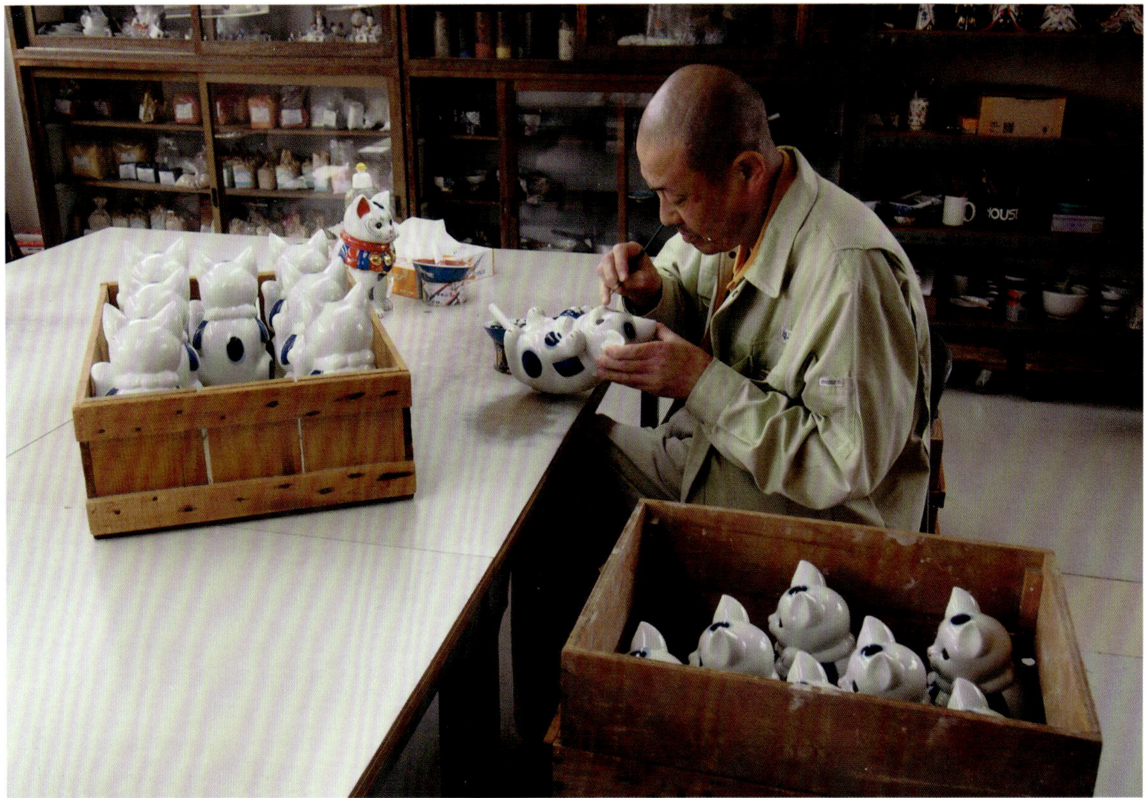

"art of the people") in Japan was developed by philosopher and art critic Soetsu Yanagi (1889–1961) in the mid-1920s, which was a time of cataclysmic social change. After centuries of isolation from the rest of the world during the Edo period (1603–1868), the years following the Meiji Revolution of 1868 saw Japan transformed into a modern nation with astonishing speed. Mass production, factory-based division of labor processes, importation of inexpensive materials and the use of cheap labor practices became standardized. At the same time, traditional crafts gradually became obsolete and extinct.

Yanagi, much like the proponents of the Arts and Crafts Movement that flourished in Europe at the end of the nineteenth century in response to the Industrial Revolution, saw value in heritage handicrafts made by anonymous artisans and he sought to reinstate the value of folk artisanship. Through what came to be known as the Mingei Movement, Yanagi put forward his belief that some of the most worthy and beautiful art is in fact made by people who aren't famous or formally recognized with titles.

As a result, utilitarian crafts that were made by anonymous artisans for commoners came to be seen as distinct from mass-produced industrial items and highbrow or aristocratic art. Items that are considered to be *mingei* usually have a practical use and are hence resilient, durable and perform functional roles in everyday life.

Facing page A member of folk band Seppuku Pistols at a gig in Tochigi Prefecture, wearing an outfit made of traditional *boro* peasant textiles (see page 24).
Above A veteran artisan at Chugai Toen studio paints Seto ware cats. Ceramic maneki-neko beckoning cats (above) are still ubiquitous in traditional pottery regions across Japan. As such, the culture of maneki-neko, mingei folk craft and artisanship has become intertwined.

A Note on the History of Japanese Folk Crafts

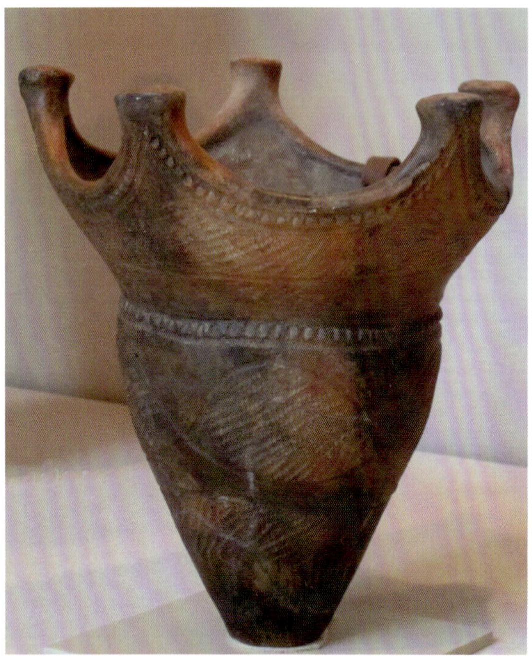

Japanese vernacular crafts have existed in some form since the beginning of life in the archipelago. Japan's history of ceramics is the oldest in the world, dating from the Jomon period (c. 14,000–300 BCE), although it would not be until around the thirteenth century that traditional ceramics came to be an essential part of the tea ceremony.

Ancient artisans did more than simply make crafts; as they traveled around the nation they founded many rural settlements and villages. The eighteenth century in particular saw a wide transmission of craft skills as artisans moved around: metalsmiths and stonemasons would go to various rural regions to work for farmers; woodworkers would be constantly on the move looking for fresh sources of wood, which is how the lathe, which has its roots in Shiga Prefecture made its way around Japan.

During the Edo period (1603–1868), many craft industries were keenly supported by both the ruling classes and the cultured merchant class, both of whom had money to spend. The city of Edo (the old name for Tokyo) became a hub for artisans from across Japan. But everything changed with the Meiji Revolution of 1868, and the rise of industrialization. The Meiji government established new manufacturing industries, so that the samurai—who had lost their status in the transition from a feudal to a modern state and were now unemployed—had work. This period of industrialization saw the import of machinery for automated manufacturing processes that could produce goods at a scale and quantity unimaginable in the world of traditional crafts. Where artisans had to work sustainably, relying heavily on nature, new forms of technology could function without any regard for environmental conditions.

The Meiji period was also the beginning of sweeping social changes, as Japan became influenced by the West. There was an unbridled fascination with and consumption of overseas goods and culture, while Japanese traditions were seen as antiquated. Factory-made Western products replaced many daily items that had until then been made by traditional processes.

This page Japan's history of ceramics is one of the oldest in the world. This earthenware pot dates from the Jomon period (c. 14,000–300 BCE).
Facing page A leather fireman's coat from the end of the nineteenth century, a time when traditional crafts were disappearing as part of Japan's first wave of industrialization.

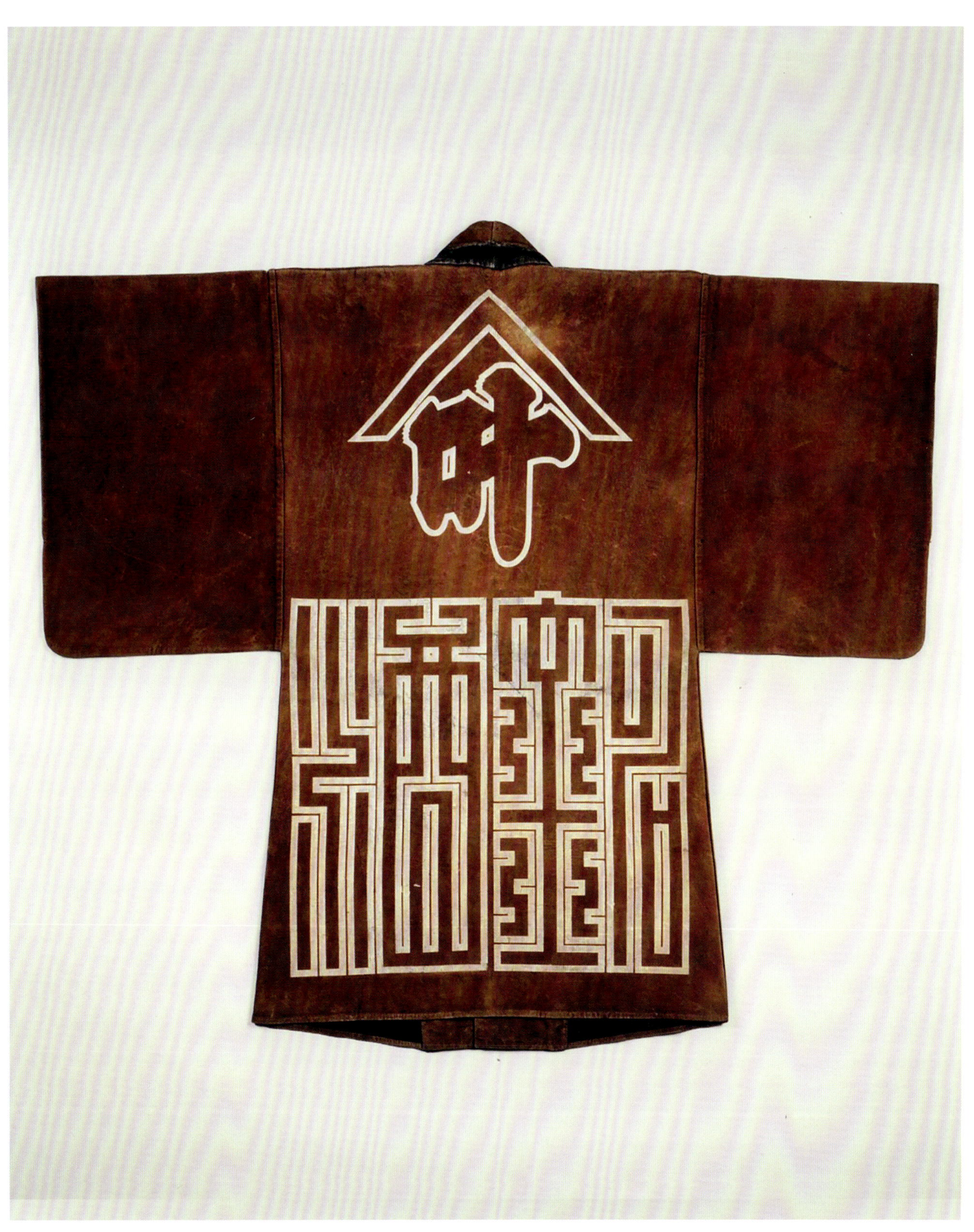

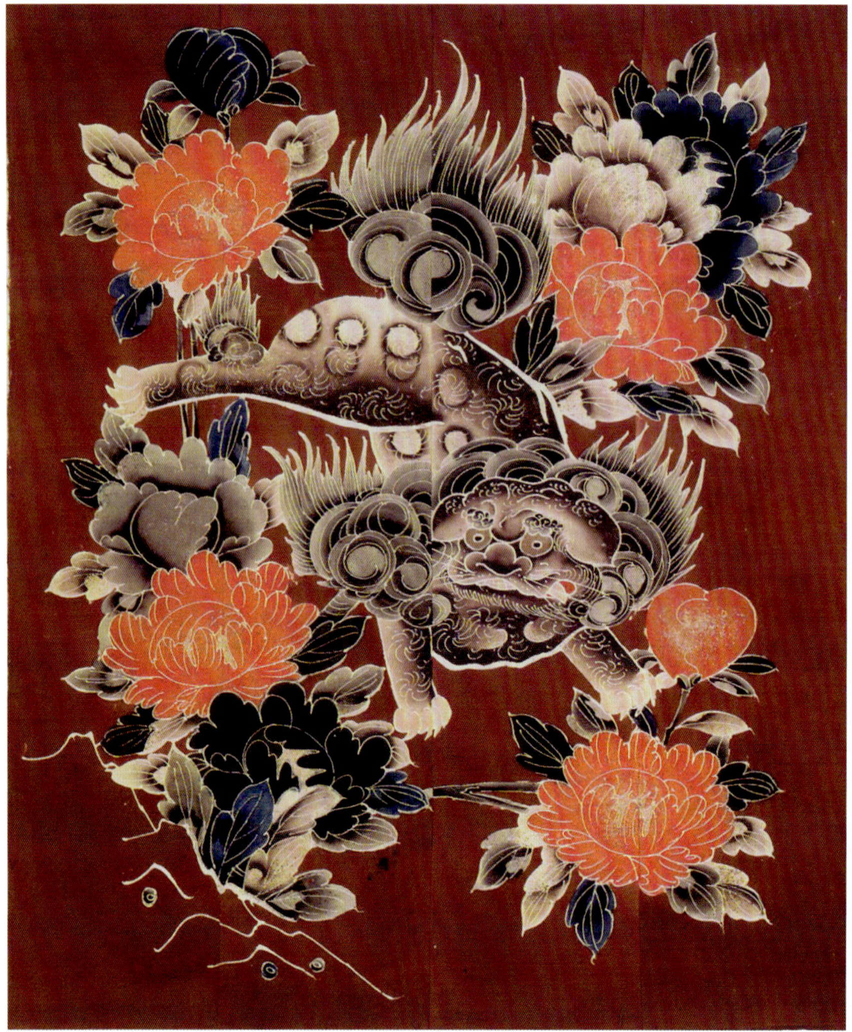

Only when the Mingei Movement began in the mid-1920s would appreciation of handicrafts and folk crafts start to trickle back. Therefore, the Mingei Movement and the "folk craft activists" associated with it were a product of their times, reflecting the social and political changes brought in during the Meiji period.

Mass production and local craftsmanship can, however, exist simultaneously. This book will highlight many of the Japanese crafts that have endured over the years, despite cultural shifts.

Above An early twentieth-century hand-embroidered quilt cover, featuring traditional motifs.
Facing page Speckle-glazed cup, water pot and sugar bowl, made by British potter Bernard Leach, a key figure in the Japanese Mingei Movement.

The Mingei Movement

Mingei Movement founder Soetsu Yanagi was initially interested in the folk crafts of Korea, a country he first visited in 1916. In 1924, he established the Korean Folk Crafts Museum in Seoul, which exhibited items from anonymous artisans. Around this time, he started collecting folk-craft pieces in Japan as well. He gathered what he thought were beautiful and "honest" crafts; his musings were rather idealistic in nature, giving aesthetic value to items he thought "ought to exist." He was very much inspired by the visual and aesthetic qualities of folk crafts, unlike folklorists of the time, who took a sociological or anthropological stance and were interested in social relationships, communities and hierarchies. Those involved in the Mingei Movement however, were concerned with the intrinsic value of the items themselves, sometimes even going so far as to display them in exhibitions without any kind of information as to who made them or where they were from.

Yanagi found wisdom in the lifestyles of common folk who had a "perceptiveness," regardless of whether they were literate, educated or not. The Mingei Movement strove to breath fresh life into folk culture, by drawing attention to heritage items and their unique regional characteristics.

In 1936, Yanagi founded the Japan Folk Crafts Museum in Tokyo, and two years later he established the Japan Folk Crafts Association. Members of the association took research trips to Japan's semitropical southern island chain of Okinawa and advocated for the cultural rights of the local Ryukyu people. They also researched the folk crafts of Japan's northern region of Tohoku, supported by the Settyo Agency set up and funded by the Ministry of Agriculture and Forestry in 1933. One of the agency's goals was to improve the economic plight of artisans in impoverished rural areas. Yanagi said, "Tohoku is certainly the region with the greatest wealth of folk crafts"—arguably a claim that still holds true today, and many of the crafts introduced in this book are from this rural region in the northeast of Japan's main island of Honshu.

The Mingei Movement had widespread influence because of the charismatic and passionate people that were associated with it. They included folklore and folk culture academics and advocates of the time, as well as environmentalists and novelists, all of whom disseminated information via schools, societies, guilds and galleries. They worked to create distribution hubs for folk crafts and to forge connections between makers and consumers. They helped bring about solidarity between the thinkers, artisans, creators and activists who were part of the movement.

Key members of the Mingei Movement were ceramicist Kanjiro Kawai (1890–1966) who was offered Living National Treasure status but refused it; British potter Bernard Leach (1887–1979), who studied Japanese *raku* pottery and wrote numerous books, including the seminal *A Potter's Book*; and Shoji Hamada (1894–1978), second head of the Folk Crafts Museum after Yanagi's death in 1961, and first director of the Folk Crafts Museum Osaka, established in 1970. He was designated a Living National Treasure, a title he accepted. Initially inspired by Leach, Hamada went to the United Kingdom with

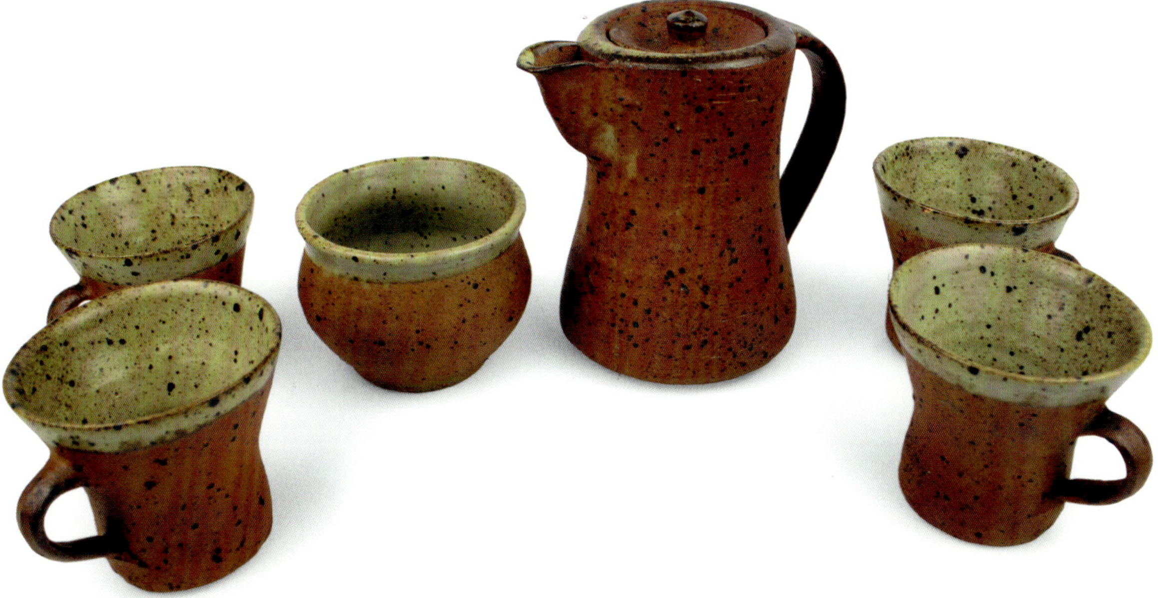

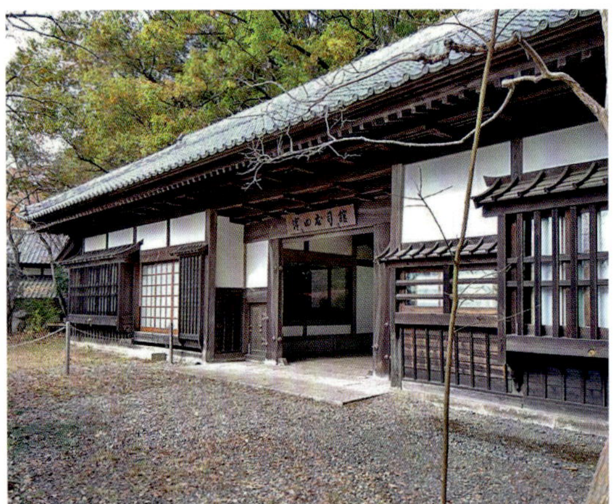

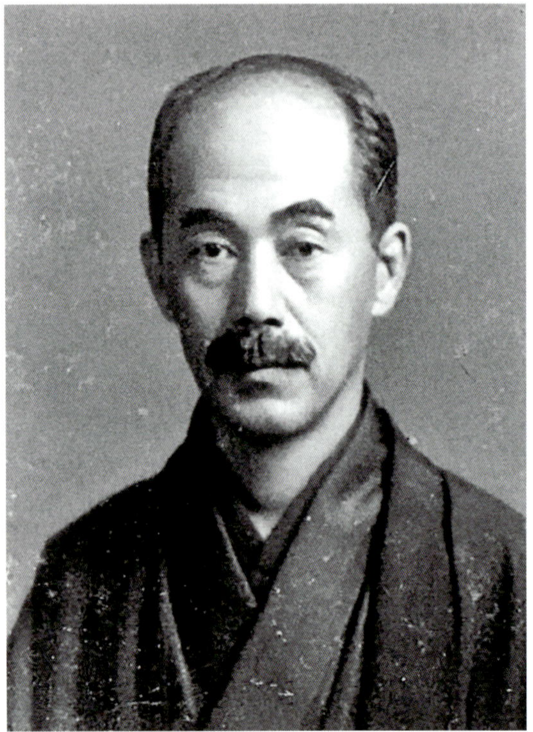

Top The Shoji Hamada Memorial Mashiko Sankokan Museum in Mashiko, Tochigi Prefecture (see page 156).
Bottom Folklorist Kunio Yanagita compiled the folklore classic *The Legends of Tono*.

him for three years before settling in Mashiko, Tochigi Prefecture. Designer and printmaker Shiko Munakata (1903–1975) (see page 151) and dyer Keisuke Serizawa (1895–1984) were other pioneering members of the movement.

While the above are considered the founders of the Mingei Movement, there were other significant players. The Shirakabaha (White Birch) Group, founded in 1910, was a group of experimental environmentalists and idealists concerned about what they saw as the reckless pursuit of profit in industrial Japan and sought out a utopian community. They made aninfluential magazine, *Shirakabaha*, an introduction for many members of the group to Western movements that also advocated for crafts. Shirakabaha members included novelists Takeo Arishima and Saneatsu Mushanokoji, and short-story writer and essayist Naoya Shiga. Another important figure in the Mingei Movement was activist, editor, writer and publisher Ryuzaburo Shikiba, who was influential during the genesis of the movement, serving as the editor of *Gekkan Mingei* magazine. This group collectively felt the philosophies of mingei provided an antidote to the industrialization of Meiji-period Japan.

Alongside the burgeoning Mingei Movement, interest in the study of folk culture was also flourishing. Printmaker Kanae Yamamoto, rural sociologist Kizaemon Aruga, scholar Eitaro Suzuki and artist, writer and agriculturalist Kenji Miyazawa were also deeply interested in peasant life and rural heritage. Folklorist Kunio Yanagita collected word-of-mouth folktales from Iwate Prefecture and collated them into the folklore classic *The Legends of Tono*. The ideas of philosophers Daisetsu Suzuki and Kitaro Nishida were also influential on Yanagi.

Other noteworthy supporters of folk culture include Keizo Shibusawa, governor of the Bank of Japan and finance minister post–World War II. He had a formidable collection of folk toys, tools and *ema* prayer plaques (see page 63). He dubbed his interest *mingugaku*, or the study of folk tools. Shoya Yoshida was a doctor who came from Tottori Prefecture. He collected mingei, worked to preserve local crafts and cultural properties, and opened the Tottori Folk Crafts Museum and shop in 1932 (see page 158).

The Mingei Movement's aesthetic sensibilities also had significant influence on contemporary artists and designers. Soetsu Yanagi was succeeded by his son, Sori Yanagi (1915–2011), an industrial designer best known for his elegant butterfly stool. He took over as the head of the Japan Folk Crafts Museum in 1977.

Sori Yanagi had direct contact with many leading artists and designers with whom he shared his passion for folk crafts, such as Isamu Noguchi, Hiroshi Sugimoto and the French architect Charlotte Perriand who worked for Le Corbusier and researched mingei culture in Tohoku. Architect Bruno Taut was similarly fascinated by Tohoku folk culture and produced many travelogues of his time up north. Even today, the global Japanese store MUJI espouses an anonymous branding strategy which is influenced by the mingei philosophy.

Below Designed by Sori Yanagi, son of Mingei Movement founder Soetsu Yanagi, the butterfly stool combines a traditional Japanese aesthetic with the molding technique of the classic Eames chair.

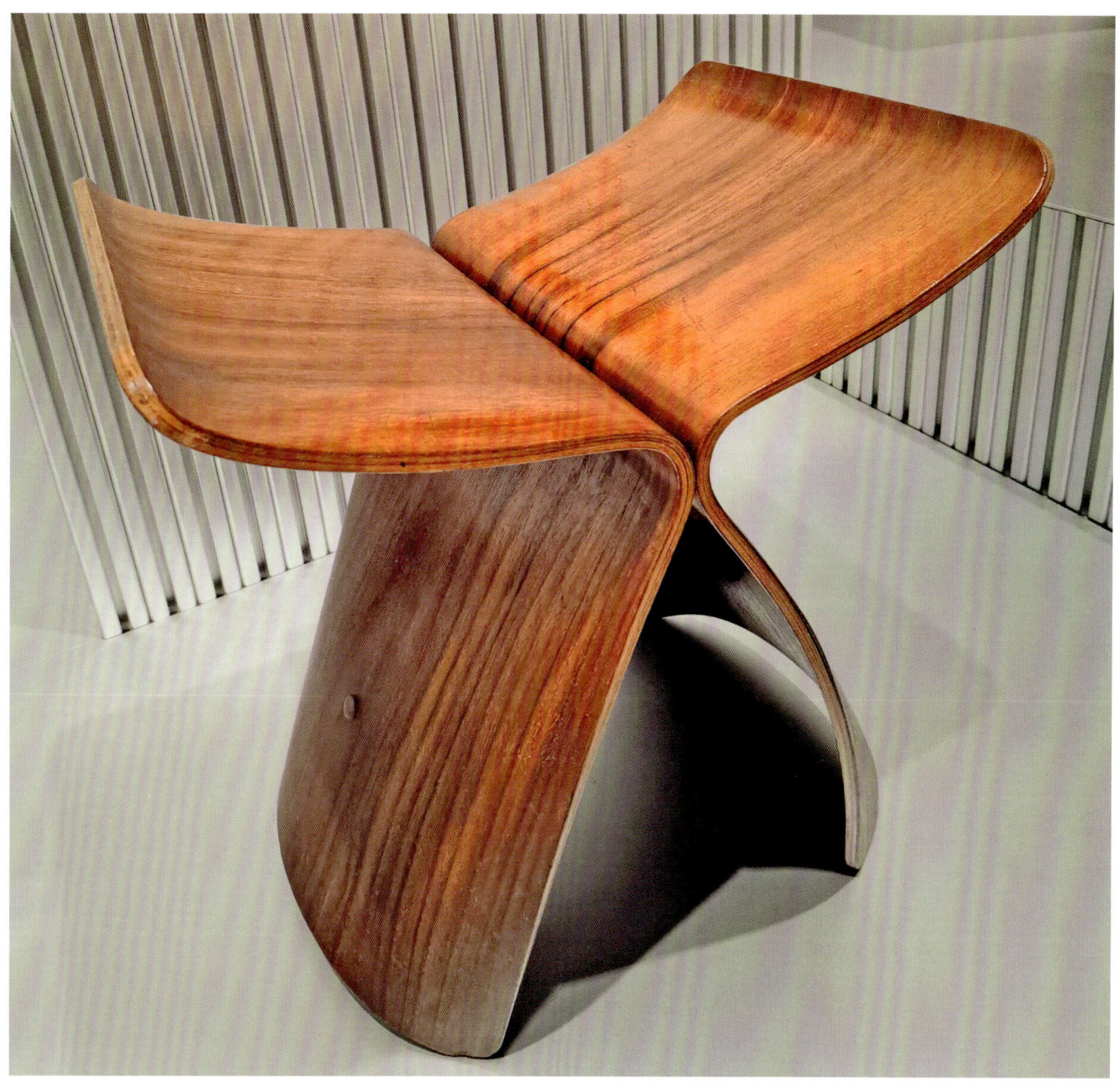

An Interview with Chiaki Ajioka

Curator, scholar and mingei folk-craft researcher

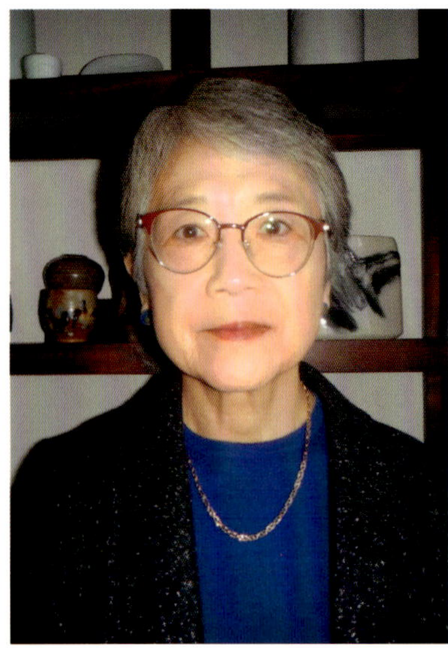

Chiaki Ajioka is a curator, scholar and art historian. She formerly worked at the Art Gallery of New South Wales in Sydney, Australia, and at the University of Sydney. She is known around the world for her research, writing and lecturing about the field of mingei folk crafts and its international influence.

Could you define mingei in your own words?
Mingei is primarily an aesthetic—the term describes traditional craft pieces that play a functional role in daily life. In the English language, mingei is often translated as "folk art," but Mingei Movement founder Soetsu Yanagi translated it as "folk craft," using the term in the English naming of the Folk Crafts Museum, for example. He also used the words "peasant art." He wanted to draw attention to the nature of the craft and the skills.

Why is mingei seen as folk art?
In terms of folk art, there is much less division between arts that involve painting or sculpture, and those that involve crafts. Because mingei objects are mostly everyday items, the term "folk art" is the easiest way to describe them. People like Soetsu Yanagi, Bernard Leach, and American art historian Langdon Warner (1881–1955), saw something deep and spiritual when looking at folk art.

If we understand mingei to be an aesthetic, then we can discuss how the specific beauty of an object can represent the culture or the inner spirituality of a people. This was something that was explored by those who first became involved in the Mingei Movement in Japan. But mingei does not have to be viewed through an academic lens—a lot of people simply love folk art! From the twentieth century onwards, many Westerners visiting Japan like to collect everyday folk-craft objects.

While Yanagi is credited as the founder of the Mingei Movement, in your research there is a fascination with the pioneer potters Bernard Leach and Kenkichi Tomimoto.
The Mingei Movement started with Leach and Tomimoto. Leach was familiar with the British

designer William Morris (1834–1896) and the Arts and Crafts Movement, which had started in the West around the end of the nineteenth century. But Tomimoto was more of a conduit, a catalyst for Leach's love of folk traditions. Before these two potters met, Tomimoto had been to London to study William Morris—he was really inspired by the decorative arts display at the Victoria and Albert Museum, where he saw slipware pottery. This inspiration that he felt was for something that was completely different to traditional Japanese ceramics.

When Leach went to Britain with the potter Shoji Hamada, they also tried to emulate these influences, so their early works use the slipware technique. Hamada worked with Leach in the countryside and the rural setting was also inspirational—he wanted to make something healthy, natural and beautiful, but with the robust quality that folk pottery had. Hamada also talked to Kanjiro Kawai who was studying highly technical Chinese ceramics and porcelain but didn't know how to develop his techniques and was stuck. Hamada told Kawai his work should be something natural and healthy, bringing forth the nature of the material.

So what is considered to be mingei is subjective?
It is subjective in the same way that tea-ceremony masters select items to be used in tea ceremony, using their connoisseurship and their eye. But Yanagi only talked about general production and how things were made—he did not talk about how he selected one particular piece, and how it was different from others.

Below The house of ceramicist Kanjiro Kawai in Kyoto is now a museum, with his works prominently exhibited.

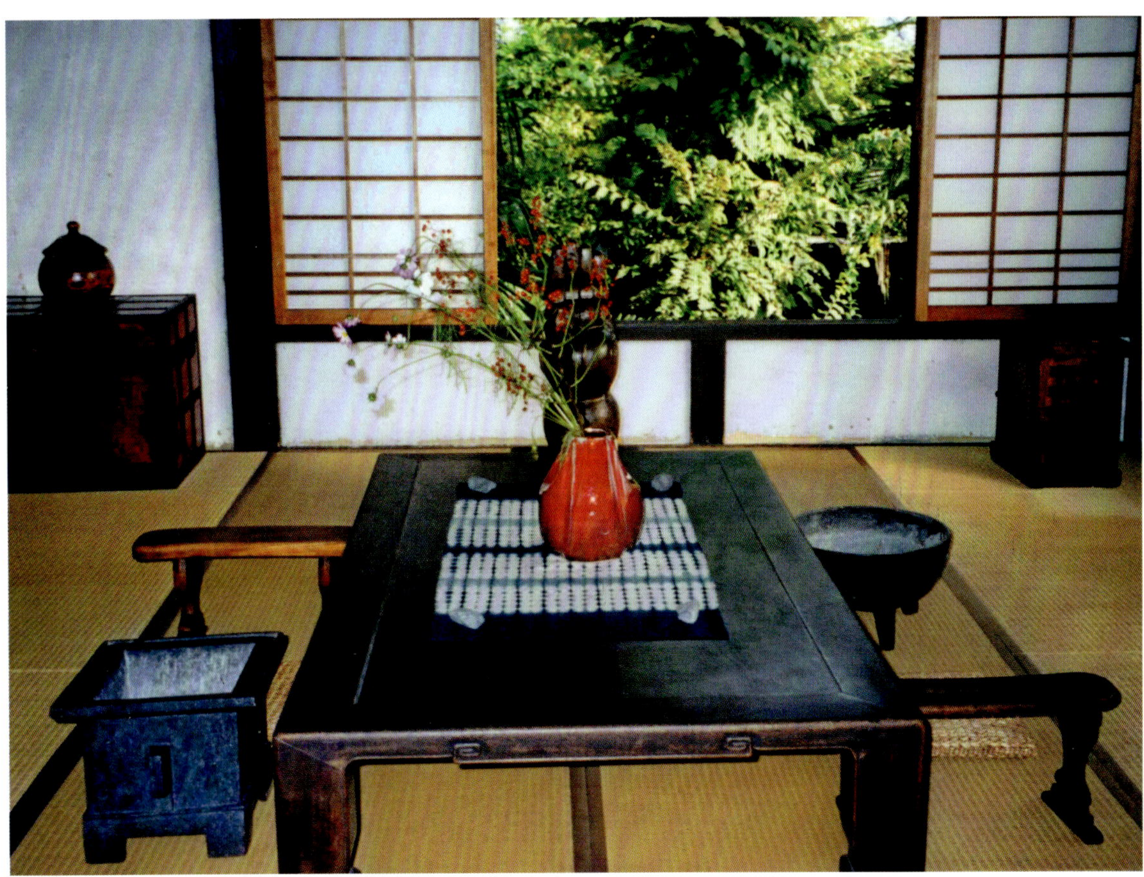

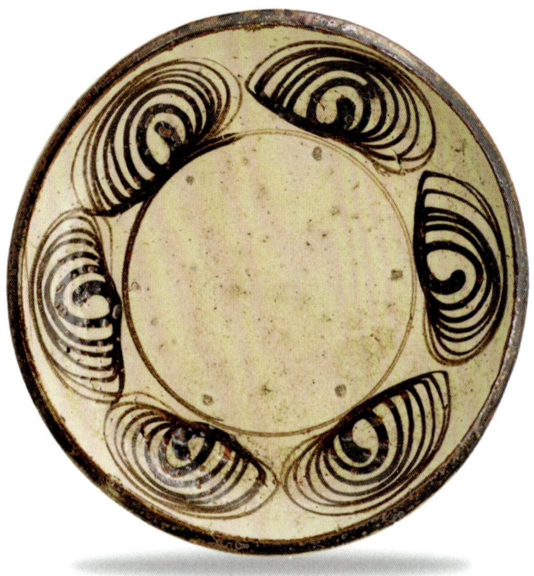

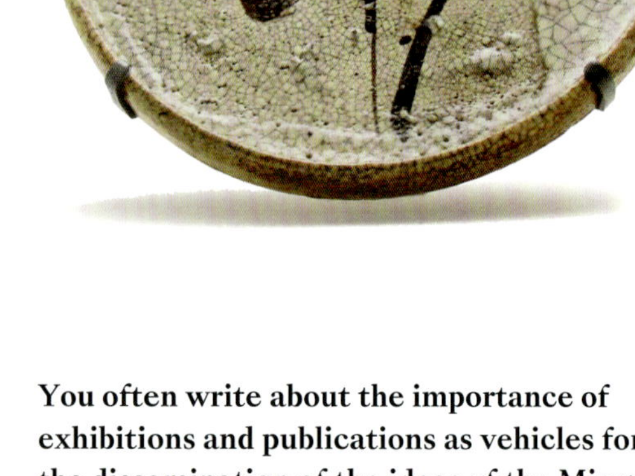

For example, I had seen the *uma no me zara* horse eye plate—a folk craft from Seto in Aichi Prefecture, one of the six ancient kilns of Japan—that has an *uzumaki* spiral pattern along the edge, which is widely regarded as on of the quintessential examples of Japanese mingei folk craft. But what struck me more deeply than that was a simple plate from potter Kanjiro Kawai's collection that I thought was just really breathtaking, it had an amazing power. That's what I mean by subjectivity. Yanagi's mingei theory was actually highly subjective and was his own response to the beauty he saw in specific pieces.

How was the Mingei Movement similar to the Arts and Crafts Movement that preceded it?
Both movements were supported by people who appreciated the aesthetic of authentic, natural objects or a simple economy of design, as well as good artisanship.

The Arts and Crafts Movement changed over time; towards the end of his life, William Morris, who provided the initial inspiration for the movement, was much more interested in social change, and in the early twentieth century the movement became more spiritually oriented.

You often write about the importance of exhibitions and publications as vehicles for the dissemination of the ideas of the Mingei Movement abroad.
The first mingei exhibition—although it didn't use the word "mingei"—was the Boston *otsue* (folk painting) exhibition in 1930 that Yanagi organized with Langdon Warner. In the same year Yanagi published an article in the journal *Eastern Art*, which was first major academic study of otsue.

If Yanagi was going to convince people outside of Japan of the importance of mingei, he knew he would need objects, and also proper academic study. I think that is why he started the magazine *Kogei* in 1931 (which eventually became *Gekkan Mingei*).

When Yanagi was in America, from 1952 to 1953, he took with him hundreds of slides showing mingei works, and that had an immense impact, because people had not seen ordinary objects in that way.

How did the interest in Japanese folk craft continue to grow in the West?
These days Westerners have a taste for Japanese products that have a characteristic often described as *shibui*—a restrained, simple, subdued aesthetic, often associated with old

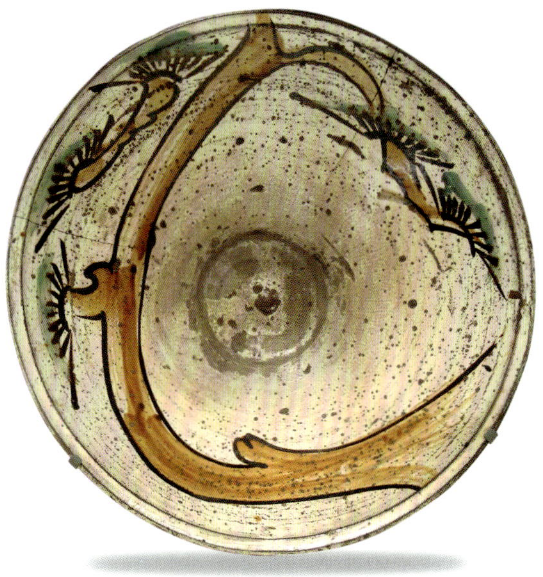

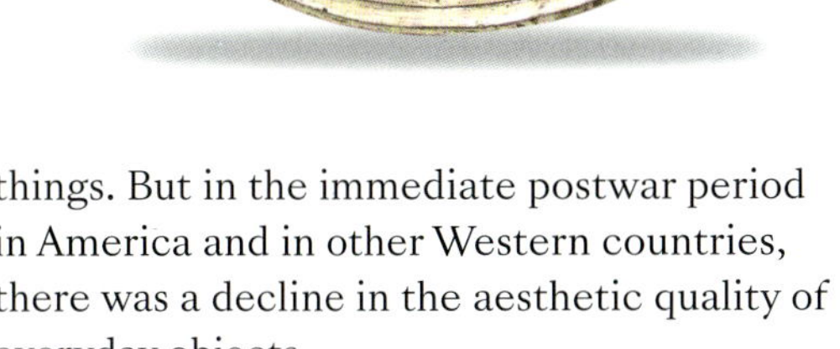

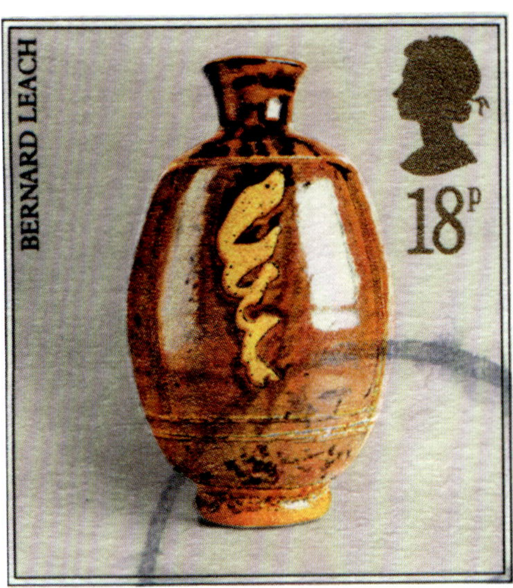

things. But in the immediate postwar period in America and in other Western countries, there was a decline in the aesthetic quality of everyday objects.

Design and lifestyle magazines in the postwar period were influential, none more so than the US publication *House Beautiful* magazine, edited by Elizabeth Gordon from 1941–1964. She wanted housewives to be more selective about what they used and how they decorated their interiors. She discovered this concept "shibui" and she interviewed a lot of people, particularly the Japan Society's manging director Douglas Overton, and Bernard Leach. This encouraged her to visit Japan; she went there four times and also interviewed Soetsu Yanagi. She saw with her own eyes the shibui aesthetic. In 1960, the *House Beautiful* "Shibui" issue covered architecture, tea, clothing and cooking. That was Yanagi's last direct contribution to the promotion of mingei, because he died in 1961. Gordon really promoted the shibui aesthetic and influenced several interior design producers in America to make products to fit with this sensibility.

What is the greatest legacy of the Mingei Movement?

Yanagi's highly developed spiritual and aesthetic arguments drew attention to ordinary objects—that is a huge contribution. I've heard American potters say that mingei is a philosophy of life. There was no theory about the beauty of folk craft before Yanagi. The Arts and Crafts Movement talked about beauty in everyday life, but didn't pin down what this beauty was. Yanagi did. This empowered a lot of craftspeople and defenders of crafts. That is perhaps the single most important contribution. It was radical, there was very strong opposition among art historians and the art establishment. They would not accept that craft is art. But fewer and fewer people think like that these days.

Facing page, left The horse-eye plate, made in the Seto kilns towards the end of the Edo period (1603–1868) is regarded as a quintessential example of mingei folk craft.
Facing page, right This dish with a design of millet dates from the sixteenth-century Momoyama period.
This page, left A bowl with a branch design, made in the eighteenth or nineteenth century in Yumino in Saga Prefecture.
This page, right In 1987, a set of four stamps were produced in the UK to commemorate the centenary of the birth of British potter Bernard Leach.

Japanese Folk Crafts Today

Folk craft is an ever-evolving concept, reflecting the cultural zeitgeist, and it is undeniable that folk craft in Japan today is very different to that defined by the Mingei Movement that started in the 1920s. There are several reasons for this. One is that craft items that were made for superstitious reasons in the past, such as the akabeko papier-mâché cow (see page 36), which was believed to protect against disease, are now often regarded as chic interior-design items, rather than having any protective qualities. Young women are just as likely to pick up a Sagara doll (see page 101) because it is adorable, rather than believing it will ward off evil. Another reason is that today's Japanese consumer is likely to live in a small urban apartment rather than in a traditional Japanese houses, with less room for artifacts. Aesthetic sensibilities have also changed dramatically, with *kawaii* or "cute" culture one of the dominant forces.

While artisans pride themselves on perpetuating lineages and keeping traditional craft techniques alive, they are also aware of the need to constantly evolve and cater to an ever-changing market For this reason, many modern-day artisans in Japan are constantly experimenting with new models, rather than focusing solely on traditional formats. Daruma figurines, for example, traditionally red, now come in vibrant colors like shocking pink; kokeshi dolls are carved in the likeness of puppies or UFOs.

But while folk-craft items may seem to have lost their traditional spiritual meaning, it is just as likely that they have become spiritual in another way. Take the traditional kokeshi doll, for example. Kokeshi artisans often talk about their dolls having a "healing presence" that calms and resonates with the soul. Materiality has significance; kokeshi fans talk about the warmth of wood.

Many consumers are also interested in vintage items that have aged gracefully, such as old kokeshi dolls that have an attractive caramel-colored patina. There is an awareness that craft items improve with time and are therefore more attractive than cheaply manufactured items that degrade quickly and have to be thrown away. Imbued in folk craft is the notion of taking care of things, using them carefully, mending them if needed, and watching them age—which gives them value.

Hiromi Chiba, of the Hirosaki Kogin Institute, a preservation society for traditional *koginzashi* embroidery used for darning (see page 128), explains that by mending cloth it can last for generations, in contrast to our modern-day environmentally catastrophic disposable culture, where product lineups are replaced not only each season, but each micro season. "Folk craft is not exactly essential to our contemporary lifestyle," says Chiba. "But nonetheless, it is hard to let it just go obsolete. It encapsulates the spirit of using things carefully, and happily there are people out there who realize this."

Mieko Taira (see page 112), an artisan who makes cloth from the fibers of the Okinawan *basho* tree says, "This generation of young consumers has "fast fashion"—for ten thousand yen

Facing page Contemporary consumers are increasingly aware of the dangers of our disposable culture. This photograph was taken at the Boro: Fabric of Life exhibition, showcasing everyday textile items belonging to Japanese peasants from 1850 to 1950 that were repeatedly repaired and recycled.

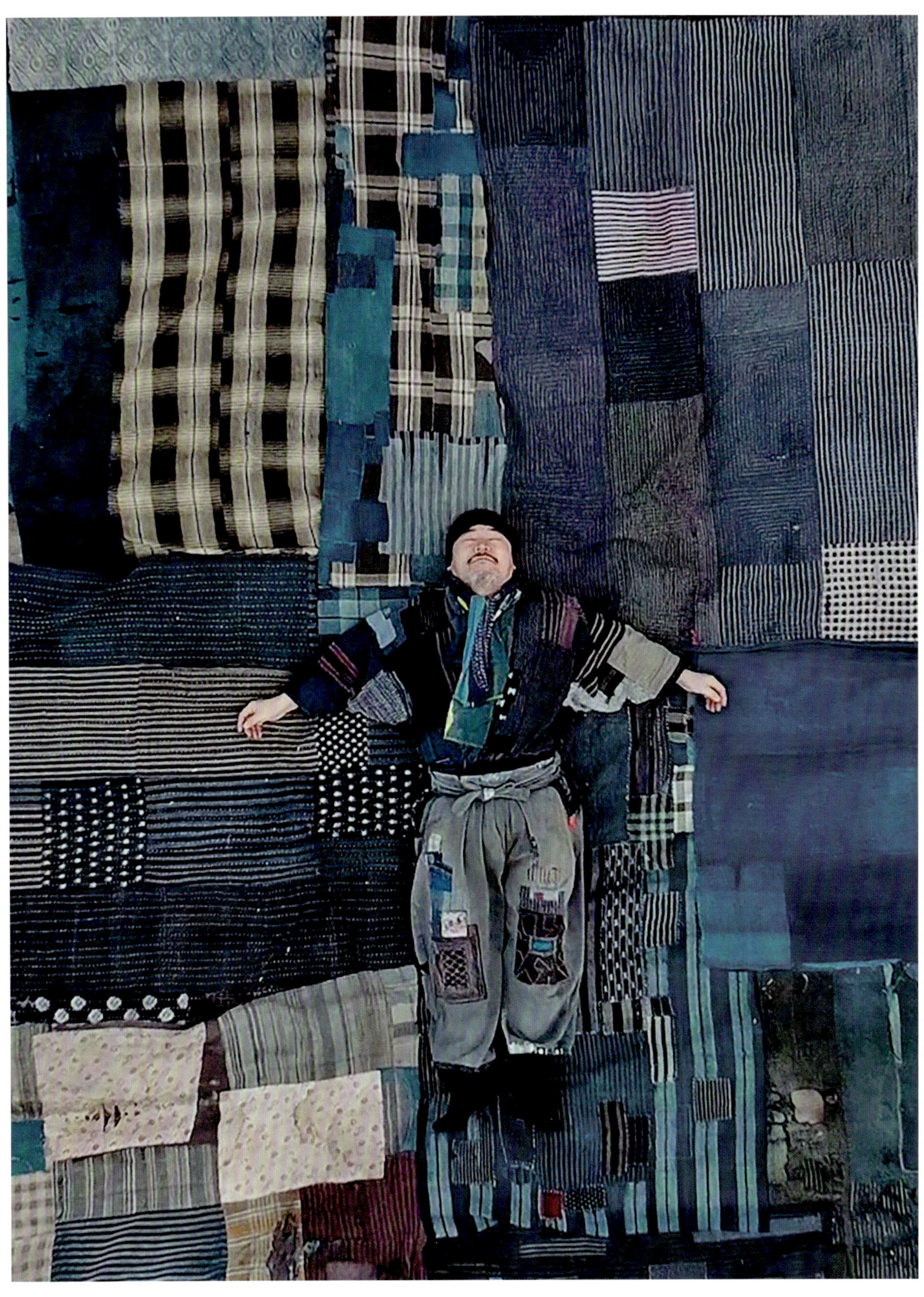

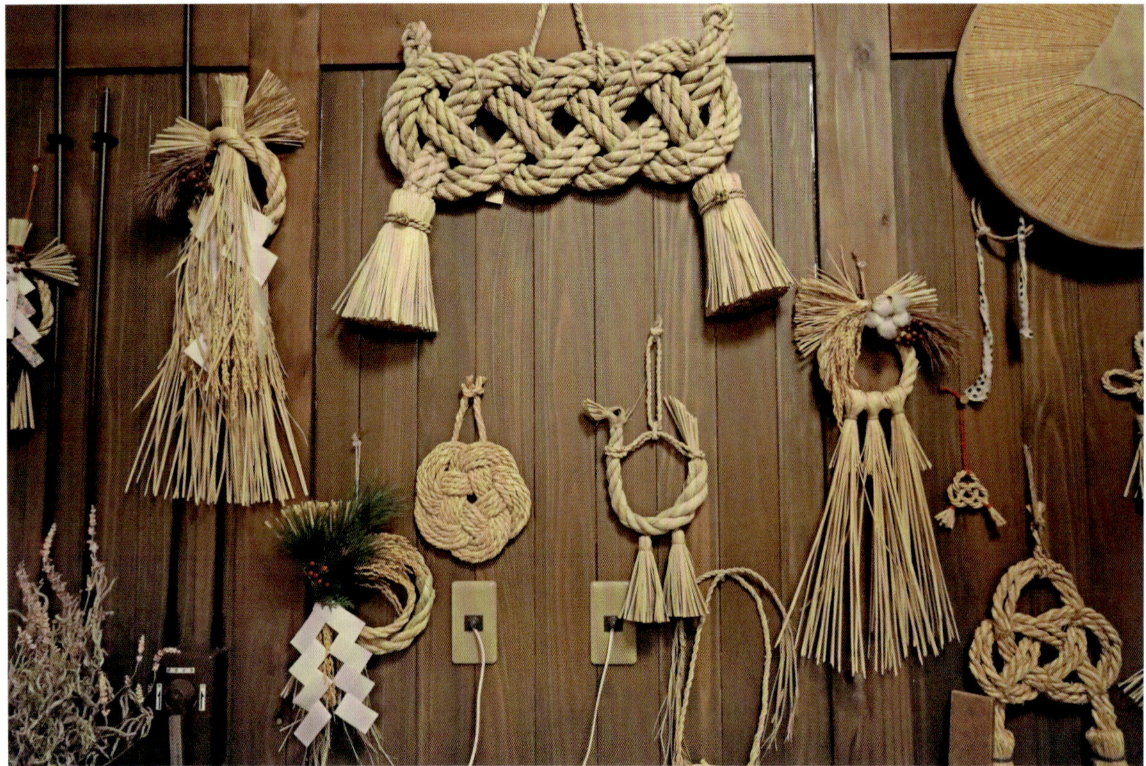

[about sixty dollars], you can get a whole new outfit. And then, after one season you can throw it away. From maker to consumer, there is no affection for or fascination with these fast-fashion items. On the other hand, bashofu cloth is made by hand, with passion, by craftspeople—this is something you can't describe with words, it is a feeling. There is a presence that is just different—I would never want to throw away any bashofu item."

Yasuhiro Koyama is a carver of traditional talismanic *otaka poppo* hawks (see page 132). He recalls the day a group of managers from a major telecommunications company visited his studio. "There were even or eight of them. They usually meet via a computer screen, and were inspired by the environment I work in, and the things I make, which are very analog and tangible, they exist in real life, which is the complete opposite of their daily life which has very little interaction with other people and nature. Just to have one of my items on their desk makes them feel they are being spiritually realigned."

While many craftspeople might be carrying on a hereditary lineage, more and more people are taking up a craft because of their own personal passion for it. A higher proportion of females than ever before can be found practicing traditional crafts. As it can be difficult to make a living from crafts, many people start as a hobby.

Hiromi Chiba says of the people who craft items using koginzashi embroidery nowadays, "First, they need to like koginzashi. And next, they need to be meticulous. It is difficult to do if you are stressed, you need to allow yourself to go into a mental state of nothingness—you need a bit of emotional latitude. You can't do it if you are too busy. Hobbyists find it pleasurable and comforting."

This page Traditional warazaiku straw crafts (see page 144). **Facing page, top** The atelier of Yasumaro Ozawa in Seto, a town that is a famous ceramics hub with over one thousand years of history. **Facing page, bottom** Otaka poppo wooden hawks, carved by Yasuhiro Koyama (see page 132).

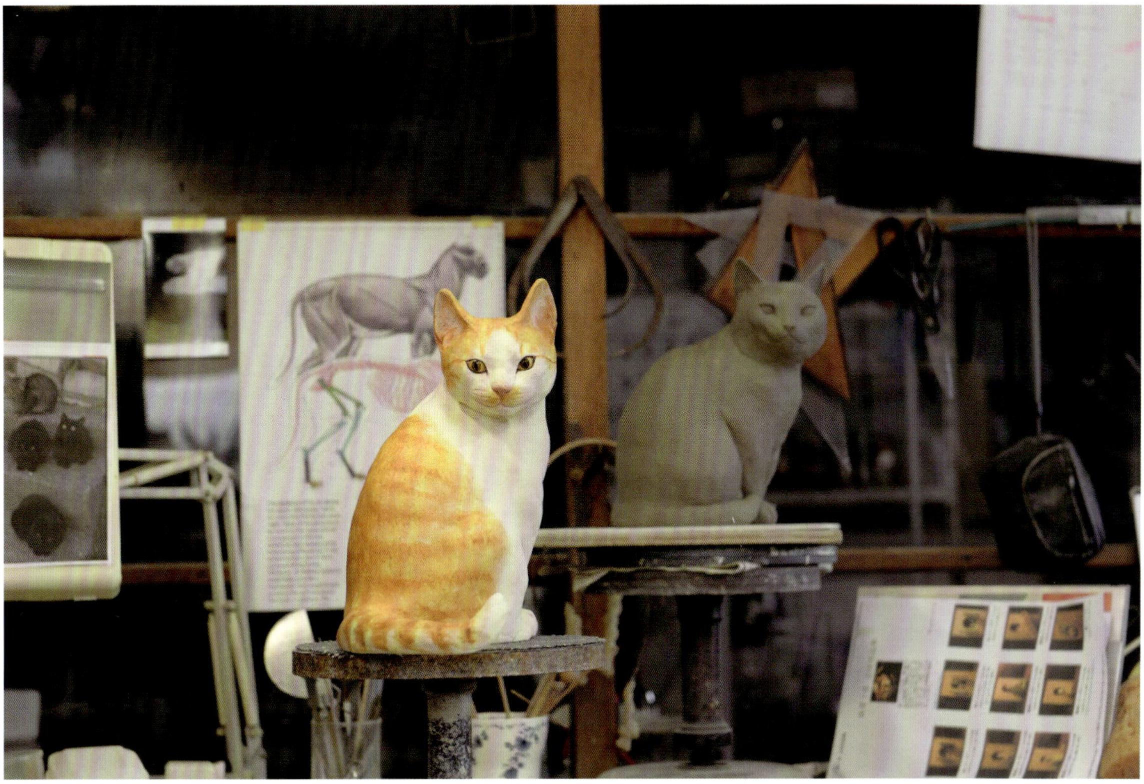

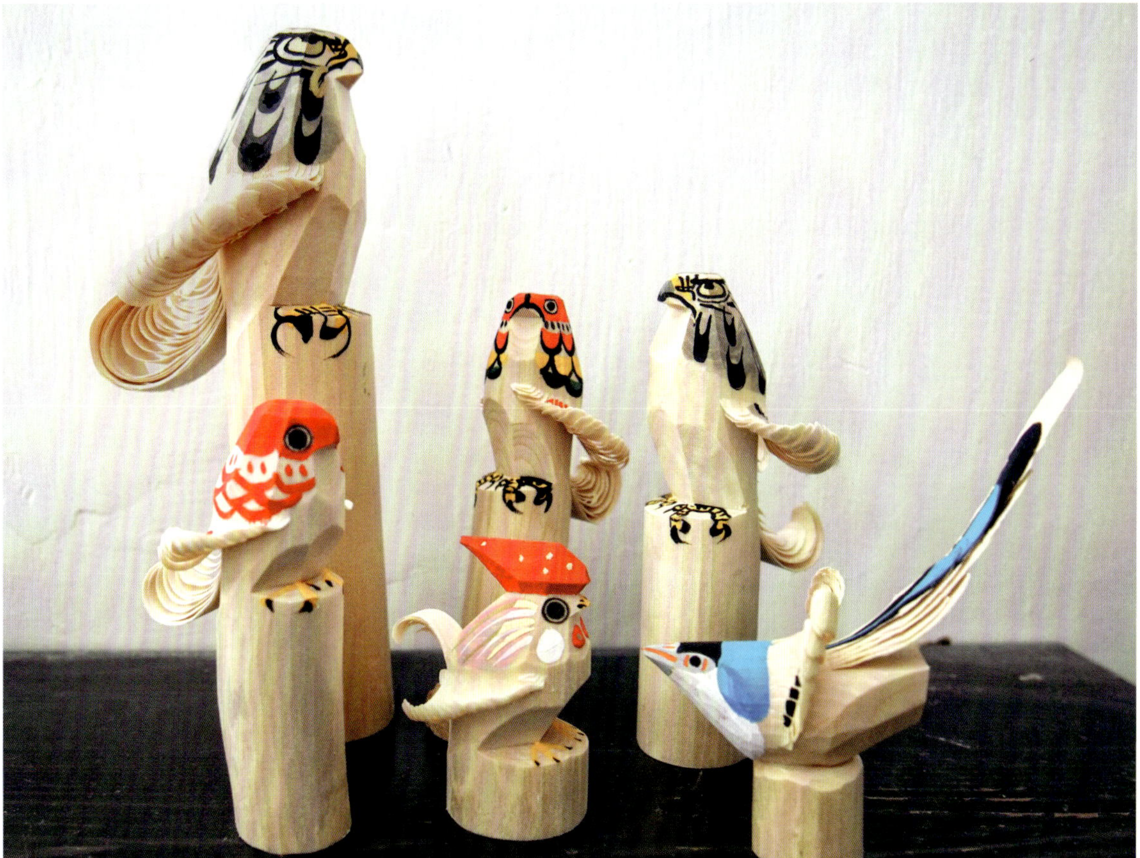

A growing interest in traditional crafts can be seen overseas as well. Stefan Johansson, curator of an exhibition of *boro* peasant textiles from northern Japan at the Museum of World Culture in Sweden says, "There is a recent interest in folk traditions. In the case of boro, it was also connected to the issue of sustainability and repairing your clothes rather than throwing them away. Learning about crafts and folk traditions can inspire you to become a creator yourself. There are fewer and fewer professions that involve creating by hand these days. Many people therefore pursue crafts as a hobby, often by getting together with others in a social environment to do so. They enjoy the artistic side and also gain an appreciation of how important it is to take care of one's possessions."

The Boro exhibition showcased items used by Japanese peasants from 1850 to 1950 that were repeatedly and ingeniously repaired and recycled. Originating at Parsons School of Design in New York, the exhibition has traveled the world.

The Future of Folk Crafts

The depopulation of rural areas of Japan as young people move to the cities for work has inevitably led to a decline in rural folk crafts. The woodworking village of Higashiomi in Shiga Prefecture, where the lathe was invented, is a hamlet of elderly folk, and there is no easy access to schools, shops or any of the facilities that young people need. This poses a significant challenge for rural artisans trying to find new apprentices. The Japanese government provides support for craftspeople through the Traditional Industry Law of 1974, whose objective is to promote traditional crafts and support initiatives that provide financial aid to people undergoing apprenticeships. However, it is hardly the ideal solution, and many crafts are not recognized as "traditional" under the government definition: needs to be used in daily life, manufactured by hand, uses a traditional technique, and uses traditional materials. Government guidelines also state that a craft-making organization has

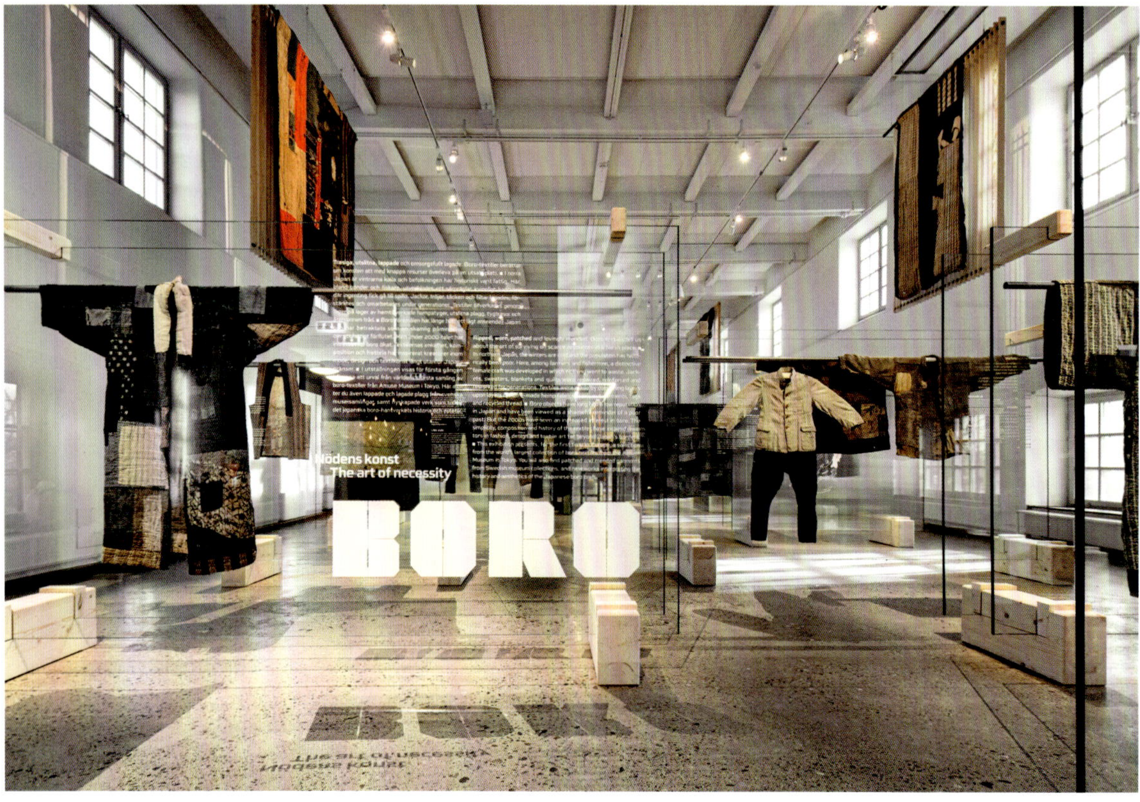

to have a minimum of thirty craftspeople. This last rule often means that many crafts do not qualify for subsidies.

Many of Japan's artisans have fought off becoming obsolete by evolving. Undoubtedly, among those who have been able to adapt there are some who have fared well. Others, particularly those that stick to tradition without any room for compromise, are on the verge of extinction. Craft is utilitarian in nature—those that are not sensitive to changes in Japanese lifestyle will invariably suffer.

In the era of social media, artisans need to have fluency in marketing and self-branding. Yuki Ogami (see page 140), an artisan at Shoyogama, a *tambayaki* ceramics atelier in Sasayama, Hyogo Prefecture, was formerly working with family members. He now collaborates with his brother who does fashion marketing, along with an art director and a spatial designer. Ogami says, "We are thinking about successors and the future of tambayaki as a whole not just about our own business."

Given that folk craft is "for the people," it is, by definition, flexible, and should be able to adjust to the needs of consumers. It is precisely this flexibility and versatility that makes folk craft so enduring and attractive. While folk crafts may seem like something from another era, their simple beauty has an appeal that transcends time. The world of folk crafts is dense with solutions and antidotes to many contemporary malaises. These ancient arts offer us new ways of thinking about how we create, utilize, consume and enjoy the items that are essential for our everyday lives.

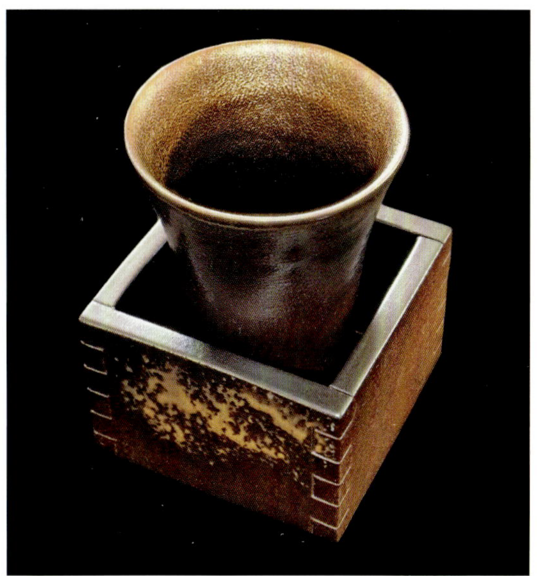

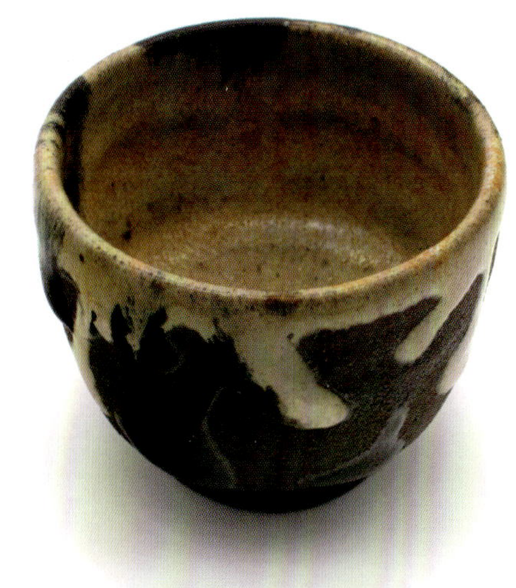

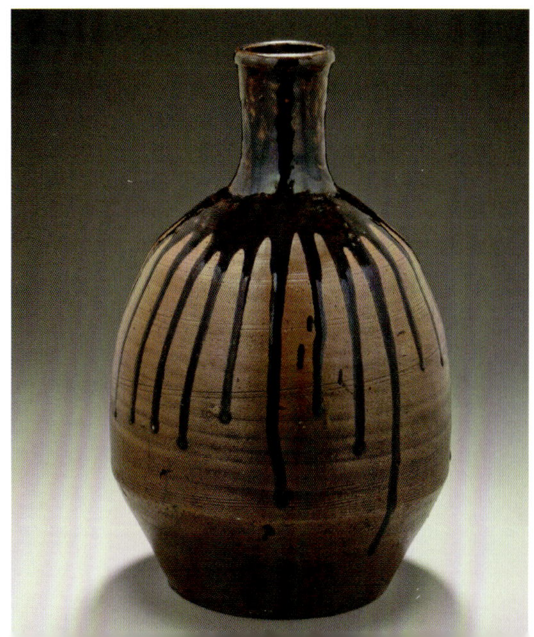

Folk crafts may seem like something from another era but their simple beauty has an appeal that transcends time.
Top A Bizen ware sake cup (see page 45).
Middle Mashiko pottery (see page 91) is known for simple pieces with a rural aesthetic.
Bottom A tambayaki sake bottle dating from the late eighteenth century (see page 140).

An Interview with Terry Ellis

Contemporary curator and tastemaker

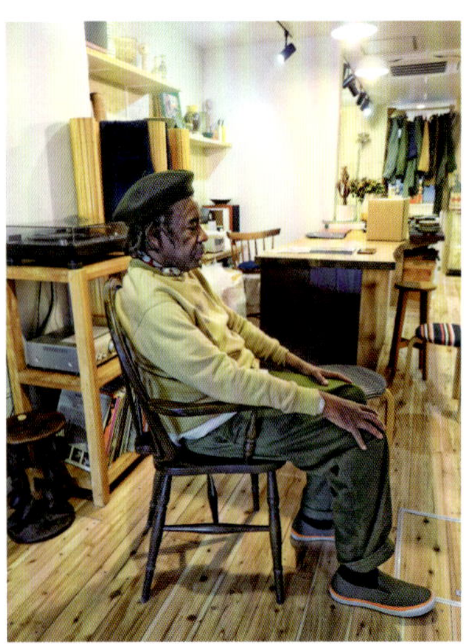

Jamaica born, London-raised Terry Ellis is a designer of craft and fashion items, and since 2022 is the owner of the Mogi Folk Art store in Koenji, west Tokyo. Formerly curator of folk-craft store fennica, part of the famous and influential BEAMS Tokyo lifestyle brand, he was an early tastemaker and instigator of a broader interest in folk art among style-savvy young consumers.

What is your connection to Japanese mingei folk craft?

I come from a fashion and retail background. I was working for the BEAMS clothing brand in Tokyo, and I saw an opportunity to expand into interiors and furniture. So we created a section in BEAMS stores called BEAMS Modern Living in the mid-1990s. We started buying vintage Scandinavian ceramics, glass and sculptural objects, to fill in the spaces not occupied by furniture. But then, for some reason, the Japanese government decided that anything imported from overseas that could be used for food had to be tested, especially ceramics, because some glazes are poisonous. As a result of this, we decided to replace the Scandinavian ceramics we'd been using with Japanese ceramics.

As part of our research into what we should buy, we ended up contacting the Japan Folk Crafts Museum. We met Sori Yanagi (son of Soetsu Yanagi), who was the director at the time, and he advised us to look into Ryukyu pottery from Okinawa, as he felt that was currently the best pottery being made in Japan. And that was the start of our relationship with mingei.

At that time, very few people under the age of fifty were interested in mingei ceramics. I think it's fair to say that BEAMS was a first point of contact with mingei for many people, some of whom have since gone on to become potters themselves.

Facing page At Mogi Folk Art (3-45-12 Koenji-minami, Suginami-ku; tel: 080-8058-1761), a folk-craft store in the west Tokyo district of Koenji, Terry Ellis has curated an eclectic selection of mingei items to appeal to young, trend-conscious consumers.

Was it a leap to go from Scandinavian to Ryukyu craft?
It may seem so, but they are both handmade, they both have their roots in modernism and they are both by and large functional objects.

When you choose craft items to sell, is your choice aesthetic, practical or both?
Both aesthetics and practicality are important. We know from studying mingei that it is locally made by unknown craftspeople, but naturally because we work in fashion, we are trying to find beautiful things.

We also consider cost, and trying to make and consume locally, but it's difficult to make absolute rules about these issues.

I am a buyer so what I select depends on what is going on at the time and what the customers are interested in and what the makers are making. So I have to have a very flexible aesthetic sensibility. I am not a creator; I am someone who makes selections from what creators are making. Basically, when we first started BEAMS, design was the zeitgeist—our customers were not interested in folk craft.

Why do you think folk art is relevant today?
There are so many things you can't do with your own hands anymore. You can't fix your own car. What do you do if your phone breaks? When I was growing up, with a bit of training or a manual you could do anything, but now you can't. That is a simplistic way of putting it, but the idea of something handmade that you haven't necessarily made yourself but could if you wanted to, and that someone who is very similar to you has made . . . this process has a humanity that is missing in the high-tech world we live in today. Even when you go to the grocery, the

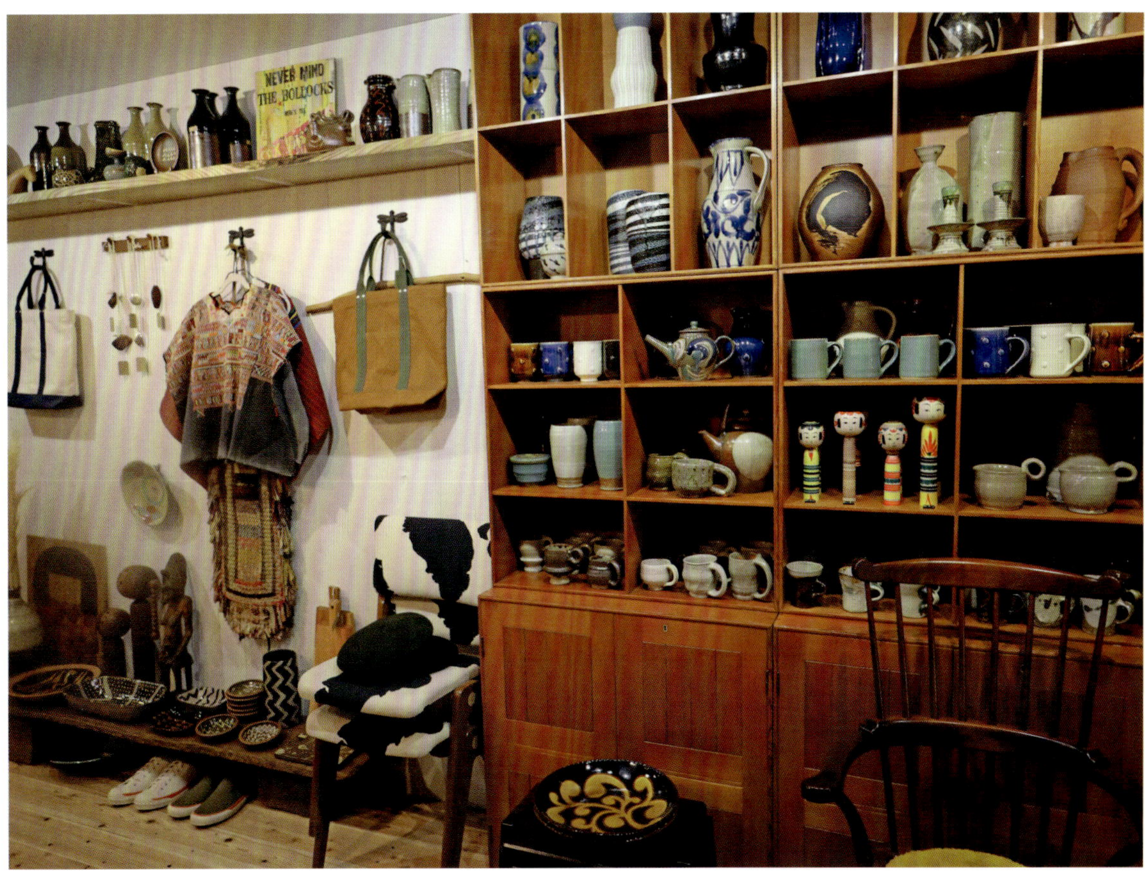

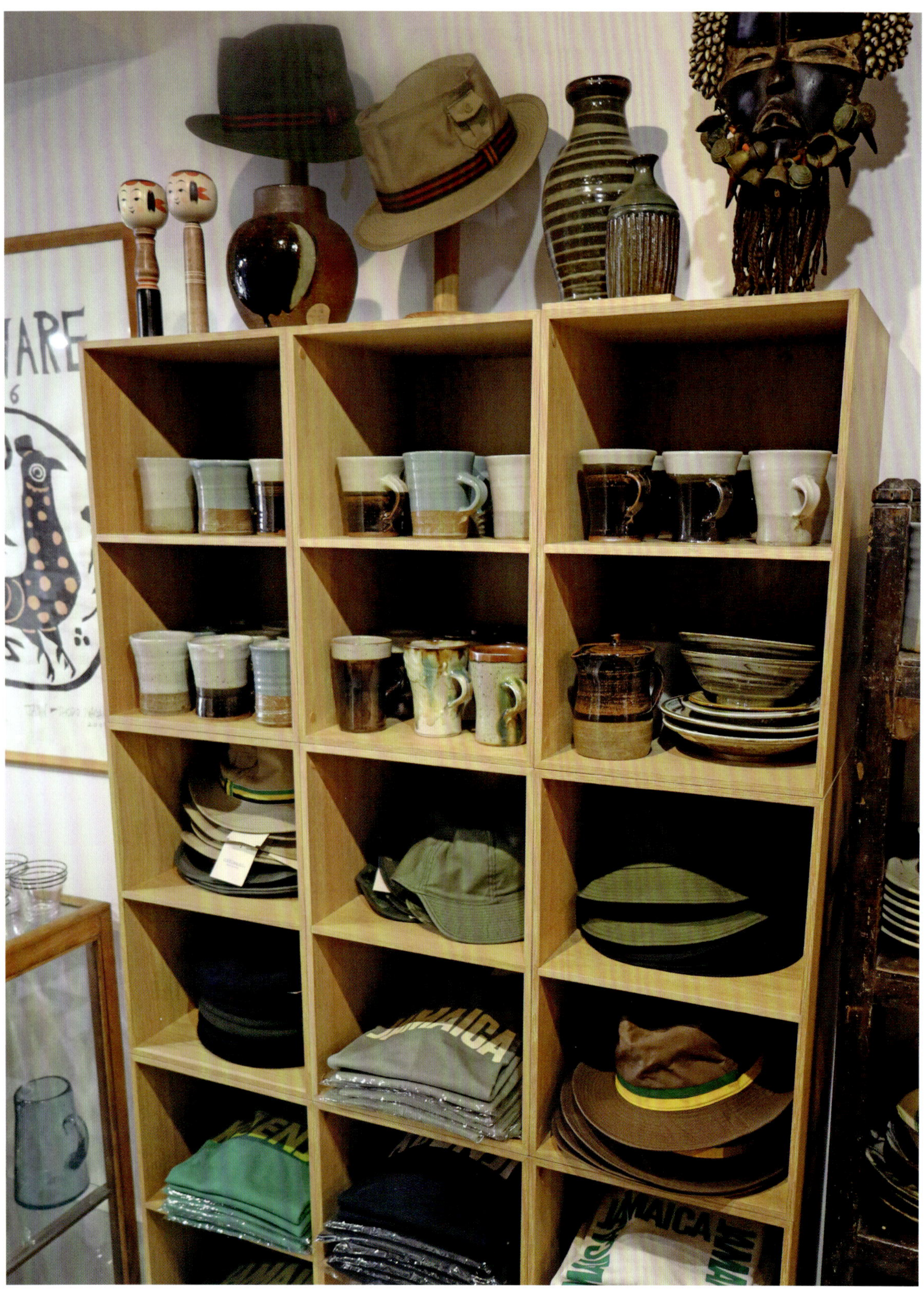
JAMAICA

transaction takes place by machine. But you can keep the high-tech out of your house if you want to. Instead, you can have things that are handmade and organic that you feel connected to. If something breaks you can mend it.

What trends have you seen lately among consumers?

At the moment we are selling a lot of plates, I think the reason is because people like to photograph the food they cook, whereas before we sold a lot of cups as people would give them gifts. I think with clothing I see more handmade or folk art fabrics like Kurume-gasuri, which is an indigo resist-dyed textile from Kurume in Kyushu. There's a kind of folksy look that's fashionable right now, and it's more to do with mingei than with music or a hippie aesthetic.

How is mingei seen abroad?

I do hear the term spoken about these days, and I think it is seen as some kind of mysterious Japanese trend that is connected to the slow-life aesthetic. I don't think it will just go away. I think there is an interest overseas in what I would call "mingei-lite." You don't need to go to a shop, you can buy online, things like white cups and objects with charming patterns. Whereas I think the original term "mingei"—referring back to the start of the Mingei Movement a hundred years ago—has a heavy image. So I think this mingei-lite is very attractive to people outside Japan. Anything can be mingei now. I particularly enjoy Afro-mingei created by American artist Theaster Gates, it's radical and fascinating, and it's definitely not mingei-lite.

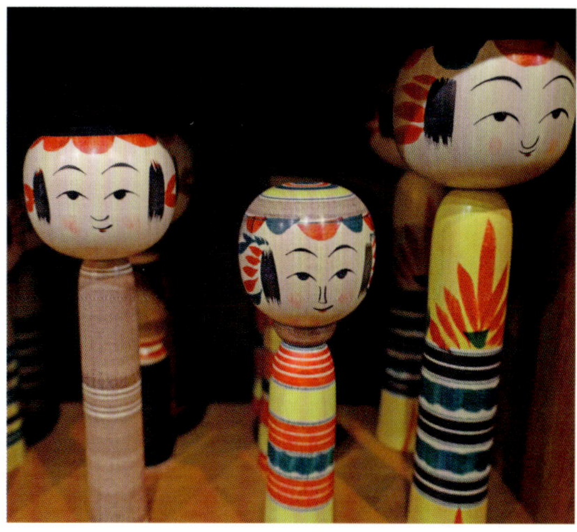

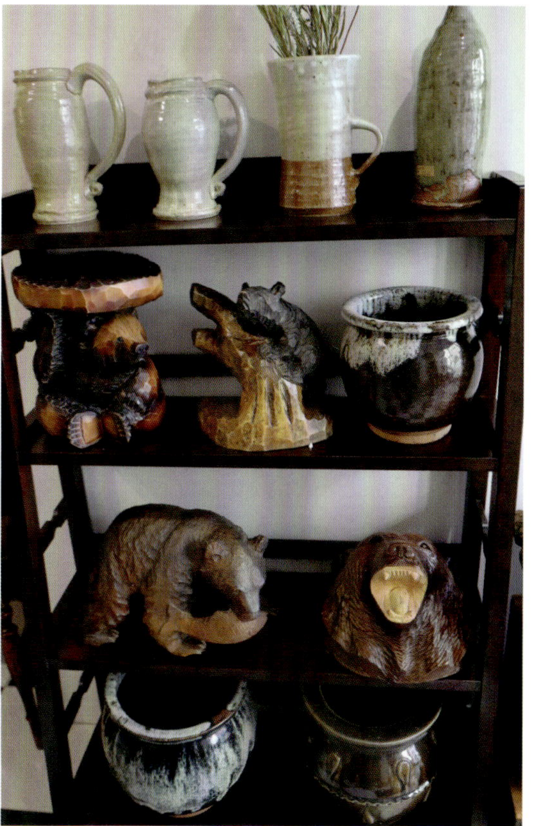

Facing page & this page A meeting with Sori Yanagi, son of founder of the Mingei Movement Soetsu Yanagi, was the start of Terry Ellis's relationship with mingei. Today his Tokyo store stocks folk-craft items such as traditional pottery and kokeshi dolls alongside contemporary clothing and accessories.

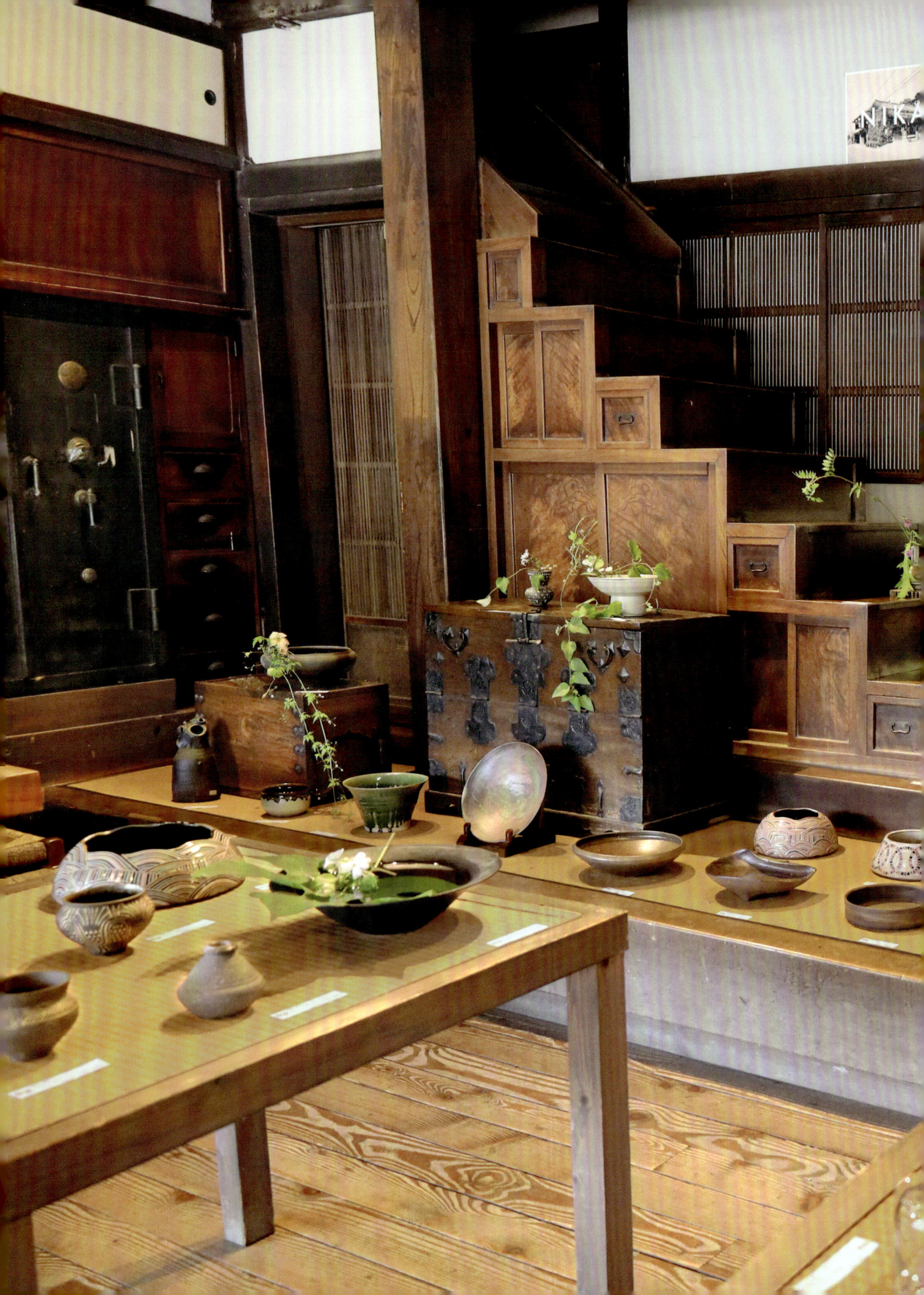

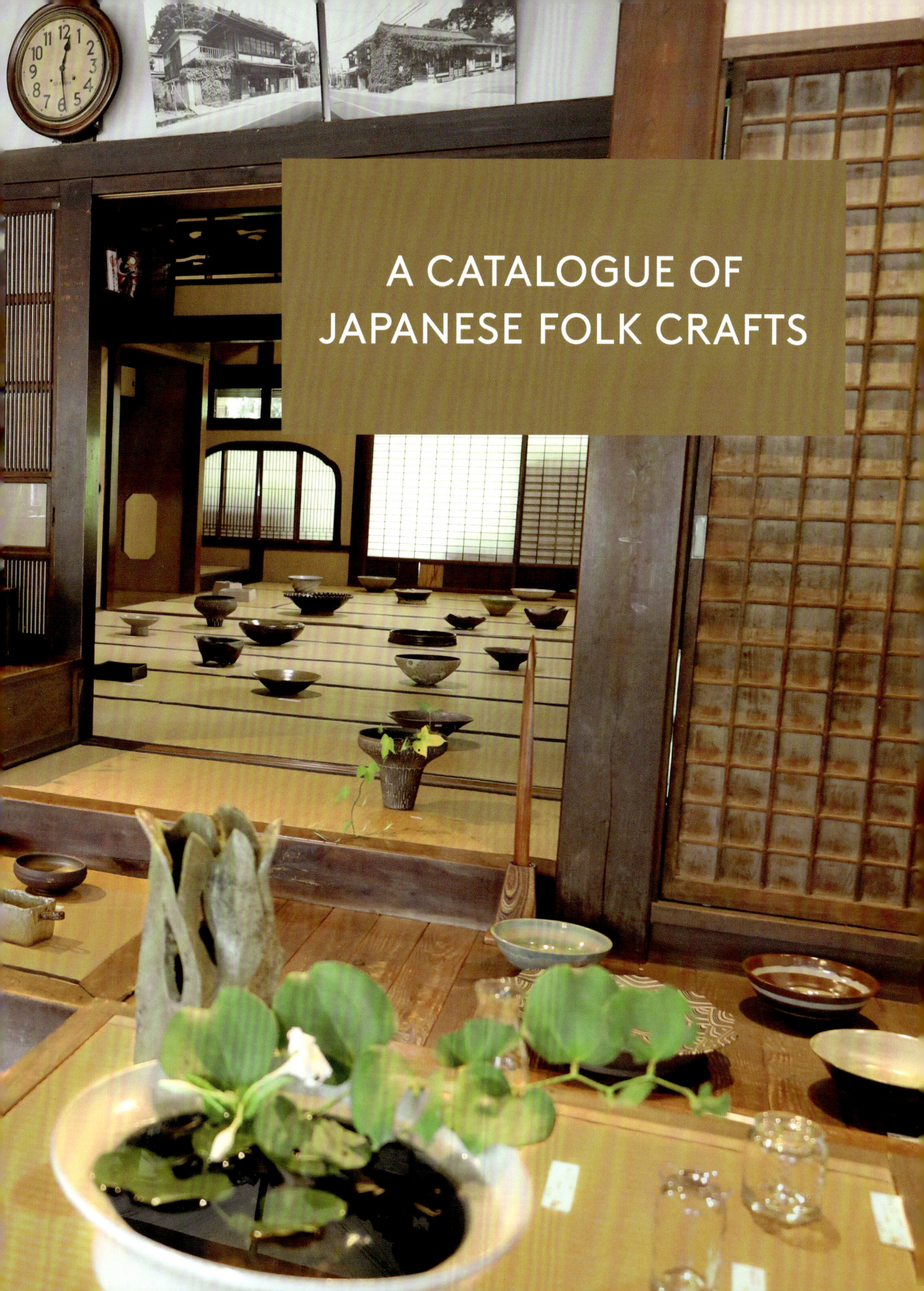

A CATALOGUE OF JAPANESE FOLK CRAFTS

Aizome Indigo Fabrics

A natural dyeing technique resulting in rich shades of blue

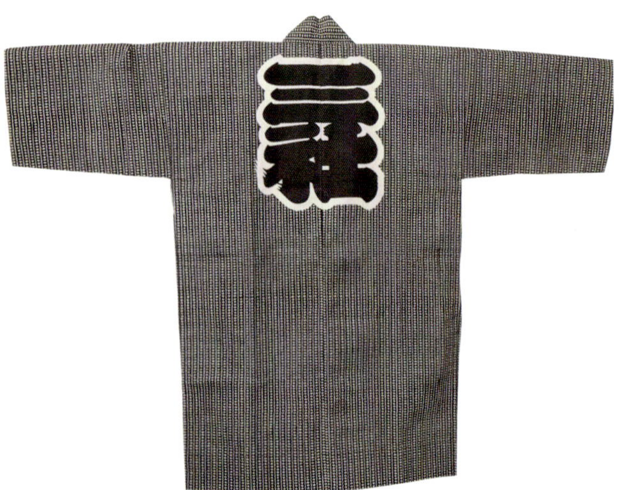

AIZOME IS A DYEING TECHNIQUE that uses the fermented leaves of the Japanese indigo plant, which produce a rich, deep-blue color.

This technique was introduced into Japan via the Silk Road during the Nara period (710–794). While the deep blue color of aizome was only worn by the nobility at first, during the Edo period (1603–1868), it became popular with commoners because of sumptuary laws that banned the usage of conspicuous colors by the townsfolk. The subdued hues produced by the indigo plant were permitted, and used to dye bedding, curtains, work outfits and *tenugui* cloths (see page 103). The dye produced by the Japanese indigo plant also has insect-repellent and odor-reducing properties, another reason for the popularity of garments dyed using this technique. Thus indigo blue became the standard color for kimonos until Japan's opening up to the outside world during the Meiji period (1868–1912) when synthetic dyes were introduced into the country from abroad.

To make indigo, good quality water is needed, from unpolluted sources, in order for it to grow well. The indigo leaves are then harvested and fermented. It is said that there are forty-eight color gradations within aizome, some of which are considered to be auspicious, such as *kachi-iro* which is a dark navy blue, almost black. The history of the kachi-iro color has its roots in the Heian period (794–1185), but it was during the Kamakura period (1185–1333), when the samurai rose to power, that the color began to be favored by the warrior class. Because the color is natural, it has a tendency to fade, but in a manner that is graceful, and many people like the way clothing made with this cloth looks after it has seen some wear.

Yukihiro Fujisawa, a third-generation indigo dyer (Fujisawa Dye Atelier Aizome Museum, 1-29-1 Kyojima, Sumida-ku, Tokyo; tel: 03-3611-6760) who dyes yukata summer kimonos, as well as ceremonial coats for festivals, explains that indigo dye is well suited to cotton or hemp fabrics because both the dye and the fabrics are derived from plants. Silk, however, derived from the silkworm, has an oily texture. Although this gives luster to the fabric, it also means that it doesn't dye well.

Above A happi coat, dyed by Yukihiro Fujisawa, made for Tokyo's annual Sanja Matsuri festival.
Facing page A magnificent indigo plain-weave resist-dyed cotton robe, painted with dyes and pigments.

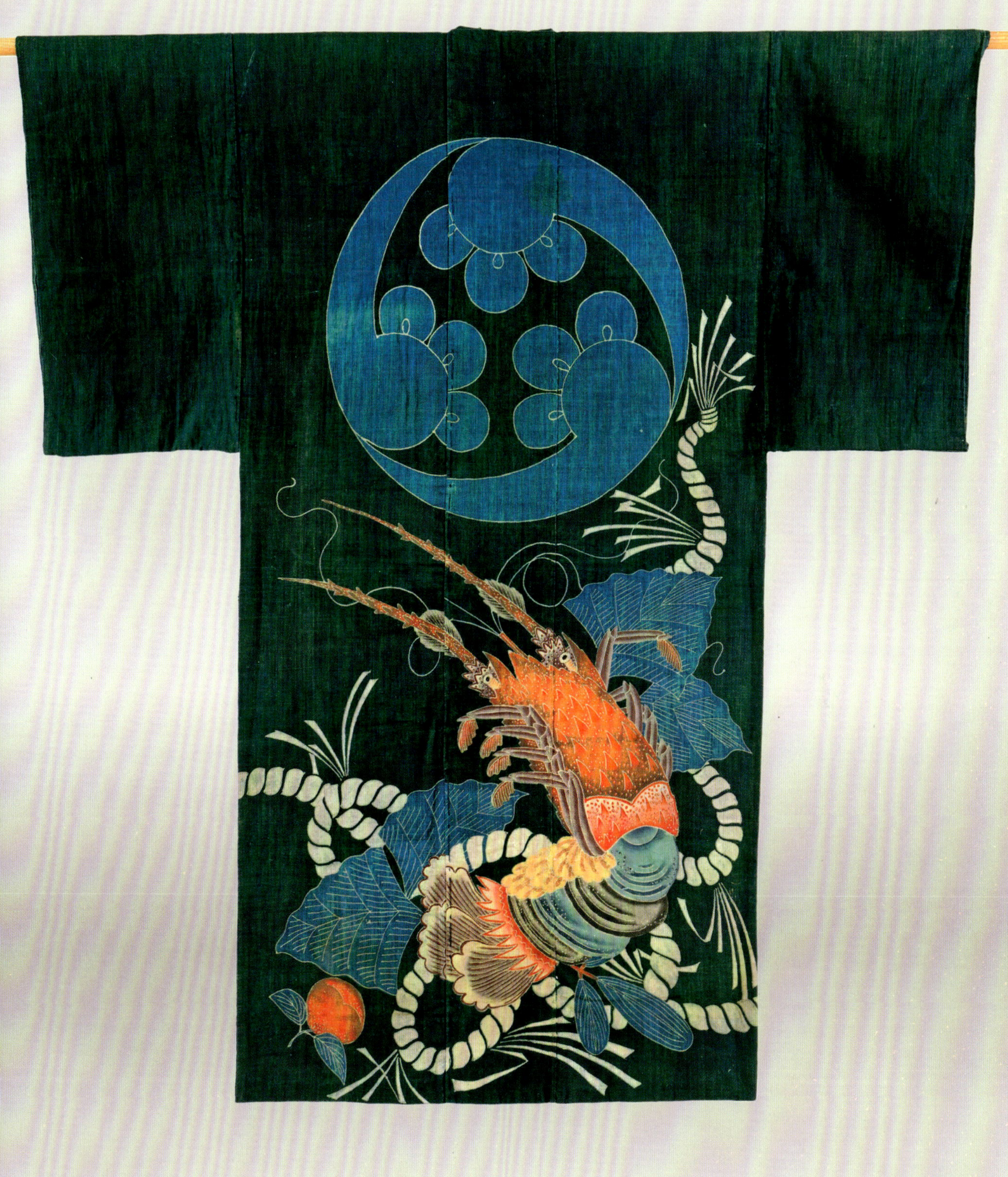

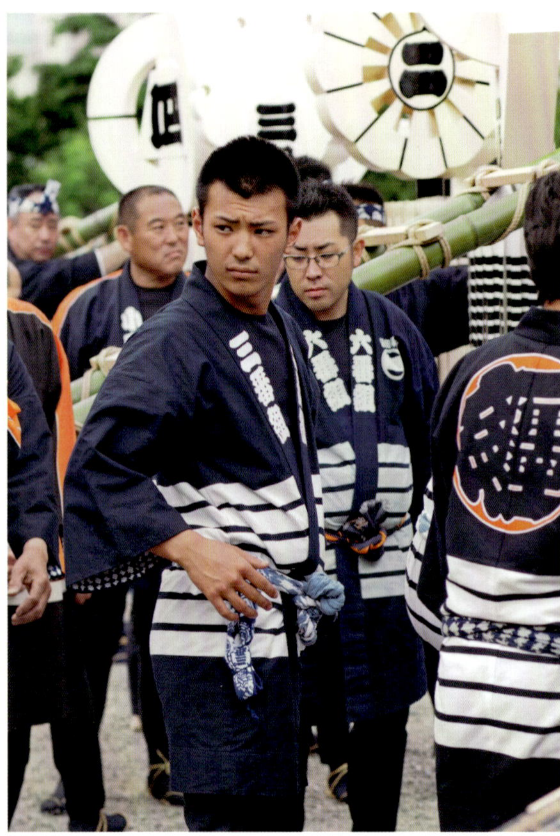

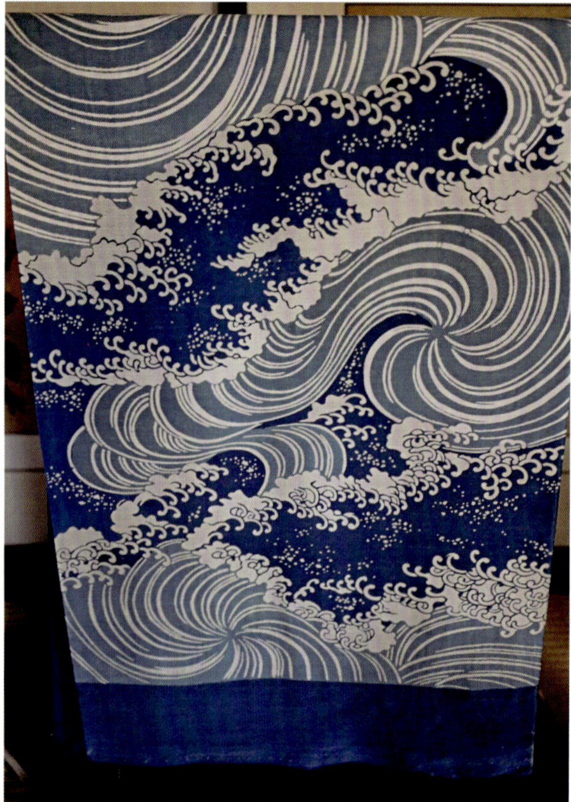

As Fujisawa's studio is located in the Sumida district of Tokyo, which is in geographic proximity to many famous festivals, including Tokyo's biggest and most iconic, the Sanja Matsuri, he produces many items related to these events, predominantly the *happi* ceremonial coat. His busiest season is from March, as the Sanja Matsuri is in May. There are also many festivals during fall in Tokyo's neighboring Kanagawa and Saitama prefectures, for which he supplies aizome goods.

Fujisawa started learning the craft of aizome when he became an apprentice in his twenties. As is the practice in the world of traditional Japanese trades, he was told to "watch and learn" rather than being taught directly. Originally he was only doing the stencil work but then he also apprenticed under a dye artisan.

Fujisawa says of the appeal of handmade things: "Artisan-made products tend to age well. Handcrafted items are not cheap, so the artisan has to take care to make a product that matches the customer's expectations. One of our popular items, for example is the *hanten*, the traditional Japanese short winter coat. The indigo color of our hanten will fade over time, but you'll get a good thirty years wear out of it. Clothes dyed using the aizome technique are like denim—as they age, they pick up a 'flavor,' and if it's a well-made item it won't fall apart, so it's money well spent. People who understand this come to us. Handmade things last a long time and have value. If there aren't people who appreciate this anymore, our job will disappear."

This page, left Festival participants wear indigo-dyed traditional outfits.
This page, right, and facing page The town of Mashiko is best known for pottery but it is also the home of the must-visit Higeta Indigo Dye Studio (1 Jonaizaka, Mashiko).

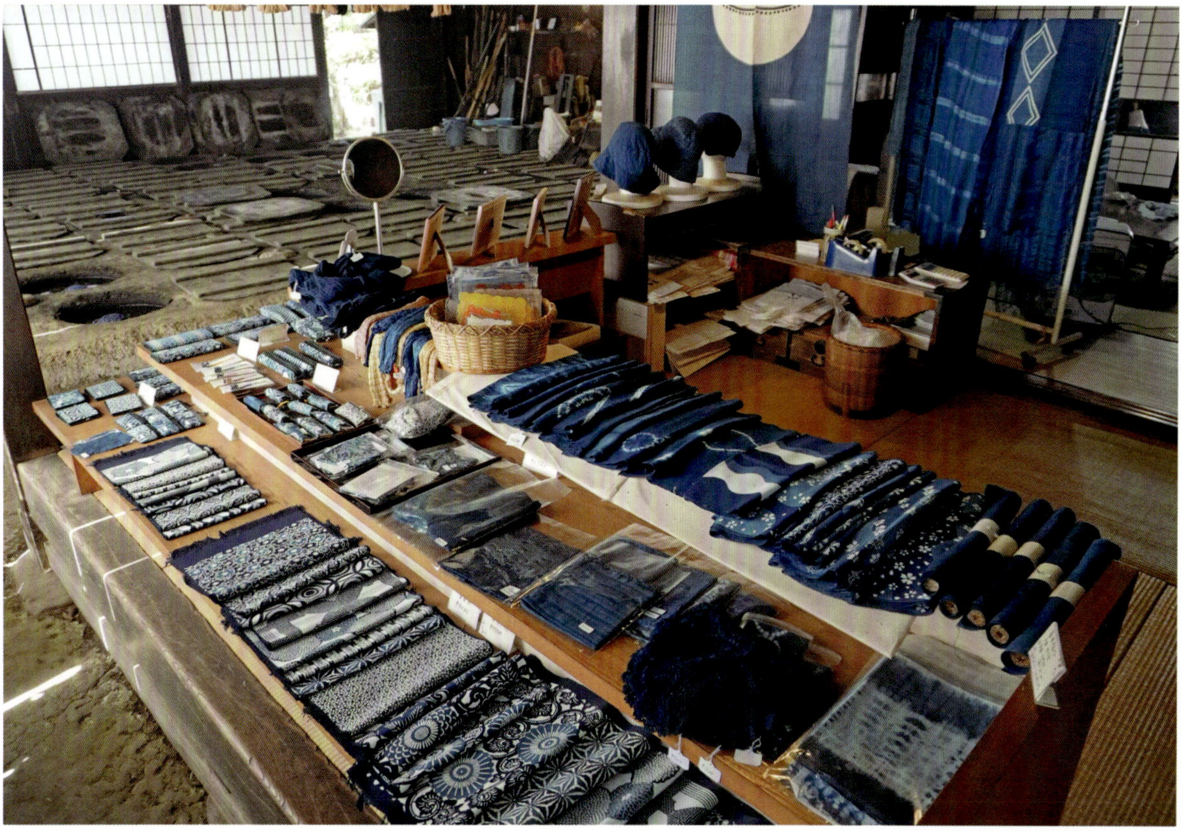

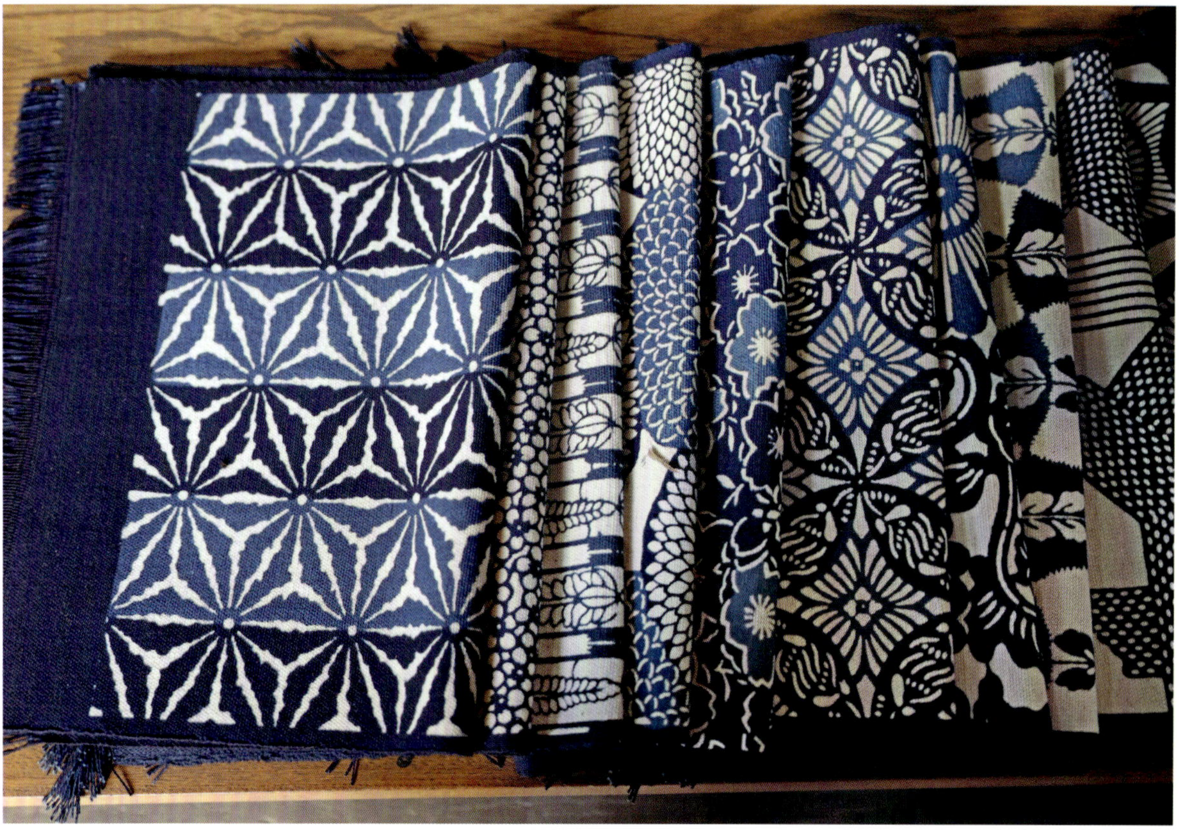

Akabeko Papier-Mâché Cows

A talisman against illness

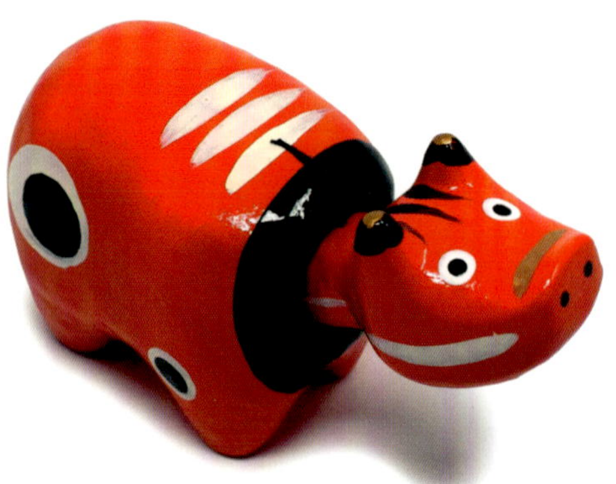

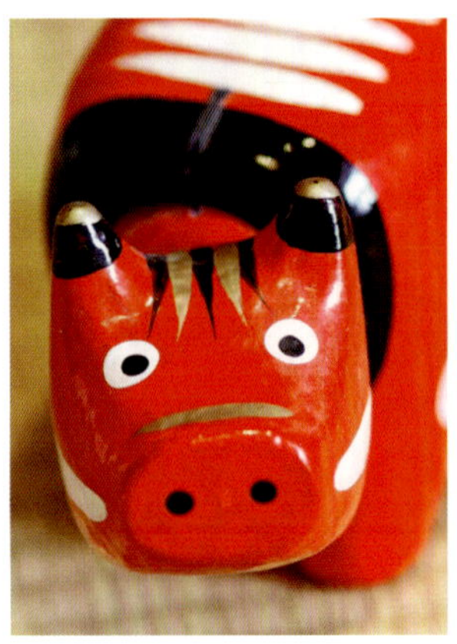

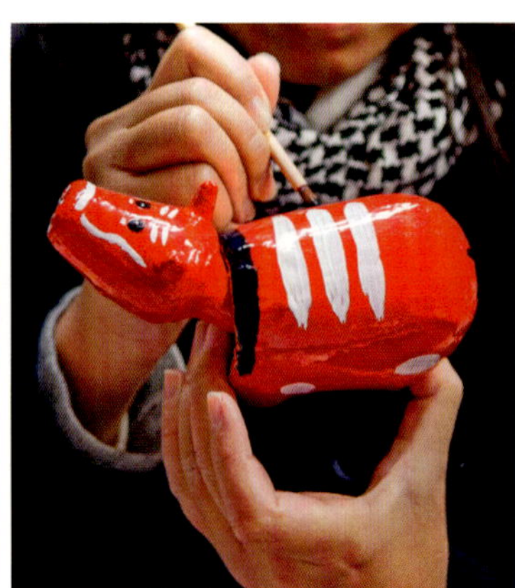

THE AKABEKO IS A BRIGHT RED, PAPIER-MÂCHÉ COW with an innocent, rather gormless facial expression and a bobbing head. The akabeko hails from the picturesque town of Yanaizu in Fukushima Prefecture. There are a few legends surrounding the cow. The townspeople built Enzoji Temple in the year 807, which required the transport of large quantities of materials, carried by cattle, including a red cow who didn't leave the site even after the temple was completed, or so the legend goes. Her apparent devotion to Buddha made her something of an attraction and upon hearing of this cow, feudal lord Gamo Ujisato ordered figures to be made in her likeness. This is said to be the origin of the akabeko toy, which, since the Edo period has been crafted from papier-mâché. The exterior is painted with a bright red lacquer, with black, white and gold accents.

The cow itself is talismanic and the traditional belief is that it protects against illness, particularly smallpox. The color red is considered to have protective qualities, and many folk toys are red for this reason.

Yanaizu is a bucolic town that sits alongside the Tadami River, and is depicted in some of the woodblock prints of Fukushima artist Kiyoshi Saito (1907–1997) . There are a number of akabeko statues across the town, including two at the splendid Enzoji Temple, which is constructed in a similar style to Kyoto's famous Kiyomizu Temple, with a lookout platform. At Enzoji there is an akabeko made of stone, and a metallic one, that visitors rub for good luck.

Nowadays the toy is made across Fukushima Prefecture, in a variety of colors including pink, pastel blue and yellow, by dedicated *hariko* papier-mâché artisans. Some add personal touches, such as decorating the bodies with the kanji character 寿 (*kotobuki*), meaning "luck." While there are many Japanese papier-mâché folk toys, akabeko are one of the most popular.

Above The cute papier-mâché akabeko is lacquered red, with black white and gold accents.
Facing page One of the two akabeko statues that can be found at Enzoji Temple in the picturesque town of Yanaizu in Fukushima Prefecture, where the akabeko folk toy originated.

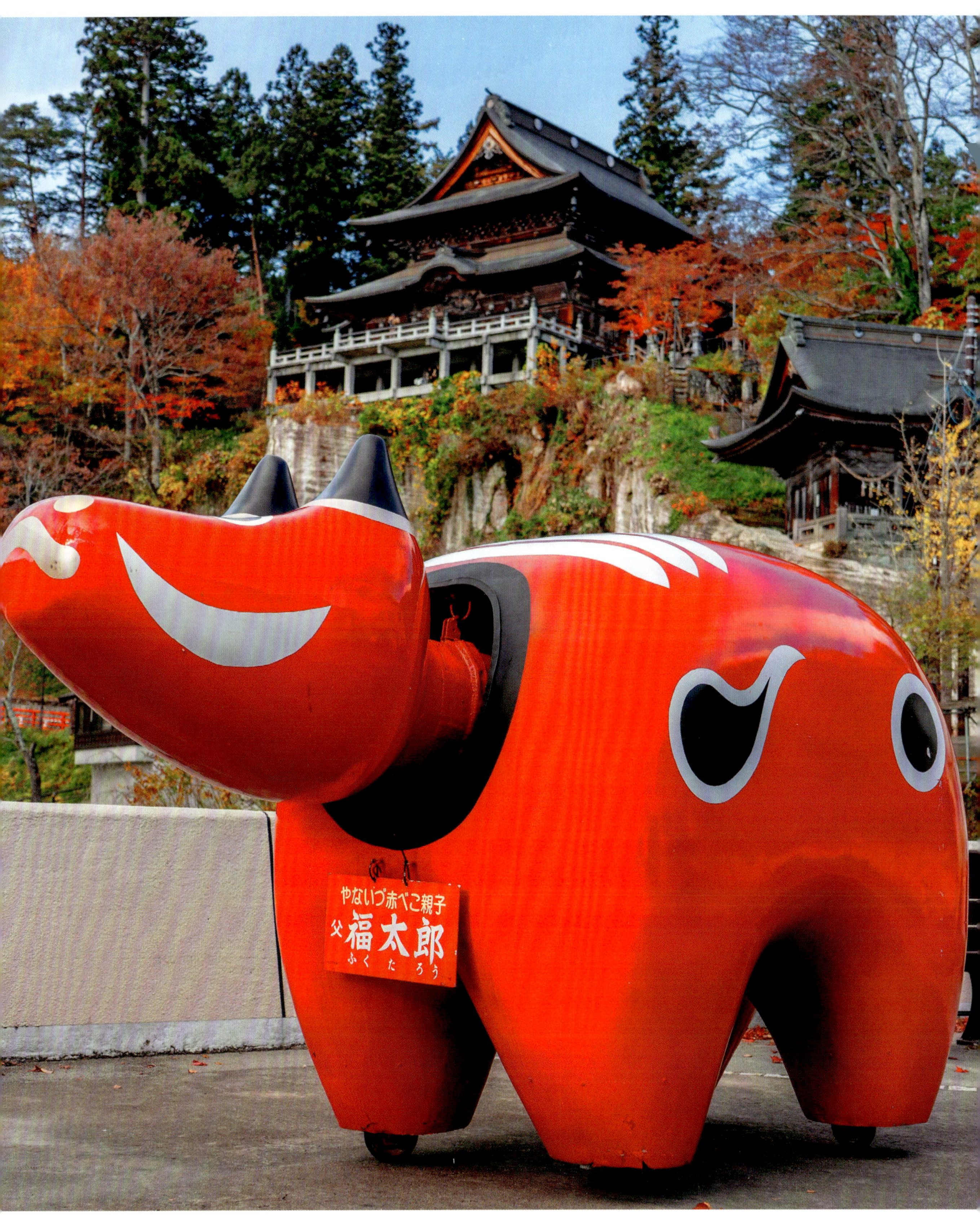
やないづ赤べこ親子
父 福太郎
ふくたろう

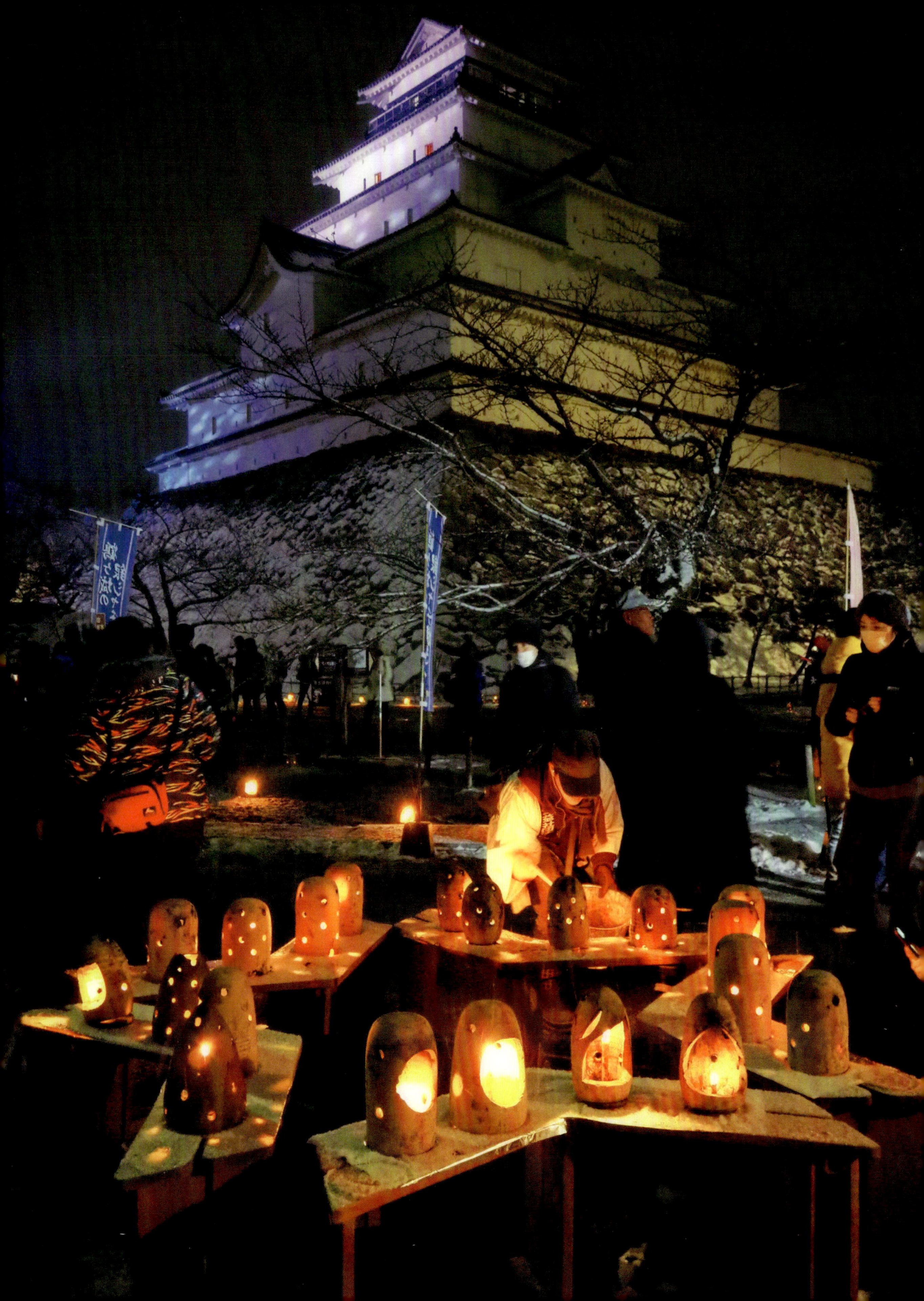

Aizu Erosoku Painted Candles

Traditional decorations for Buddhist altars

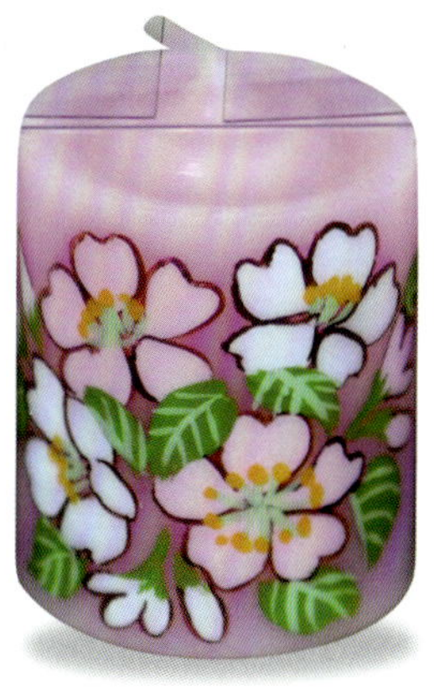

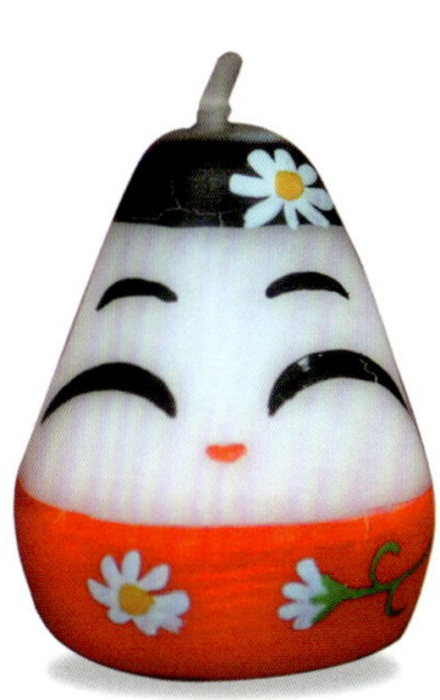

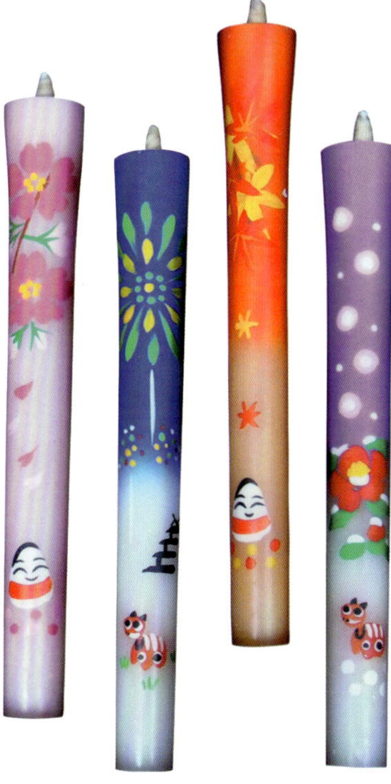

AIZU EROSOKU (LITERALLY "PAINTED CANDLES") are decorative candles, that have been produced in the Aizu region of Fukushima Prefecture for over five hundred years. The candle production is incredibly labor intensive and each candle is made by dipping it in wax over thirty times, which gives delicate "growth rings" similar to trees. The wicks are also hand-rolled.

Historically, erosoku were used on Buddhist altars, so they are made with plant-derived wax, which produces less soot. They were traditionally adorned with auspicious motifs and local flower types, such as adonis blossoms. Nowadays they are also painted with images that are associated with Fukushima, such as the akabeko cow (see page 36), or goldfish in pink hues.

The best place to see Aizu erosoku is at the ethereal Aizu Erosoku Festival that takes place during winter at Tsurugajo Castle, when over ten thousand candles are placed around the snowy castle grounds.

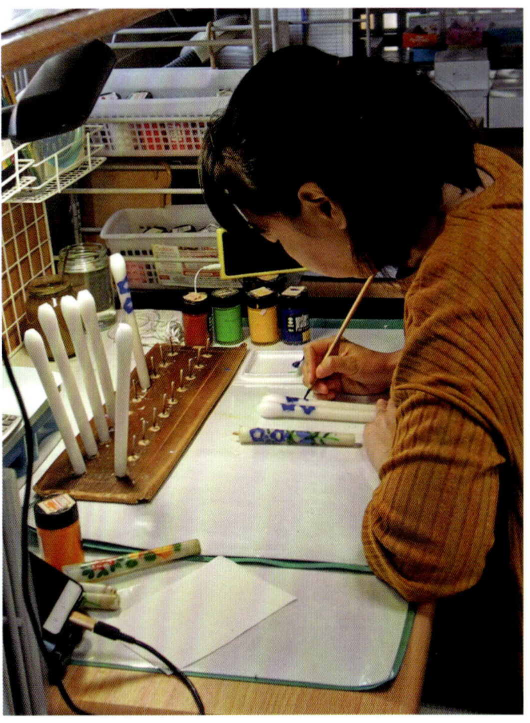

Facing page Candles at the Aizu Erosoku Festival.
Above & left Aizu erosoku candles are painted with a variety of auspicious motifs from flowers to the akabeko cow.

Asa Japanese Hemp

Playing an important part in traditional rituals

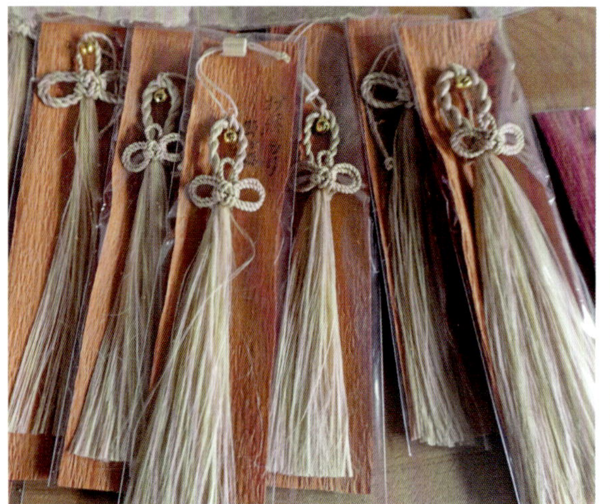

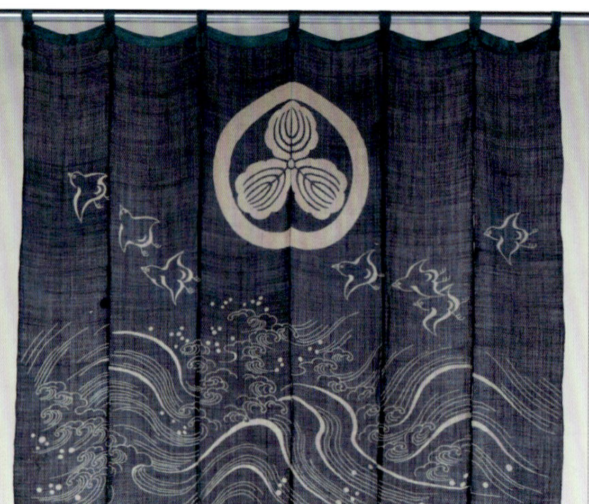

JAPANESE HEMP has a long history that is believed to originate in the prehistoric Jomon period (c. 14,000–300 BCE). Evidence for this comes from hemp seeds found at the Okinoshima site in Chiba Prefecture, which are thought to be 12,000 to 15,000 years old.

The use of hemp in Japan has traditionally been incredibly wide, ranging from fishing lines, string, and fabric, to food. Hemp was a prominent fiber crop as it was easy to grow even in poor soil conditions. According to Junichi Takayasu, curator at the Taima Cannabis Museum in Tochigi Prefecture, "Archeological evidence shows that cannabis hemp was the primary fiber crop from the Jomon period to the end of the nineteenth century."

In feudal times, hemp was widely used to make clothing for commoners, and was cultivated by many households. Light, soft and fire resistant, it was also used for clothing for firefighters of the Edo period (see page 11). It was also used in architecture, for example as material for *kayabuki* thatched roofs (see page 70) and for farming tools, such as rope. People started to show gratitude to this plant and it became sacred as a result.

Hemp is still used today for many sacred items associated with the Shinto religion. "The rope to ring the bell of a Shinto shrine is made of hemp and some places also use hemp for the *shimenawa* rope talismans," says Takayasu. "The ritual wand used by the priest for purification rituals is made of cannabis fibers. It is thought that a strange purification power comes out from the fibers, and that this can cleanse people of defilement that can't be seen with the eyes. Purification processes like these are an important part of the Shinto religion. Hemp is regarded as having purifying qualities, and that is the reason it is so prominent in the Shinto faith. When the emperor ascends the throne in Japan, he also wears clothing made of hemp that has been specially grown for this purpose."

Hemp also still utilized in present-day Japan for traditional cultural practices: it is used to

Above left Talismans made of locally produced hemp on sale at Yashuasa studio (see page 43) in Tochigi Prefecture. Hemp is thought to have talismanic and purifying qualities. **Above right** An indigo resist-dyed plain weave hemp *noren* door hanging from the Meiji era (1868–1912). **Facing page** An indigo hemp jacket from the Meiji era with reinforced cotton stitching.

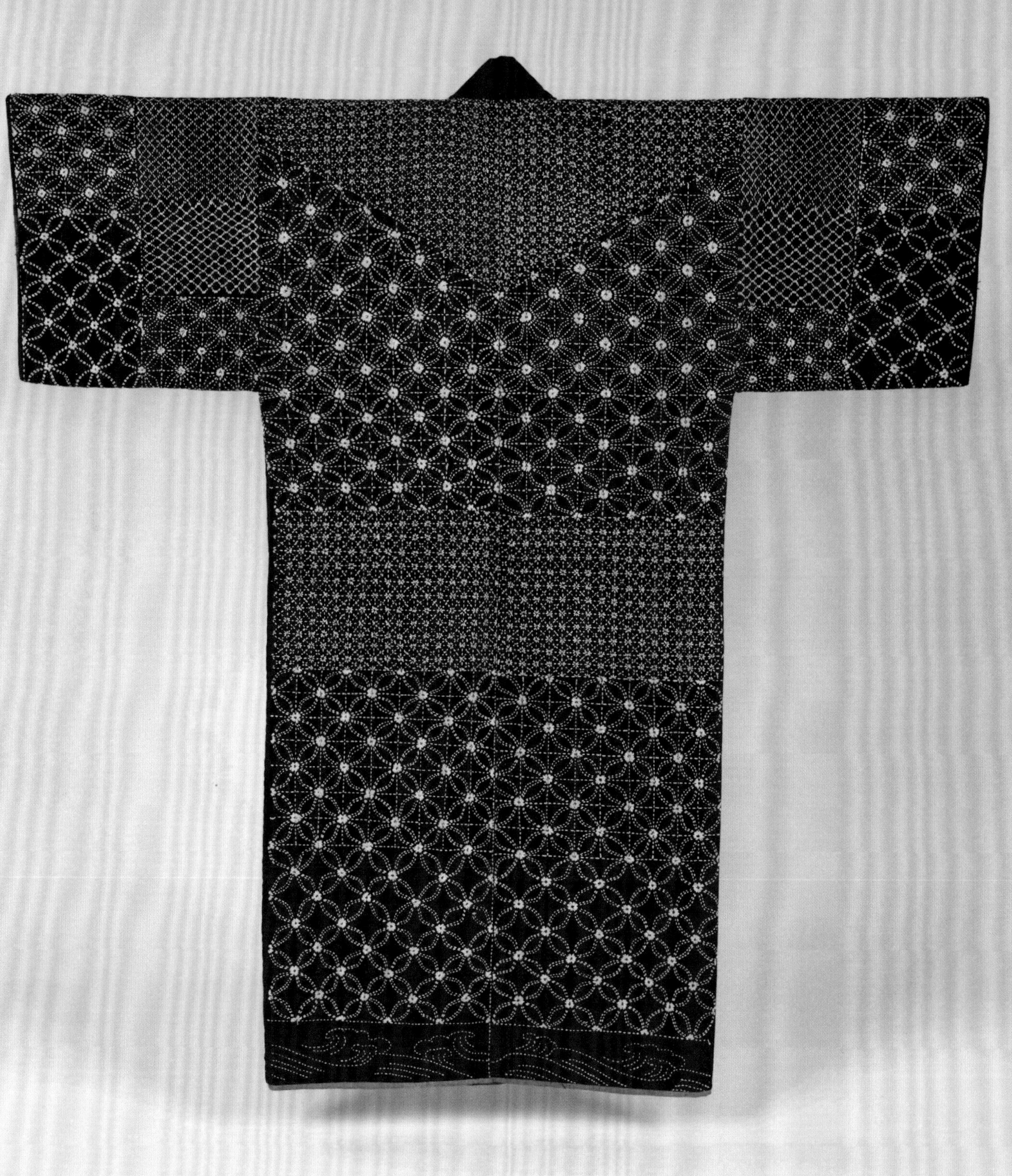

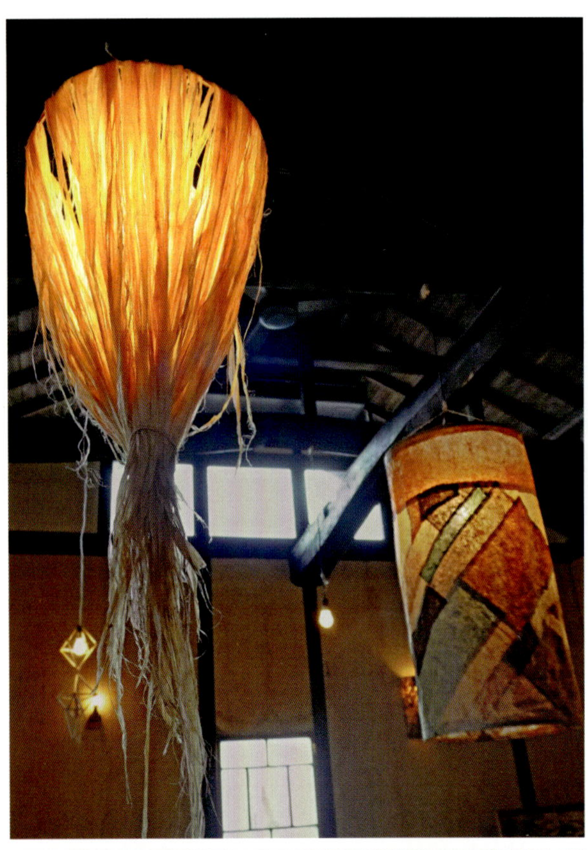

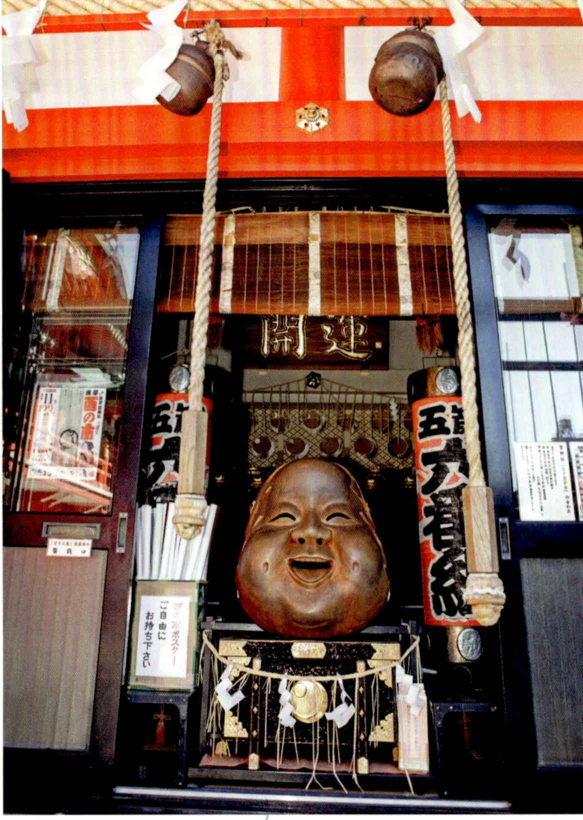
ご自由に
お持ち下さい

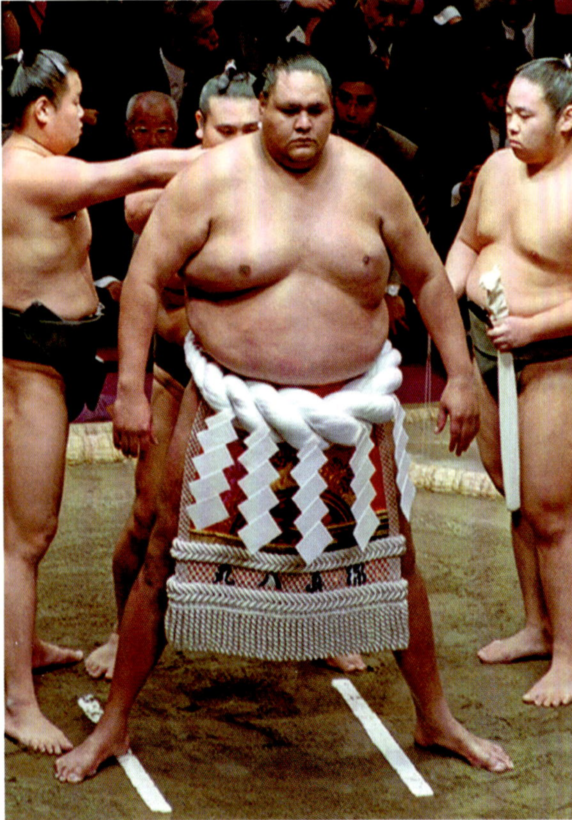

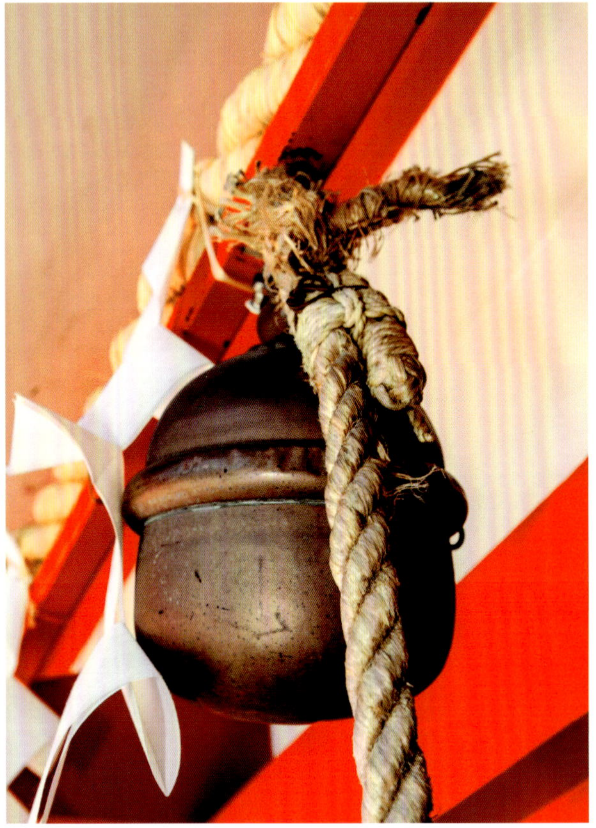

make the bow strings in *kyudo* (archery) and for the loincloth of the top-ranked *yokozuna* in sumo wrestling.

Hemp is able to grow well in a wide variety of environments, including locations that have extreme climate conditions. It thrives, for example, in the mountains of the northern prefecture of Fukushima where the average yearly temperature is 48°F (9°C) and the soil is still frozen in May. Hemp is fast growing, and doesn't require as much fertilizer and herbicide as cotton crops, which makes it environmentally friendly.

Despite this, many hemp products used in Japan these days are imported from China. Sometimes products labeled as hemp are actually ramie or flax linen. Currently in Japan there are thirty-three farms that grow cannabis hemp, and thirteen of these are in Tochigi Prefecture. These farms are licensed to grow a strain of hemp called *tochigishiro* which is low in THC, the main psychoactive component of cannabis, and hence has no narcotic potency.

Yashuasa (600-1 Shimonagano, Kanuma, Tochigi, 0289-84-8511) is an eighth-generation hemp production studio that is located in Tochigi Prefecture, headed by hemp artisan Yoshinori Omori. They produce *seima* fibers (made from hemp bark) from which they make contemporary items such as paper, wall hangings, wallpaper and lampshades. However, 70 percent of what they produce is for use in Shinto shrines.

Omori explains that in Japan, hemp plays an important part in many of life's rituals, from birth until death. "These rituals are such an ingrained part of our lives, that I don't think people actually realize they are using hemp," he says. "For example, when a child is born, hemp thread is traditionally used to tie the umbilical cord. Then there is the traditional gift known as *tomoshiraga* that is given at weddings. This is a decorative bunch of hemp thread that represents the hair of an elderly couple and the purpose of this gift is to wish the newlyweds a long life together."

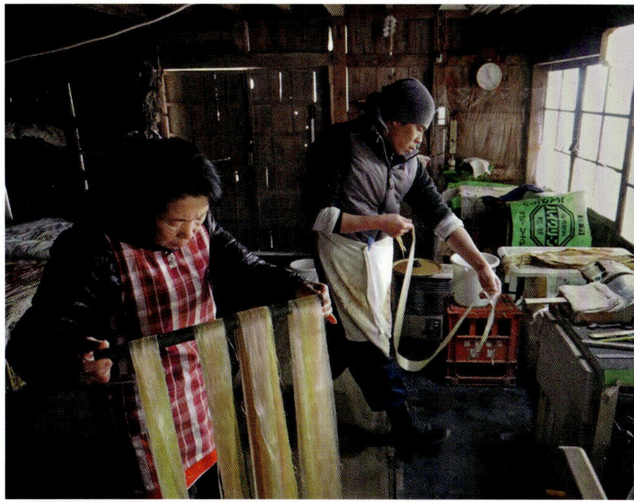

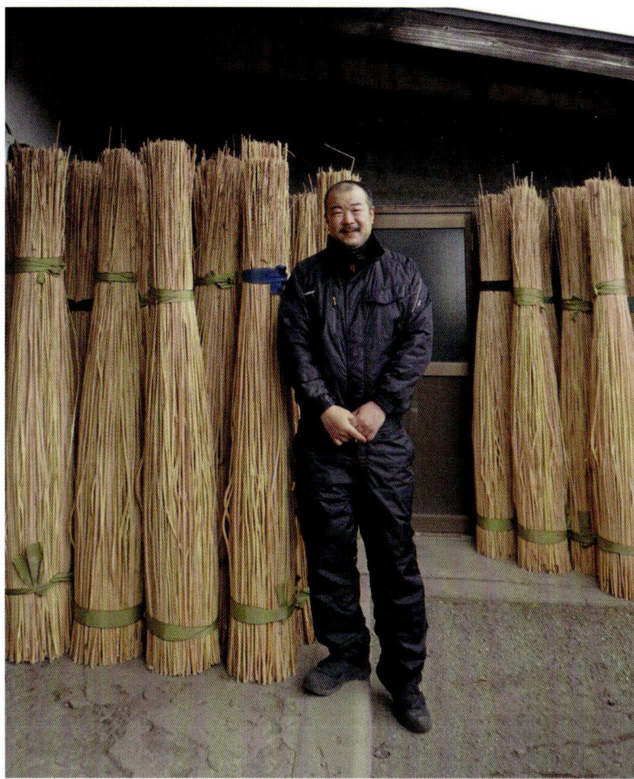

Facing page Domestically produced hemp is used to make a wide variety of items, from lampshades (top left) at Yashuasa studio, to shrine decorations like these ropes at Otori Shrine (top and bottom right), to sumo accessories (bottom left).
This page, top Artisans at Yashuasa studio make seima.
This page, bottom Yoshinori Omori is an eighth-generation hemp artisan.

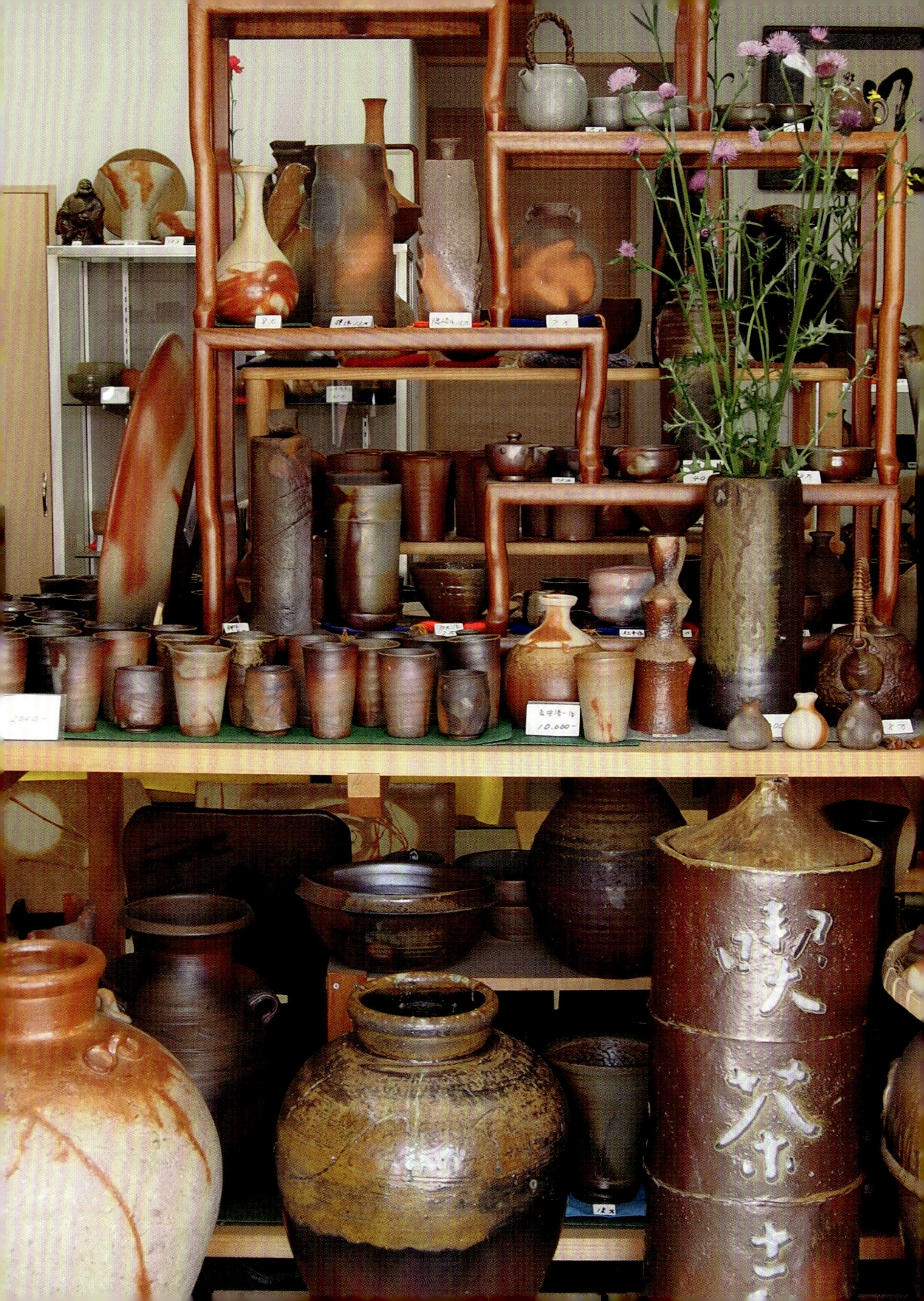

10,000-

Bizen Unglazed Pottery

Simple pieces with an earthy, rustic appearance

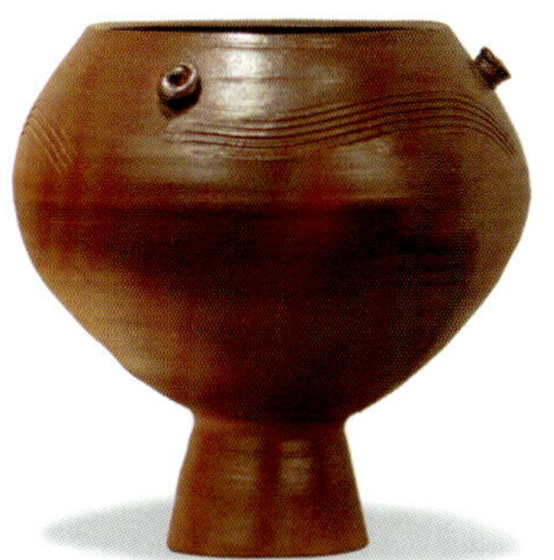

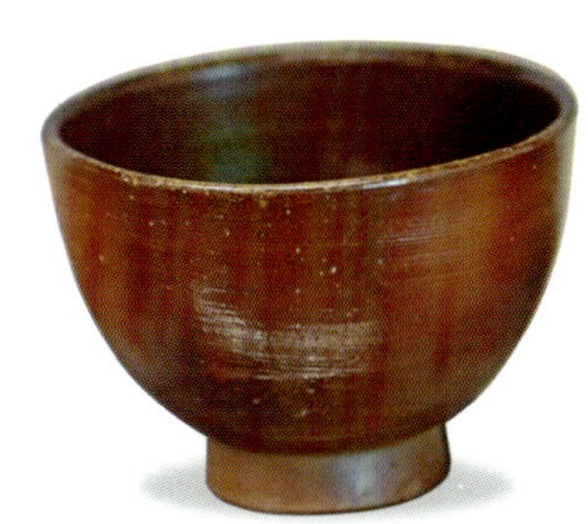

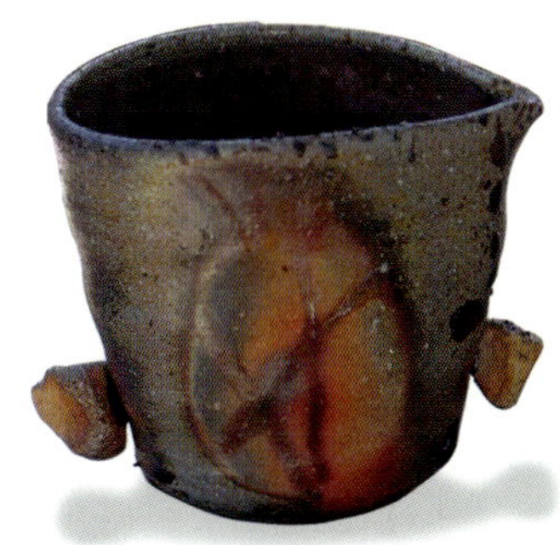

BIZEN WARE IS AN UNGLAZED FORM OF POTTERY crafted in the town of Bizen in Okayama Prefecture in the west of Japan. The pottery is made using a local clay called *hiyose* that contains iron, as well as soil extracted from rice paddies.

This type of pottery is unique yet durable, and is characterized by its brown-red hue. The lack of glaze gives it an earthy, rustic appearance and the designs are simple and charming. Each piece is fired at high temperature, traditionally using red pine, giving it molten ash patterns from the wood burning in the kiln. Rice straw is also wrapped around the pottery pieces before the firing process, and this creates the red and brown patterns.

Bizen ware is fired at a slow pace over a long period of time, up to twenty days in some cases. Many kilns undertake the process only twice a year as it is incredibly exhausting, due to the enormous amount of preparation that is required. A major part of this preparation is having enough wood on hand to fire the kiln continuously. The firing process requires constant supervision and wood needs to be added to the kiln day in day out—in some cases every fifteen minutes.

The production process has its roots in Sue pottery, a form of stoneware fired at high temperatures that was introduced to Japan in the fifth century by immigrant artisans who came to the country from Korea. The history of Bizen ware dates back to the Heian period (794–1185), when it was used to make roof tiles and other practical items for daily use, such as bowls and plates. Bizen is one of the six ancient Japanese kilns that have over a thousand years of history (the others being Seto, Echizen, Tokoname, Shigaraki and Tamba).

The unassuming sensibility of Bizen was lauded by renowned sixteenth-century tea master Sen no Rikyu, who espoused a minimalistic aesthetic in his tea ceremonies. Because of this, Bizen ware is often used in tea ceremony, to this day.

Bizen ware is predominantly made in the district of Imbe, an incredibly picturesque area of Bizen that has over a hundred galleries and

Facing page & above Bizen pottery is characterized by its brown-red hue, and a lack of glaze, which gives it an earthy, rustic appearance.

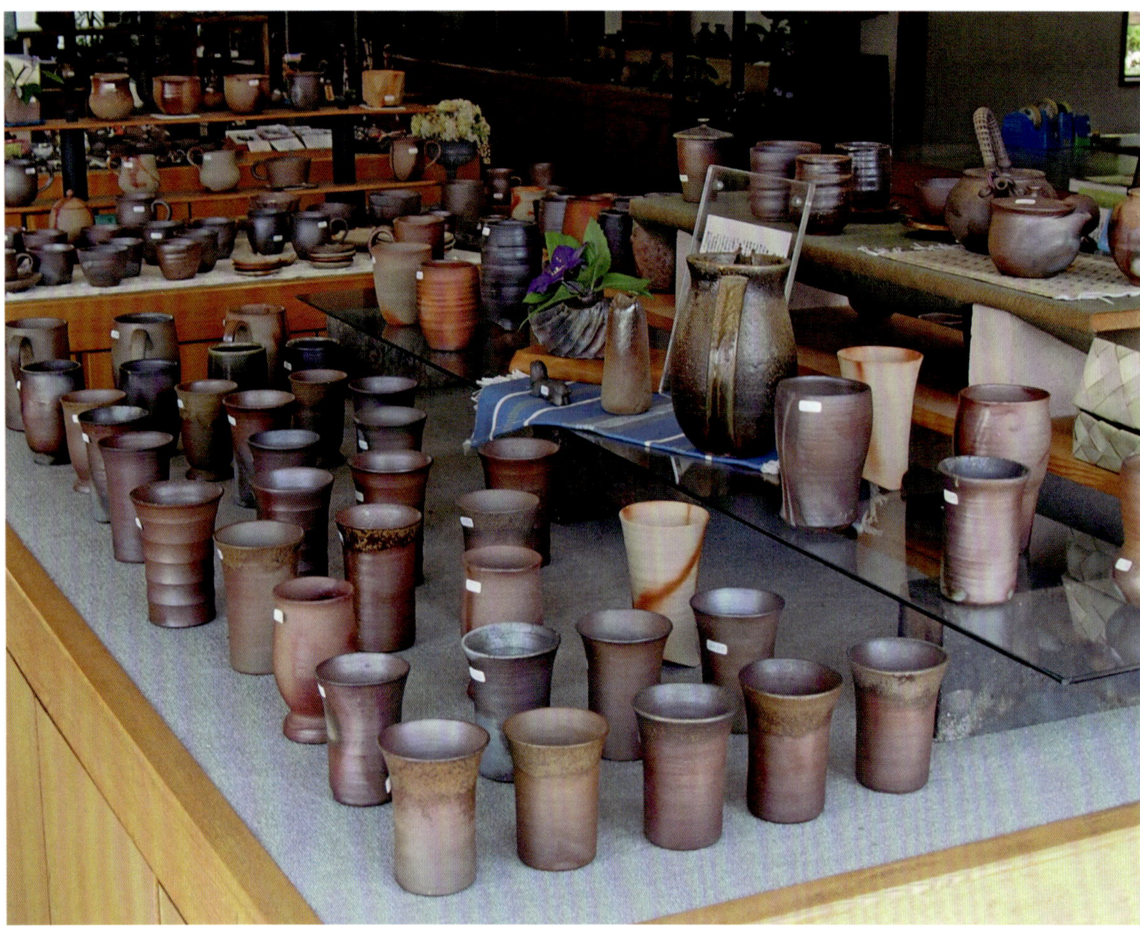

kilns scattered through its streets. The area around Imbe Station has kiln chimneys protruding out of buildings. The studios and shops have Bizen-tiled roofs giving the entire town a bygone charm. Local shops display a wide selection of Bizen ware—ranging from cups and plates to vases and ornaments—all of which have a *wabi-sabi* appeal that fits with the philosophical notion embraced by Sen no Rikyu that imperfection is beautiful. Bizen pottery items are uneven in shape and the colors are irregular. However, they undoubtedly exemplify a certain type of beauty.

Wasyugama (1754-3 Kojima Akasaki, Kurashiki; wasyugama.com) is a Bizen kiln that specializes in classic Bizen ware. Artisan Takaaki Owashi also runs an Airbnb next door to the kiln, so that it is easy for guests to see potters in their ateliers, as well as try their hand at making pottery themselves.

"Nowadays many people enjoy using Bizen ware to serve coffee or beer," says Owashi. "It's because the mouthfeel of the pottery is particularly suited to these beverages and makes them taste even more delicious!"

This page The town of Bizen is full of shops that display a wide selection of Bizen ware.
Facing page Bizen ware is sometimes used for decorative items such as masks. Like most mingei folk crafts, however, it is more often used for practical items for daily use. These days, many Bizen artisans craft items to suit contemporary tastes such as exquisite coffee cups.

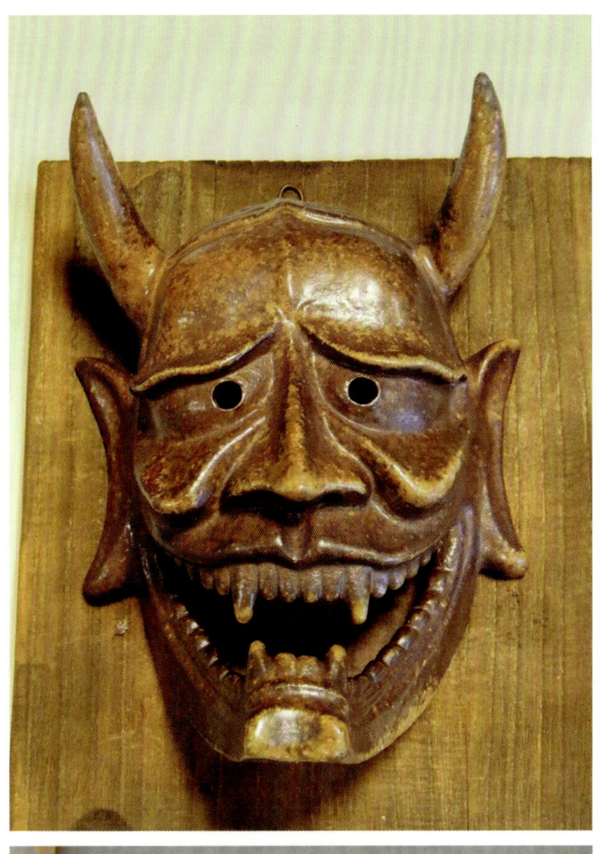
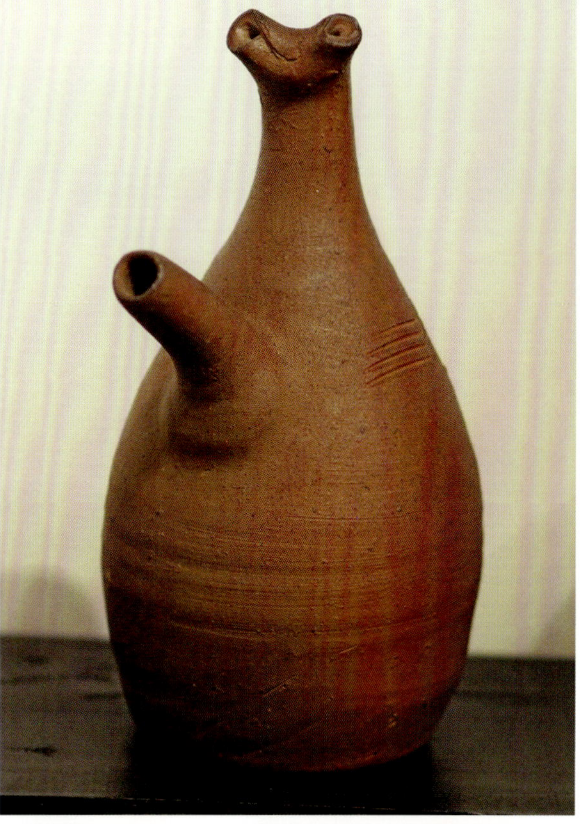
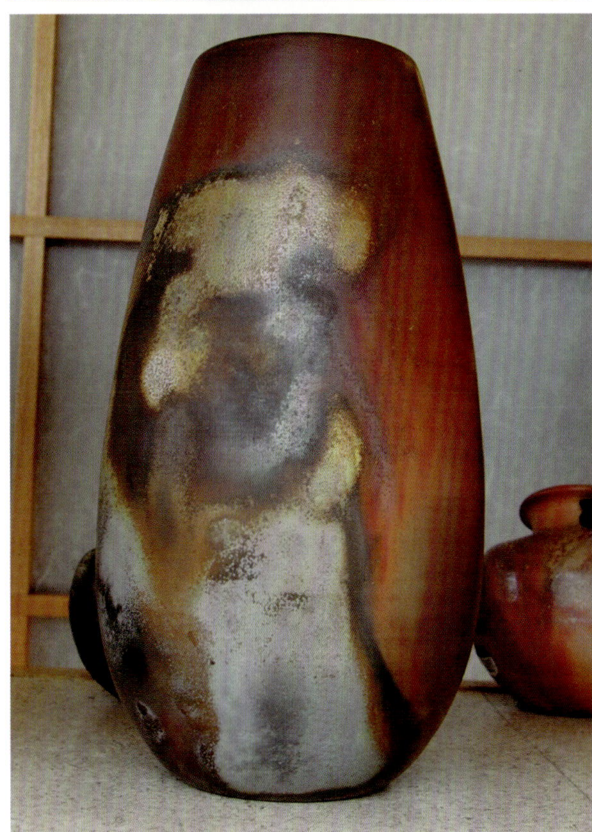
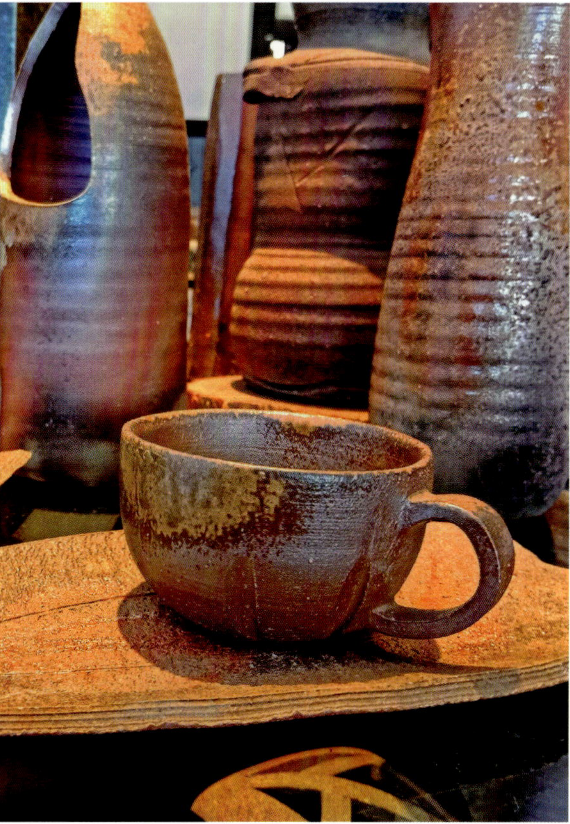

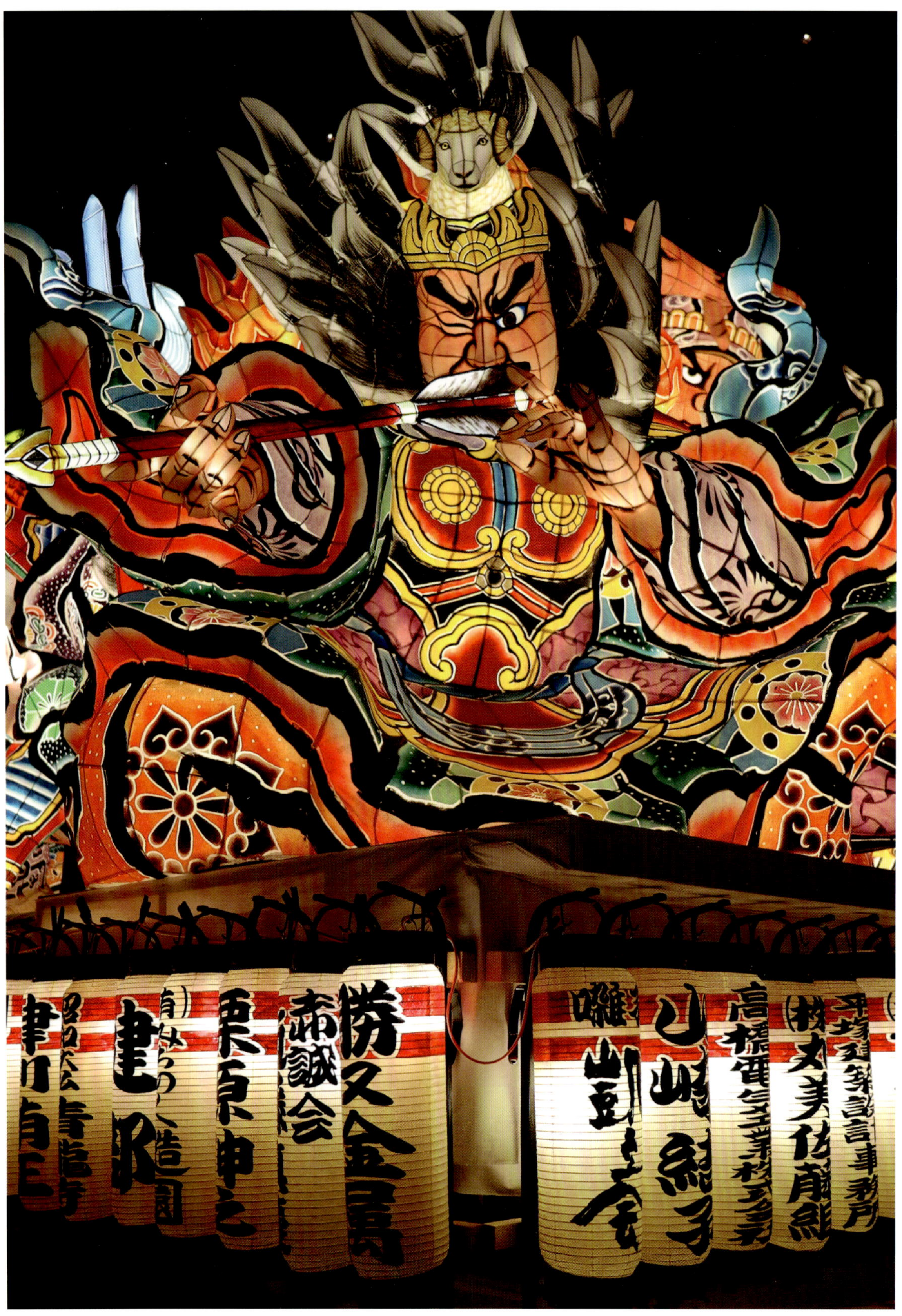

Chochin Paper Lanterns

Ubiquitous decorations for everything from temples to restaurants

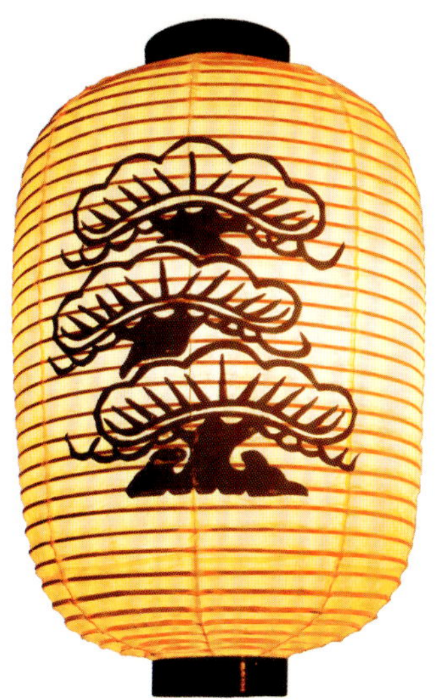

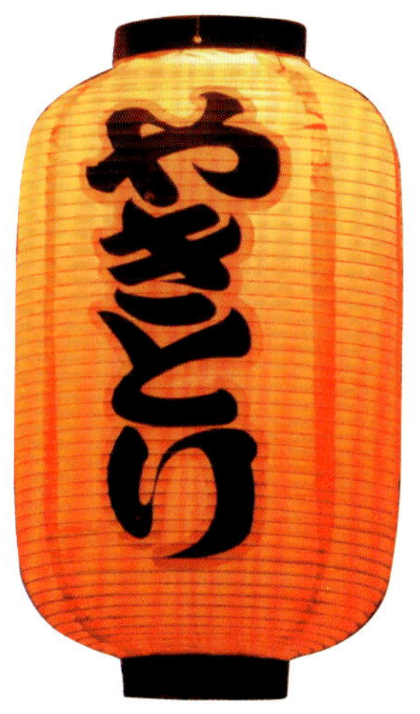

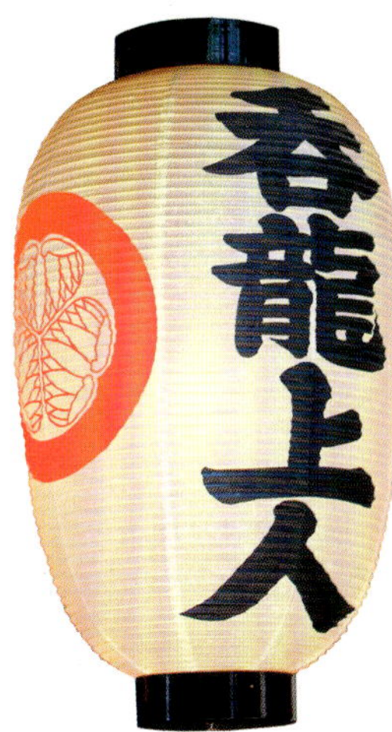

A COMMON SIGHT outside temples, eateries and at festivals, chochin lanterns are traditionally made from a bamboo frame wrapped with washi paper or silk although today they are also made of modern materials such as plastic. Chochin lanterns date from the Muromachi period (1333–1573), but it was during the Edo period (1603–1868) that a type of lantern that could be folded up and stretched out like an accordion—making it easy to carry as well as a chic accessory— became popular, as did the custom of carrying a lantern inside the sleeve pocket of a kimono. Japan's largest chochin is the ginormous 1,500 pound (700 kg) lantern at the front gate of Sensoji, Tokyo's oldest temple. It can be collapsed to let floats pass during the Sanja Matsuri festival.

There are several dedicated lantern festivals across Japan, which are important for artisans, who may spend up to a third of the year making chochin just for these events. Visiting one of the festivals listed below is a great way to appreciate the Japanese craft of lantern-making.

THE NIHONMATSU LANTERN FESTIVAL

This 350-year-old festival takes place in October in Nihonmatsu, Fukushima Prefecture, with seven floats covered in three thousand red lanterns that emit a warm glow. The lantern-covered floats are paraded through the town, and the locals wear dramatic full-length yukata kimonos.

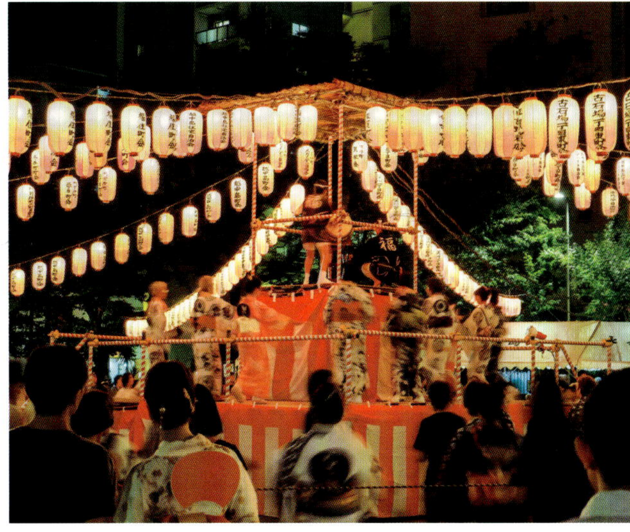

Facing page A giant Nebuta lantern float is decorated with chochin lanterns on the underside.
This page Chochin lanterns illuminate a traditional summer Bon Odori festival.

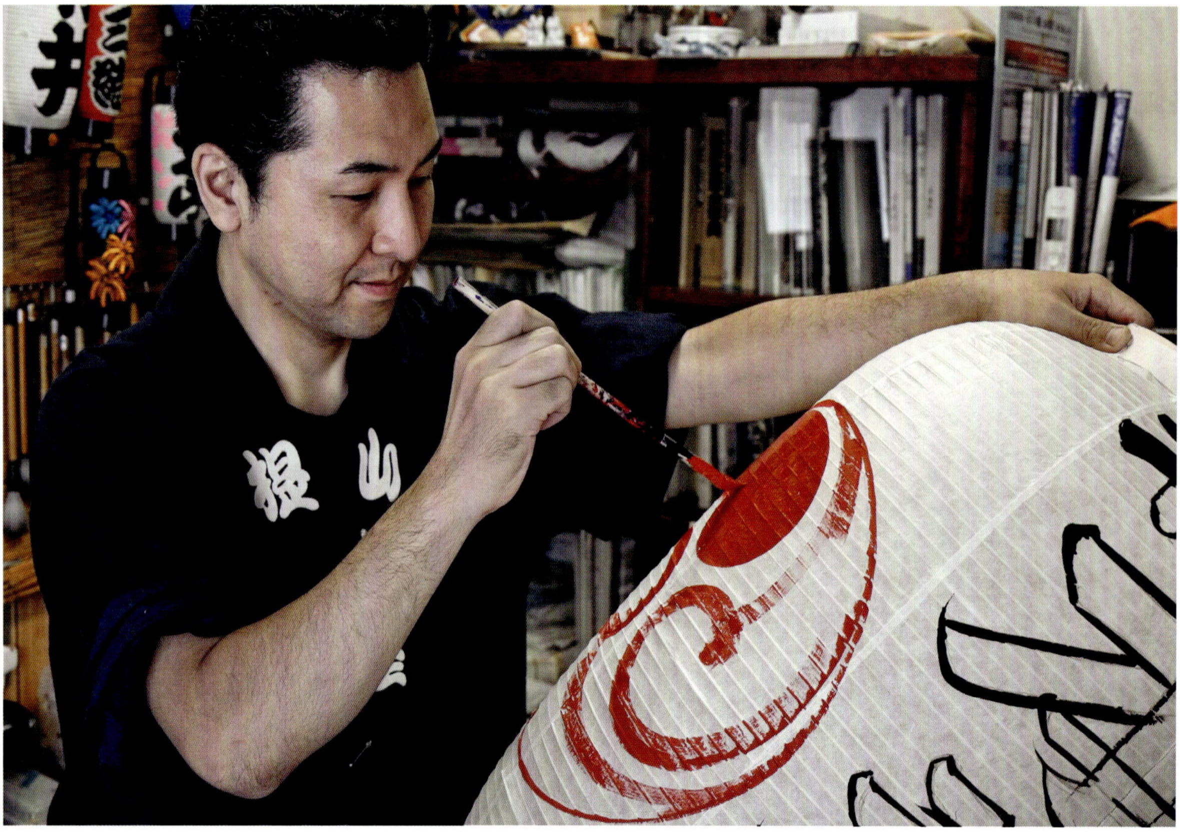

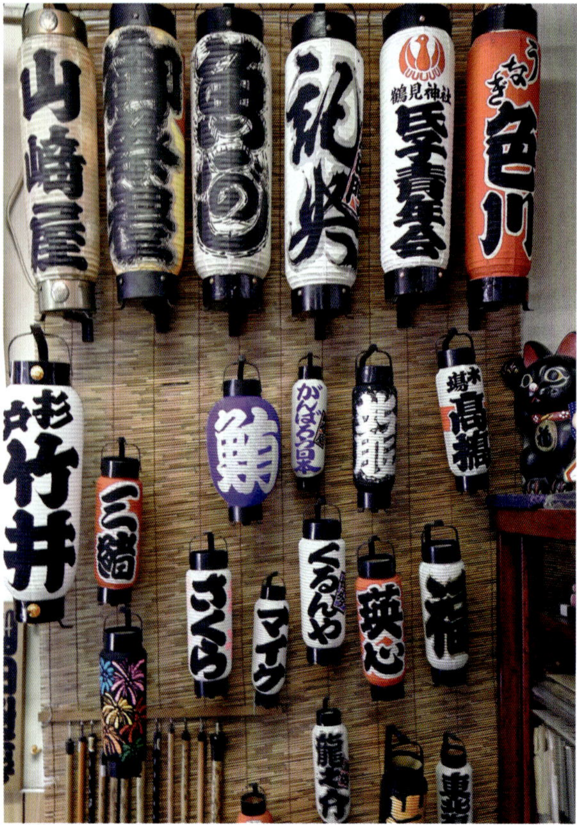
山崎屋
鶴見神社
色川
竹井
さくら
マイク

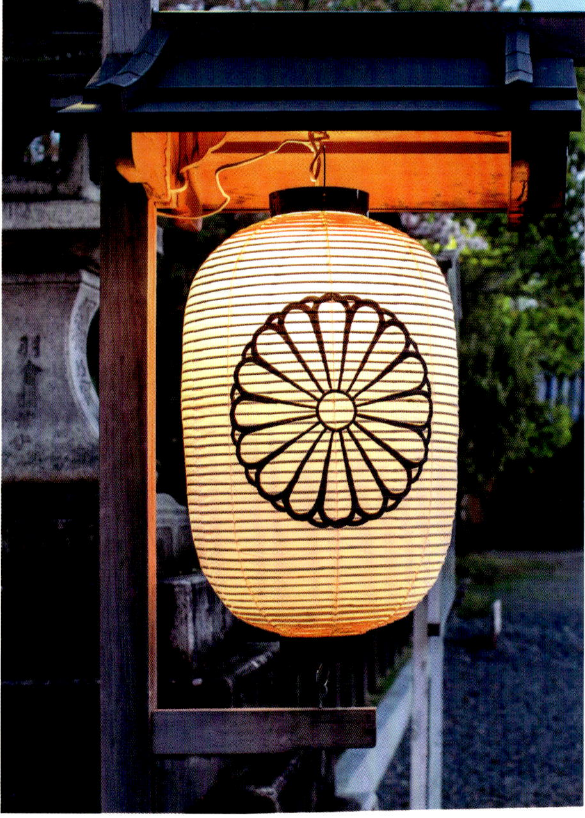

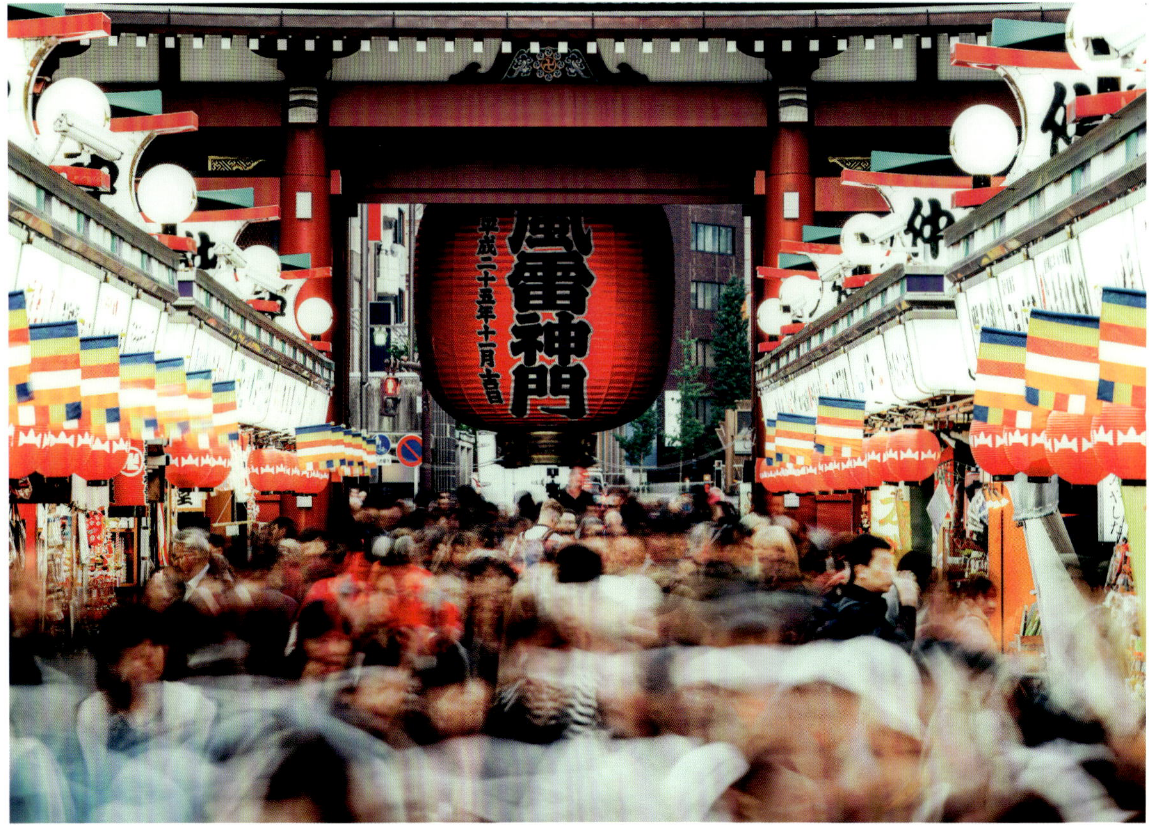

THE AKITA KANTO FESTIVAL

The Akita Kanto Festival is held every August in Akita City, and is performed as a ritual to cleanse evil spirits and to protect against disease. The paper lanterns are shaped like the *komedawara* bags used to store rice. They are hung from giant bamboo poles, in clusters that resemble ripe stalks of rice, and are carried with great dexterity through the streets of Akita.

THE YANAI GOLDFISH LANTERN FESTIVAL

The goldfish lanterns of the city of Yanai in Yamaguchi Prefecture have red and white bodies, cute faces, round black eyes and large tails. They are made of washi paper, which is pasted onto split bamboo, then dyed. It is said that the festival started when a candle merchant in Yanai, inspired by the lanterns he had seen at Aomori's Nebuta Festival, created goldfish lanterns for children. Even today, during the festival, children dressed in yukata summer kimonos carry lighted goldfish chochin lanterns through the evening streets of Yanai.

THE NEBUTA FESTIVAL

The largest of the summer festivals in Aomori Prefecture, the Nebuta Festival in Aomori City takes place every August. There is a parade of two dozen large lantern floats, bearing enormous lantern sculptures made of painted washi paper molded over wire frames. These lanterns take about a year to make, and are embellished with iconography ranging from mythical creatures, dogs, folkloric characters and kabuki protagonists. While the enormous lanterns are not the chochin collapsible type, this is Japan's most resplendent lantern festival and shows the heights of lantern-painting craftsmanship.

Facing page, top and bottom left The Yamazaki-ya Genshichi lantern store in Tokyo's Asakusa district has an array of hand painted lanterns. **Facing page, bottom right** A temple lantern brightens the dusk. **This page** Japan's largest chochin lantern is the 1,500 pound (700 kg) lantern at the gate of Tokyo's Sensoji Temple.

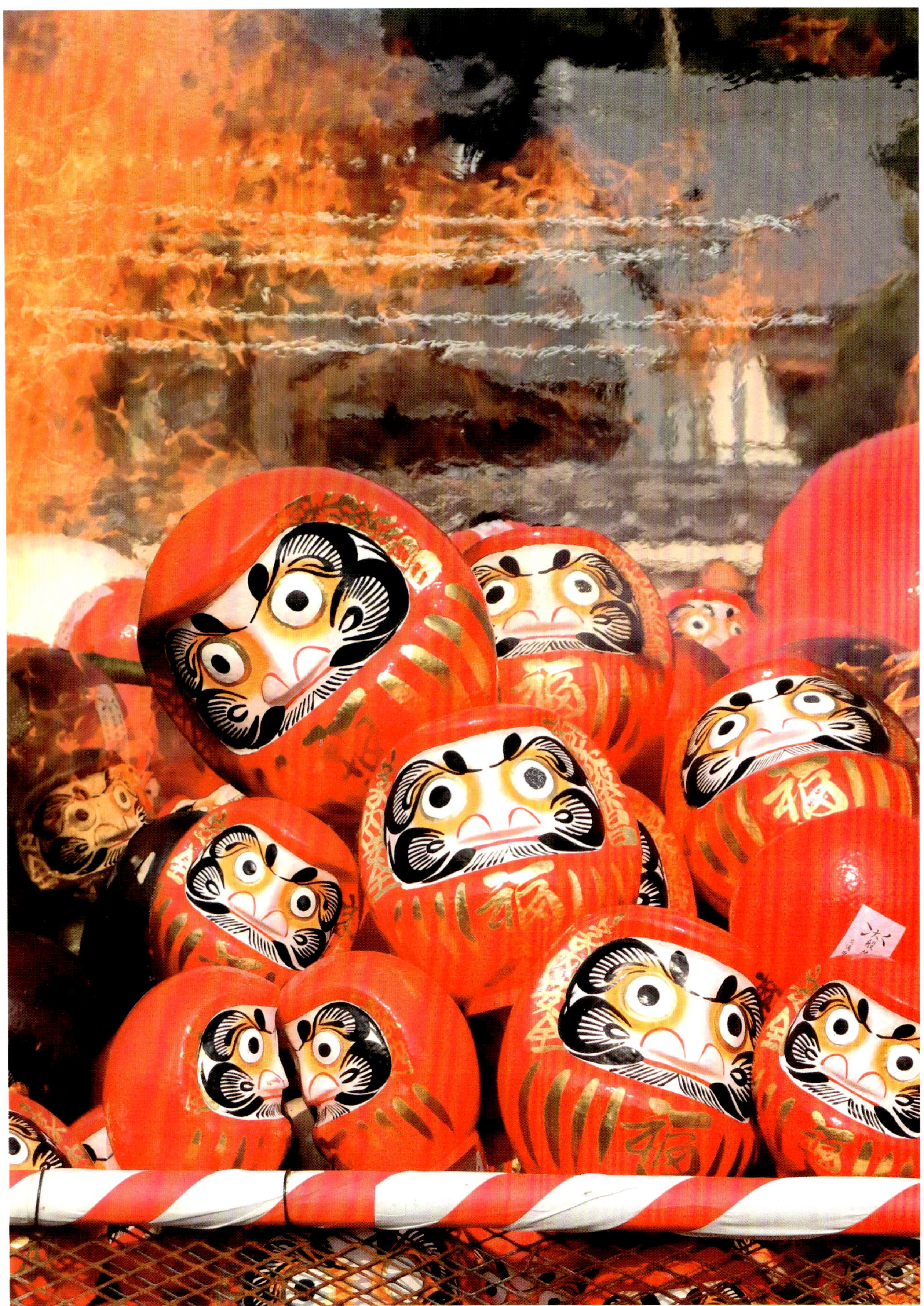
福

Daruma Good-Luck Figurines

Japan's iconic folk figure, based on a likeness of Bodhidharma

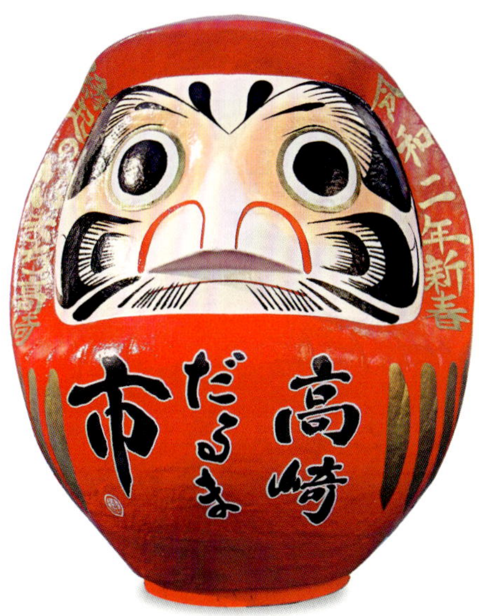

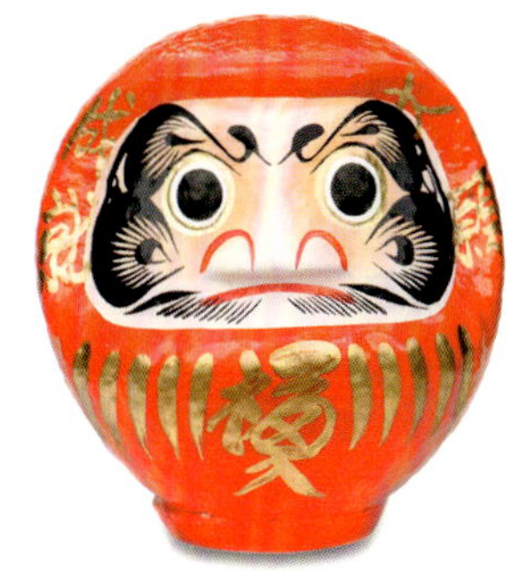

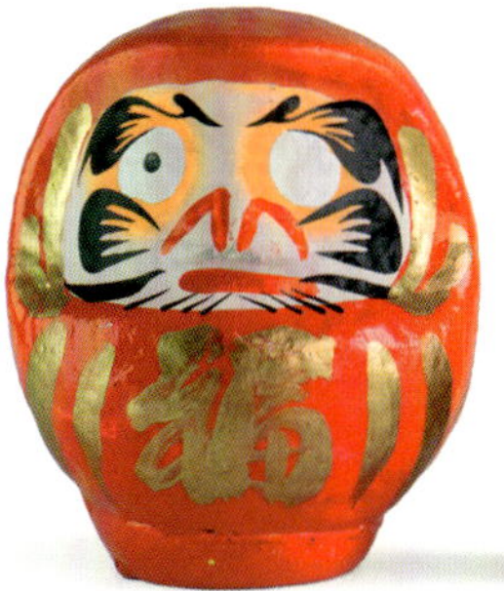

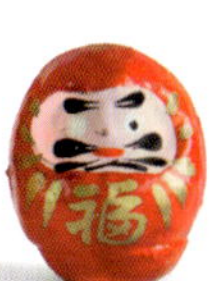

DARUMA ARE A TYPE OF FOLK FIGURE symbolizing good luck, based on the likeness of Bodhidharma, the founder of Zen Buddhism. Daruma were popularized in the Edo period and are one of the most iconic dolls and souvenirs of Japan. While there are various manifestations of Bodhidharma in Japanese art, some of which are more realistic depictions, the face of a Daruma usually has wide eyes and a dramatic beard, drawn with calligraphic flourishes. The eyebrows are painted to resemble a crane, and the beard to represent a turtle, both motifs that symbolize longevity.

Bodhidharma was said to have lived in a cave for nine years where his legs atrophied and fell off, so the Daruma has no legs. The roly-poly doll is made so that it always stands upright, returning to an upright position even when pushed over, as though to illustrate the famous Japanese saying in praise of perseverance: "fall down seven times, stand up eight."

For this reason, Darumas are commonly bought for people looking achieve a certain goal, such as passing school entrance exams. The eyes are often left blank: one eye is filled in when the person purchases the Daruma and sets a goal; the other eye is filled in once the goal has been achieved.

Daruma are traditionally painted red, which is considered an auspicious and talismanic color. Nowadays, however, you can find a wide range

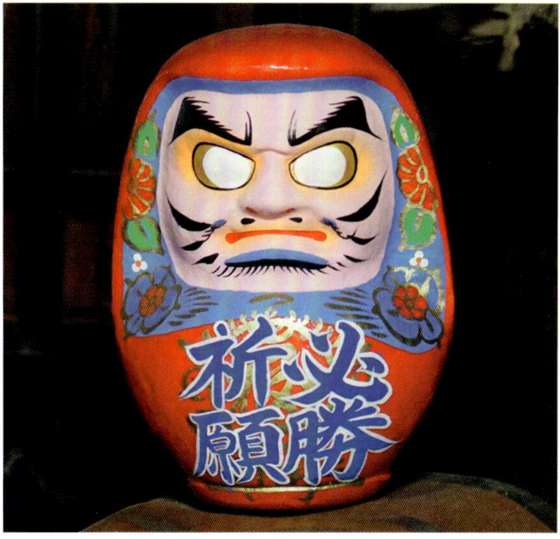

Facing page Daruma are burned in a temple ritual to thank old items for their service. **This page** Daruma usually have wide eyes and dramatic beards and eyebrows. Eyes are often left blank, to be filled in by those praying to achieve a goal.

This page Seto ware daruma cats, made by Chugai Toen studio.
Facing page, top The city of Takasaki in Gunma Prefecture is the undisputed mecca for daruma production. There are many studios and festivals devoted to the roly-poly doll.
Facing page, bottom Kokeshi doll artisans, who have excellent brushwork skills, craft some of the most exquisite daruma.

of colors, with various meanings. Yellow and gold symbolize wealth, green is for health, pink is for love and white is for luck in exams.

The first Daruma are thought to have been created by a priest in Takasaki in Gunma Prefecture, which remains an important production center for Daruma to this day. Another major production site is Shirakawa City in Fukushima Prefecture. Oftentimes, temples or cities will hold a festival at the beginning of the year with hundreds of Daruma dolls for sale. There are several major temples devoted to Daruma with displays of the dolls, including Shorinzan Darumaji in Takasaki, Horinji in Kyoto and Katsuoji in Osaka. Temples such as Nishiarai Daishi in Narita, near Tokyo, host dramatic Daruma-burning rituals, where old Daruma are placed in a large pit and set alight, while priests circle around and chant prayers. This type of ritual, known as *kuyo*, is a kind of memorial service to thank items that are no longer wanted for their service. Lucky charms such as Daruma are often replaced once a year.

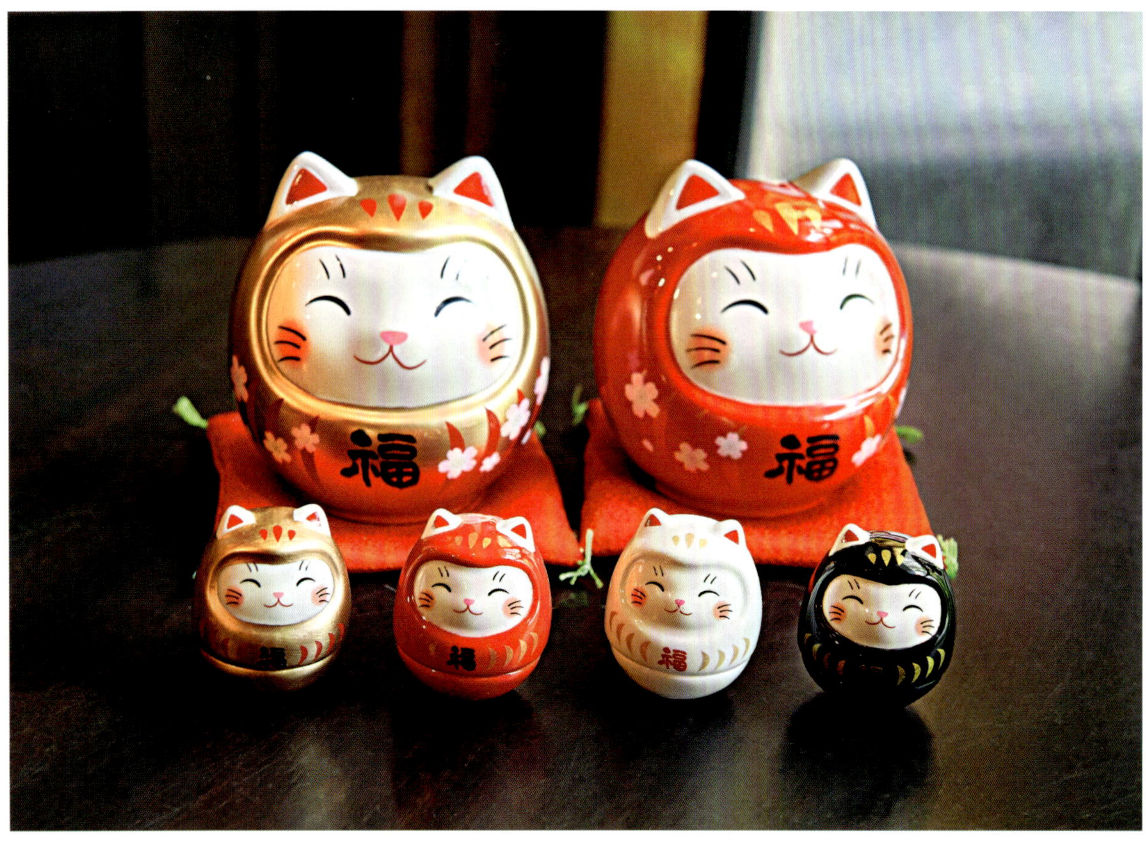

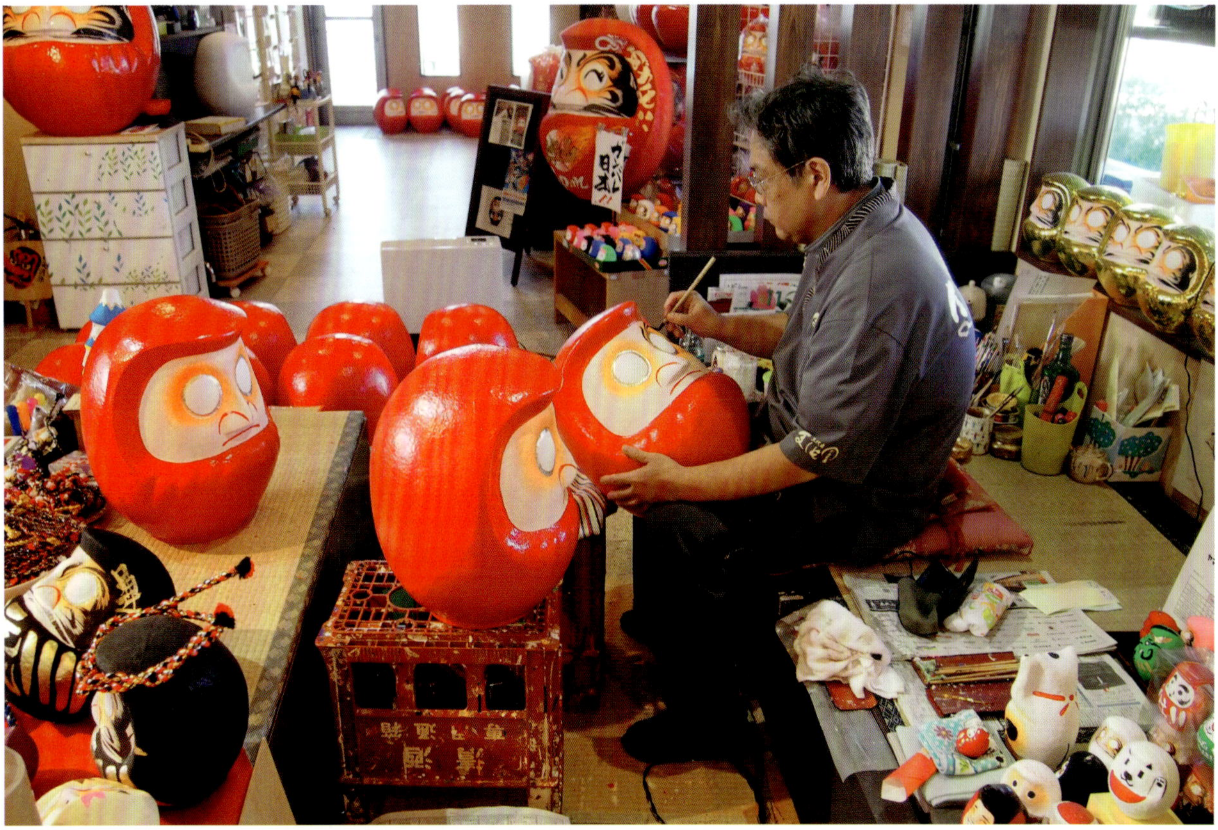

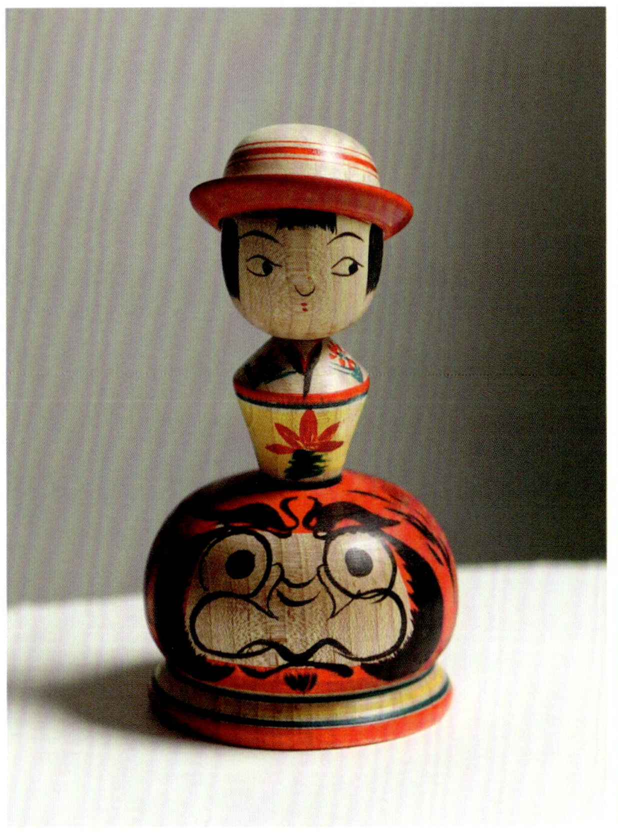

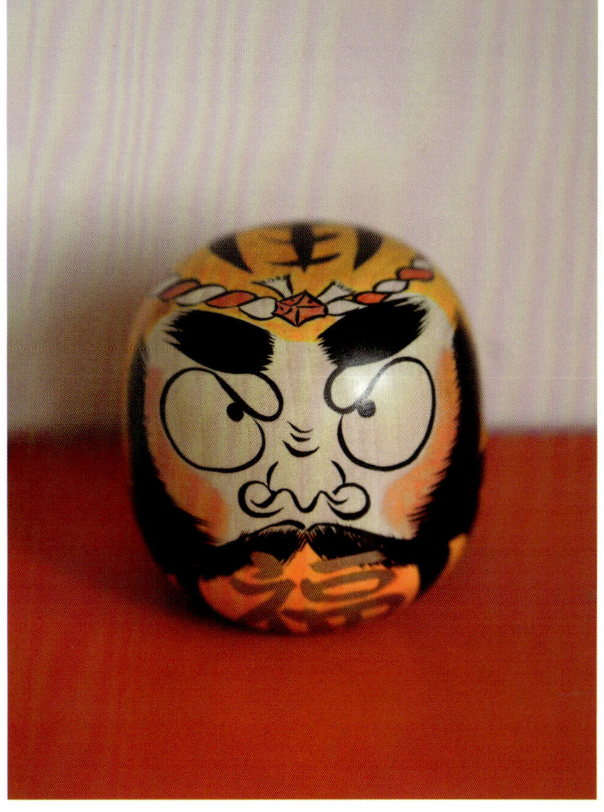

Dosojin Guardian Figures

Shinto spirits from Nagano, with protective powers

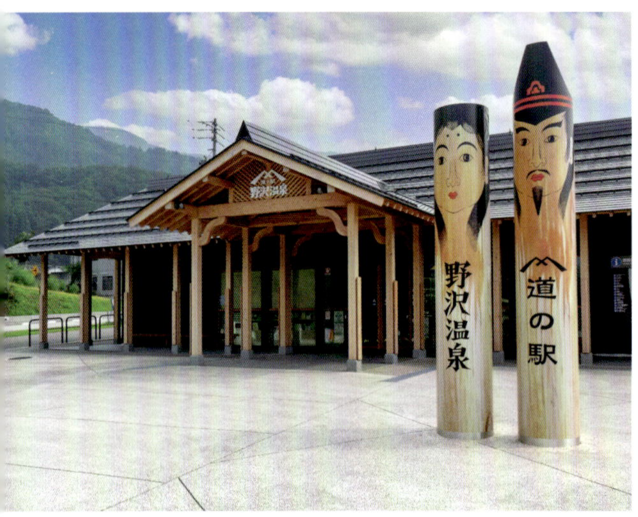

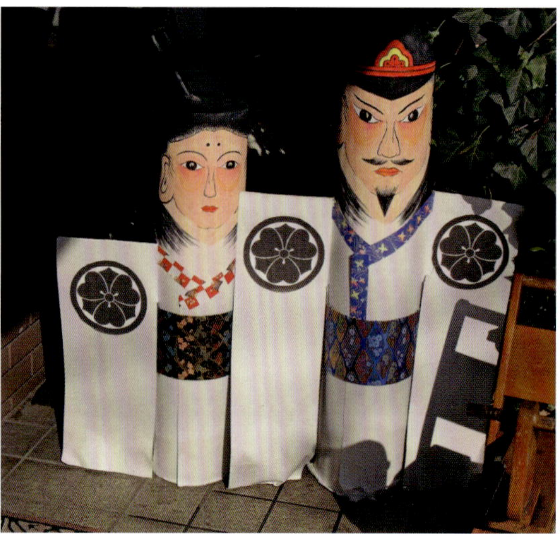

IF YOU GO TO THE MOUNTAIN HAMLET of Nozawa Onsen in Nagano, you will immediately notice the pairs of wooden statues, in the shape of a man and a woman, everywhere you go, displayed at tourist offices, cafés, restaurants and on sale at souvenir shops. The pair are the Shinto guardian deities of Nozawa, called *dosojin*. They protect people on journeys, as well as people who are journeying through changes in their lives, and are thought to be connected to Jizo, the Buddhist god who protects travelers and children. While dosojin are found in various manifestations in different parts of Japan, in Nozawa they are represented as a couple with their own story: a man and a woman who were so ugly that they couldn't find love. But when they found each other their luck changed, they got married and had children. The couple depicted on the Nozawa statues are not unattractive, but both have unusually strong features such as full lips and glaring eyes. Their faces top a column of wood that has no arms and legs. In some cases, the face covers most of the wooden columns.

The Dosojin Fire Festival, held in Nozawa every January 15, celebrates love, marriage and the first child, as illustrated in the story of the town's most famous couple. The festival is also held to wish for a good harvest and to protect against malevolent spirits. Villagers construct a thirty-foot (ten meter) high shrine without using nails. During the festival, men aged forty-two climb on top of the shrine and those aged twenty-five gather around the bottom. Villagers try their hardest to set fire to the shrine, which eventually goes up in flames. The whole process can take up to four hours and watching the shrine being consumed by a raging fire against a snowy backdrop is a sight to behold.

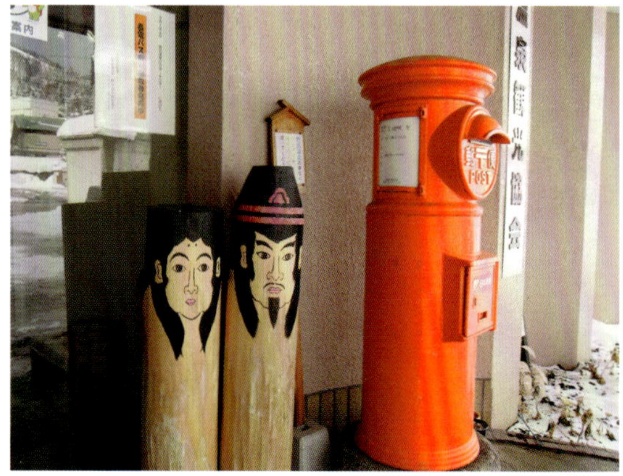

In the mountain hamlet of Nozawa Onsen in Nagano Prefecture, dosojin figures are everywhere.

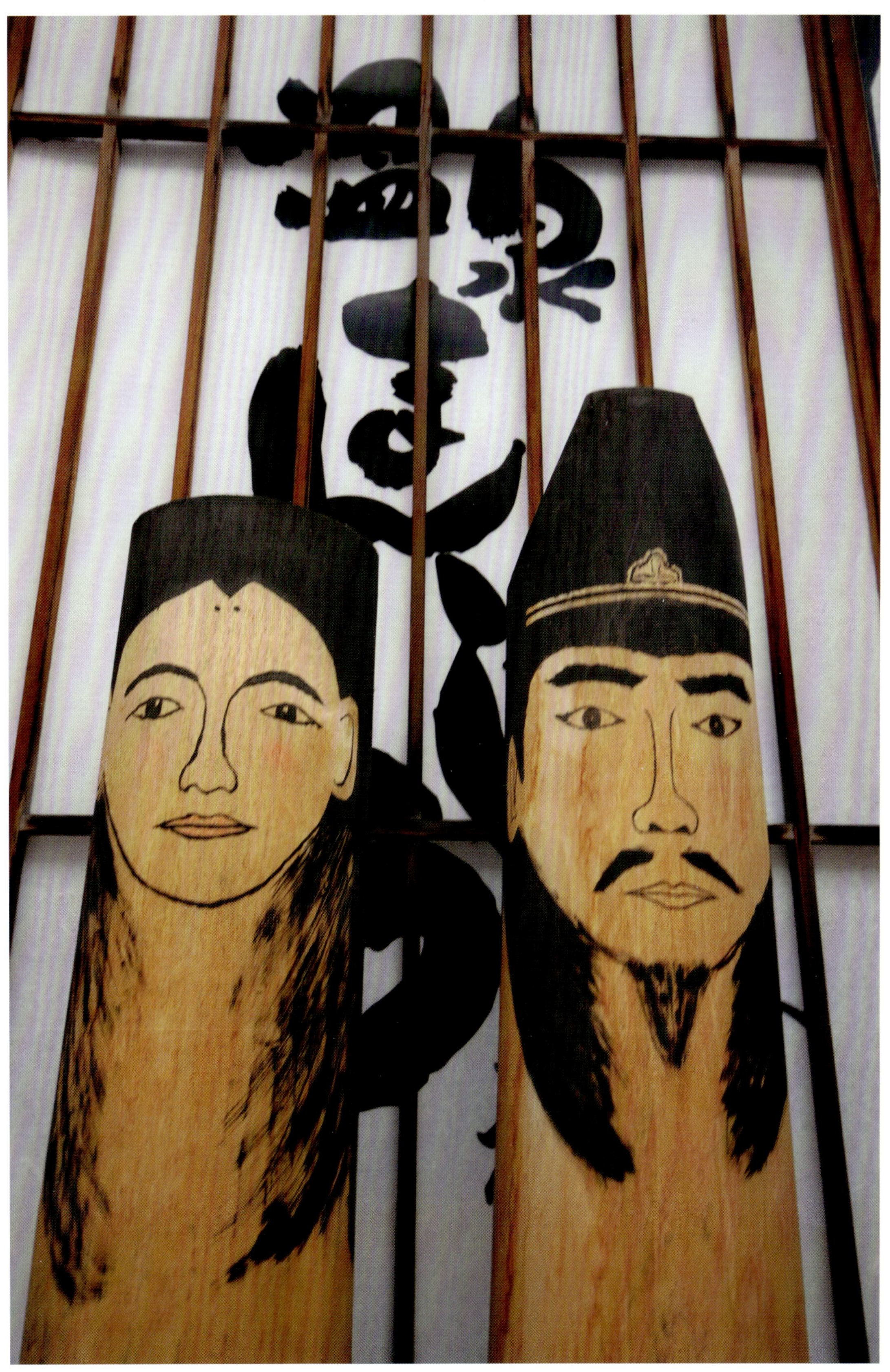

Edo Furin Glass Wind Chimes

Delicate hand-blown baubles that protect against evil

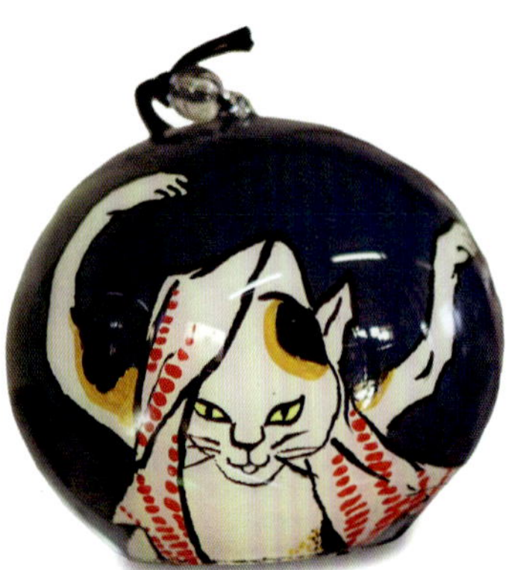

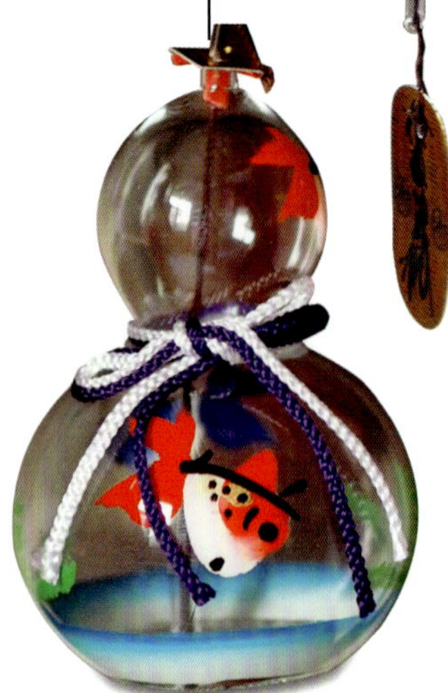

EDO FURIN ARE DELICATE, hand-blown glass wind chimes, with slightly jagged edges that produce a distinctive high-pitched tinkling sound. The sound is said to be "cooling" and the furin is one of the most iconic symbols of summer—as soon as the weather turns hot, you'll hear wind chimes on the streets of Tokyo.

Historically, furin were made of phosphor bronze and used as protective amulets by the nobility and samurai. It was only in the eighteenth century that they began to be made of glass, using Dutch glass-making techniques brought to Japan by traders. These days most furin are imported from China, where they are produced in bulk, using a mold. There are only two Edo furin studios left in Tokyo: Shinohara Furin Honpo (4 -22-5 Minami Shinozakimachi, Edogawa -ku; tel: 03-3670-2512) and Shinohara Maruyoshi Furin (4-25-10 Taito, Taito-ku; tel: 03-3832-0227).

The furin produced by hand in Japan are made with glass that is heated to roughly 2,370°F (1,300°C), melted, and blown using a glass rod. First a small sphere is blown, then another is blown inside that sphere. The bottom of the furin is cut to give a jagged edge. They are painted from the inside with classic auspicious motifs, such as pine. Initially they were said to protect against evil and made in colors like red. Nowadays, the color red is said to evoke heat so the most common motifs have become goldfish, hydrangeas and morning glory flowers, which are typical icons that evoke summer.

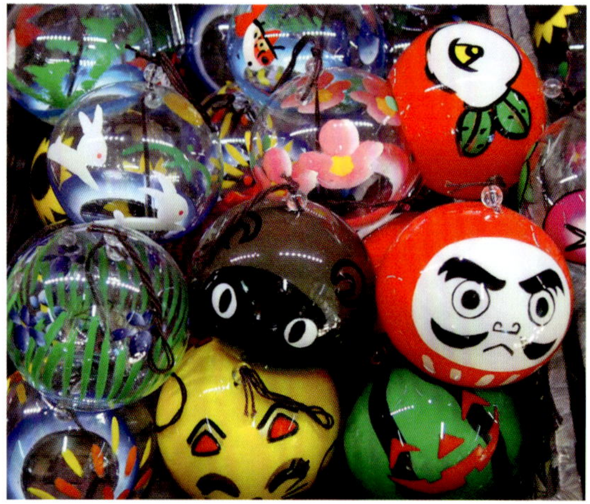

Traditionally painted red, these days Edo furin come in a wide variety of designs. A piece of paper is hung from the *zetsu* (clapper) that catches the wind and makes the chime tinkle.

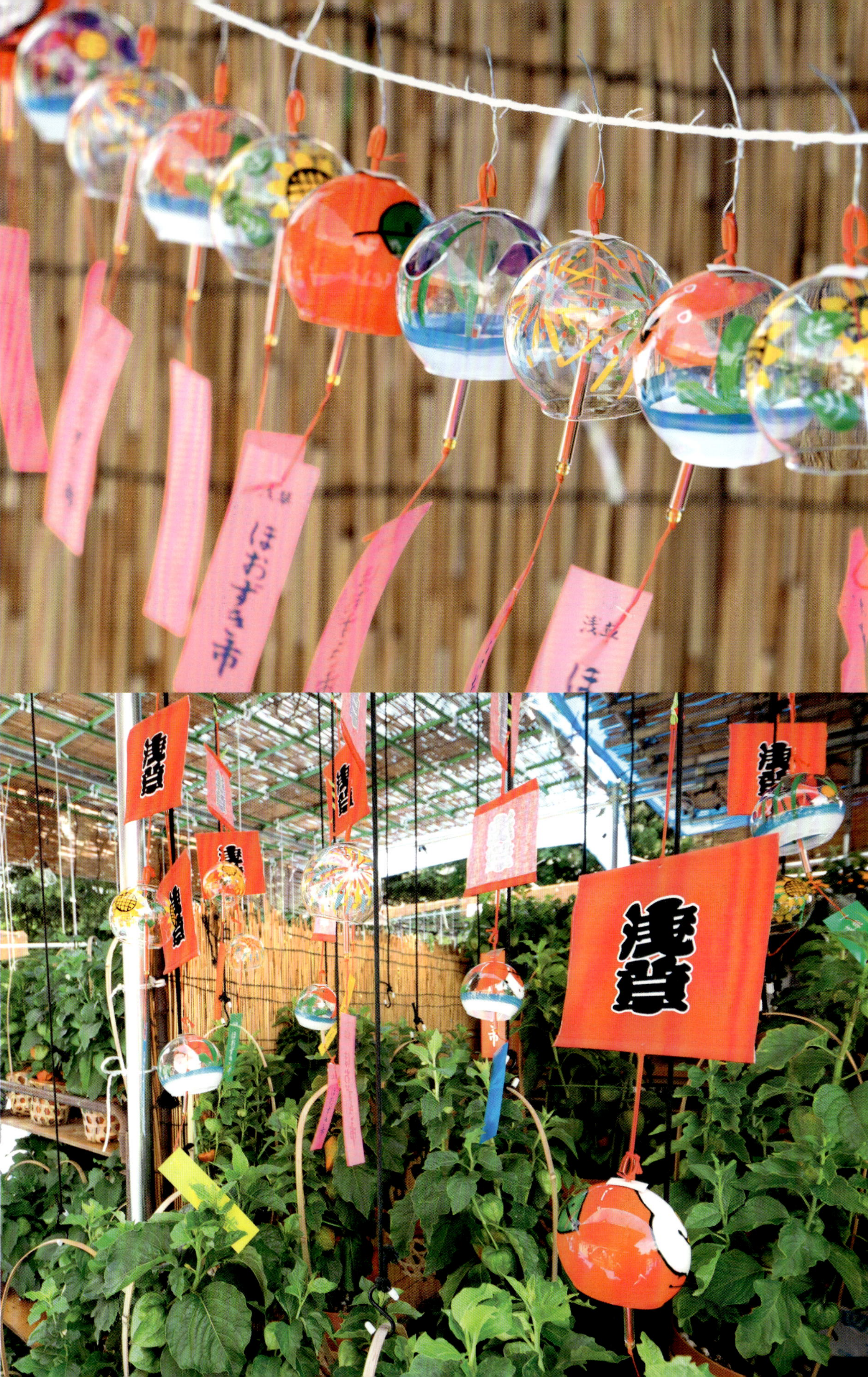
ほおずき市
浅草
浅草

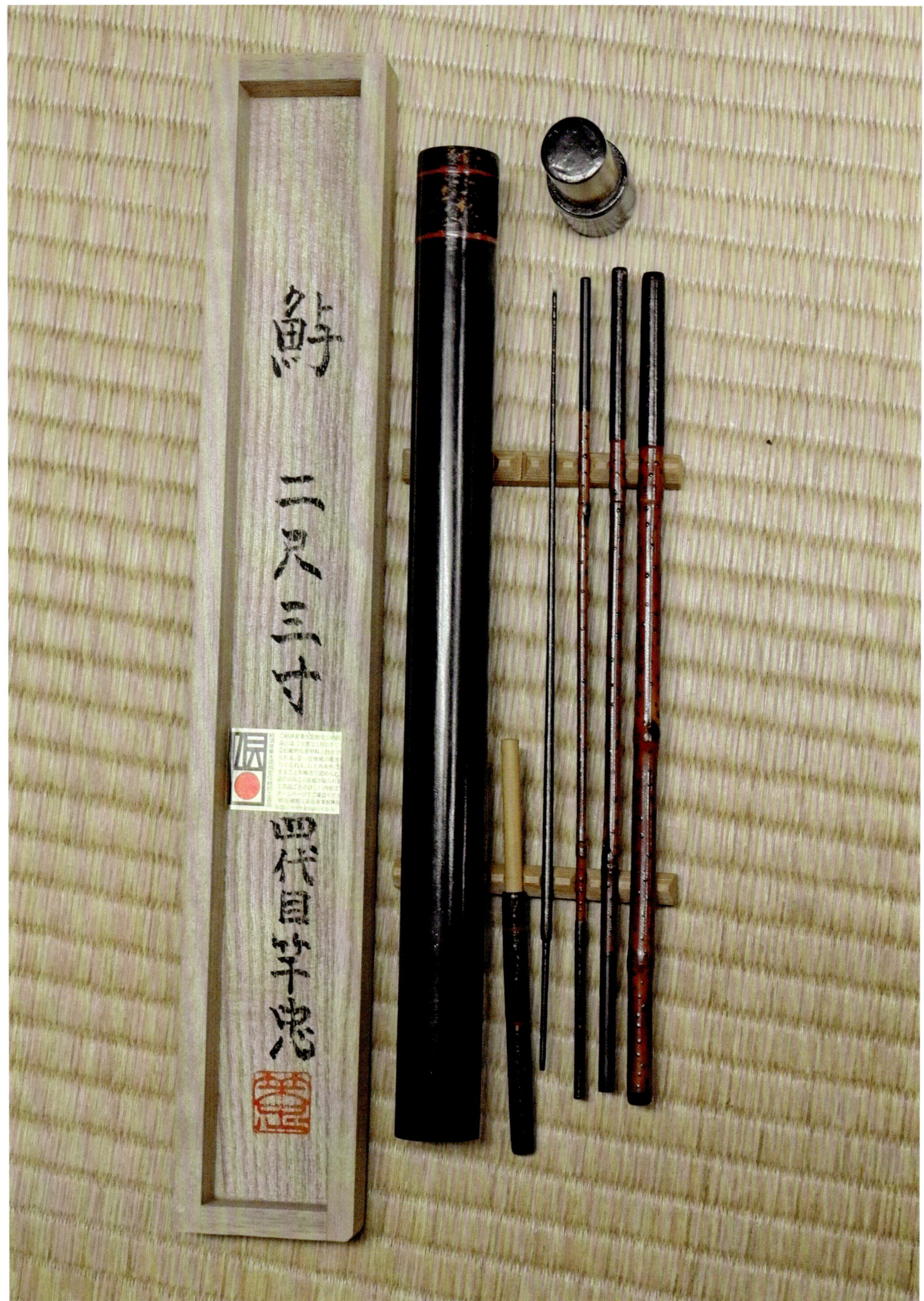
鮒　二尺三寸
四代目竿忠

Edo Wazao Bamboo Fishing Rods

Traditional rods dating back to samurai times

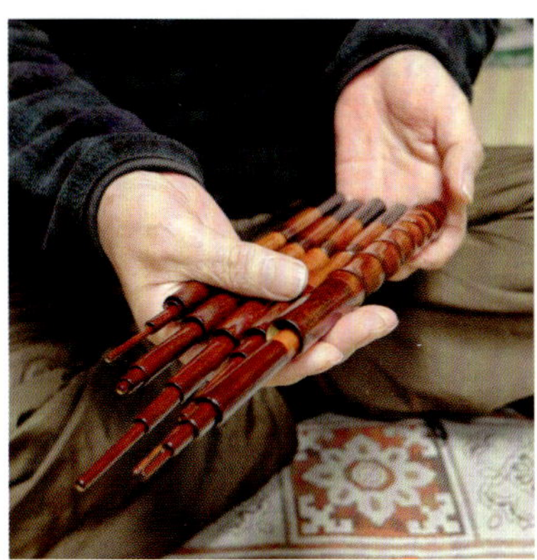

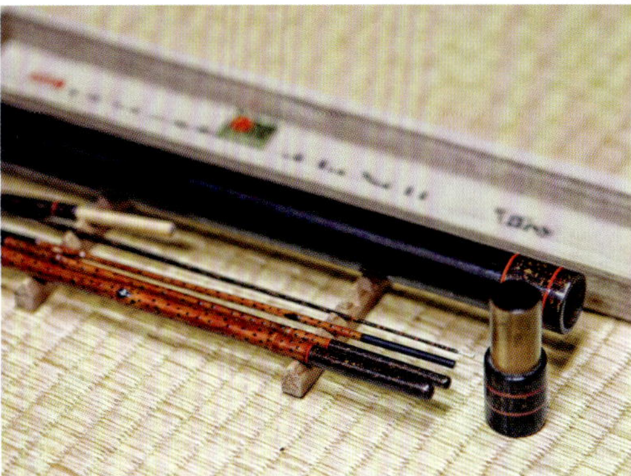

EDO WAZAO ARE SIMPLE, COLLAPSIBLE BAMBOO FISHING RODS that lack a reel, but are finely crafted from flexible bamboo that can absorb the fighting pull of the fish. The rods are made to catch all kinds of fish, from *tanago* (Japanese bitterling) to *wakasagi* (Japanese pond smelt) which is caught by ice fishing on frozen lakes in Hokkaido. The fishing rods were first made in 1778 by a man called Tosaku Taichiya, who sold them at a temple stall in Tokyo's Ueno district. The term *Edo wazao* refers to rods made by artisans in his lineage that are crafted in Tokyo and in the neighboring prefectures of Chiba and Saitama. While they are seen as a fine craft nowadays, and purchased by fishing aficionados across the world, they were once a commoner's tool to obtain food, and can be spotted in scenes of downtown Tokyo life depicted in the woodblock prints of artists like Utagawa Toyokuni II.

Kisaburo Nakane (artisan name Saochu IV) (5-11-14 Minami-Senju, Arakawa-ku, Tokyo; tel: 03-3803-1877) is an Edo wazao craftsman with over six decades of experience. Each rod he crafts is made of bamboo and coated with a natural *urushi* lacquer which gives an elegant finish. Nakane says of the aesthetic value of the rods: "They are better if they are attractive. Japanese crafts need to be aesthetically 'cool.' You can't teach taste, but humans are drawn to beautiful things, so I strive to make beautiful rods. You can find traditional fishing rods in other areas of Japan such as Sendai and Shonai, but the artisans only make rods for the fish caught in that region. With Edo wazao, you need to make particular kinds of fishing rods that suit the local conditions. In Tokyo, the Sumida, Arakawa and Tamagawa rivers flow into Tokyo Bay. This mixing of fresh and salt water means you get a huge variety of fish. I need to make different types of fishing rods to catch these different types of fish.

"There are different ways to enjoy fishing: you can catch a really tiny fish or a huge fish, depending on the rod and the person. The tremble you get in your hand [when a fish bites], even with a small fish, is an incredible feeling."

Facing page An example of a fishing rod set that can be assembled. **Above** Edo Wazao artisan Kisaburo Nakane holds some beautiful samples of his finely crafted fishing rods.

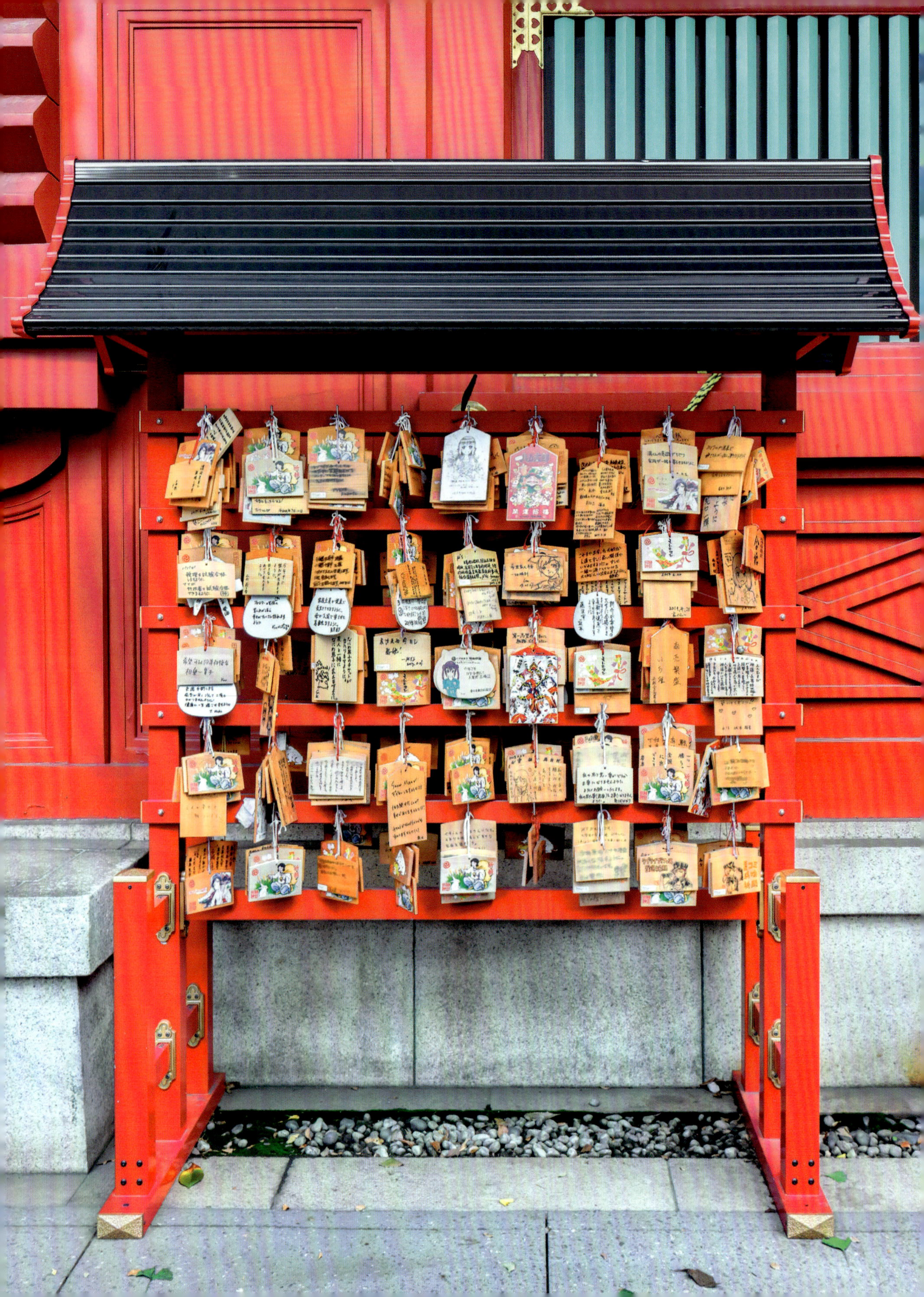

Ema Prayer Plaques

Colorful wooden plaques for prayers and wishes

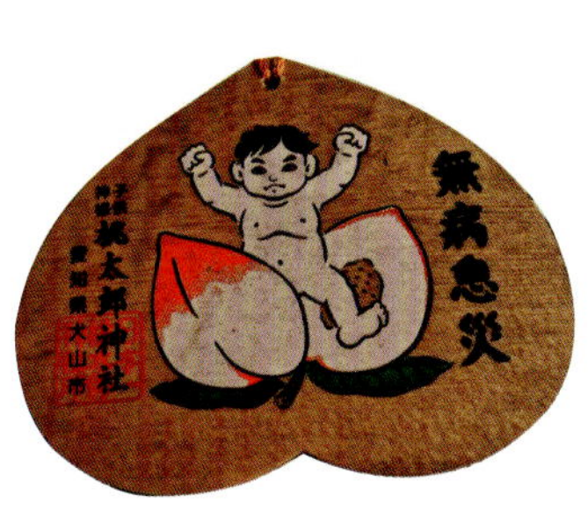

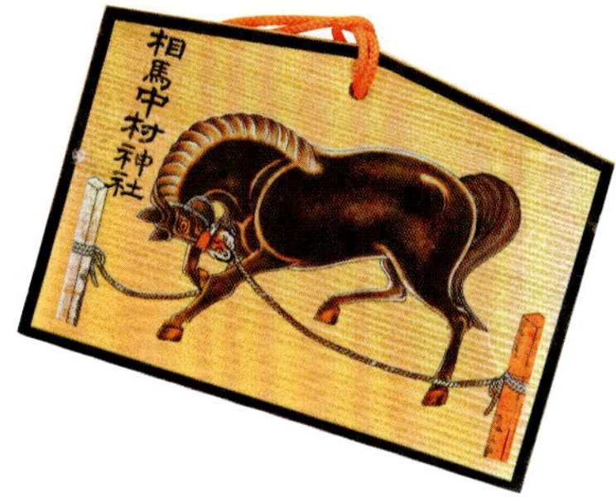

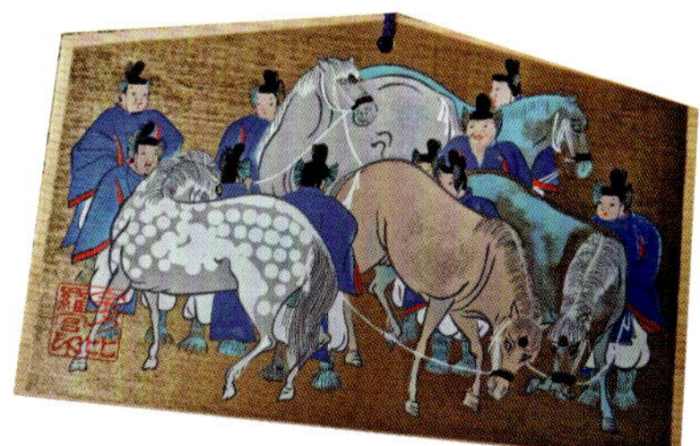

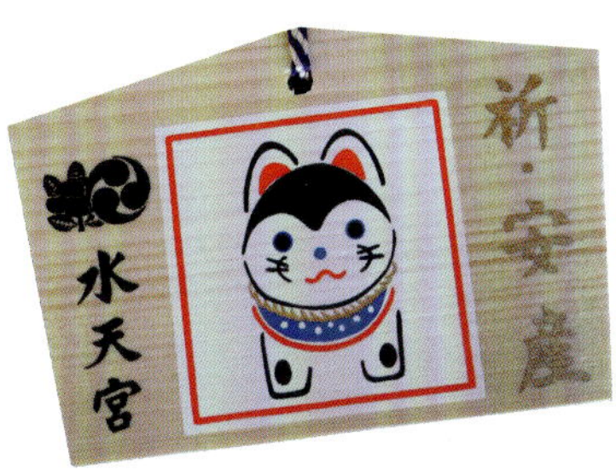

EMA ARE SMALL WOODEN PRAYER PLAQUES found at religious sites across Japan. They are decorated on the front with an illustration—often that year's Chinese zodiac animal— and the back is left blank for people to write their wishes.

The word *ema* in Japanese quite literally means "picture horse." The tradition of dedicating a sacred horse—called *shinme*—to a Japanese shrine, is an ancient one. Even today, Tokyo's Meiji Shrine, and Ise Grand Shrine in Mie Prefecture have stables where these horses are kept.

Fumihiko Murai of the Yokohama Equine Museum (1-3 Negishidai, Naka-ku, Yokohama; tel: 045-662-7581), which has an excellent collection of horse-related folk toys and talismans explains: "In the Shinto religion, horses have traditionally been regarded as protective talismans, as well as a bridge between the world we live in and the world we cannot see. Many interesting local customs have grown up around this. For example, at Niukawakami Shrine, deep in the hills of Nara Prefecture, people would bring a black horse to the shrine if they were praying for rain, and if they were praying for dry weather they'd bring a white one."

However, as not everyone was able to bring an actual horse to a shrine, horse figures made of clay, straw or wood were used as a substitute from around the end of the third century. By the end of the eighth century, these horse effigies were believed to be amulets with supernatural powers.

This custom gradually evolved into ema plaques depicting horses. The oldest ema artifact dates back to the Nara period (710–794). In the Muromachi period (1333–1573), the variety of motifs used on the plaques became wider. From the fourteenth century onward, ema also started to proliferate in Buddhist temples, not just in Shinto shrines. Even today, across the nation, places of worship display these wooden plaques with hopes, prayers and words of gratitude scrawled on the back. Some religious sites even have specific halls, called *emado*, dedicated to housing ema prayer plaques.

Facing page A typical display of ema prayer plaques at a neighborhood shrine. **Above** Originally decorated with images of horses, ema plaques today bear a wide range of motifs.

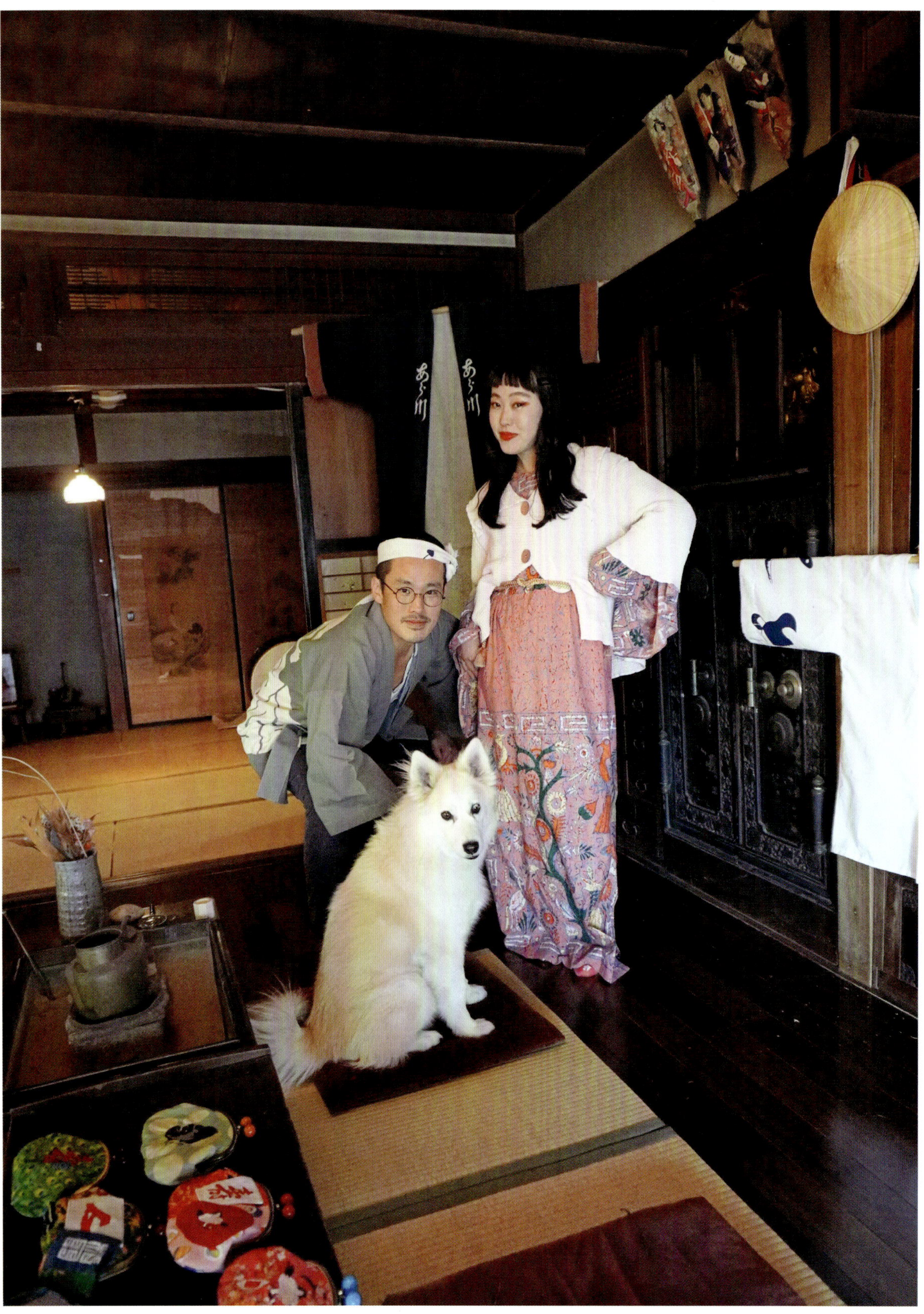

Gamaguchi Coin Purses

The clasped "frog's mouth" opening brings good luck

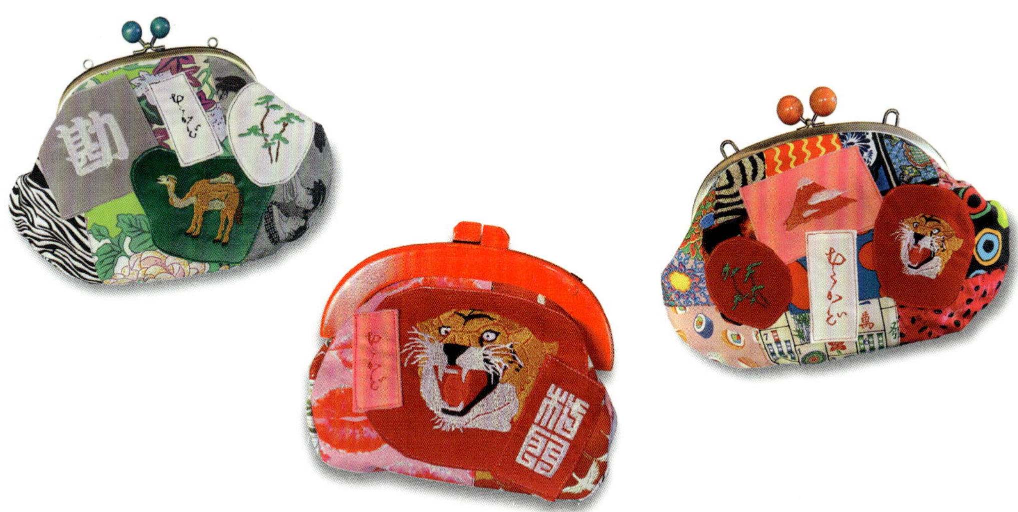

GAMAGUCHI ARE A TYPE OF COIN PURSE with an opening that is said to look like a frog's mouth. In Japanese the word for frog is *kaeru* which also means "to return" and this "frog's mouth" opening suggests that luck and money will return to the owner.

The gamaguchi coin purse is the predecessor of full-scale Western-style bag manufacturing in Japan. The first purse in this style was brought to Japan from France in 1872 by a merchant who had been traveling around Europe under the authority of the Japanese government. The purses became particularly popular at the beginning of the twentieth century as they went well with Western clothing, which was then becoming fashionable. As the twentieth century progressed, nylon and vinyl became popular materials for making gamaguchi. There were a number of gamaguchi artisans in downtown Tokyo jostling with each other for business.

Chiaki and Yuta Murakado own the brand Murakado (murakado.com) and make gamaguchi coin purses and koiguchi shirts (see page 77) from their house in Tochigi Prefecture. They have a funky sense of style and are part of a movement of young, fashionable people who are interested in folk craft and rural living. They are in a punk band, the Seppuku Pistols, whose aesthetic sensibilities, both visual and aural, borrow heavily from Edo-era folk culture.

"A gamaguchi makes this great 'snap!' sound," says Yuta. "And that's what's good about it. We were working on a film called *Hakai no hi* [Days of Destruction] about practitioners of the Shugendo religion. Finger snapping is an important part of their rituals, and I think this sound resonates with people on a cellular level. It is the same as the gamaguchi snap, which you subconsciously hear over and over again."

Chiaki adds, "A regular purse has a zip but a gamaguchi has a mouth that opens and closes. When open, the mouth takes in a lot of good things, and for those things not to fall out, the mouth closes. To have an open and closed mouth is symbolically the same as the effigies outside shrines."

Facing page Chiaki and Yuta Murakado make gamaguchi coin purses from their house in Tochigi Prefecture. **This page top** Gamaguchi purses made by the Murakados. **This page bottom** Gamaguchi are popular souvenirs for tourists today.

Hagoita Shuttlecock Paddles

The wooden paddle that became a good-luck symbol

HAGOITA ARE LAVISHLY DECORATED wooden paddles that were originally used to play the shuttlecock game *hanetsuki* , an imperial court game that was popular in the Muromachi period (1333–1573). Early shuttlecocks had gold and silver embellishments, befitting their noble surroundings, and were thought to look like dragonflies which are the predators of mosquitoes. For this reason *hanetsuki* came to be played at the start of the year to protect against disease and to wish for a year of good health. By the Edo period (1603–1868), the hagoita paddle had become popular as a gift.

Kazuhiro Nishiyama, of the atelier Hagoita no Kogetsu (5-43-25 Mukojima, Sumida-ku, Tokyo; tel: 03-3623-1305) says, "There is a custom for parents or grandparents to buy a hagoita to celebrate baby girls, during the child's first year. These types of hagoita feature cute motifs. There is another type of hagoita with kabuki motifs. There is an annual year-end, three-day hagoita market at Tokyo's Sensoji Temple, attracting fans from all over Japan, where kabuki enthusiasts can buy hagoita that feature their favorite characters.

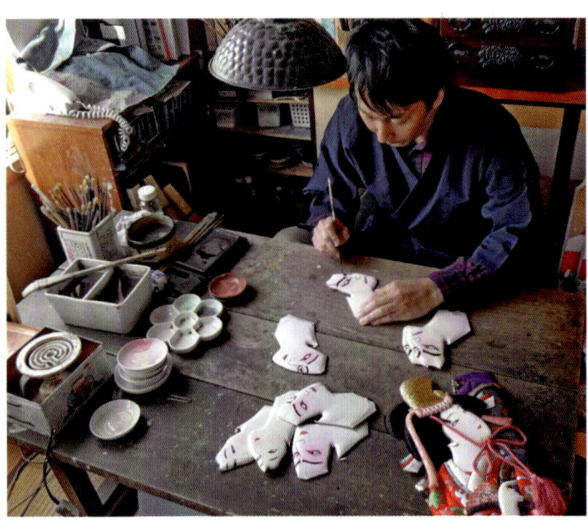

"The upper part of the paddle is called the *oshi-e*. It is made of cardboard, to form the structure, then padded with cotton to give it volume, and wrapped with fabric. Then the decorations are applied to form a picture. In the Edo period, the hagoita were simpler than the ones now. There was no cardboard then, so they used layers of washi paper instead. From the end of the nineteenth century cotton was ubiquitous and hagoita became more voluminous after that."

While they were originally made with kimono cloth, during the postwar era there was a boom in doll culture, such as the dolls used in displays for Hina Matsuri (Girls' Day). Fabric was manufactured specifically for the doll outfits, and this fabric is used for hagoita today.

Like kumade lucky rakes (see page 83), the main place to buy hagoita, apart from the ateliers, is at temple fairs. The end-of-year market at Sensoji Temple is a raucous and atmospheric event. Nishiyama explains a typical sales ritual: "For a 10,000 yen shuttlecock, we sellers will say, 'We're knocking the price down to 8000 yen.' The customer feels they have lucked out, and we are grateful to them too. Then, they tip us for more than we discount them for. With this gesture, both parties feel good. It's a kind of feudal-era style of buying things. Afterwards we clap in a three-three-four rhythm, a total of ten claps, a nice round number. It is a gesture to signify that we rounded off a good deal."

Left Kazuhiro Nishiyama at work in his Tokyo atelier.
Above Hagoita paddles featuring cute motifs are often given as presents to celebrate the first year of life of a new baby girl.
Facing page Kabuki characters are a popular decoration for hagoita paddles.

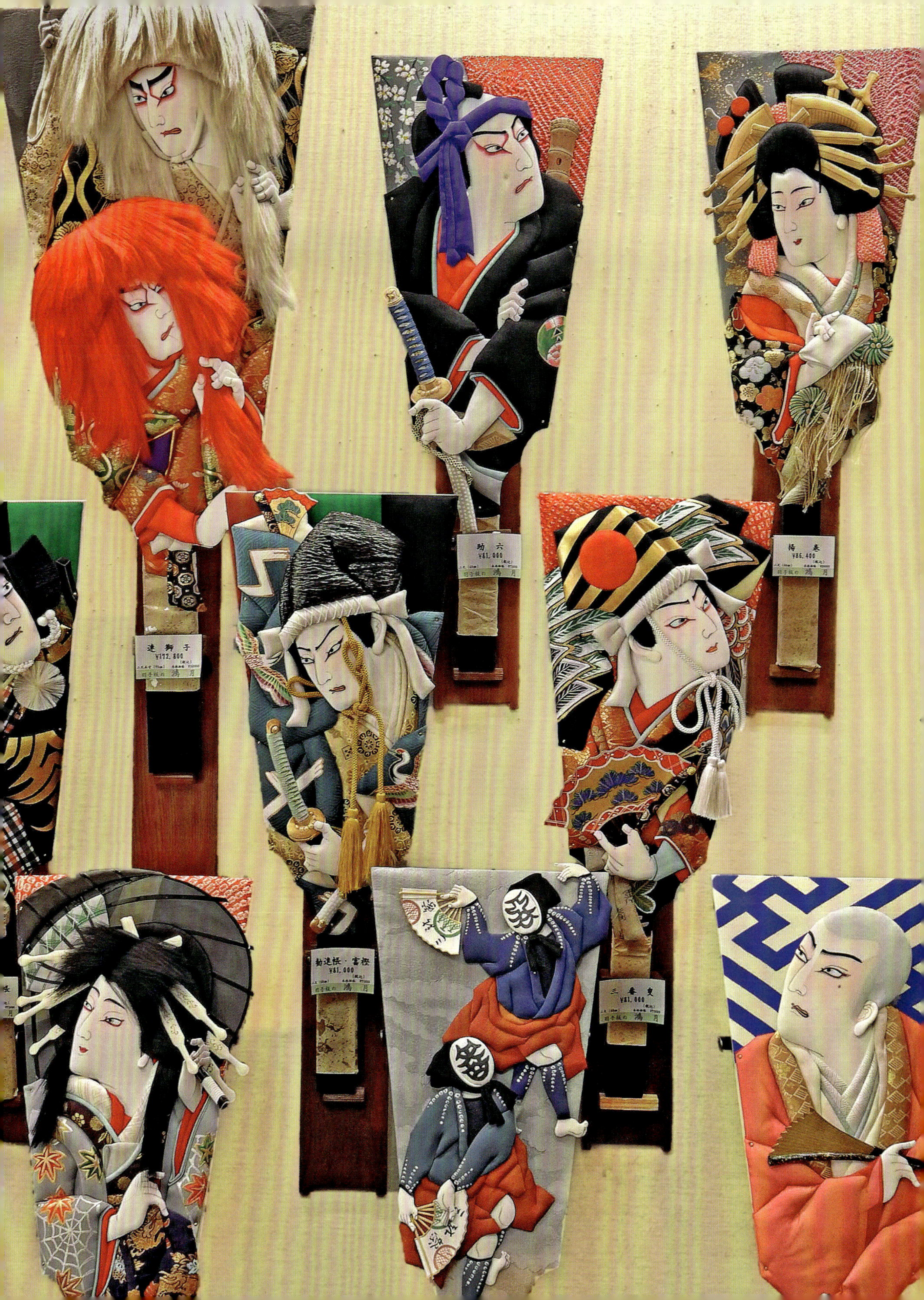
連獅子
¥172,800
助六
¥81,000
揚巻
¥86,400
勧進帳・富樫
¥81,000
三番叟
¥81,000

Inuhariko Papier-Mâché Puppies

Adorable mascots that bring good health

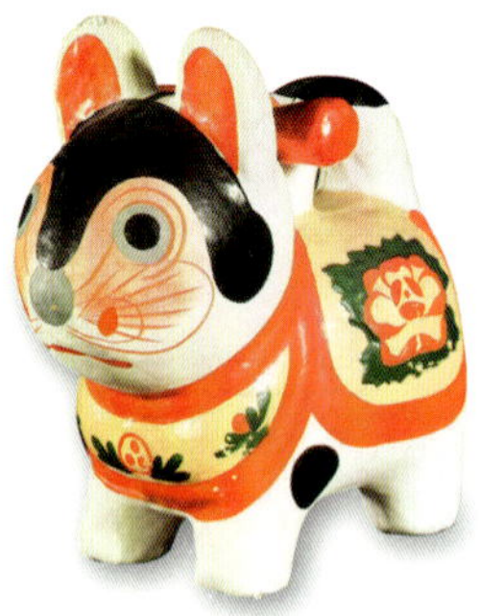

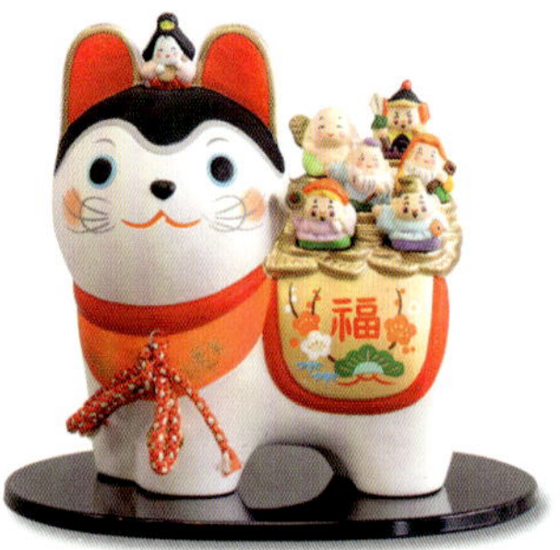

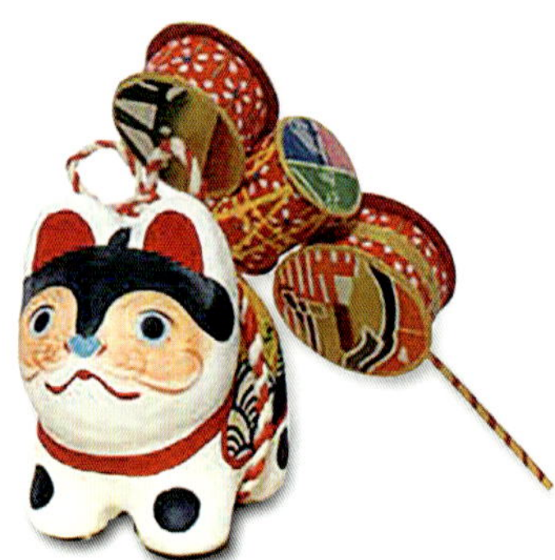

INUHARIKO ARE ADORABLE papier-mâché pups. During the Heian period (794–1185), a dog-shaped box was used as a protective talisman, in the hope that children would grow up to be as strong and healthy as a dog. In the Edo era (1603–1868), rather than a box that was shaped like a dog, the figure of dog itself—the inuhariko—became a popular ornament.

Quite often the inuhariko wears a *den-den daiko* drum on its back or a bamboo basket on its head. When joined together, the kanji characters for "bamboo" and "dog" look like the kanji for "laugh," so it is hoped that by displaying an inuhariko, a household will be filled with laughter. They are often painted with seasonal flowers like the peony, or with the kanji character 福 (*fuku*), meaning "good fortune."

A custom has grown up in Japan whereby a new baby would be gifted an inuhariko by the mother's family on the occasion of the baby's first shrine visit—known as *miyamairi*—that usually takes place in the first month after the child's birth to pray for blessings and good health. The inuhariko is often given back to the shrine at the time of Shichi Go San festival, when the child turns three.

The inuhariko is made of papier-mâché in craft villages such as Dekoyashiki village in Fukushima Prefecture. They are typically made by artisans who also craft other auspicious papier-mâché figures such as maneki-neko cats (see page 86) and akabeko cows (see page 36). Beverly Maeda, featured on page 120, is a popular artist who crafts inuhariko in vibrant colors.

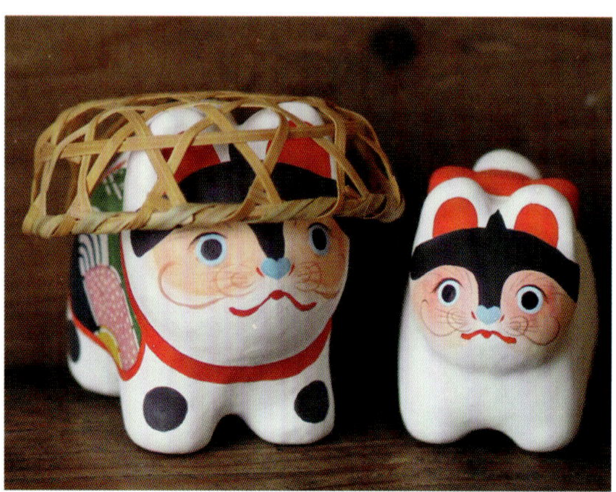

This page A vintage inuhariko, ca. 1950, displayed at the Brooklyn museum (top left); bearing lucky gods (top center); carrying traditional drums (top right), and wearing a bamboo basket (above). **Facing page** Inuhariko are displayed at a shrine in Osaka.

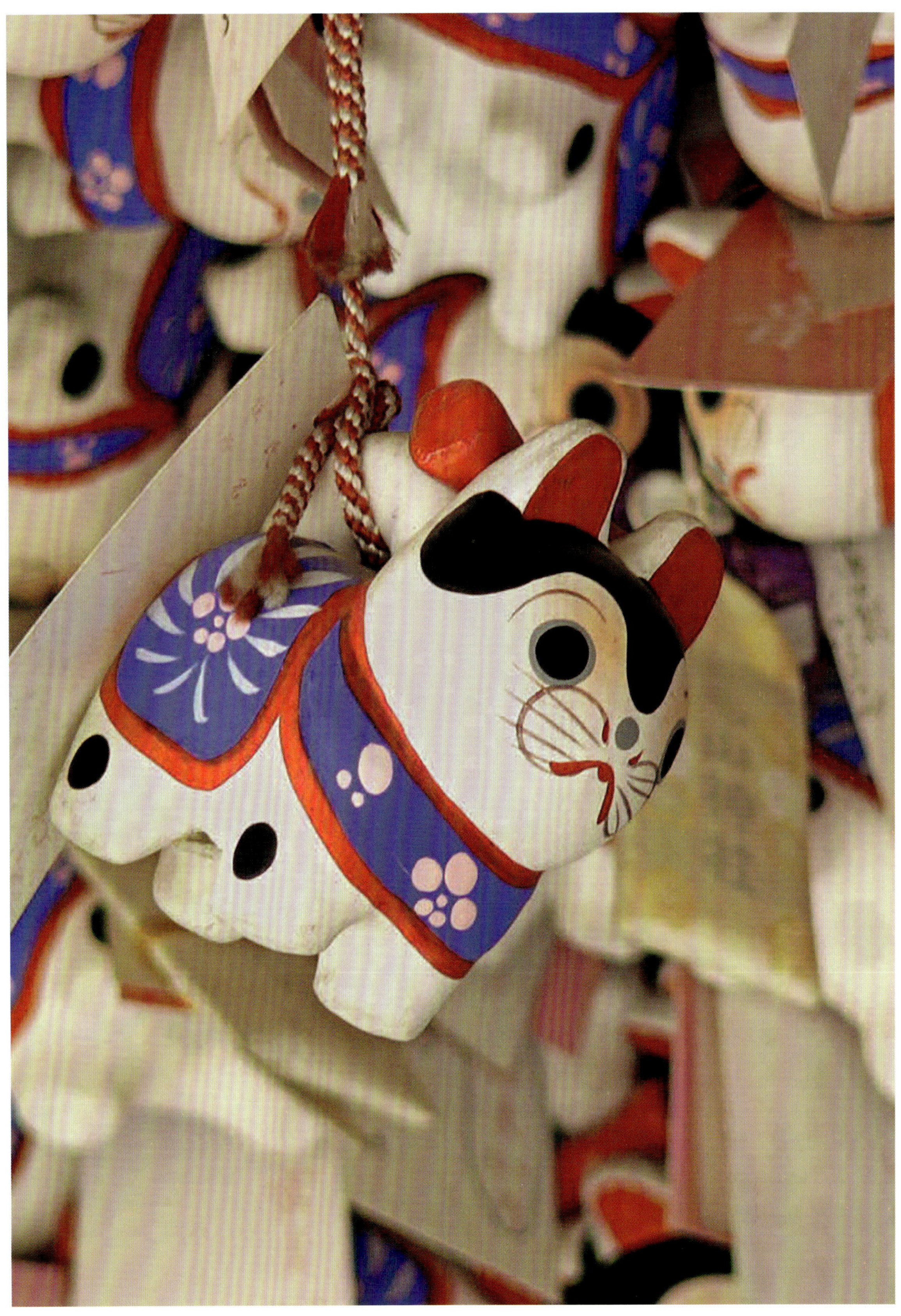

Kayabuki Roof Thatching

Beauty, charm and artisanship, with UNESCO recognition

KAYABUKI IS A GENERAL TERM used in Japanese to describe thatched roofs made from a variety of materials—including *kaya* (miscanthus), rice straw, wheat straw, silver grass, reeds or hemp—which are laid on a framework that is usually made of bamboo. These thatched roofs are becoming an increasingly rare sight in Japan, but can still be found on traditional *minka* farmhouses in rural areas, as well as on temples and shrines in Tohoku, such as Dewa Sanzan Shrine, one of Japan's holiest places, in Yamagata Prefecture.

Kayabuki roofs are usually found in locations with cold winters; the roofs tend to be steeply pitched so that heavy winter snow will slide off. The roofs are resilient in all seasons, providing excellent ventilation and protection against rain, snow and heat.

The roofs need a high degree of maintenance at an exorbitant cost, and need to be replaced every decade or so. There are two different methods for maintaining a kayabuki roof. The *sashigaya* method focuses on replacing damaged parts, whereas *fukikae* is a method whereby the entire roof is replaced. Traditionally, old roofing material was often used as fertilizer for the plants that go on to be used for the next set of thatching material. Before World War II, the construction and maintenance of kayabuki thatched roofs was predominantly a community affair and there were many thatching artisans.

During Japan's period of economic growth from the 1960s to the 1980s, the relocation of youth to the cities and the consequent depopulation of rural areas led to a decrease in kayabuki roofing. These days few specialized artisans remain, and owners of thatched-roof houses may have to call in thatchers from distant locations when re-roofing or repairs are necessary.

Environmental damage has also led to a paucity of certain types of reeds that have been traditionally used for thatching, and it is not unusual these days to see minka houses with aluminum roofs.

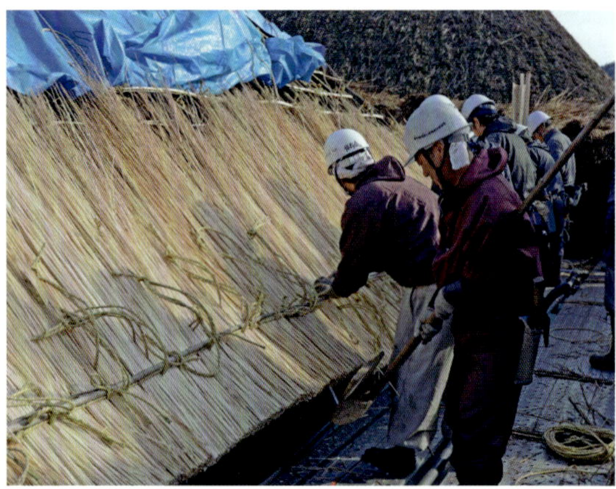

Despite these challenges, the craft of kayabuki roofing was designated by UNESCO as an Intangible Cultural Heritage in 2020, which will hopefully lead to increased efforts to preserve this artisanal skill.

Top Few specialized artisans remain in the field of kayabuki roofing.
Below Steeply pitched roofs ensure that heavy winter snow will slide off easily.
Facing page The village of Ouchi-juku in Fukushima Prefecture is famous for its thatched-roofed houses, which date from the Edo period.

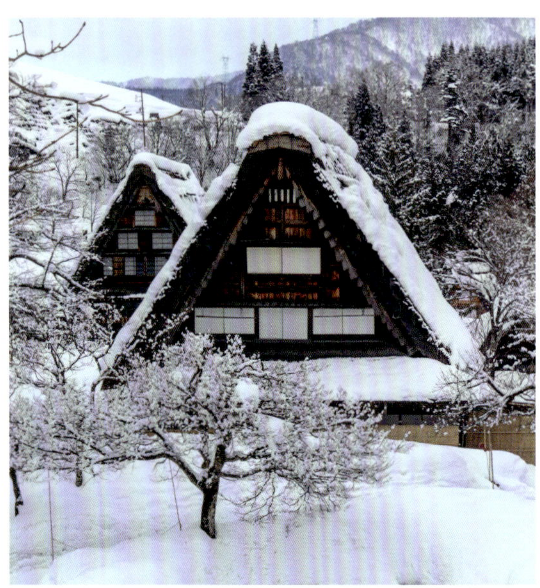

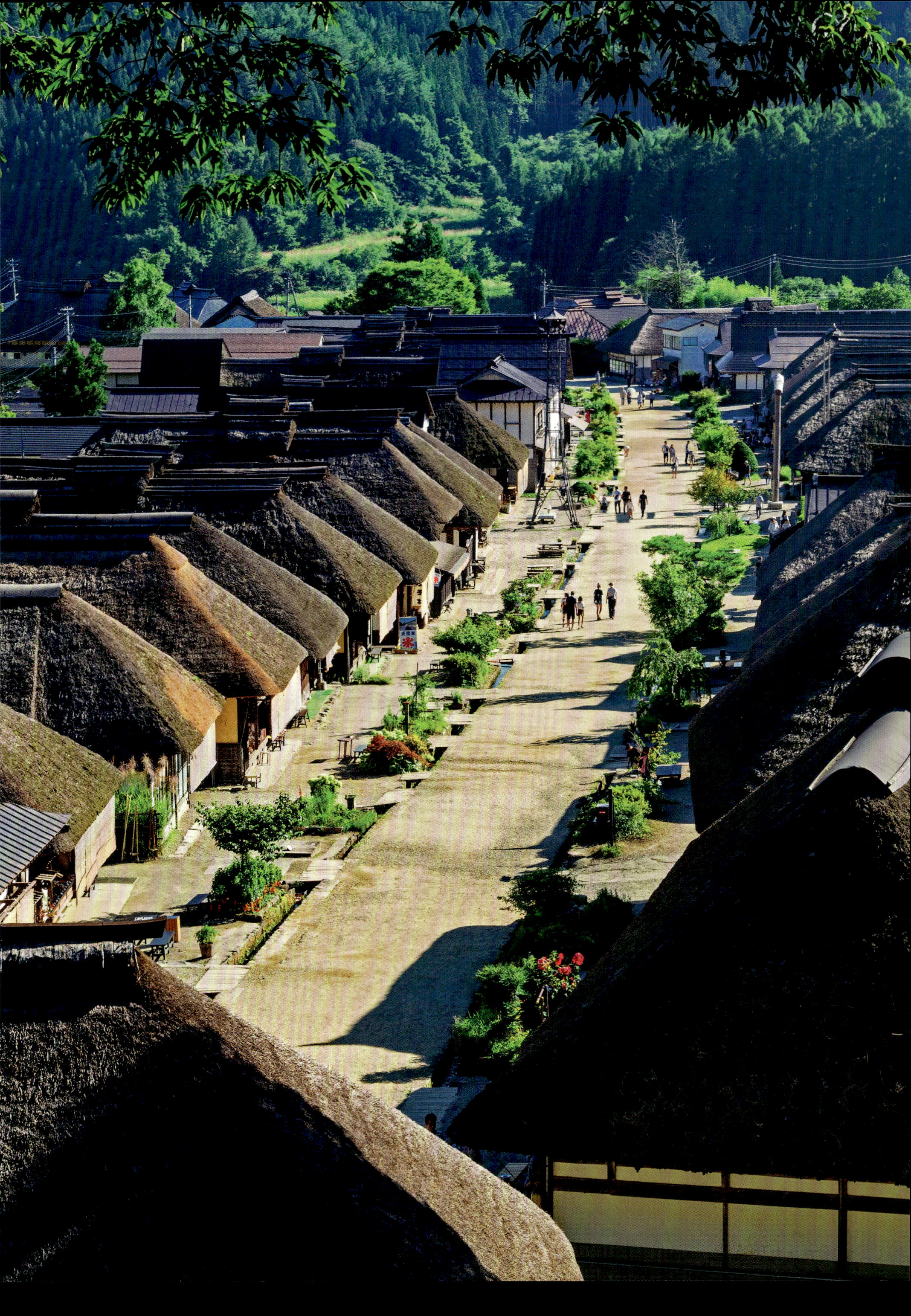

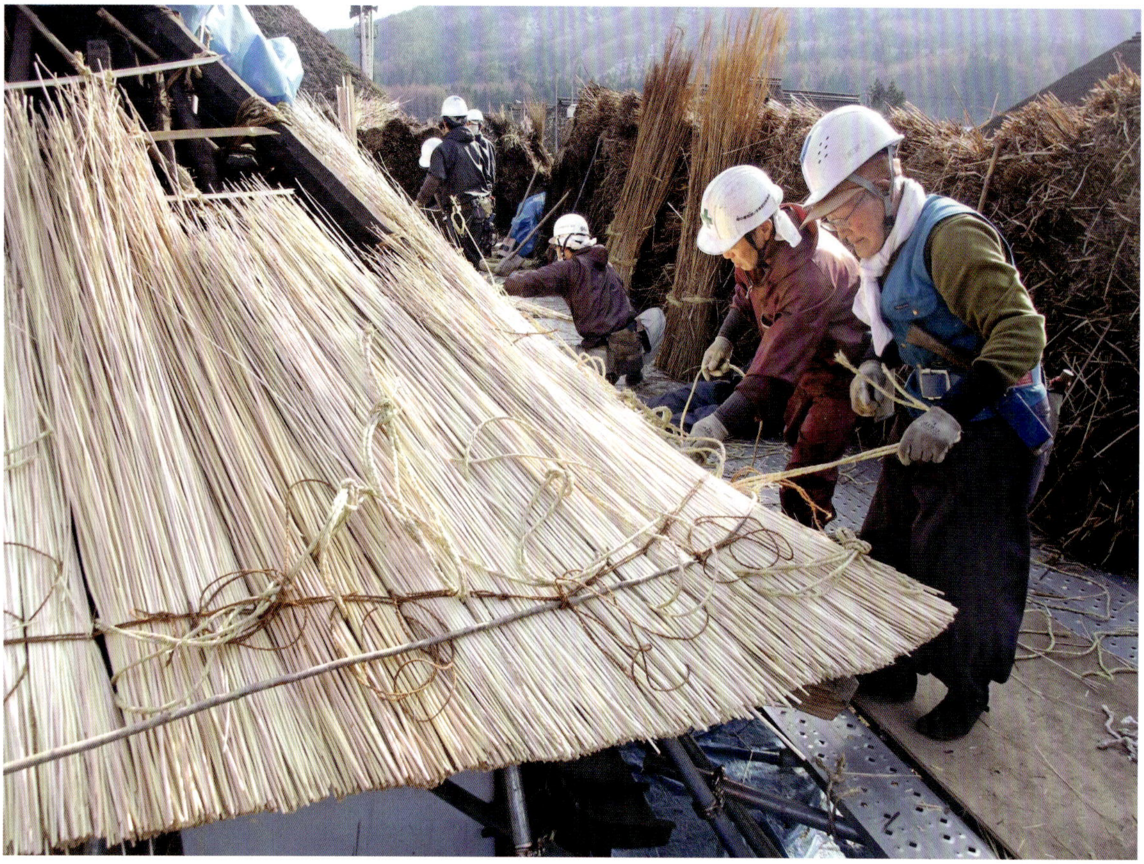

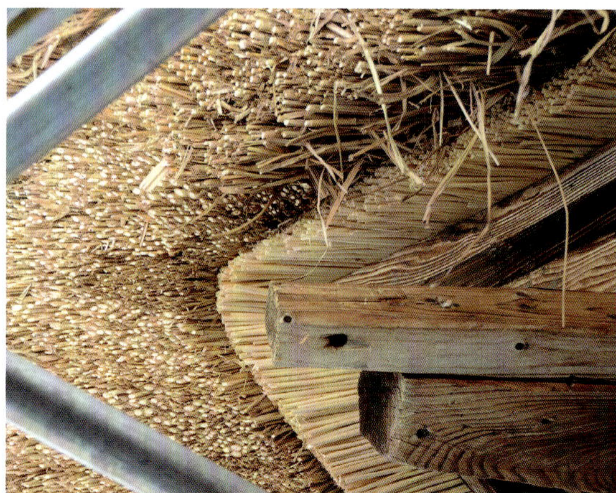

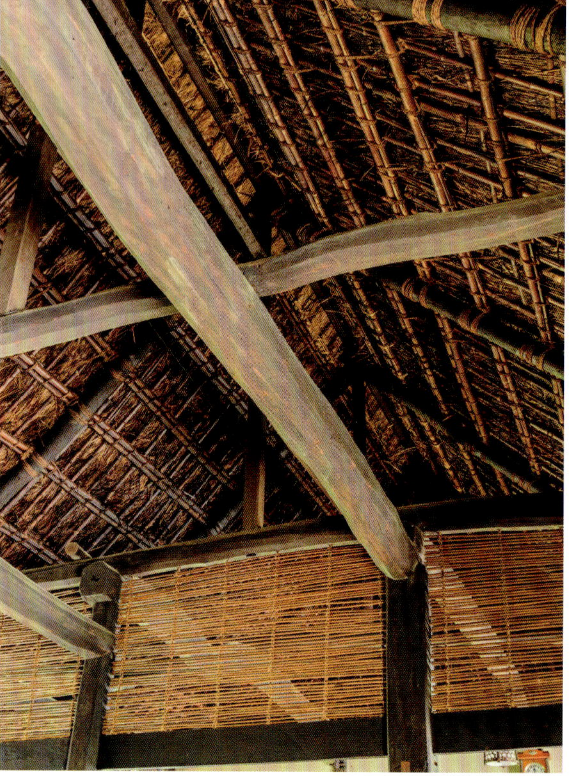

This page Kayabuki thatch is made from a variety of materials, including *kaya* (miscanthus), rice straw, wheat straw, silver grass, reeds and hemp—the latter of which is fire resistant—laid on a framework that is usually made of bamboo.
Facing page One of the nine thatched houses in Suganuma Village in Gifu Prefecture, which was designated a UNESCO World Heritage Site in 1995.

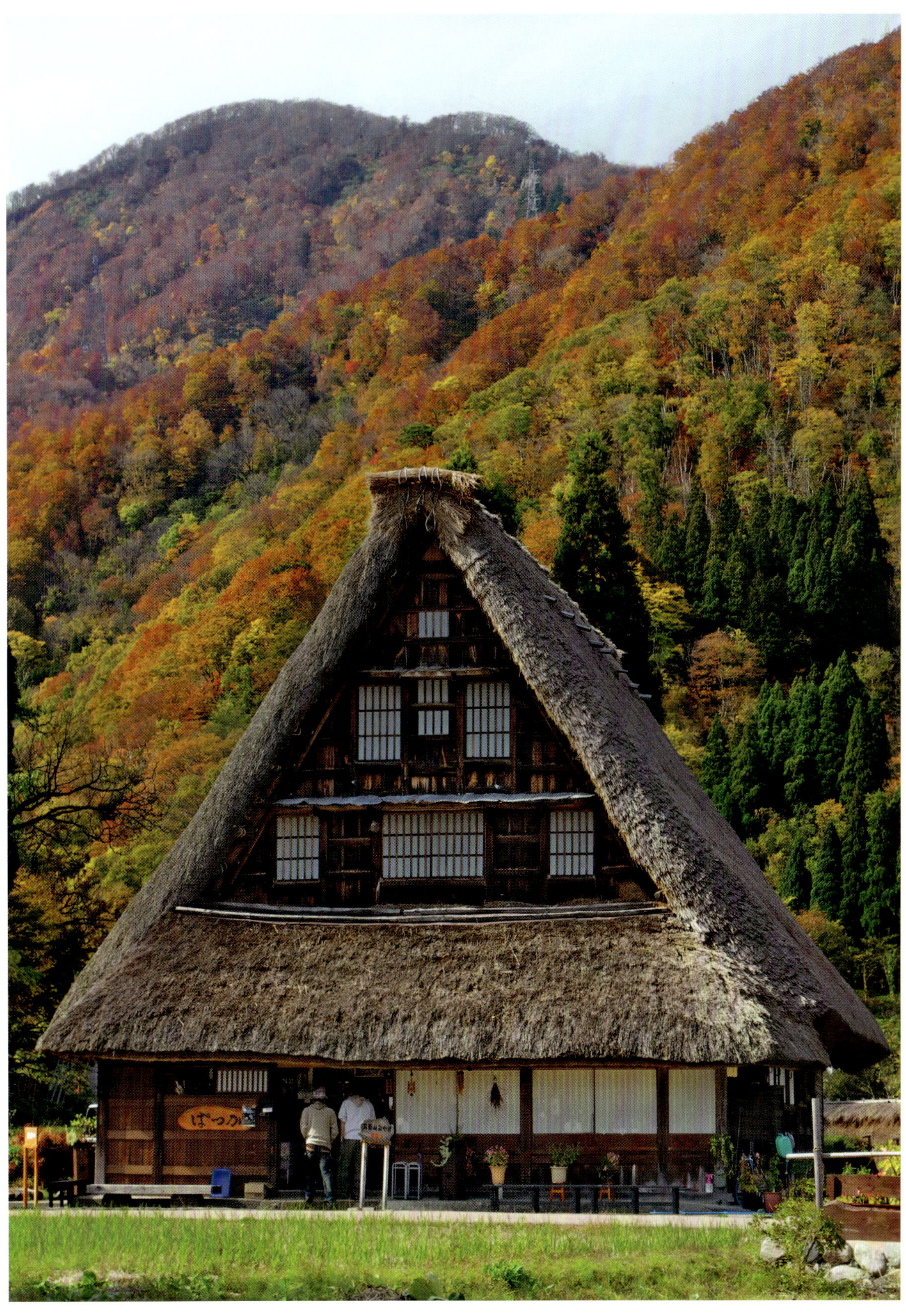

Kendama Ball-and-Cup Toy

A simple game of skill that everyone in Japan plays

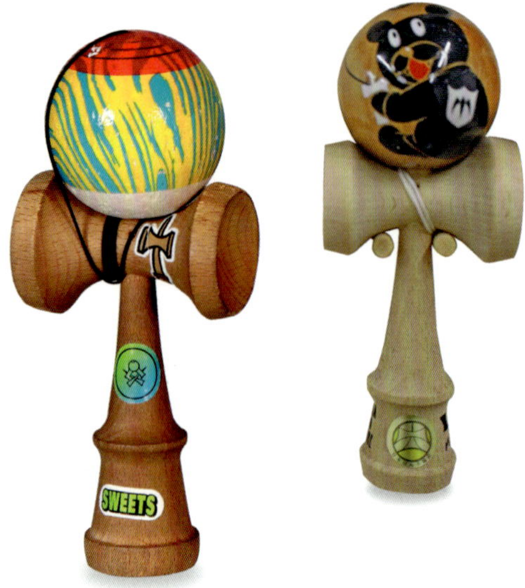

THE PHENOMENALLY POPULAR KENDAMA is a traditional wooden ball-and-cup game. It is a simple toy, similar to the French bilboquet and requires balance, quick reflexes, and good hand-to-eye coordination. People usually just play it for fun, with the basic aim being to balance the ball on one of the wooden cups at the side, or to spear it onto the pointed end. More competitive players can challenge themselves to master complicated techniques to complete tricks. There is hardly a Japanese person who would not have played kendama at least once.

While no one actually knows when kendama first came into existence, it is thought to have arrived in Japan from Europe via the Silk Road at some time during the Edo period (1603–1868). The predecessor of today's kendama had a more chalice-shaped cup; the current form was designed and developed by Ekusa Hamagatsu in Hiroshima in 1919. However, there are a variety of sizes and materials used for kendama. Nowadays they are mostly made in Yamagata Prefecture, an area blessed with rich woodlands, by the company Yamagata Koubou, who also make official competition models. While kendama were traditionally made with a hand-held lathe, Yamagata Koubou's manufacturing process is mechanized using bespoke machinery.

Kendama has become a street-culture phenomenon across the world, with competitions for enthusiasts. In 2006, the first kendama maker was established in the US, and there are now several globally popular brands, including Cereal and Sol. Social media is an important platform for sharing tricks and another reason for the continuing fascination with kendama.

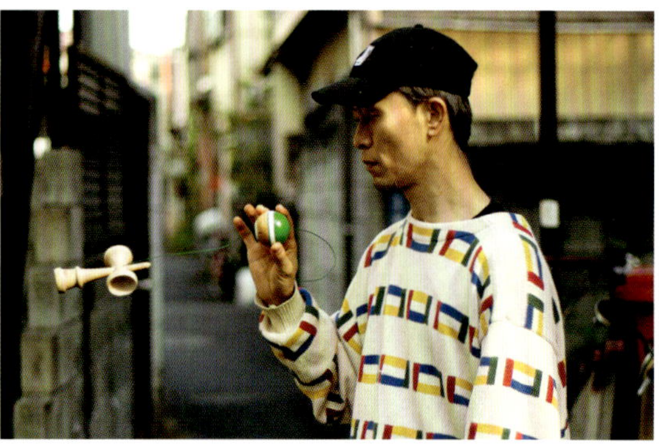

This page top Kendama come in many attractive designs. **Above** Kendama designer, maker and community organizer, Ayumu Haitaini. **Facing page top left** A kendama collaboration between Haitani, and Denki-yu sento bathhouse. **Top right** A vintage kendama. **Bottom** Yamagata Koubou kendama.

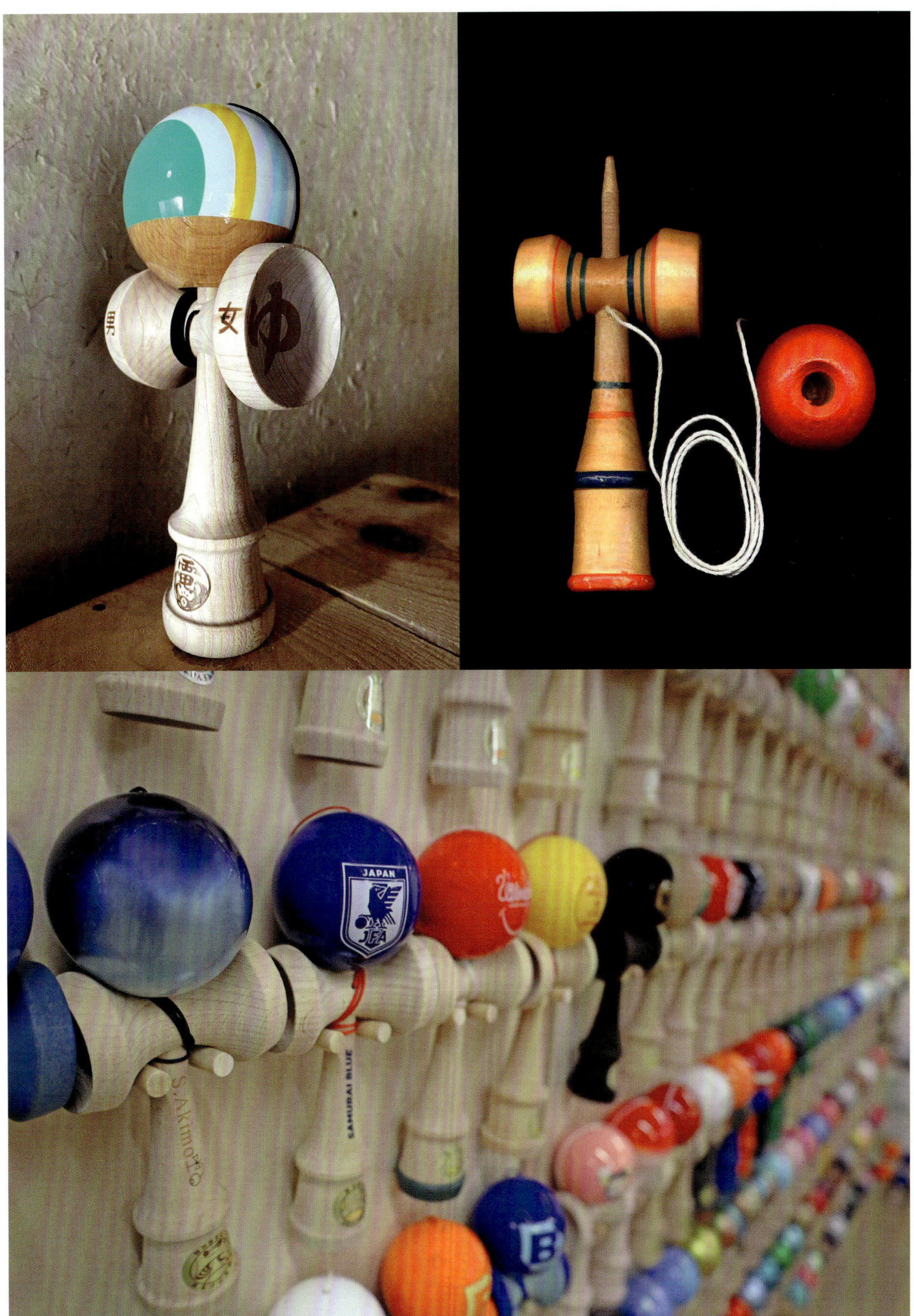
男
女
ゆ
JAPAN
JFA
SAMURAI BLUE
S.AkimoTo
B

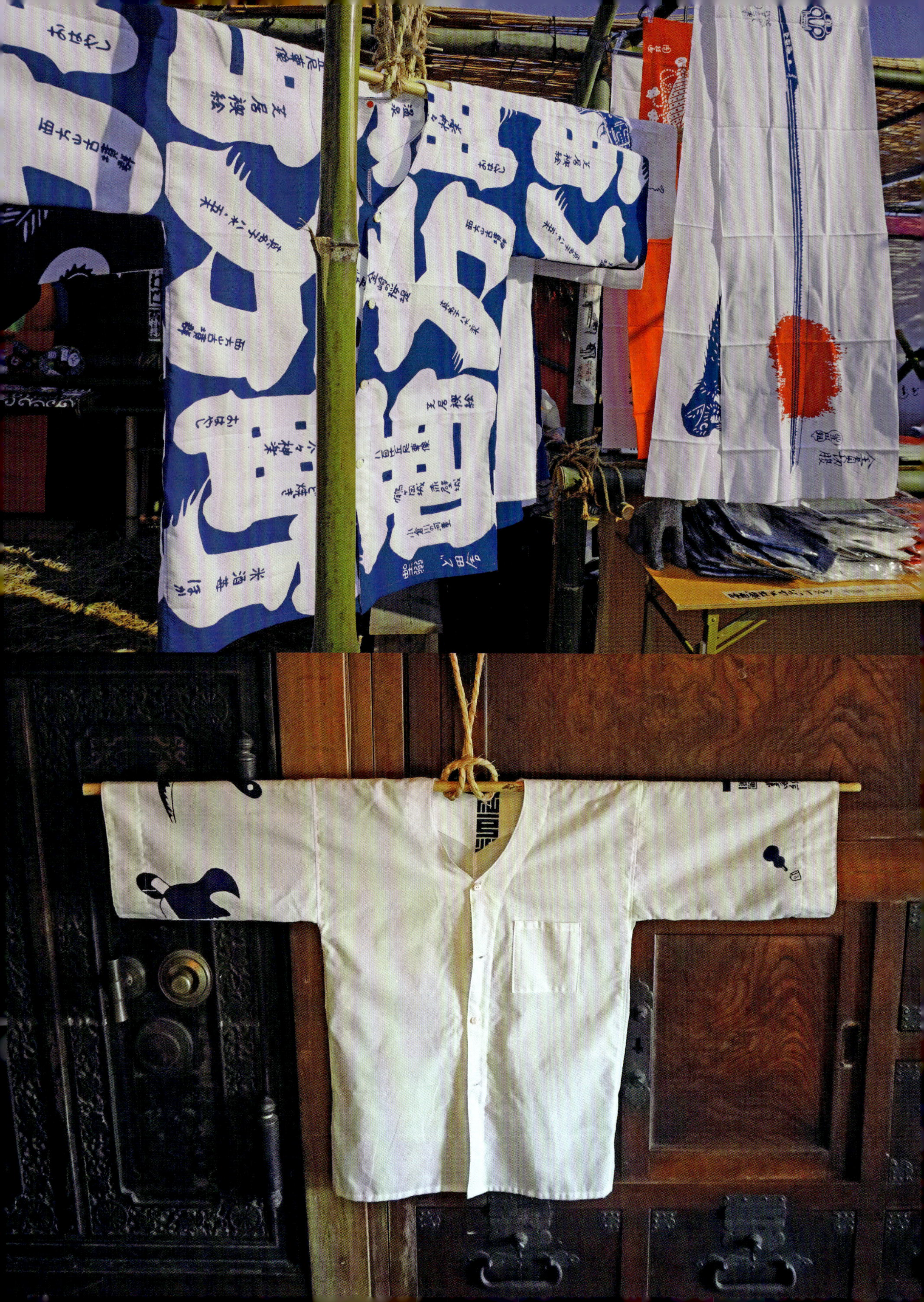

Koiguchi Cotton Festival Shirts

Simple shirts with bold patterns worn on festival days

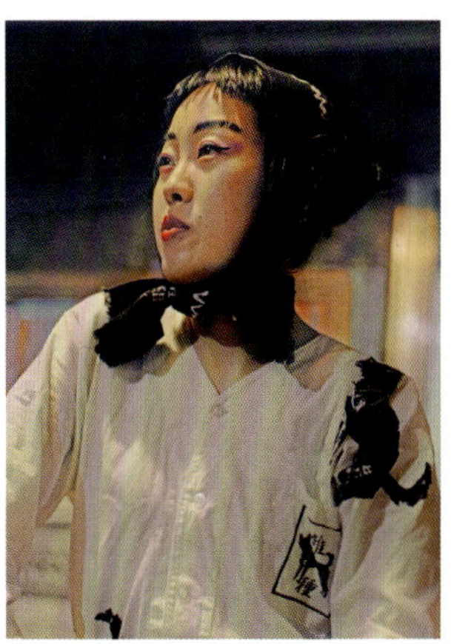

KOIGUCHI SHIRTS are made in a shape that follows the silhouette of the body, and they have sleeves that taper into an opening that is *koiguchi* (carp's mouth) shaped. Made of cotton, they are quick drying, absorbent and light. Traditionally they were decorated with symbolic and auspicious motifs such as dragons, or Fujin and Raijin, the gods of thunder and wind. These shirts are commonly worn at festivals, and it is said that some people wore them in lieu of full body tattoos and that the shirts themselves originally imitated tattoos, fitting closely to the contours of the body, just as a tattoo would. At festivals, koiguchi shirts are usually worn with a happi coat over a belly girdle and a loincloth.

Yuta Murakado is a maker of traditional koiguchi shirts. His shirts are composed of five cotton tenugui cloths (see page 103), with no collar and three-quarter-length sleeves; the shirts are fastened with cat-eye buttons. He sews the shirt so that the armpit is open to create a loose and comfortable fit across the chest. Thanks to new creators like Murakado, these traditional shirts have found a new young and stylish fan base who wear them as they might wear a Hawaiian shirt.

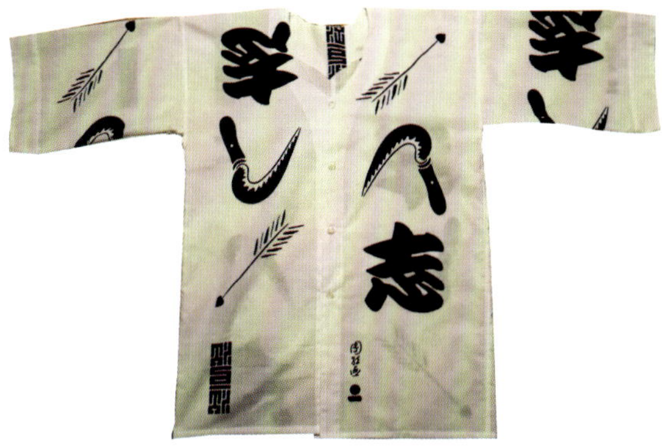

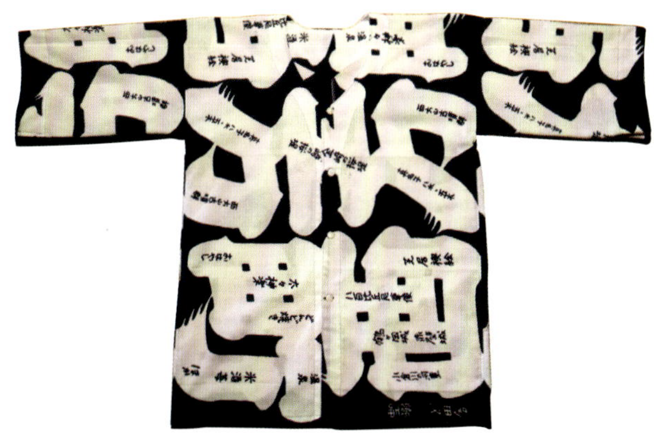

Koiguchi shirts are typically worn at traditional festivals. Considering that almost all shrines and temples host festivals at least once a year, there are hundreds of thousands of festivals throughout the year across Japan. These festivals are an important source of income for artisans, many of whom spend the majority of the year producing handcrafted items for these events.

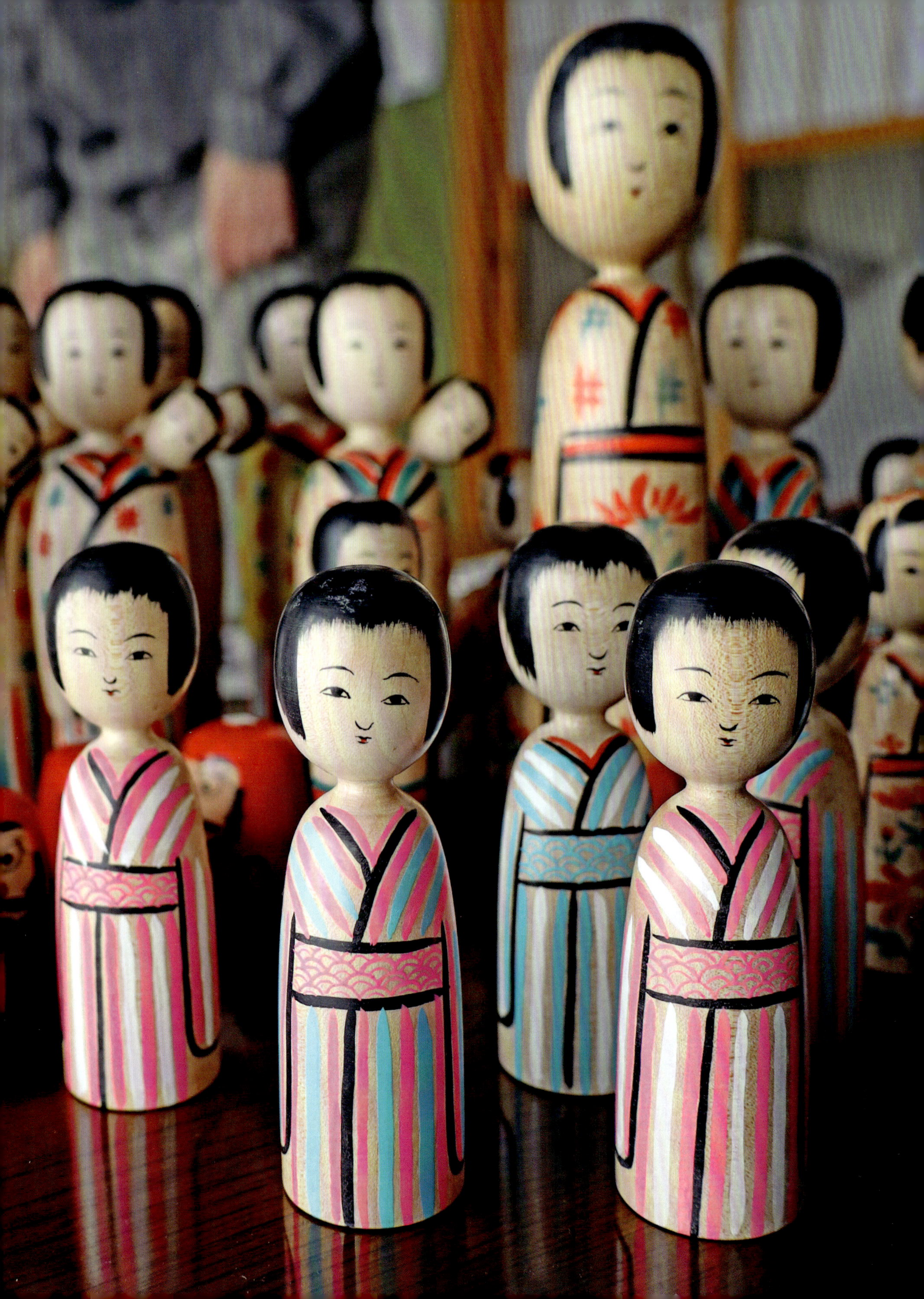

Kokeshi Dolls

Simple wooden dolls from northern Japan

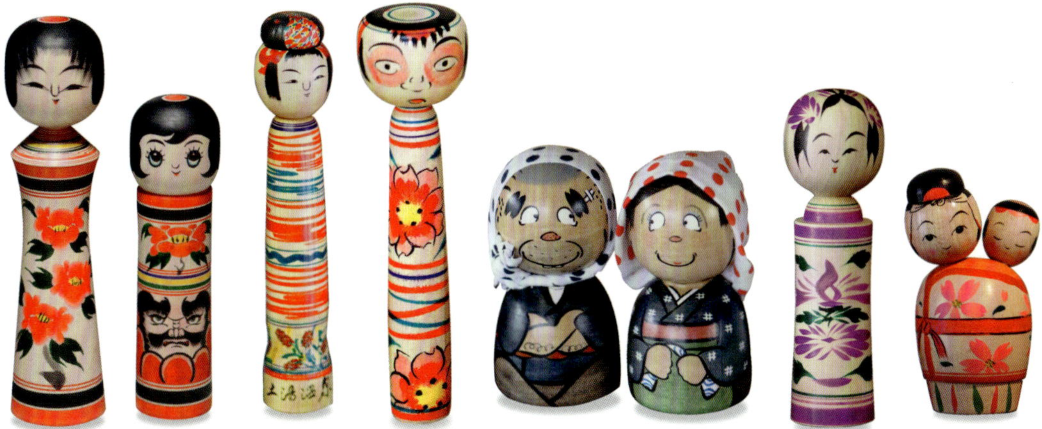

KOKESHI ARE TRADITIONAL DOLLS that are made of wood and characterized by their lack of arms or legs. They are produced in the Tohoku region of Japan in the north of the main island of Honshu and were originally a children's toy, although they are more often used as an interior-design element nowadays.

They are one of the best-known forms of Japanese folk craft and loved for their simple, elegant and minimalist designs. For lovers of kokeshi, the dolls' artisanal and handmade nature represents the romance of a bygone past when craft items were made one at a time, with care and attention. Kokeshi fans often have an emotional response to the dolls; their facial expressions are rather ambiguous, which many find comforting. Famed kokeshi artisan, Yasuo Okazaki says, "When you come home from work, and you are tired, kokeshi make you feel healed and comforted."

There are two main classifications of kokeshi: the traditional historic types and modern types that emerged post–World War II. Traditional kokeshi are predominantly made in Japan's northern region of Tohoku by craftspeople who underwent an apprenticeship with a recognized artisan. There are twelve traditional styles, each with their own characteristic patterns, body shapes and facial features. They are delicately painted in shades of yellow, red, green, and purple. The most common of these twelve styles is the Naruko kokeshi, made in Naruko Onsen in Miyagi Prefecture. These exquisite dolls are painted with calligraphic precision in vibrant reds and greens. The most common motif is an abstract expression of a chrysanthemum which is painted onto the body. Their demure faces have a faint smile.

Modern kokeshi are quite unlike the traditional type in that there are no formal rules as to who can make them, how they look or where

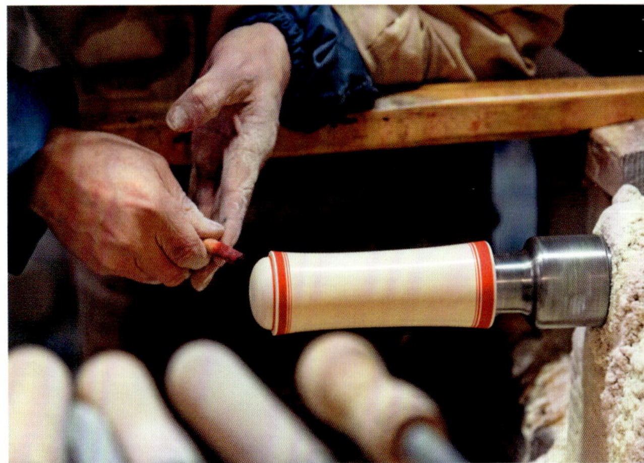

Facing page Traditional Kijiyama-style kokeshi made in Akita Prefecture. **Above, top** Kokeshi dolls come in a wide variety of traditional and modern styles. **Above, bottom** Kokeshi are made one at a time, with care and attention.

they are made. They can range from kitsch tourist souvenirs that resemble local landmarks through to fine-art pieces that resemble abstract sculptures.

Although no one knows who exactly made the first kokeshi, the oldest documented evidence of the dolls dates back to the 1860s in villages around the Sakunami Onsen hot-spring area near Sendai. Woodcraftsmen called *kijishi* who made and sold items such as plates, soup and rice bowls and candlestick holders would use leftover wood to make wooden dolls, using a lathe-like turning device called a *rokuro*. They would sell these humble dolls to visitors to the hot springs, mainly farmers and their families who would take time off during the snowy winter months to relax and recuperate at hot-spring resorts.

The Mingei Movement, which started in the 1920s, drew attention to kokeshi dolls. Folklorists associated with the movement, such as Keizo Shibusawa (1896–1963) and Yotaro Arisaka (1896–1955) carried out research into rural folk culture, including folk toys such as kokeshi. As a result of their work, many people, often educated males from elite backgrounds, traveled to Tohoku to discover a nostalgic "forgotten past." This philosophical interest in folk toys and craft continues to this day.

During Japan's postwar domestic travel boom, hot-spring resorts became vacation spots for urbanites, and kokeshi became popular souvenirs. To this day, kokeshi continue to be one of the most popular Japanese mingei crafts.

This page Artisan Naomi Umeki, trained in the traditional Zao style, crafts irresistible kokeshi cats with classic abstract chrysanthemum motifs. **Facing page, top** Kokeshi artisan Toru Izu at Ginzan Onsen adds the finishing touches to one of his creations. **Facing page, bottom left** Modern kokeshi do not have to conform to traditional rules. Jacob Hodsdon and Lisa Holt-Hodsdon craft art pieces that highlight the texture of the wood. **Bottom right** Traditional Naruko kokeshi dolls by Yasuo Okazaki.

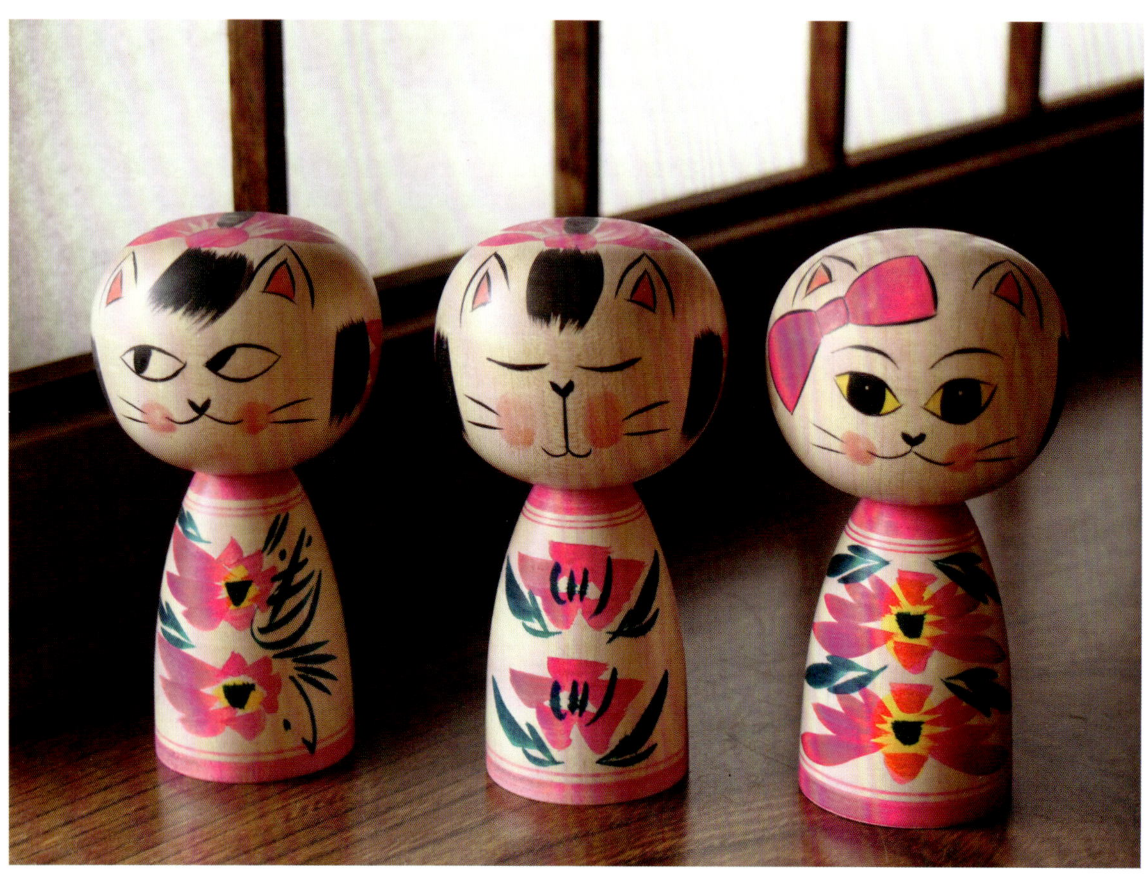

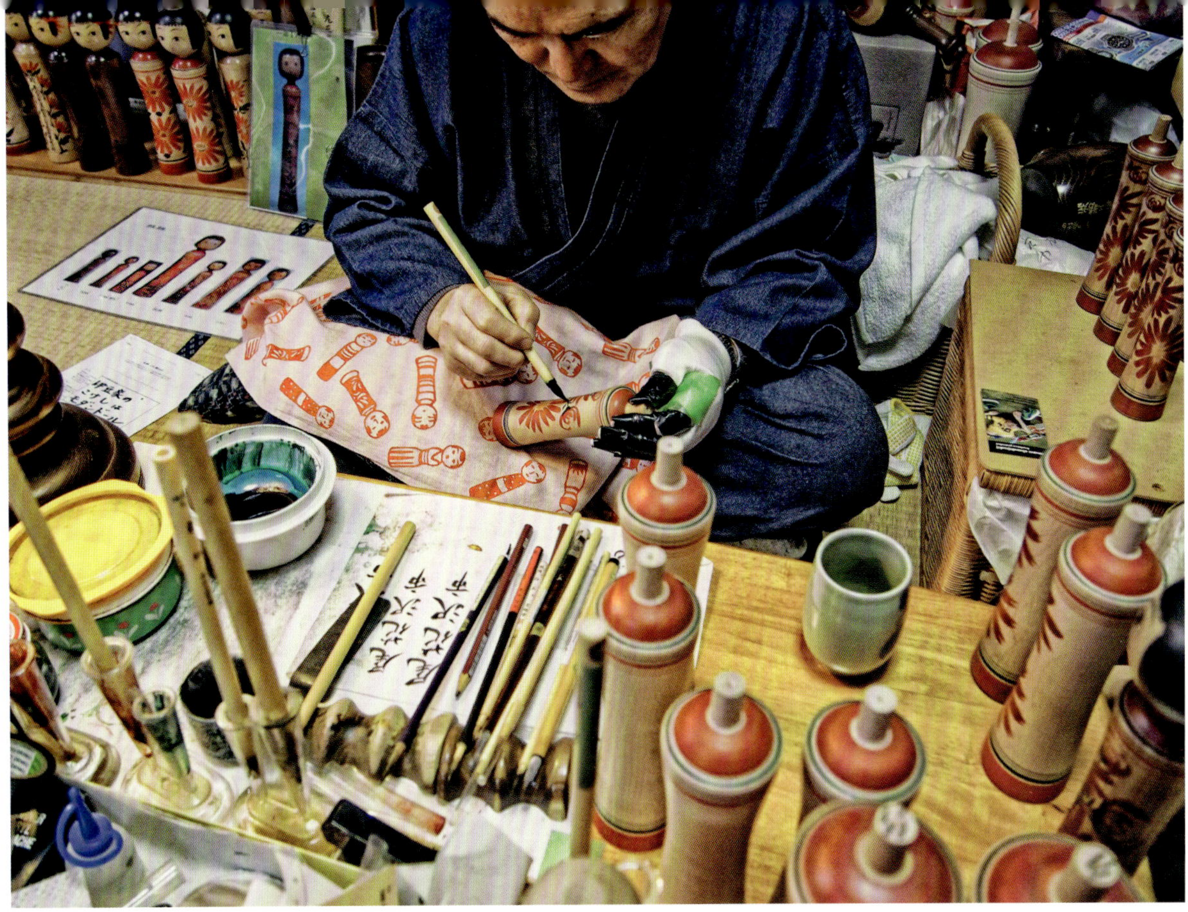

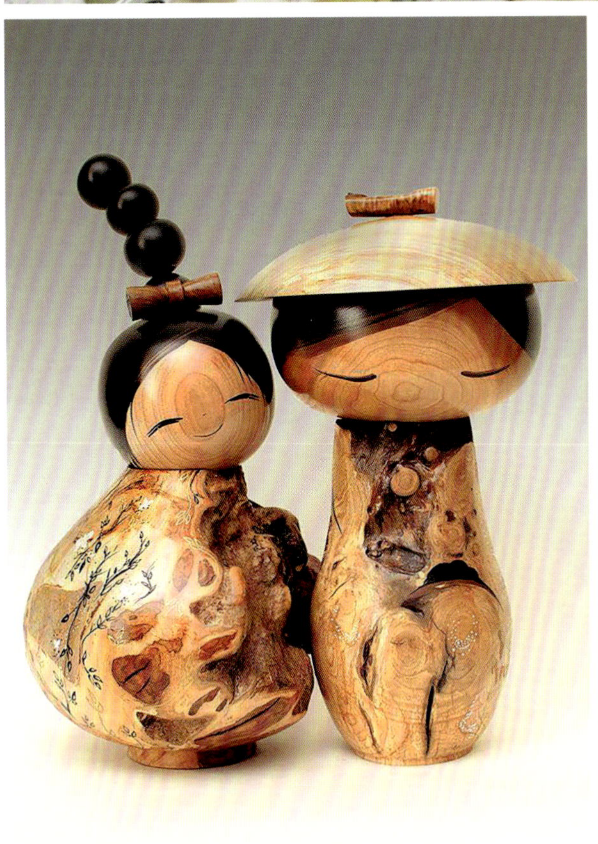

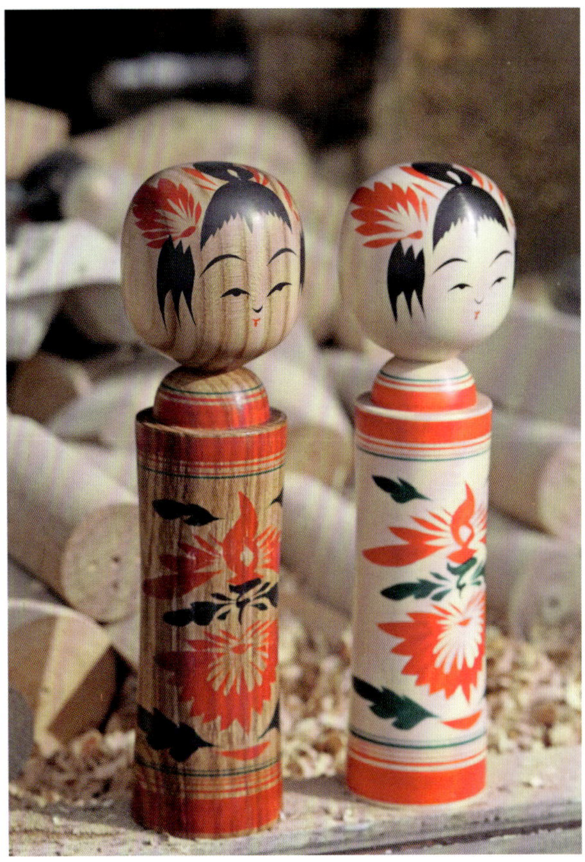

Kumade "Bear's Paw" Rakes

A talisman to rake in success and money

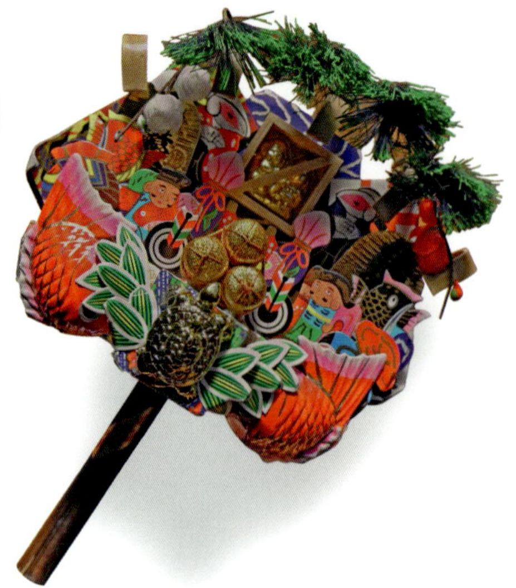

KUMADE ARE TALISMANIC RAKES made of bamboo that are embellished with decorations, ranging from mythical creatures to deities. The word *kumade* in Japanese literally means "bear's paw" and they are said to rake in luck and success. Throughout Japan they are a common sight at shops, eateries and bars. In the past, they were predominantly made with four prongs, representing the claws of a hawk. Five-pronged rakes then became the norm. Nowadays, their fundamental shape is more akin to a regular Japanese bamboo garden rake.

Kumade are displayed in shops and restaurants in a location where they are visible to customers. They are also found in the home—in the *tokonoma* alcove where artistic items are displayed; as part of the home shrine; affixed to a wooden beam; or placed in a window.

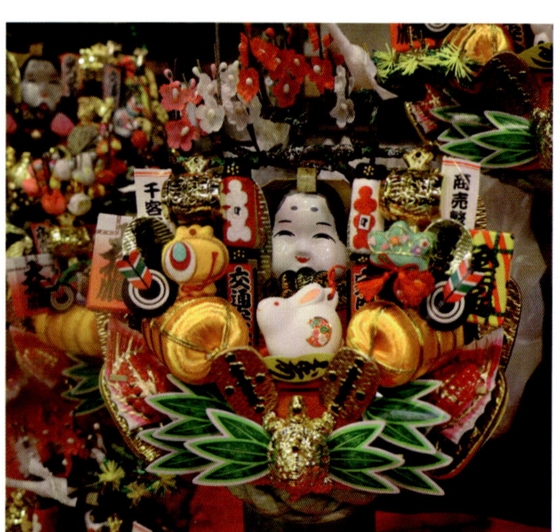

Numerous motifs are used on kumade, all of which are celebratory, such as the *shochikubai* arrangement of pine, bamboo and plum; or an *okame* mask with the face of a smiling woman. The crane and the turtle, which represent longevity are also common. Some kumade feature sea bream as their Japanese name (*tai*)is connected to the word *medetai*, meaning auspicious. The sea bream is often being carried by Ebisu, one of Japan's Seven Lucky Gods.

Like most talismans, kumade rakes are replaced every year (often with larger ones). They are mostly sold at Tori-no-ichi festivals held in shrines and festivals across Japan in November every year, a tradition that dates from the 1700s. Otori Shrine in Tokyo's Asakusa district holds one of the most spectacular, with dozens of picturesque stalls in the shrine precincts, and the road leading to the shrine is decorated with lanterns. From August onward, kumade artisans are busy preparing for this yearly event.

Like many artisanal crafts, environmental factors are key to the survival of kumade. They are usually displayed in family-run independent shops, such as groceries or fishmongers, and small restaurants of the type found in traditional *shotengai* shopping streets. As chain supermarkets, convenience stores and out-of-town shopping malls proliferate, the continued existence of craft items like kumade is threatened.

This page Kumade are heavily decorated with auspicious items. **Facing page** Kumade markets often take place at local shrines, usually in November. Tokyo's most famous markets are at Hanazono Shrine and Otori Shrine.

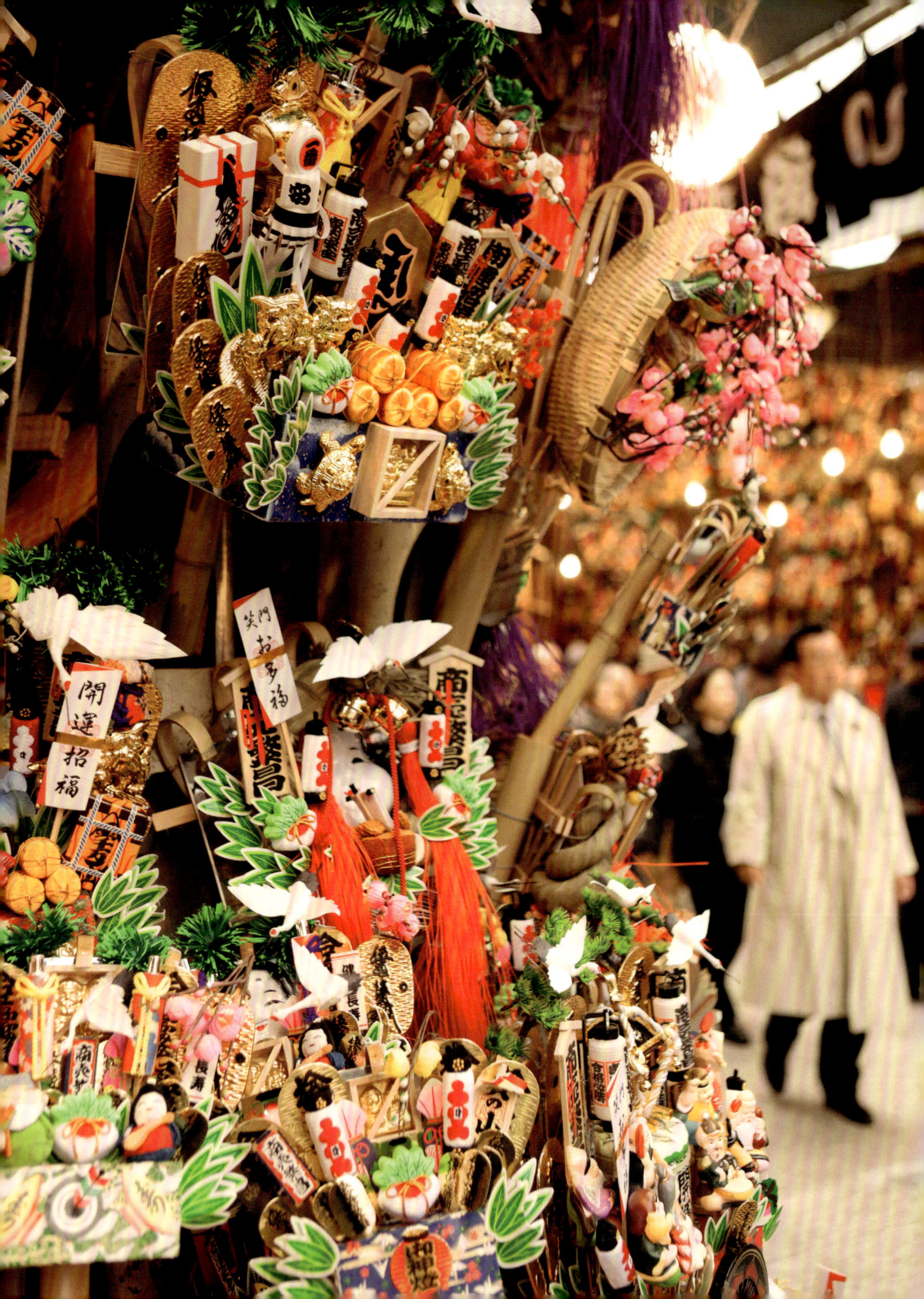
笑門
お多福
開運
招福

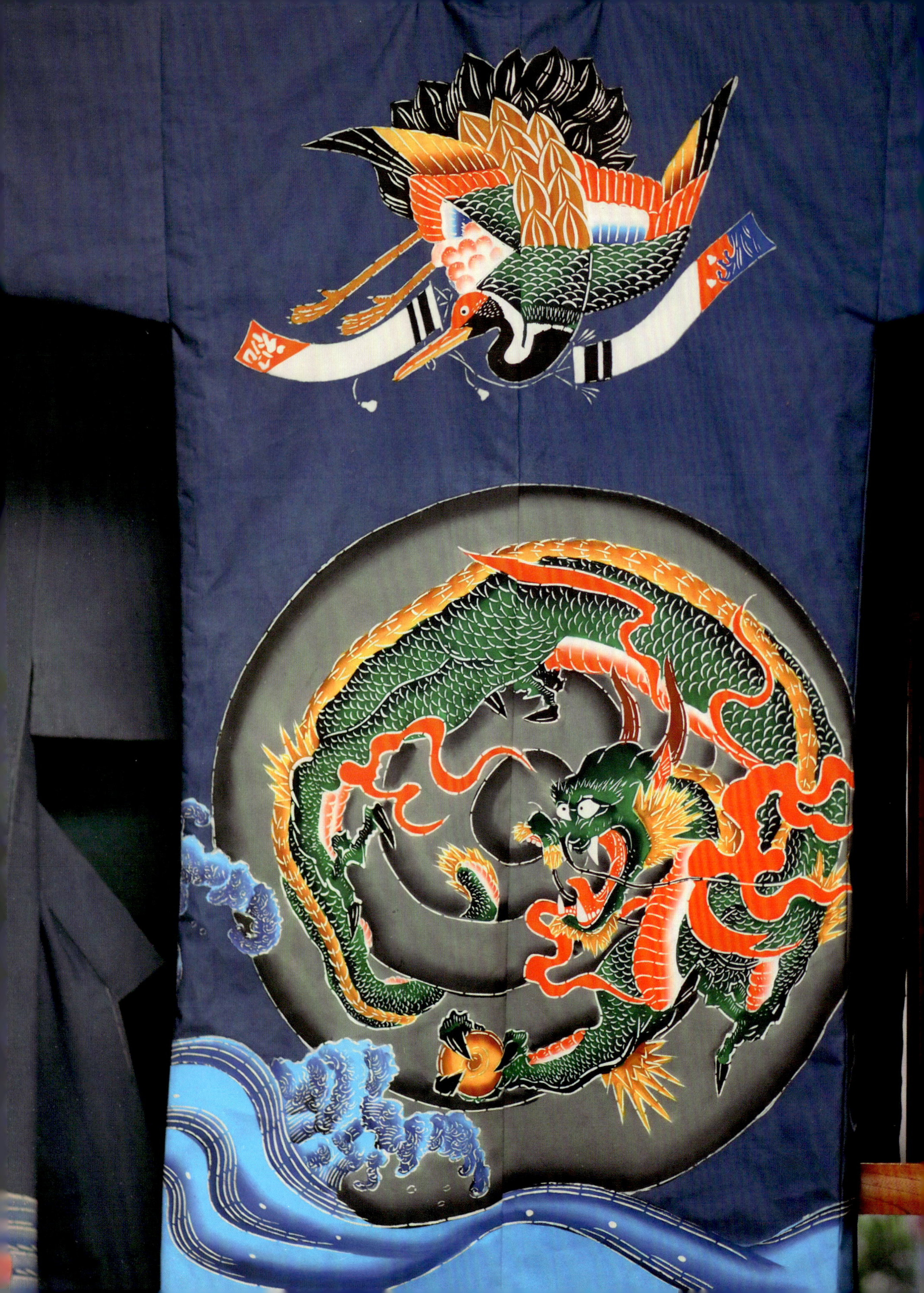

Maiwai Fisherman Coats

Colorful hand-dyed coats to celebrate a good catch

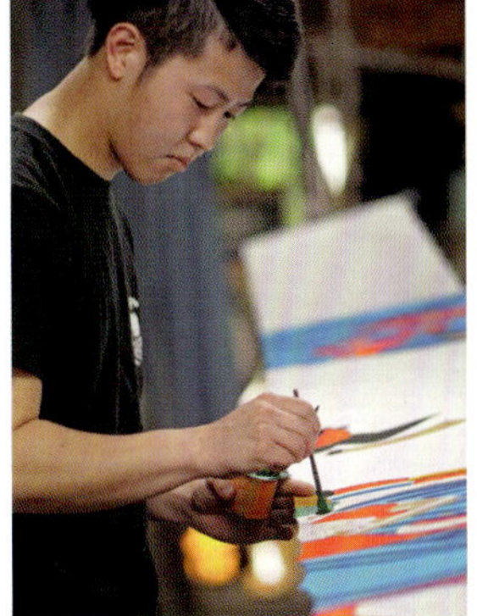

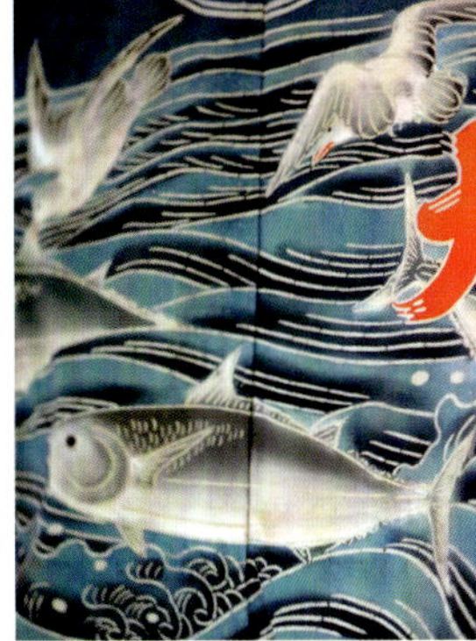

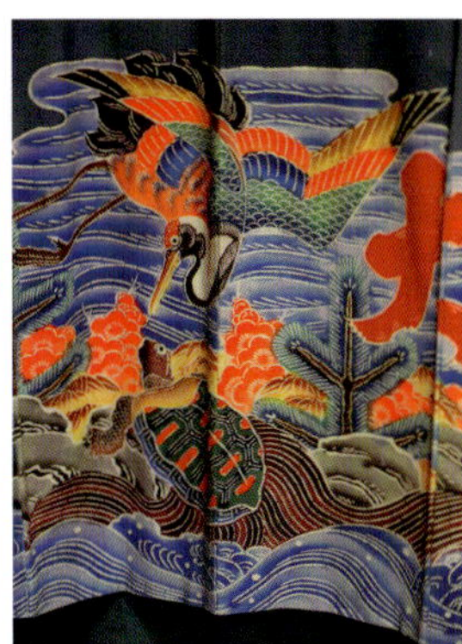

MAIWAI ARE COLORFUL FISHING KIMONOS traditionally worn by fishermen when there was a good catch, a custom that began in the Edo period (1603–1868). Kosuke Suzuki, third generation maiwai maker (620-1 Yokosuka, Kamogawa, Chiba; tel: 04-7092-1531) says, "It was an era when death was always around the corner, so people liked to live for the moment. If they had money, they would enjoy spending it on luxury items like these. The motifs on the coats were things like the types of fish they caught." The tradition is said to have started in Chiba Prefecture and it then spread along the Pacific coast.

Artisans who make maiwai kimonos carry out all stages of the decoration process themselves. They design the illustration, and then they make stencils for each part of the illustration from soaked persimmon paper. Using the stencils, they apply a sticky rice glue to the cloth to do a resist dye. The number of stencils used to create a pattern varies from two for a *hanten* short coat, to eight for a regular kimono.

Basic pigment colors are used to dye the cloth such as ultramarine, Prussian blue, rouge, cinnabar, india ink, and indigo, but using gradations, artisans can create new hues. The pigments are mixed with soy bean paste so that the colors fasten to the fabric.

The motifs are dramatic and bold. The crane and turtle, which signify longevity, are popular illustrations, as are gods offering protection, such as the goddess Benten or the fishing gods Daikoku and Ebisu. The background is usually embellished with a wave. These days the coats are used for ceremonial occasions such as local festivals, rather than to celebrate a good catch.

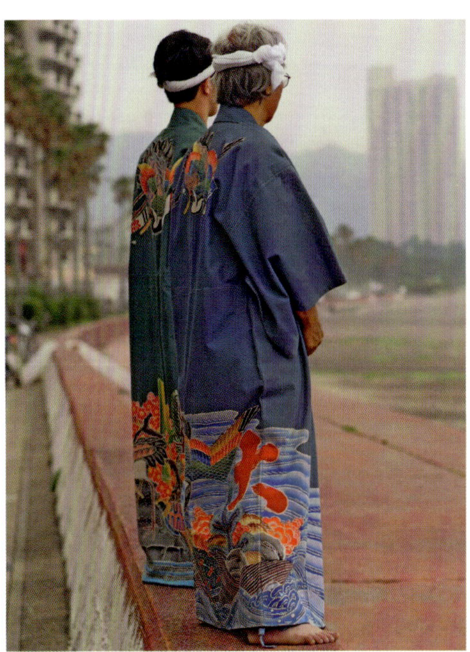

Vivid colors stand out against the subdued indigo of the background. Kosuke Suzuki's son, Riki, works on a design (this page top left). Above, Kosuke and Riki wear maiwai fishing coats.

Maneki-Neko Lucky Cats

Auspicious figures that grant wishes and bring good fortune

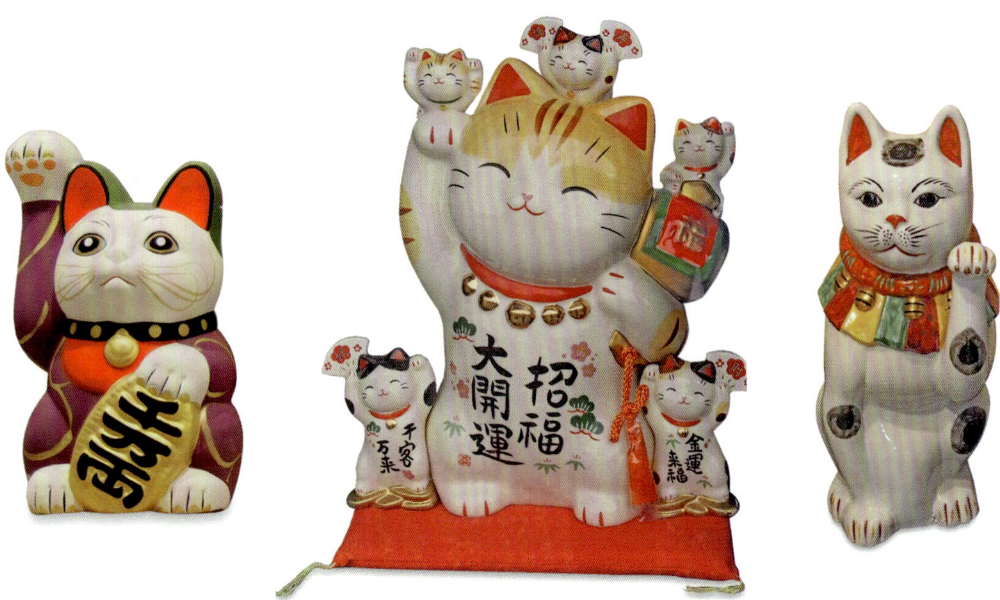

CATS IN JAPAN have a special place in folklore and religion. They were originally kept as protectors of rice and silk as they staved off mice. It is believed cats first came to Japan from China, around 550 AD, in ships that were bringing the Buddhist sutras—cats would catch the mice that otherwise might have eaten these important religious documents. For this reason, cats have always been venerated at Buddhist temples in Japan, and it is argued that without the cats that came on those early ships, Buddhism would not have flourished in Japan.

There is a widespread belief that cats are auspicious and have the power to grant wishes. In the Edo period, the culture of maneki-neko beckoning cats proliferated and they are still extremely popular today. While the ceramic variety is most common, maneki-neko are also made of *hariko* papier-mâché, or wood. They also come in various shapes and sizes: some have their right paw raised for money and luck; others have the left paw raised to beckon lots of customers to a business. Pink is for love, white is for happiness, black and red are for protection, yellow is for money and marriage, gold is for business and money, and green is for success in education.

A woodblock print by Utagawa Hiroshige I, entitled *Characters from Plays as Merchants and Customers* from 1852 is thought to be the first existing evidence of maneki-neko—pictured in the print is a market scene in Tokyo where one of the vendors is selling clay beckoning cats of the type crafted at Imado kiln in Tokyo. Imado ware cats are characterized by a stamp on their backs which says *shime* ("close"), a play on words to ensure that the luck contained in the cat will stay there.

Fushimi kiln in Kyoto was also a hot spot for the manufacture of maneki-neko in the Edo period and they were sold at religious sites around the city. Many people who went on pilgrimages to Kyoto brought these talismans back home with them and as a result their popularity spread across Japan.

Above The ceramic variety of maneki-neko is the most common.
Facing page Gotokuji Temple in Setagaya, Tokyo, is home to a vast number of beckoning cats.

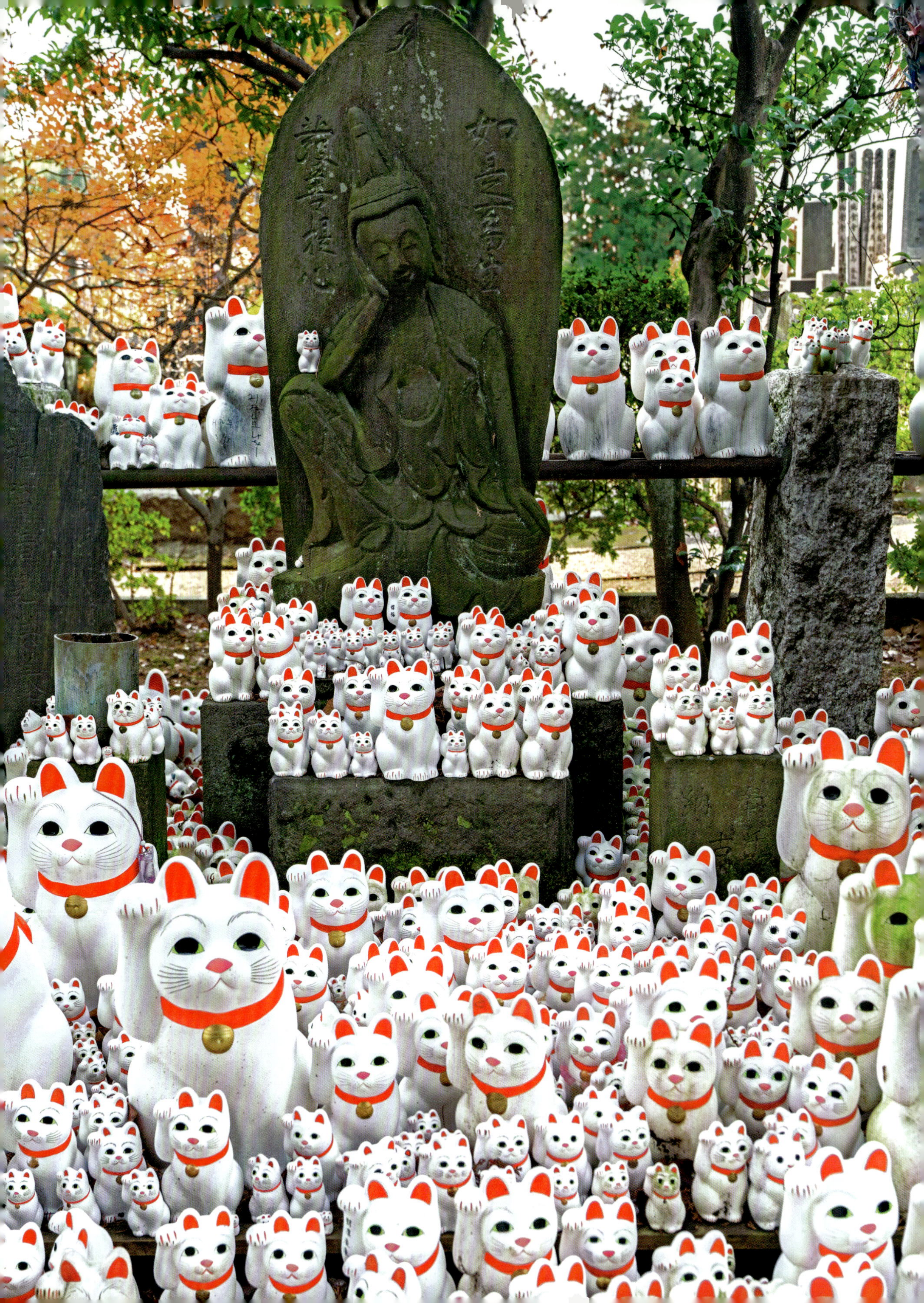

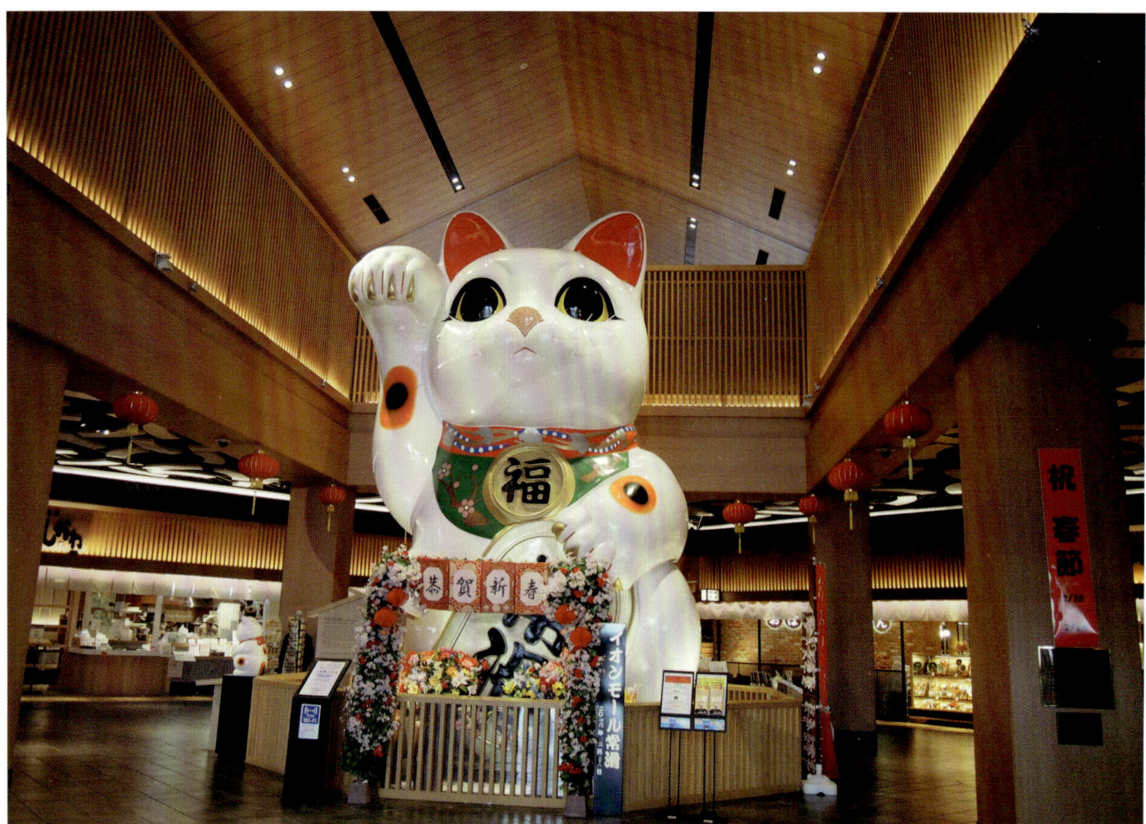

Ceramic maneki-neko are still ubiquitous in traditional pottery regions across Japan. As such, the culture of maneki-neko, mingei folk arts and artisanship has become intertwined.

The place in Japan with the strongest maneki-neko identity is Seto, in Aichi Prefecture with more than four hundred kilns. It has over a thousand years of history as a pottery hub and maneki-neko have been made there since the 1800s. Seto's Maneki-Neko Museum (2 Yakushi-machi, Seto; tel 0561-21-0345) is the largest of its kind in Japan, with over five thousand pieces. Once a year, usually in September, the city holds a massive maneki-neko festival where makers from across Japan exhibit and sell their beckoning cats.

Tokoname is another Aichi Prefecture town with an ancient kiln and a strong maneki-neko identity. The town is charming in appearance with many cat statues and ceramics studios. The Tokoname maneki-neko is the most ubiquitous maneki-neko type, distinguished by its large eyes, and can be seen at eateries across the globe, where its role is to beckon in passing customers. The Baigetsu kiln in Tokoname is responsible for around 80 percent of the market share of maneki-neko.

This page A huge maneki-neko at Aeon shopping mall in Tokoname, Aichi Prefecture.
Facing page First appearing in Tokyo in the nineteenth century, and then in Kyoto, the production of maneki-neko cats gradually spread around the country, picking up regional characteristics that reflect the skills of the local craftspeople. The maneki-neko on the facing page are crafted by artisan Junichi Hashimoto in the style of Kamogata clay dolls that are typical of Okayama Prefecture.

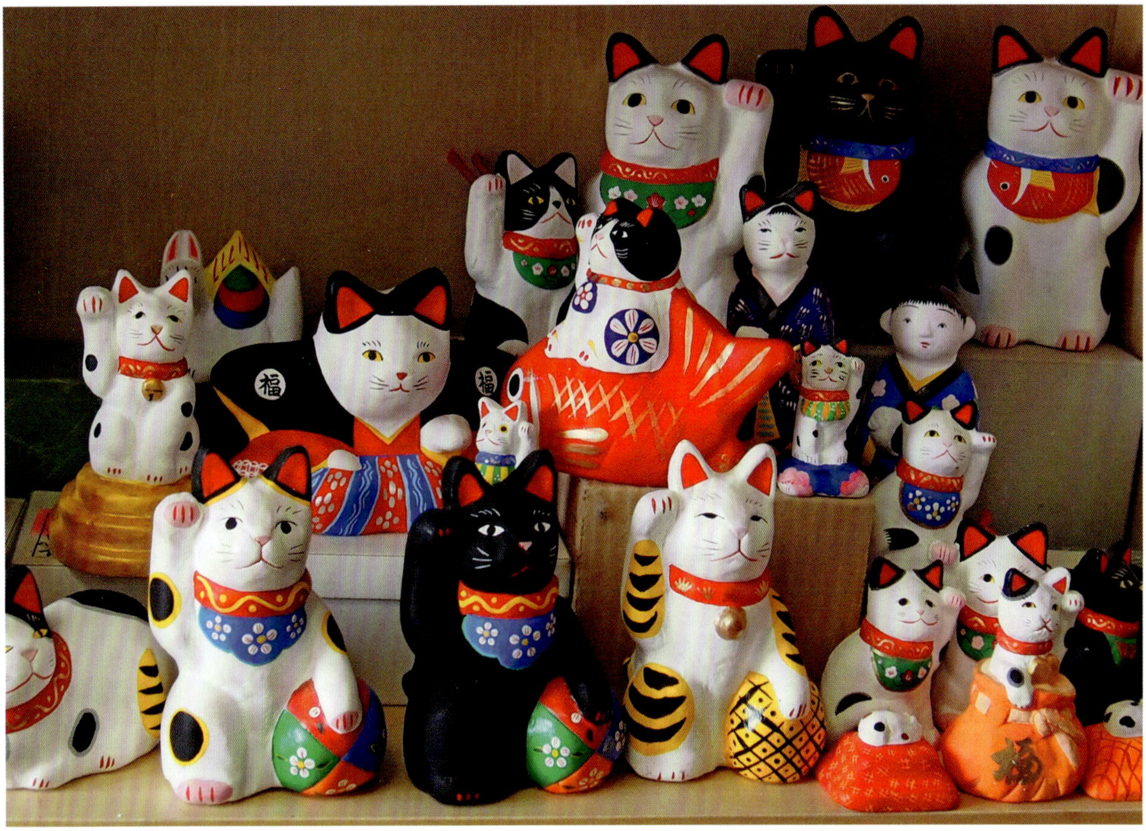

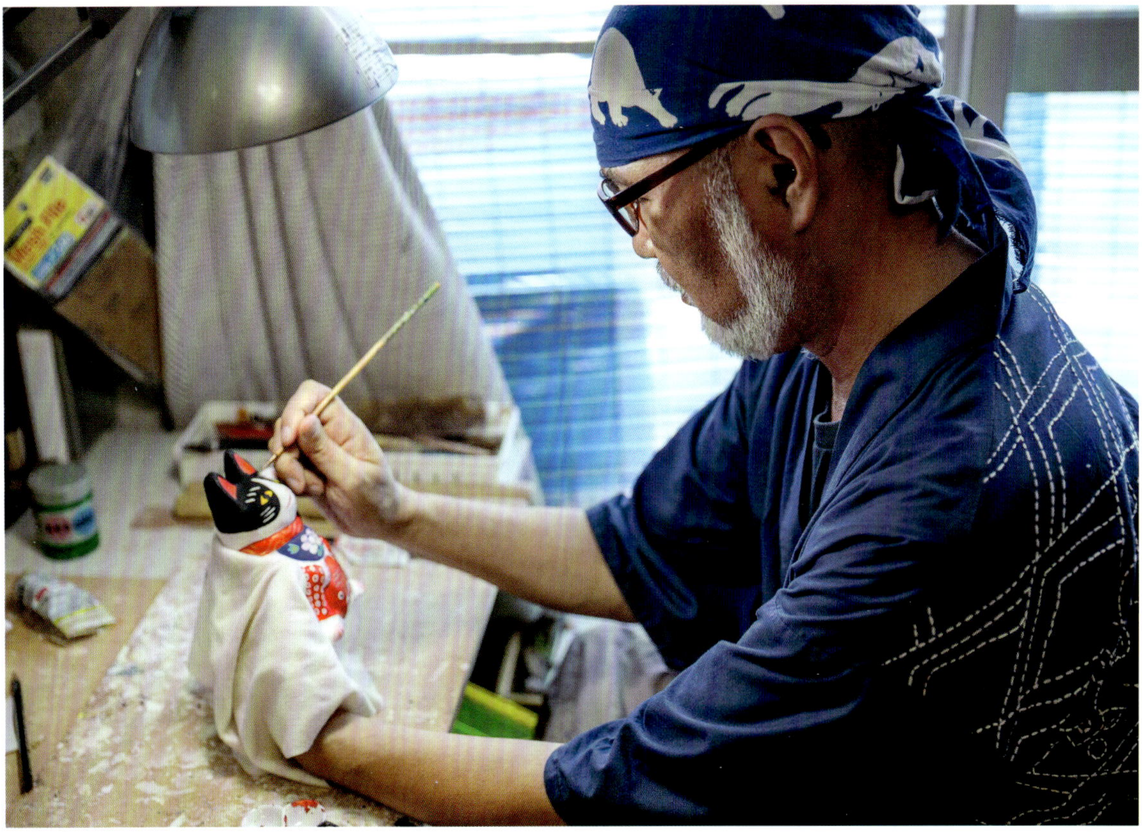

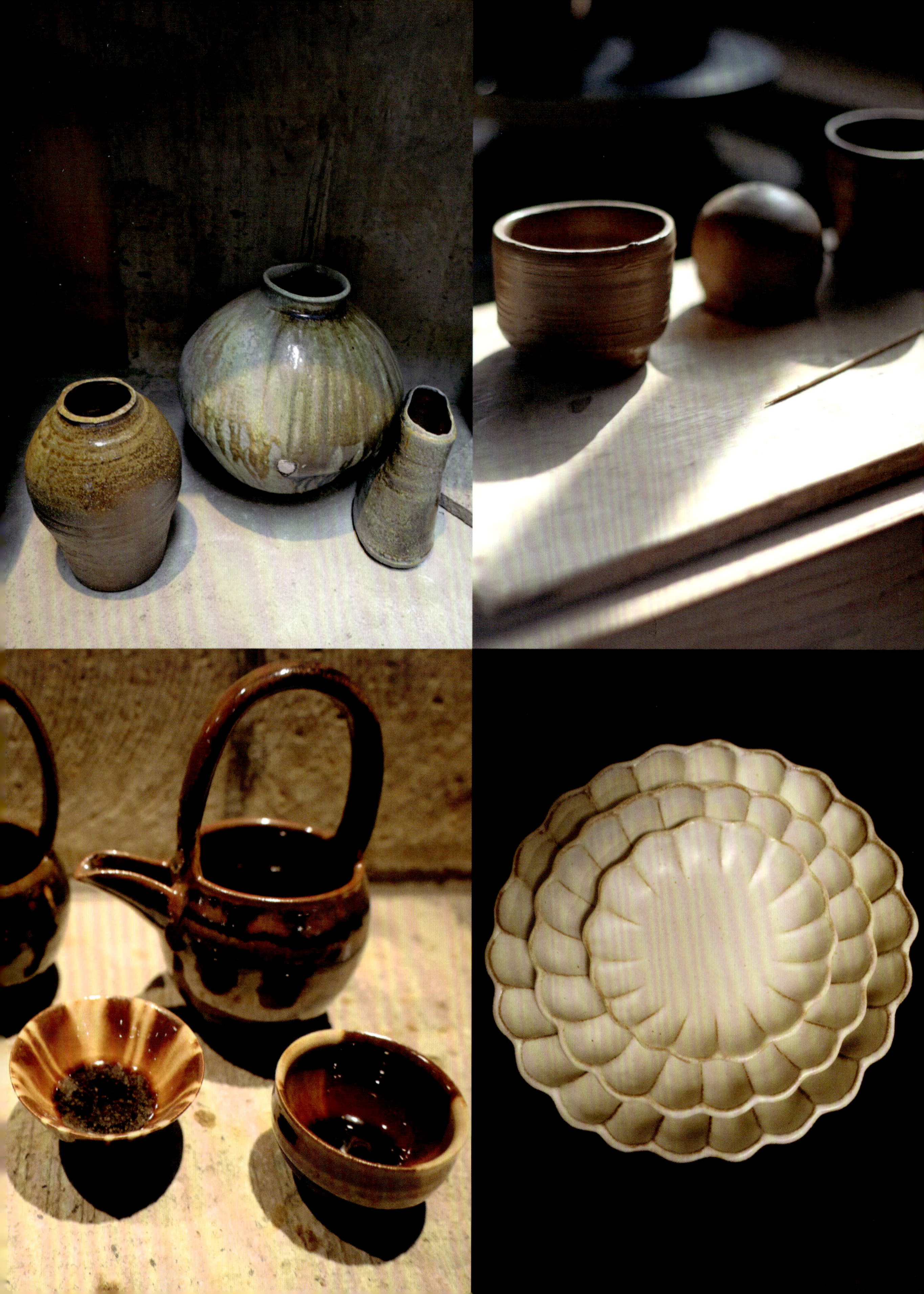

Mashiko Ceramics

Pottery with a distinctive color and glaze

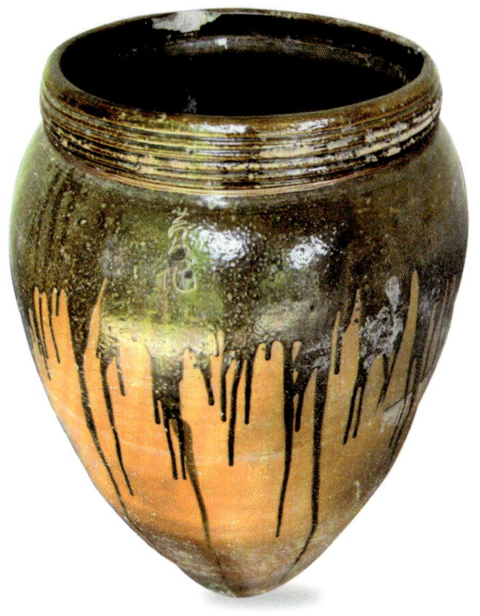

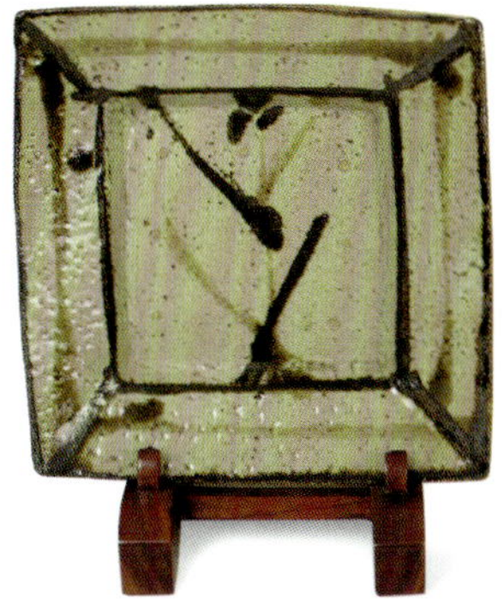

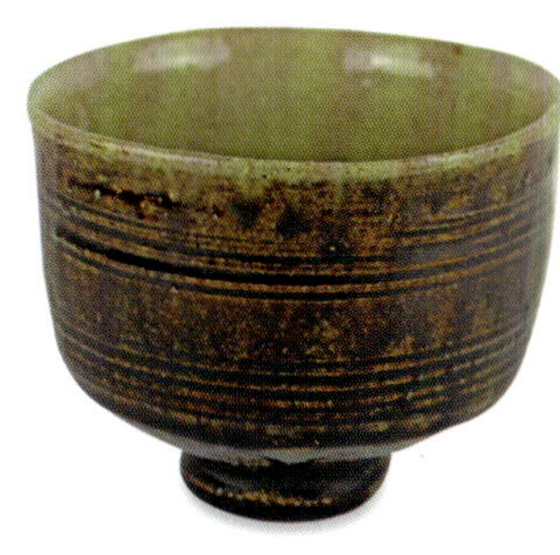

MASHIKO CERAMICS ARE MADE in the mountain town of Mashiko, Tochigi Prefecture, only sixty miles (100 km) from Tokyo. Mashiko ware is characterized by the fact that the local clay is used as is, without mixing with other materials. The clay has high levels of silicic acid and iron, which make it quite heavy and thick. It has a red-brown color and the glazes are made of powdered stone and iron powder.

Mashiko is known for being quite open to outsiders and accepting apprentices to become potters. However, it has a long and storied history. Mashiko ware got its start when potter Keizaburo Otsuka started making everyday items there during the Edo period. By the late nineteenth century, Mashiko had become predominantly a production region for kitchenware items. Shoji Hamada, one of the founders of the Mingei Movement, set up his studio here. He is known for utilitarian items such as plates and cups, embellished with bold, abstract and playful patterns. He used his fame to revive the area, and his student, Tatsuzo Shimaoka, designated a Living National Treasure in 1996, also worked in Mashiko from 1953 until 2007. Nowadays there are around three hundred ceramicists working in Mashiko town, which is well worth a visit (see page 156).

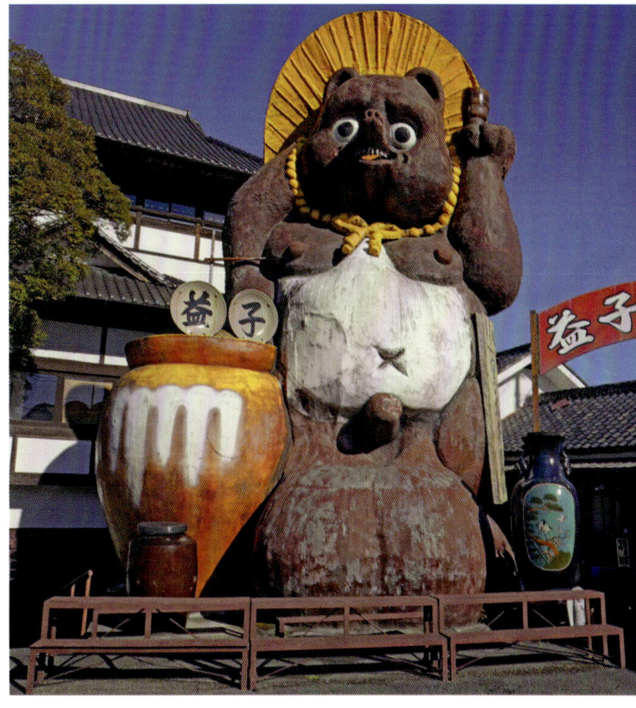

Facing page & above Mashiko ware is diverse and local artisans craft a wide range of everyday practical items. **Right** Pottery raccoons are a common sight around the town of Mashiko.

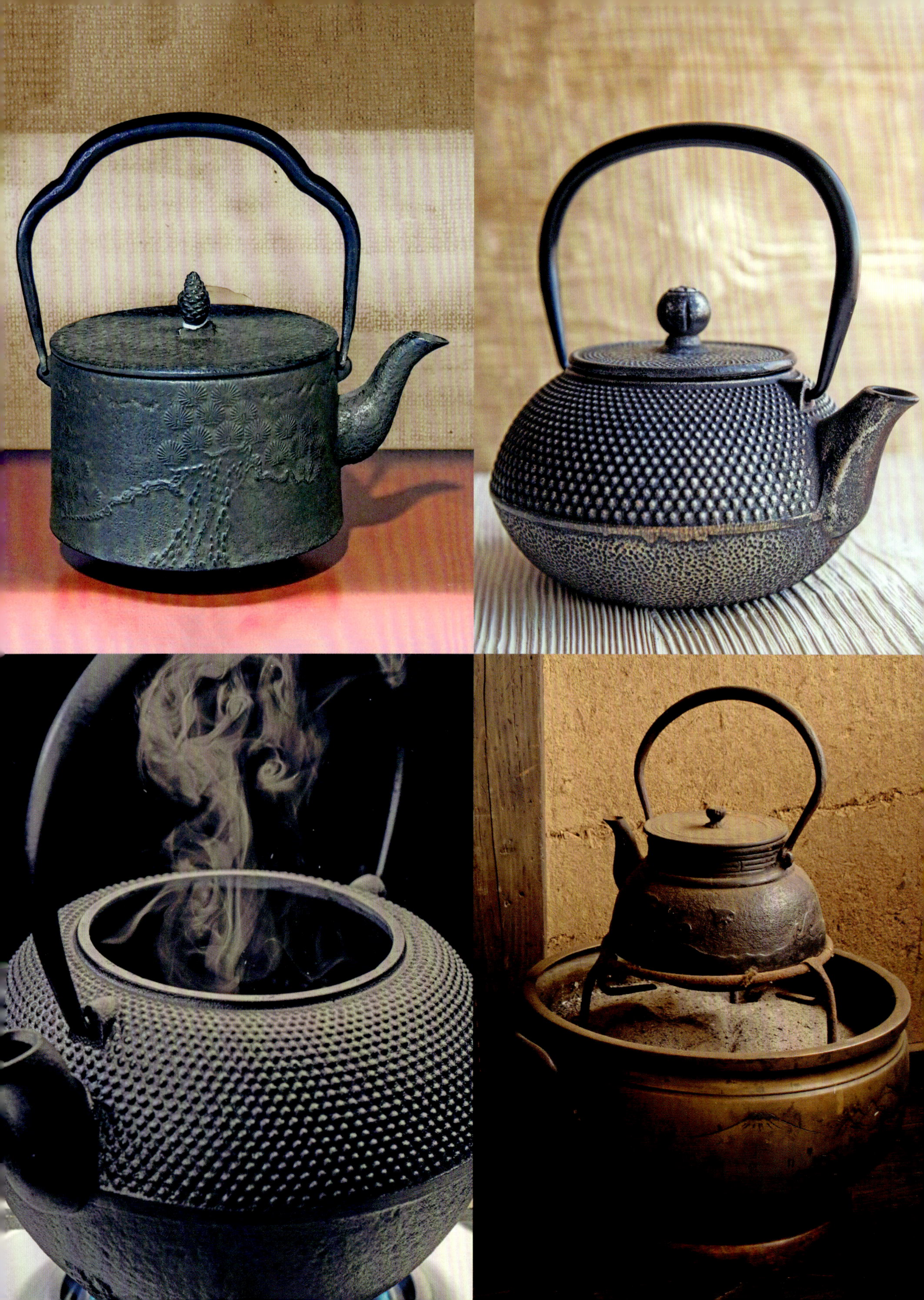

Nambu Tekki Ironware

Traditional cast-iron pots from Tohoku

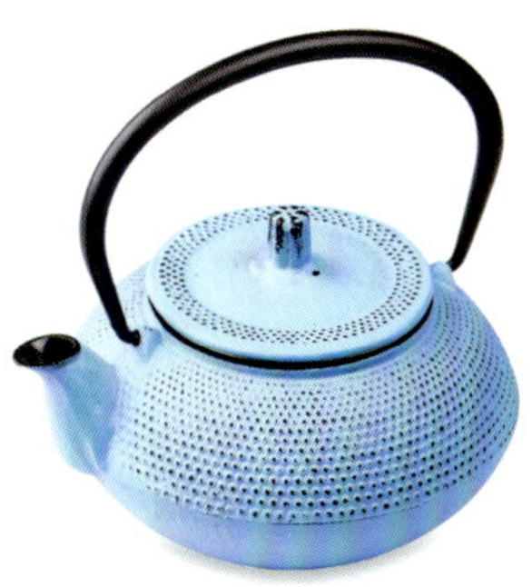

ONE OF THE MOST distinctive folk crafts from northern Japan's Tohoku region is Nambu tekki ironware. Beautiful, durable and practical, these cast-iron kettles and pots are highly sought-after. Other ironware products include kitchen products, furin wind chimes (see page 58) and paperweights. While iron artifacts from Tohoku date back to the twelfth century, high quality Nambu tekki products have been crafted in Iwate Prefecture since the 1600s (when the area was known as Nambu), owing to the easy availability of iron ore. Ironware is made in several regions of Japan but Nambu tekki crafted in Iwate Prefecture is of exceptional quality.

The cast-iron pots are exquisite to the eye. The exterior of the pots have a textured *arare* (hail) pattern that expands the surface area of the pots. Another feature of Nambu kettles is that they are coated with urushi lacquer at the end, which gives a beautiful deep color. Other than that, the design is quite simple. These days they are sometimes made in pastel colors to match contemporary homes.

In feudal times ironware pots were used in tea ceremonies in the Nambu domain. In 1659, Nizaemon Koizumi, an ironware artisan from Kyoto, was asked to move to Nambu in order to make kettles. These superior items were also presented to the emperor as gifts. The third generation of Koizumi's lineage started making smaller-sized pots, and these ended up becoming hugely popular.

Boiling water in Nambu tekki pots releases small amounts of iron, which gives the water a soft, mellow texture, and is beneficial for those who are iron deficient. It is also said that the use of ironware removes chlorine from water. The more the pots are used, the better they become in quality. The best-known company making Nambu tekki pots is Iwachu, based in Morioka (2-23-9 Minamisenboku; tel: 019-635-2505). A section of Iwachu's atelier is open to visitors, who can watch master craftsmen pour molten iron, apply lacquer and embellish the molds, with meticulous attention to detail.

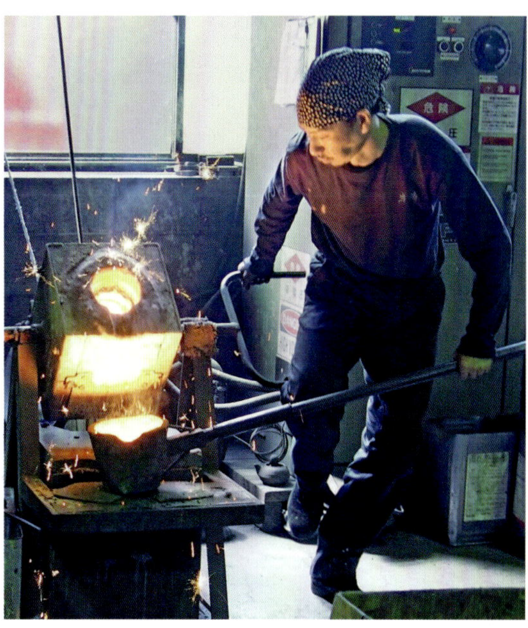

Facing page & above High quality cast-iron products have been crafted in Iwate Prefecture since the 1600s. **Right** Iwachu is a highly regarded ironworks company in Morioka City, producing kettles, kitchenware and other household objects.

Omamori Protective Amulets

Good-luck charms that are carried on one's person

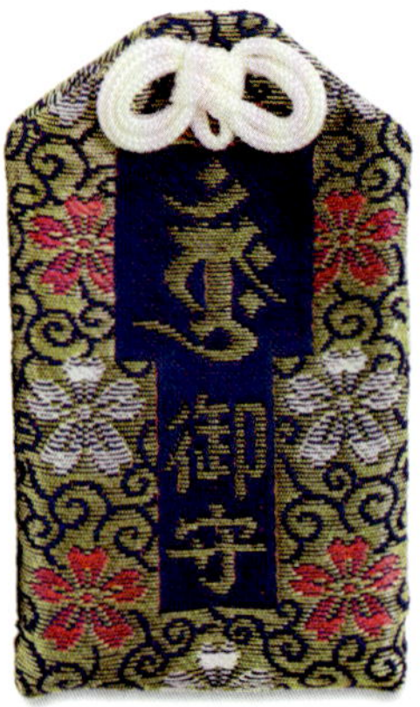

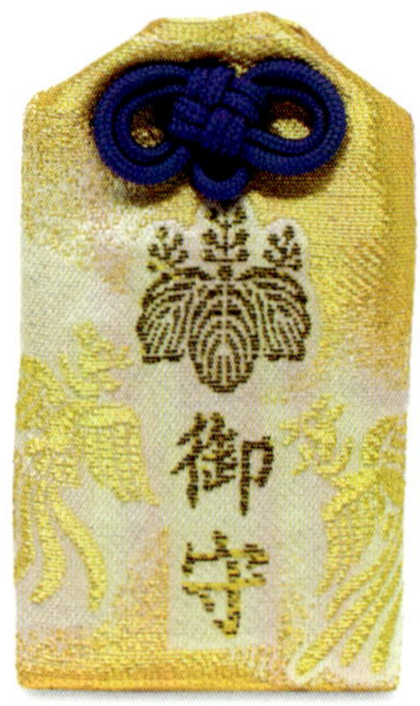

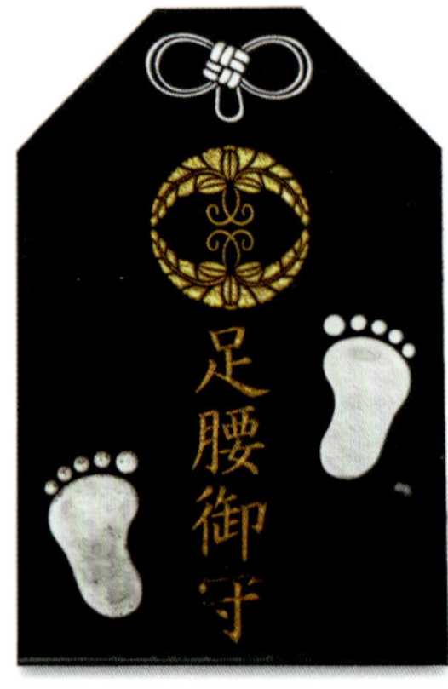

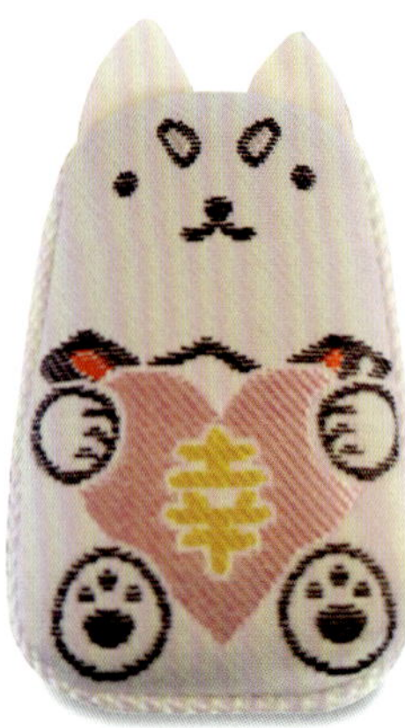

OMAMORI ARE PROTECTIVE AMULETS associated with both Shintoism and Buddhism that are carried on one's person, perhaps hanging from a bag. They are an ubiquitous sight in Japan and people will typically buy one when visiting a shrine or temple, not just for spiritual purposes, but also as a memento of their trip.

Omamori are usually themed: some are for luck during exams, others are for finding love or safe travels. They all contain a prayer inside, although one should never open an omamori as it is believed that the good luck will escape.

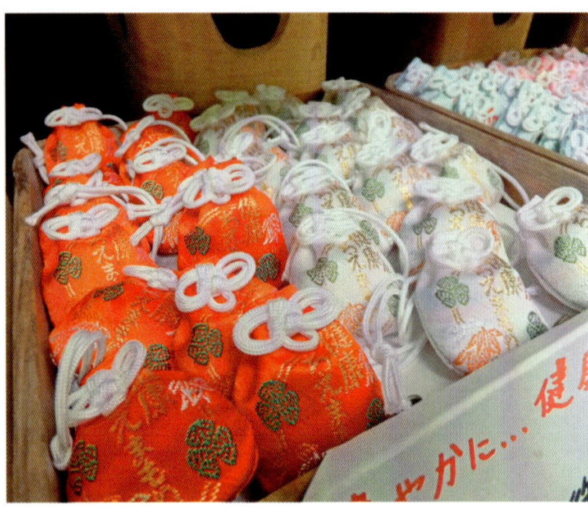

They are typically made of silk, with the prayer inside written on paper or wood. They are available at both shrine and temple stores and they might have the principle deity of the shrine on the front, or a local folkloric character. Contemporary omamori might be shaped in the likeness of something, typically a well-known character, such as Hello Kitty, or a cute animal. There are even manga-themed omamori sold at Kanda Myojin Shrine, which is situated close to Tokyo's anime and manga mecca, Akihabara.

If an omamori gets damaged or is dirty, it is believed that this damage has been sustained by the omamori during the process of protecting the bearer from harm. The lifespan of the omamori is considered to be a year, after which it should ideally be returned to the place it was bought from and replaced with a new one.

This page Omamori are sold at temples and shrines and can be found in an array of traditional and contemporary designs. **Facing page** An old Buddha statue at Shofukuji Temple in Fukuoka is decorated with an omamori.

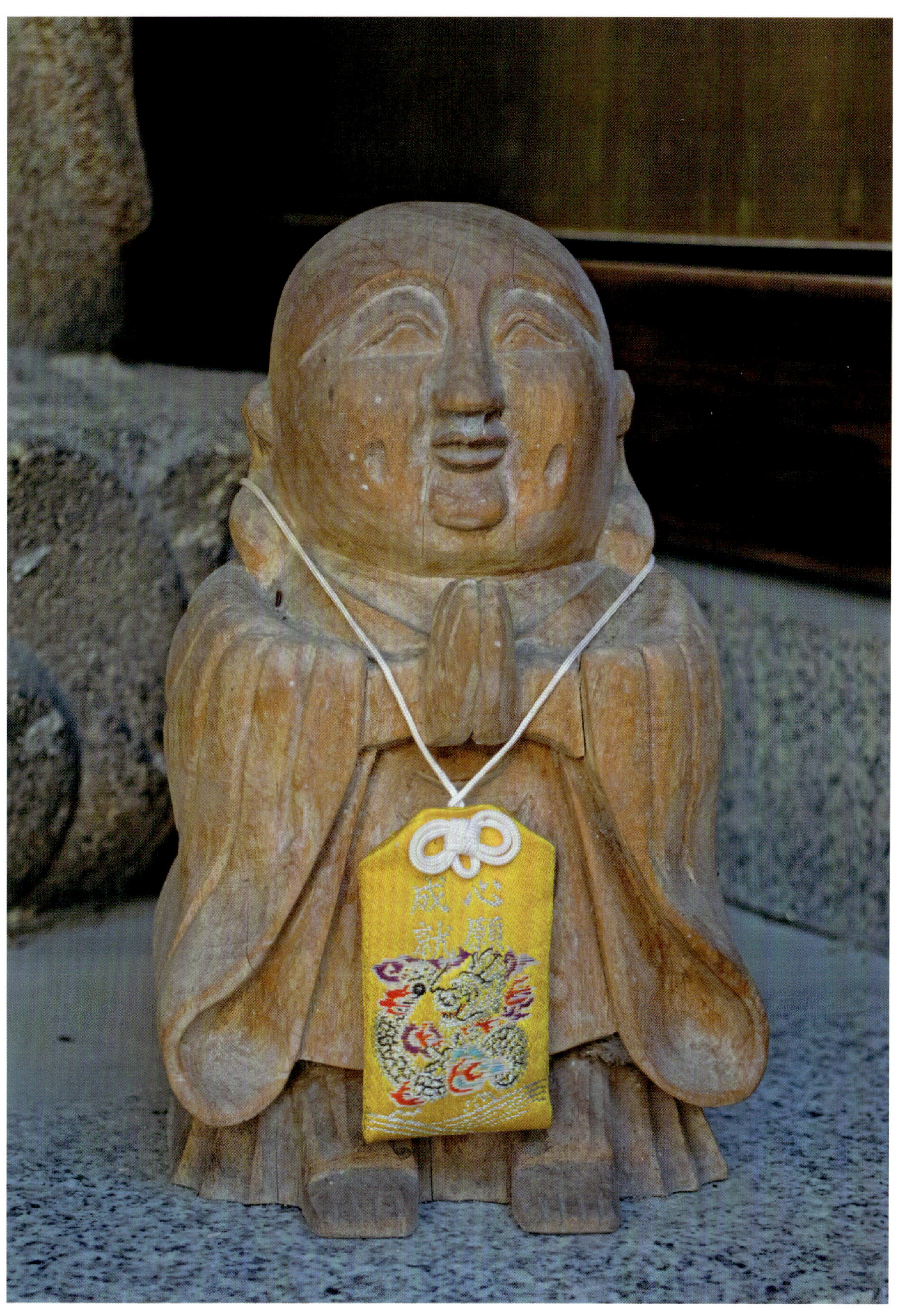
心願成就

Ontayaki Pottery

A tradition made famous by Soetsu Yanagi and Bernard Leach

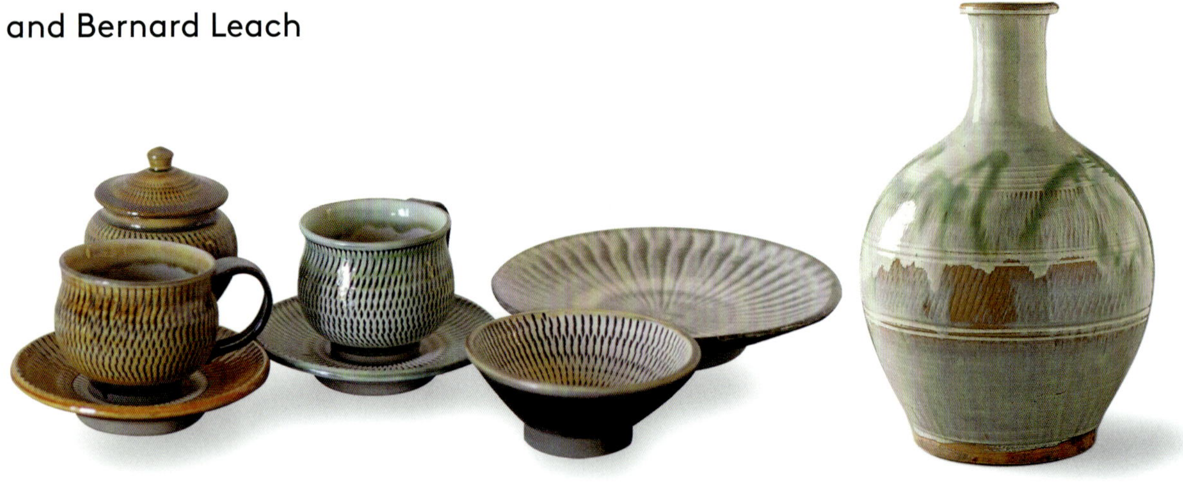

ONTA IS A BUCOLIC MOUNTAIN HAMLET located in Japan's southern island of Kyushu. The hamlet consists of only a small handful of households, and the majority of these are pottery families. Ontayaki—as pottery from Onta is called—got its start in 1705 when potter Yanase Sanemon and two other families started to make vessels for everyday use, such as bowls, plates and cups. Ontayaki is known for the various different techniques which are used to embellish the pottery, such as *tobikanna* which are incisions made with a piece of iron, or *hakeme* which are marks made with a brush. The resulting patterns give ontayaki its distinctive beauty.

Contemporary potters creating Ontayaki ware stick to old-school methods, and reject modern technology. Their lathes are still powered by foot pedal, the climbing kiln is wood fired and the mortar is driven by river water.

Despite Onta's remote location, public awareness of the Ontayaki pottery tradition became widespread when Mingei Movement founder Soetsu Yanagi praised the utilitarian and unpretentious aesthetic of this folk art. Ontayaki was lauded as the epitome of the mingei philosophy. The items are never signed by individual potters, but are known under the collective name of the village.

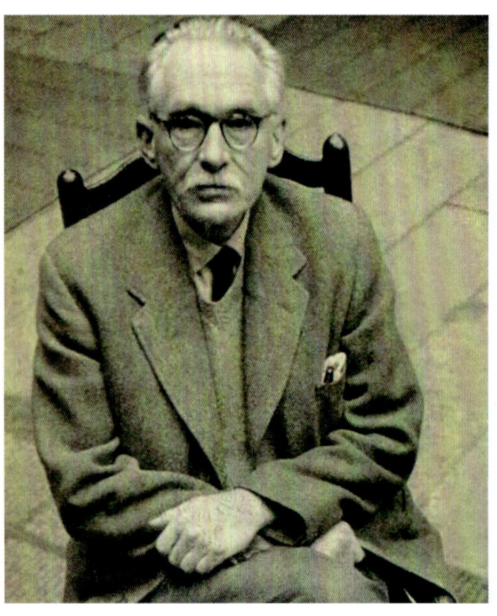

Famed potter and Mingei Movement founding member Bernard Leach lived in the hamlet from 1955 for a decade, bringing international fame to Onta.

This page, top, and facing page Ontayaki pottery was hailed as the epitome of the mingei philosophy, which valued anonymity—pieces are not signed by individual potters but given the name of the village. **Above** Bernard Leach lived in Onta for a decade, bringing fame to the village.

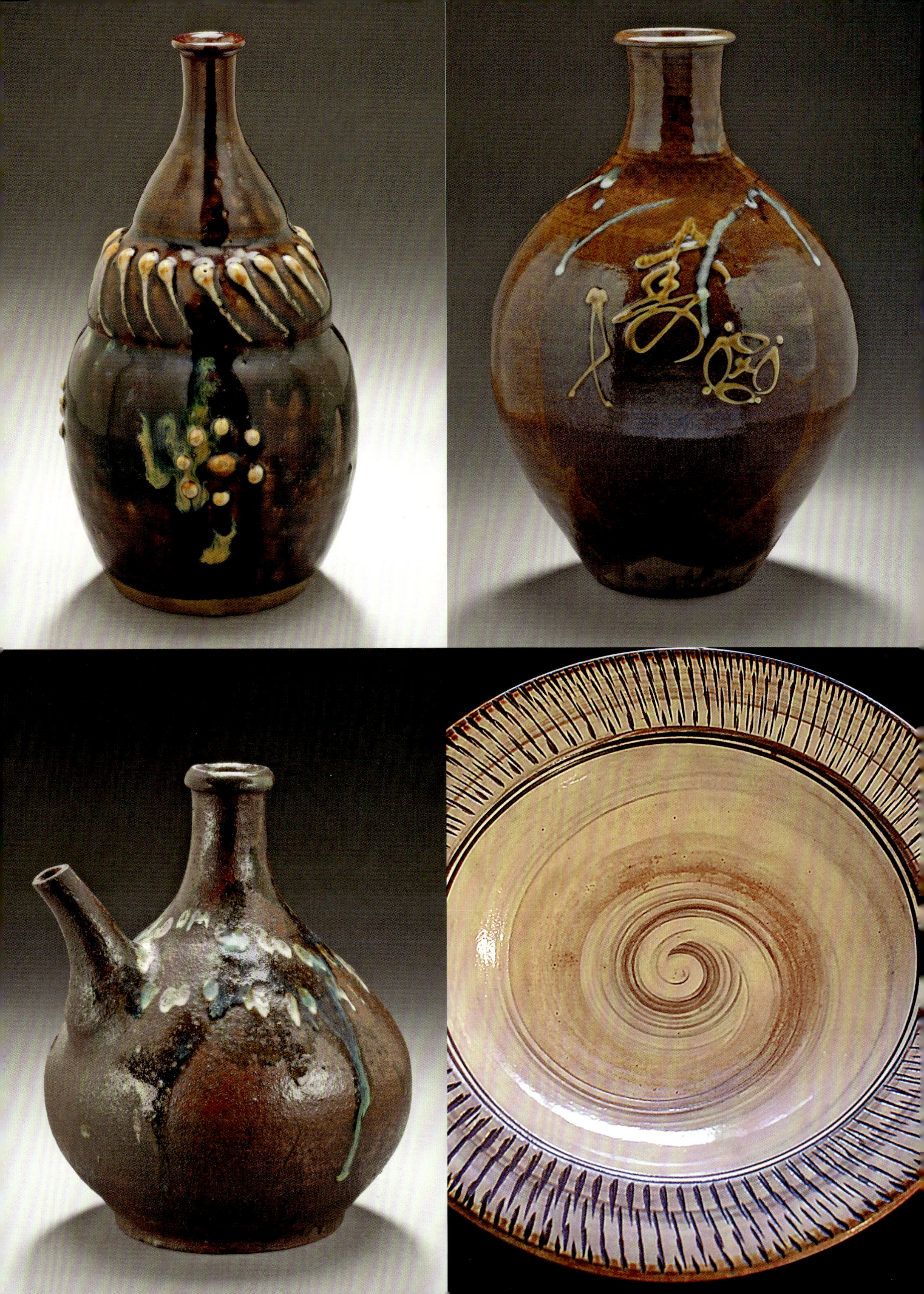

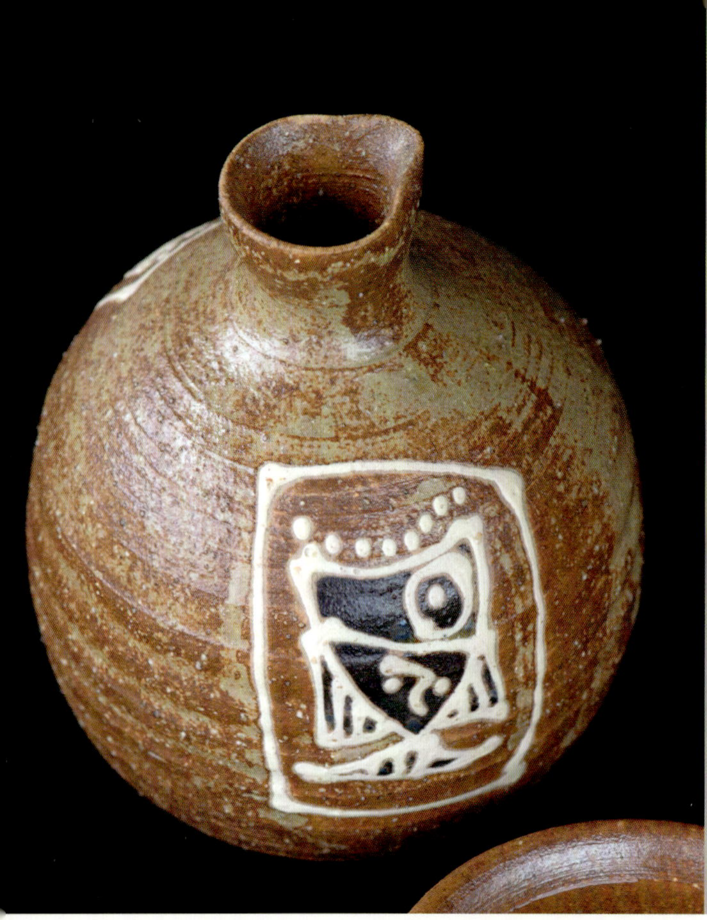

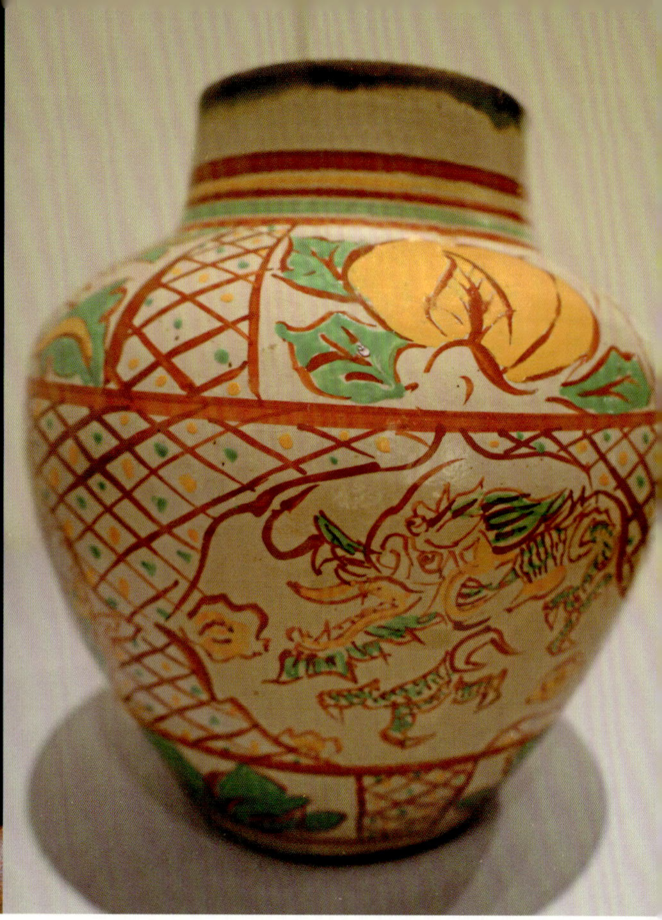

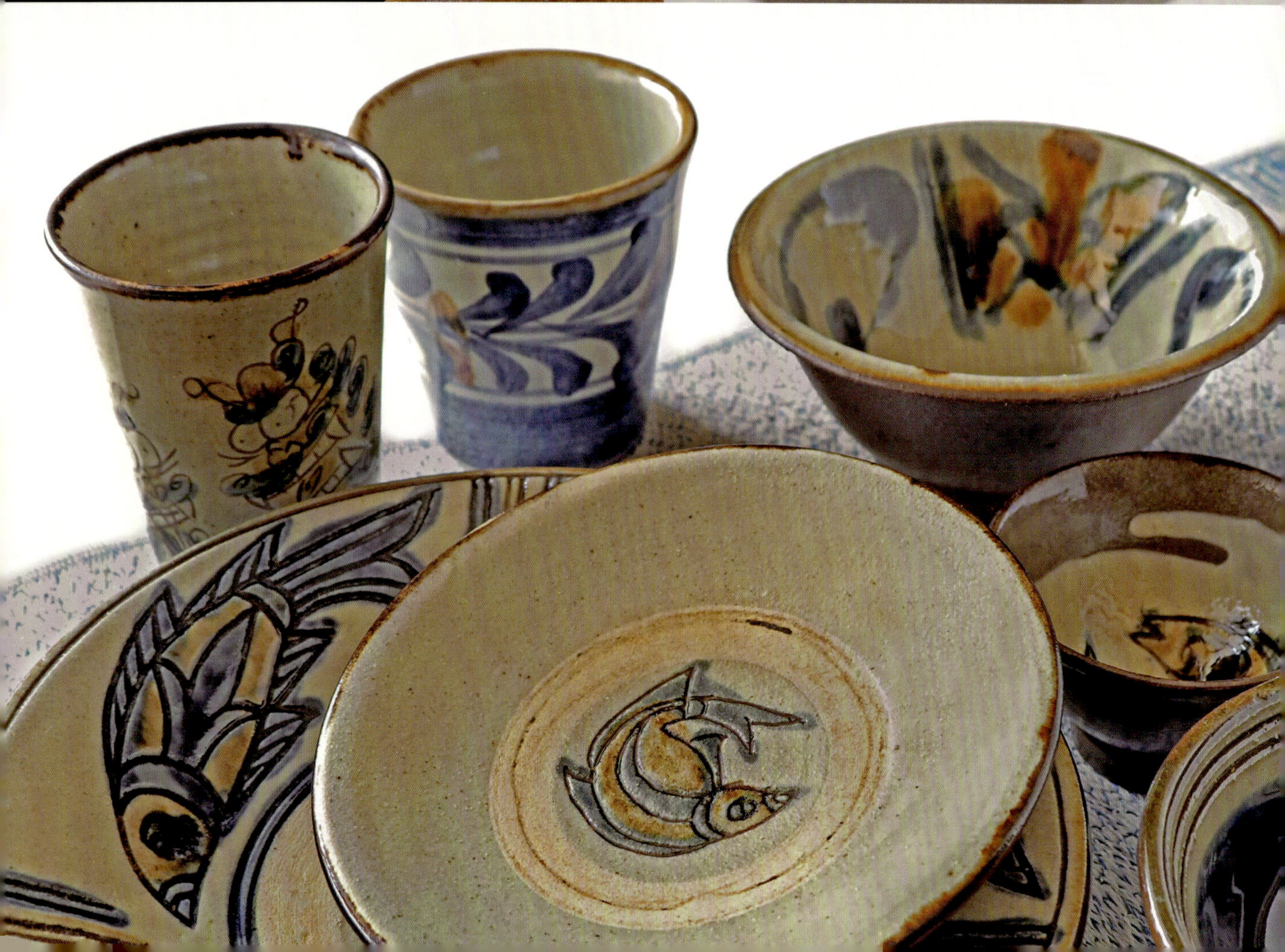

Ryukyu Pottery

Tableware and fine-art pieces from Okinawa

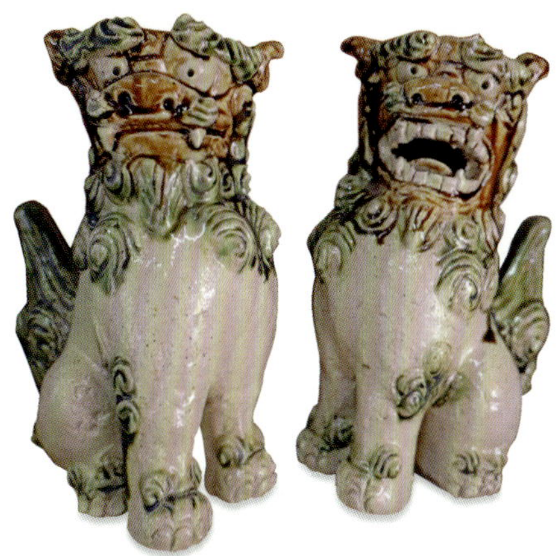

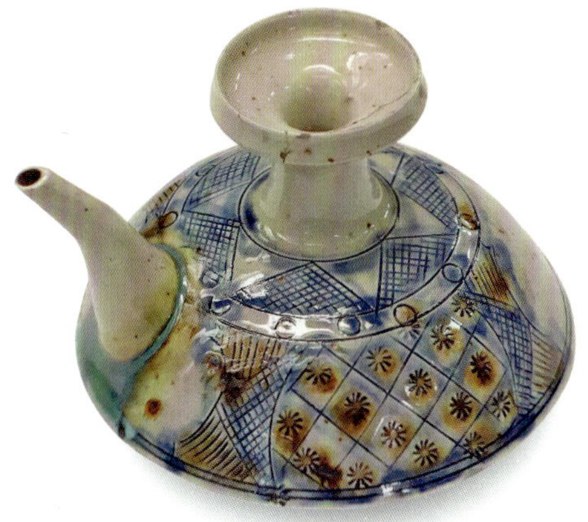

RYUKYU POTTERY, MADE IN OKINAWA and also known as *yachimun*, is characterized by dense and solid forms, and is used for plates, mugs, sake bottles and cups, and flower pots. The pottery is amalgam of influences from Southeast Asia, with vivid hand-created designs. Motifs include auspicious local plants and marine life.

There are two types of Ryukyu pottery: *joyachi* (glazed pottery), which is also made into fine-art pieces, and *arayachi* (unglazed pottery) which is often used to make jars for storing miso, and awamori, the local liquor.

Another use of both joyachi and arayachi is for *shisa*, a type of guardian lion-dog statue, first imported from China around the fourteenth century. Shisa are an ubiquitous sight in Okinawa, on roof gables and the gates of houses. They are usually in pairs: the female is depicted with a closed mouth that keeps in good spirits, the male scares evil spirits away and has an open mouth. There are variations on the shisa found across Japan, usually displayed outside Shinto shrines, and sometimes called *komainu*.

While Okinawa is known now as a resort and leisure destination, the folk art and craft of the region has been a source of inspiration for mingei aficionados ever since the genesis of the Mingei Movement. In 1939, Soetsu Yanagi shot two films there, one of which, called *Ryukyu no mingei* (Ryukyu folk crafts) looks at folk craft in the region and features Ryukyu potters.

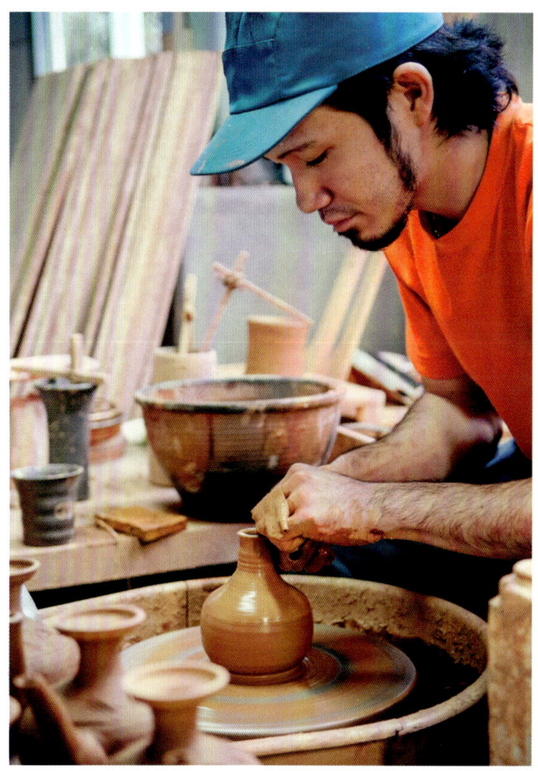

Facing page & above Ryukyu pottery is simple, thick and rustic. It is generally used for household items as well as for shisa lion-dog statues.
Right A potter at work at a studio in Naha, Okinawa's capital city.

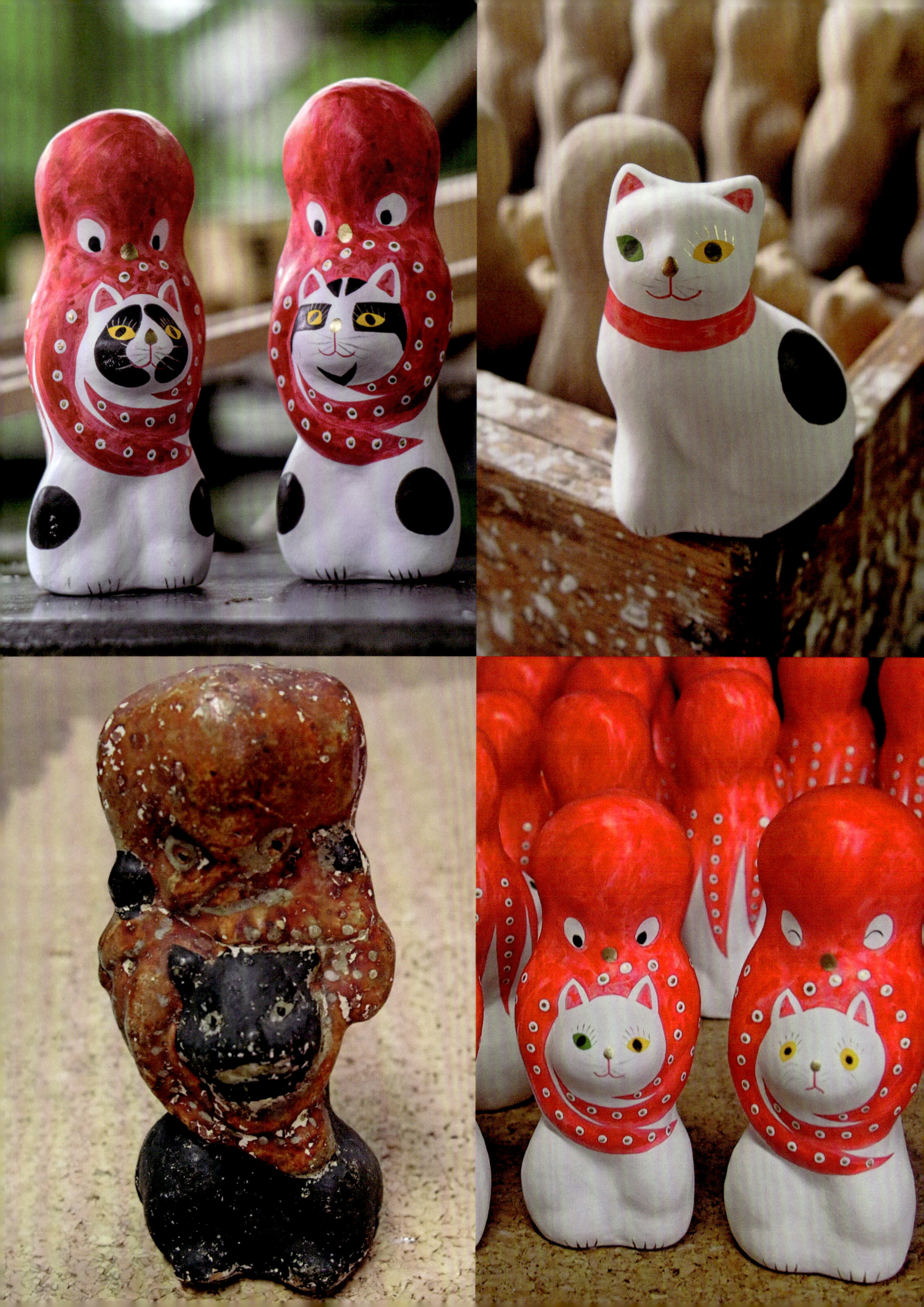

Sagara Dolls

Lucky figurines, often a cat with an octopus on its shoulders

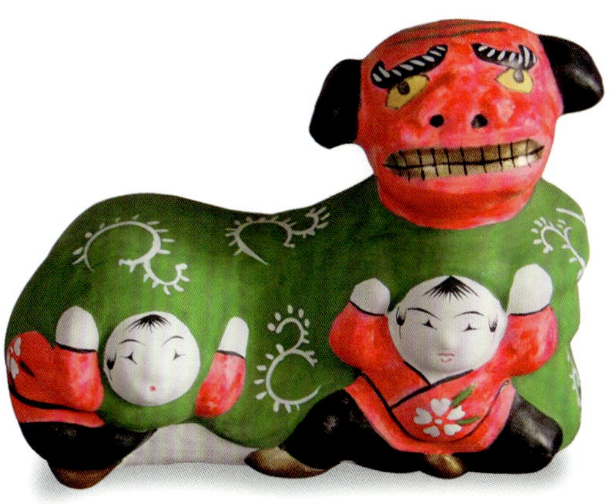

SAGARA DOLLS ARE MADE FROM CLAY in Yamagata Prefecture, and are experiencing a boom in popularity among trend-conscious youth for their cute designs. The most representative motif is a cat with an octopus wrapped around its shoulders.

The history of Sagara dolls dates back to around 1790, when samurai Atsutada Seizaemon Sagara from the Yonezawa clan was ordered by his lord to study doll making, as a way of bringing money to the region. He went to Kyoto, Edo (now Tokyo) and Ise. He learned to carve religious figurines and became interested in the traditional clay dolls from Kyoto's Fushimi district. He also learned pottery techniques from the Soma region. Sagara dolls are a result of all these factors combined.

According to eighth generation artisan Ryuma Sagara (3-3-64 Shimohanazawa, Yonezawa, Yamagata; tel: 0238-23-8382), the original motifs for Sagara dolls were often kabuki characters or one of Japan's Seven Lucky Gods. These days, the most popular motif is the cat, riding the wave of the current cat boom in Japan.

Sagara dolls look simple, but take around two months to craft, as all aspects of the production are carried out by one person. They are made from locally sourced clay, which is then fired at a lower temperature than is usual for ceramics so that they do not crack or melt.

The dolls are thought to be talismanic. Ryuma Sagara explains that if there is danger, the clay doll will "adopt" the bad luck, breaking itself in the process. For instance, if someone fell down a flight of stairs but didn't get injured, they might go home to find a mysterious crack in their Sagara doll. Many dolls feature an octopus wrapped around a cat, as the word *tako* means both "octopus" and "many blessings."

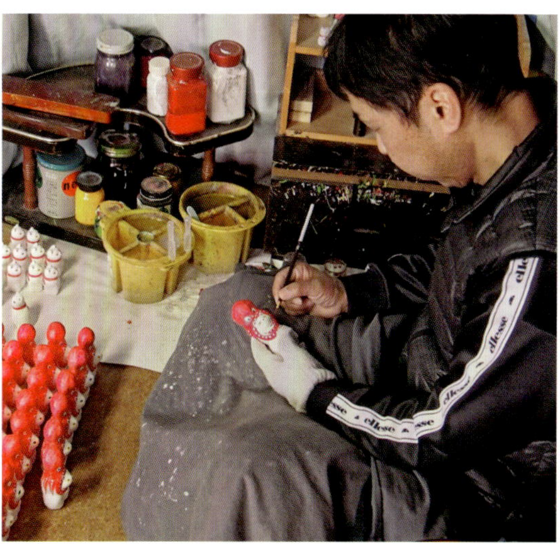

Facing page The most common motif for Sagara dolls is a cat with an octopus wrapped around its shoulders. The example bottom left dates from the Edo period. **Right** Eighth-generation artisan Ryuma Sagara at work.

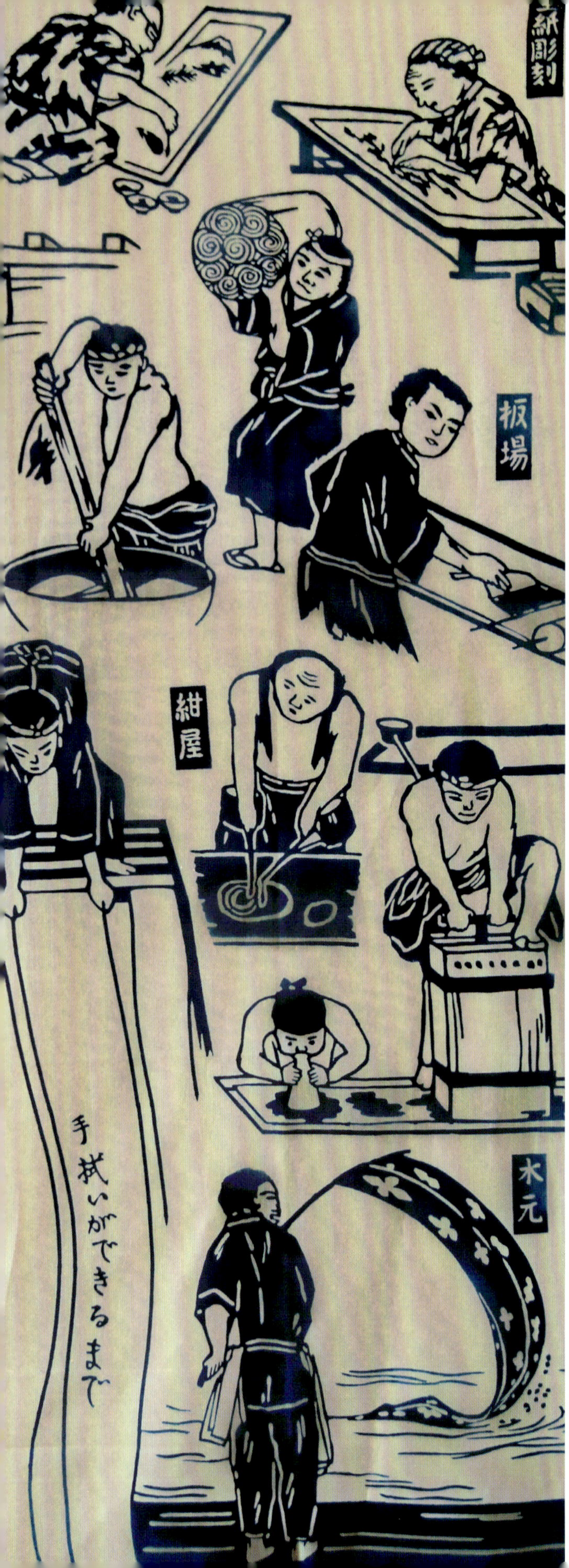

紙彫刻
板場
紺屋
水元
手拭いができるまで

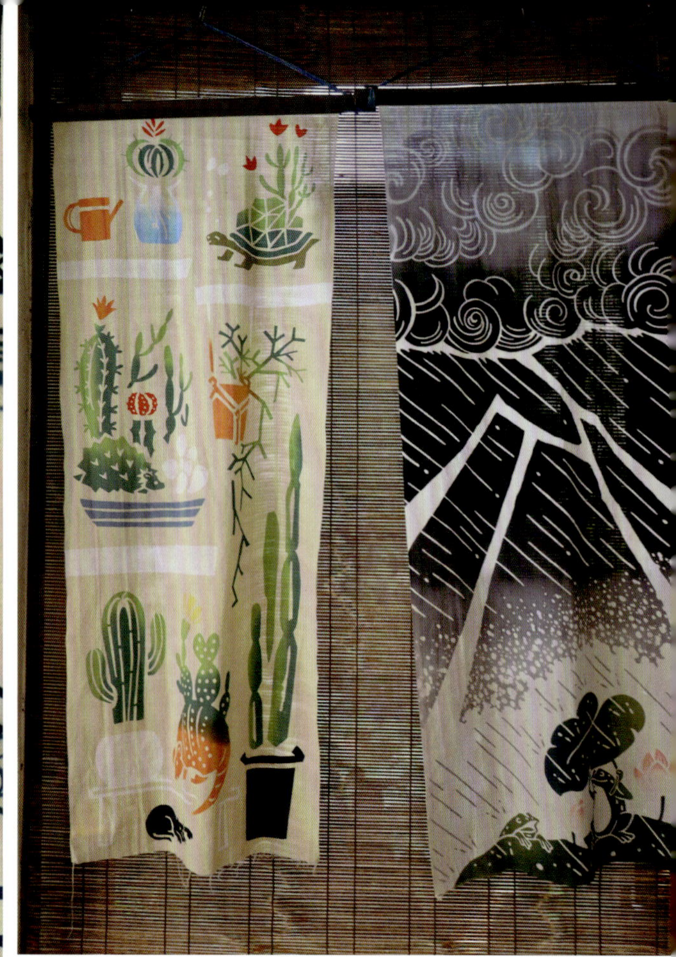

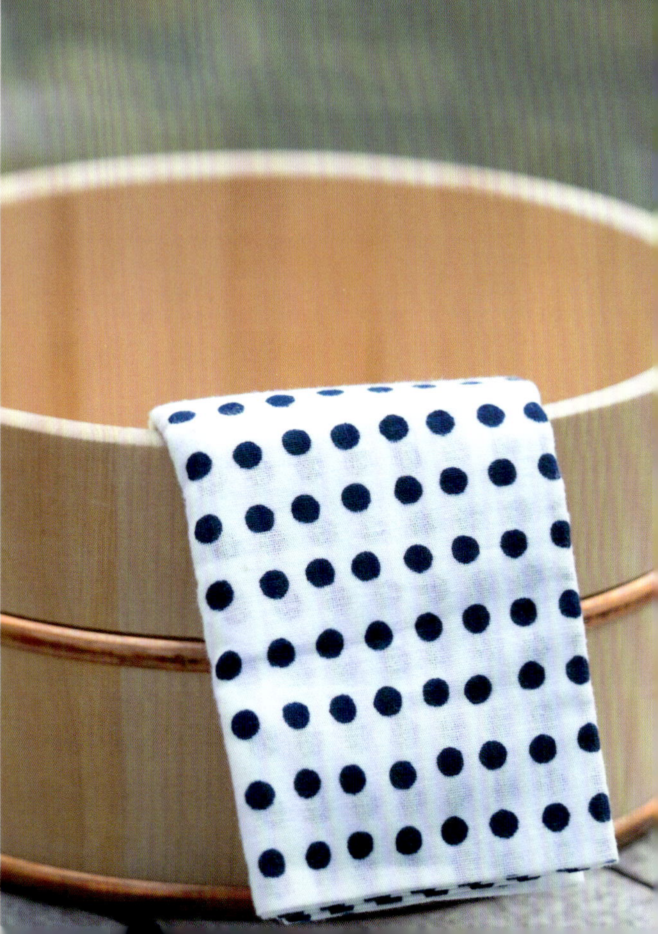

Tenugui Dyed Cotton Cloths

A traditional cloth for utilitarian daily use

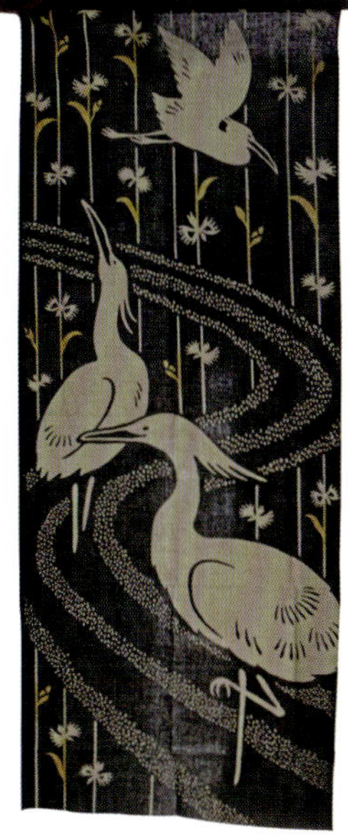

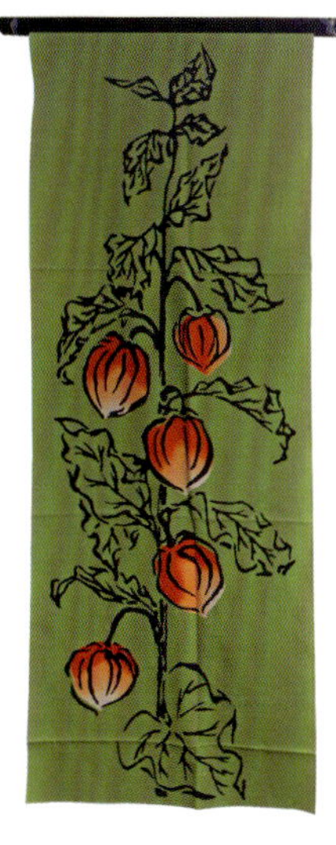

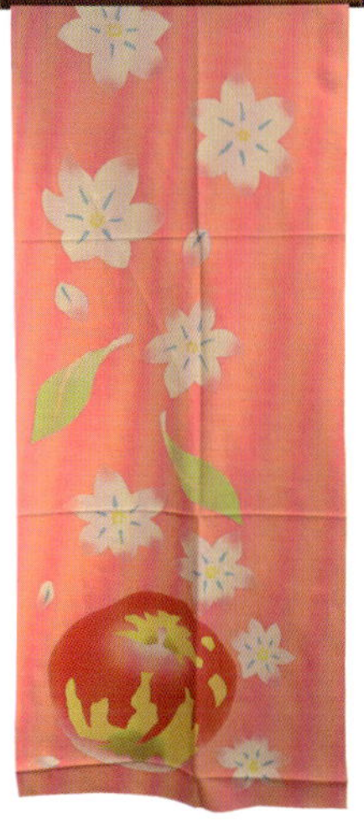

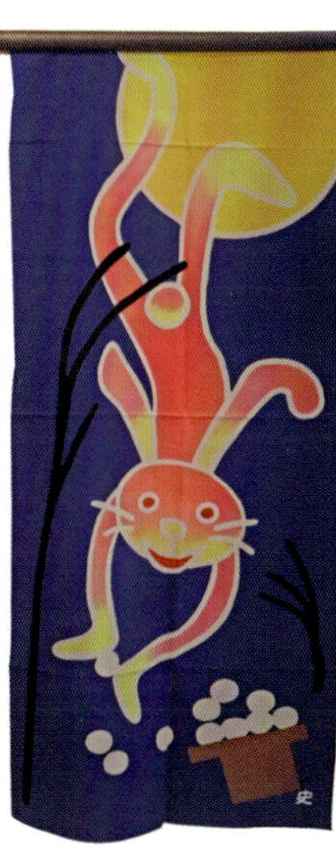

TENUGUI ARE STRIPS of embellished cotton cloth measuring around 14 x 35 inches (35 x 90 cm), dyed with bold patterns, and with a variety of uses from wiping kitchen surfaces, wearing as a scarf, toweling the skin dry, to wrapping and carrying things. As an item for daily use they are washed regularly and become softer in texture. They have been around since the Heian period (794–1185), but were popularized in the Edo period (1603–1868) as cotton became widespread among commoners.

Tenugui are also featured in traditional arts like rakugo and kabuki theater. Famous kabuki actors and sumo wrestlers would give out tenugui with their name printed on them, like a kind of business card. The practice of making bespoke tenugui, decorated with the name of a company or store, is still common today.

Since the nineteenth century, tenugui have been dyed using the *chusen* method: in small lots that use hand-cut stencils. This means that the items are not printed superficially on the top, but the dye seeps through the cloth giving delicate gradations in color. The ends are finished so that they don't fray. Yukata summer kimonos are also made from rectangular cotton cloth, so often the same craftspeople make both.

Many traditional tenugui patterns have verbal puns or auspicious motifs, such as the hemp pattern which symbolizes a wish for children to grow fast, just like the plant. Decoding the iconography of these tenugui cloths is just one of the ways to enjoy them. And because of these beautiful handcrafted designs, many people frame tenugui for decorative purposes, rather than buying them for practical use.

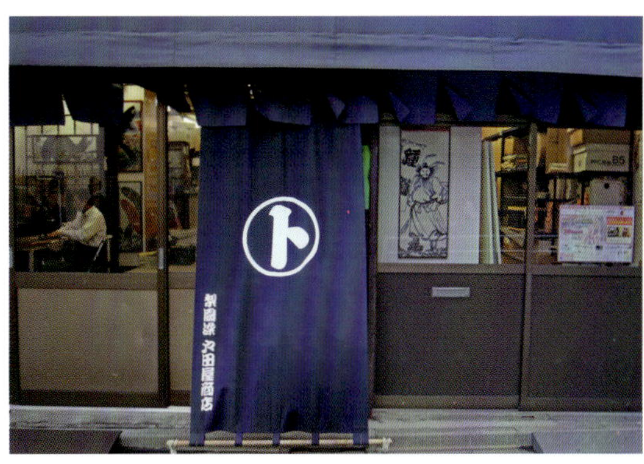

Facing page & above Tenugui patterns range from simple patterns, seasonal motifs and auspicious symbols, to comical and irreverent themes.
Right The Todaya Rienzome shop in Nihonbashi, Tokyo, founded in 1872, specializes in tenugui.

Tohoku Toy Horses

Messengers to the gods

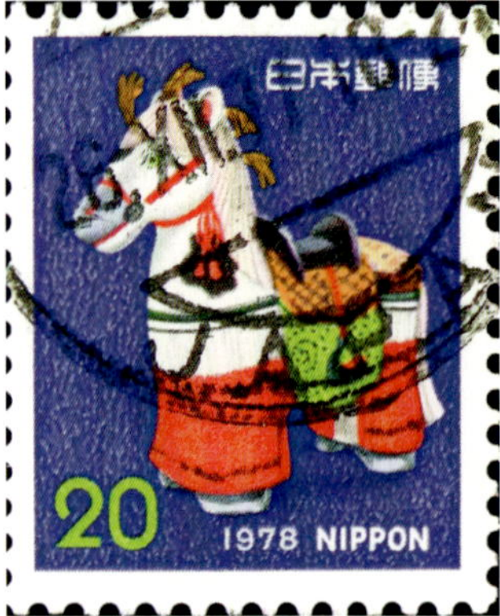

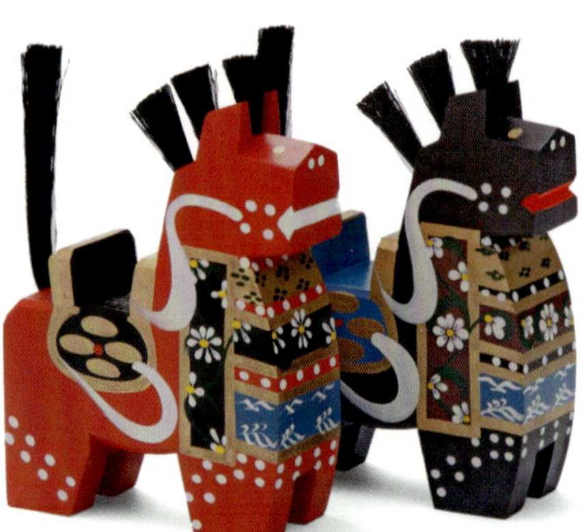

HORSE FOLK TOYS come mainly from Japan's northern Tohoku region where the culture of the horse has traditionally been strong, in agriculture and for transport. Farmhouses in Iwate Prefecture have stables built into the house to protect horses from cold weather, giving rise to a culture where horses are part of the family. Wooden horse toys are a homage to these important and auspicious animals.

There are three main types. The angular Miharu Goma is from Koriyama in Fukushima Prefecture, former domain of the Miharu clan. Legend has it that a group of mythical horses came to the aid of shogun Sakanoue no Tamuramaro when he was in battle. The Miharu horse represents those horses and is given to children in the hope that they grow up healthy and happy. Originally made from pieces of wood left over from crafting Buddhist effigies, it is believed to have protective qualities and the ability to carry messages to the gods. The Miharu Goma is thought to be one of the three most beautifully shaped wooden horses in Japan along with the Yawata Uma from Aomori and the Kinoshita Koma from Miyagi.

The Yawata Uma is a toy horse that comes from Hachinohe, Aomori Prefecture. The town's Kushihiki Hachimangu Shrine has a long tradition of horseback archery, which is still practiced today at its yearly festival, and the souvenir horses commemorate this. Yawata Uma horses have a saddle of the type a bride would have used when riding to the home of her new husband, and is often given as a wedding gift. Images of the iconic horse are displayed all over Hachinohe.

The Chagu Chagu Umakko toy horse is often made by woodworkers of other crafts, such as kokeshi. They resemble the horses that are paraded during the Chagu Chagu Umakko Festival in Morioka, Iwate Prefecture, where over a hundred horses are dressed in colorful costumes and are taken on an eight mile (13 km) walk from Onikoshi Sozen Shrine to Morioka City. The name comes from the sound of the bells the horses wear. The folk toy also wears large bells.

Above and facing page, bottom left The Yawata horse bears a saddle to carry a bride to the home of her new husband. **Facing page, top** The Chagu Chagu Umakko toy horse wears colorful costumes, and bells. **Facing page, bottom right** A Miharu horse from Fukushima Prefecture.

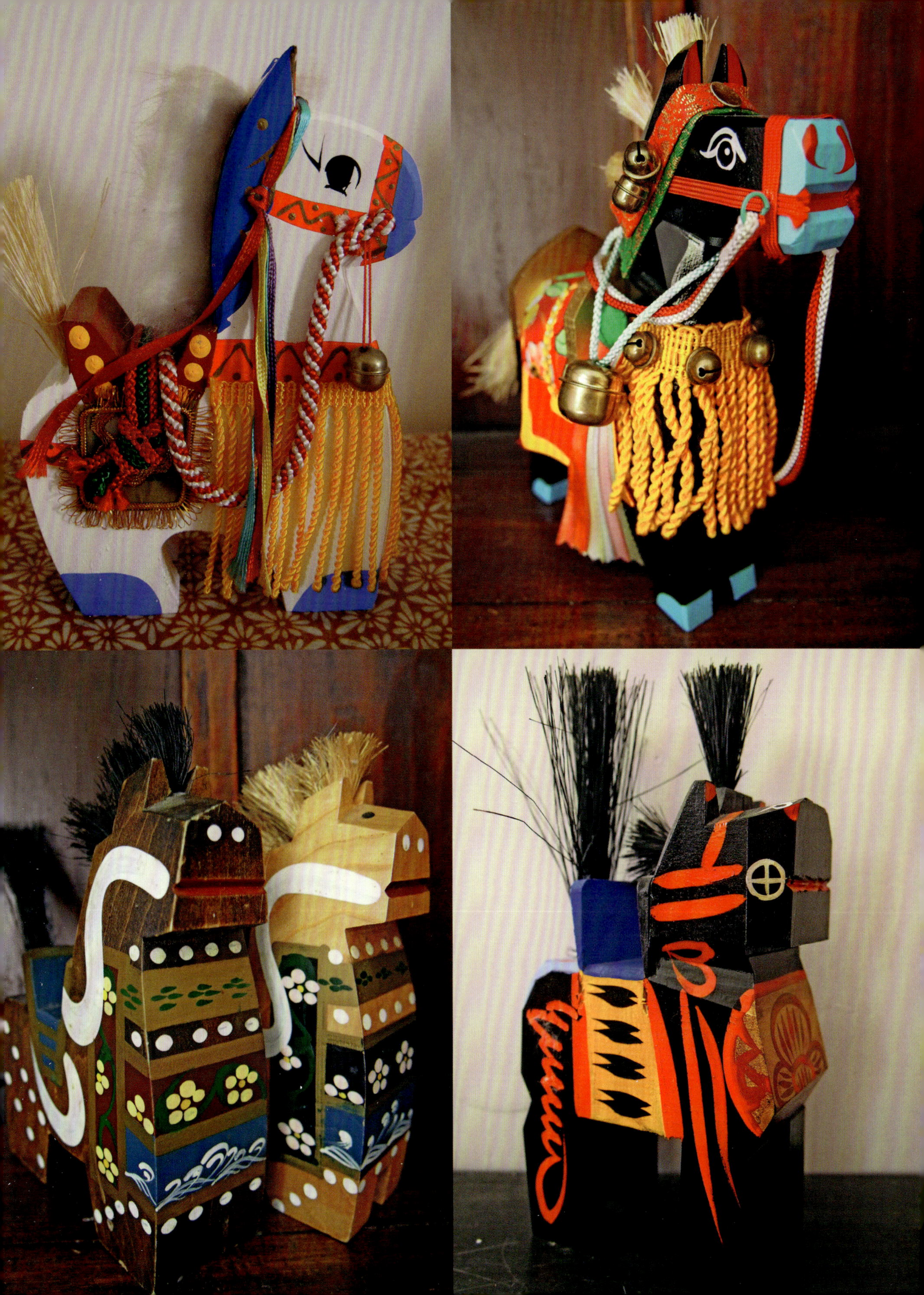

Washi Handmade Paper

An ancient craft still going strong

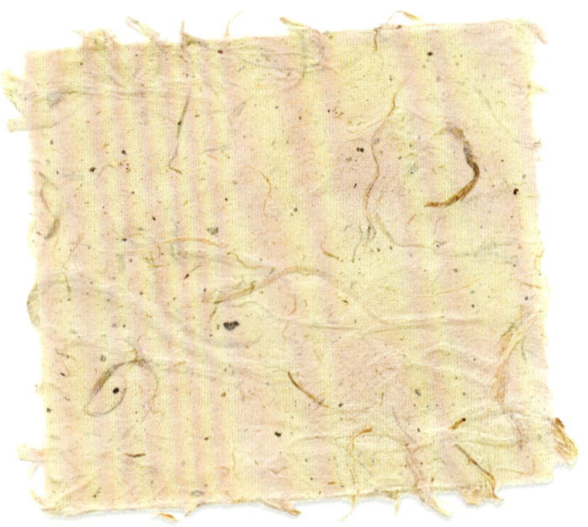

TRADITIONAL HANDMADE WASHI PAPER is an indispensable part of Japanese everyday life, from interior design, to food culture, to lighting. It can be seen in products such as masking tape, shoji screens, lampshades, printing paper, origami and wrapping paper. It is fibrous and strong, absorbs water without damage and yet retains a textural warmth. Colored washi is soft and billowy. Washi is surprisingly resilient, and there are numerous artifacts made of washi dating as far back as the Nara period (710–794) that still exist in good condition today.

Kiyoshi Takagi, from Ozu Washi, a historic washi-making company based in Tokyo, says of its qualities, "If washi gets wet, it won't tear easily, and you can write on it using *sumi* ink without it blurring or smudging. If you go to the Shoso-in treasure house of Todaji Temple in Japan's ancient capital of Nara, you can see

Washi paper has a soft texture yet is conversely much stronger than Western paper. Washi is made of the fibers of the inner bark of the ganpi, kozo (paper mulberry) or mitsumata plants.

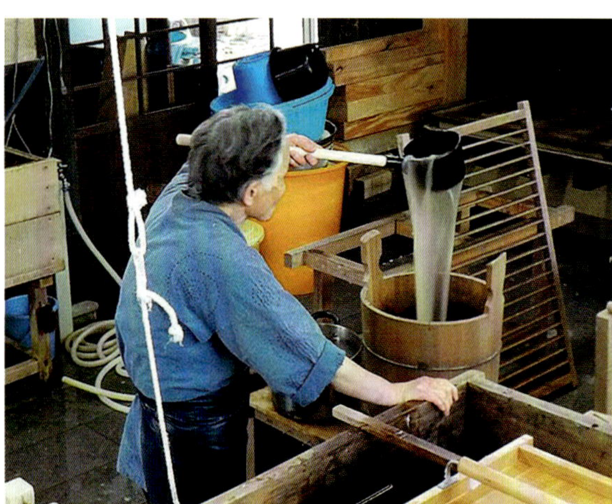

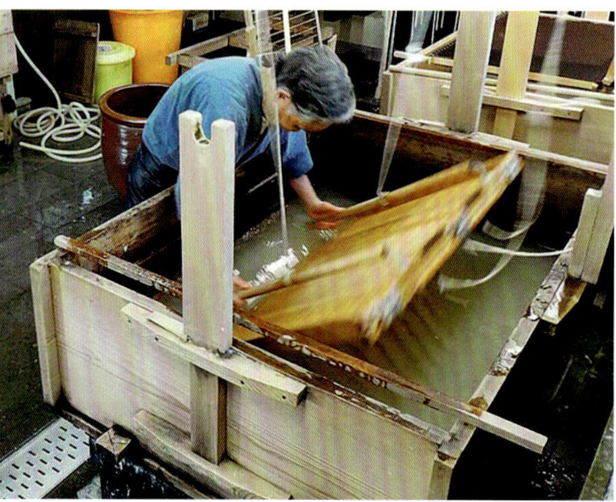

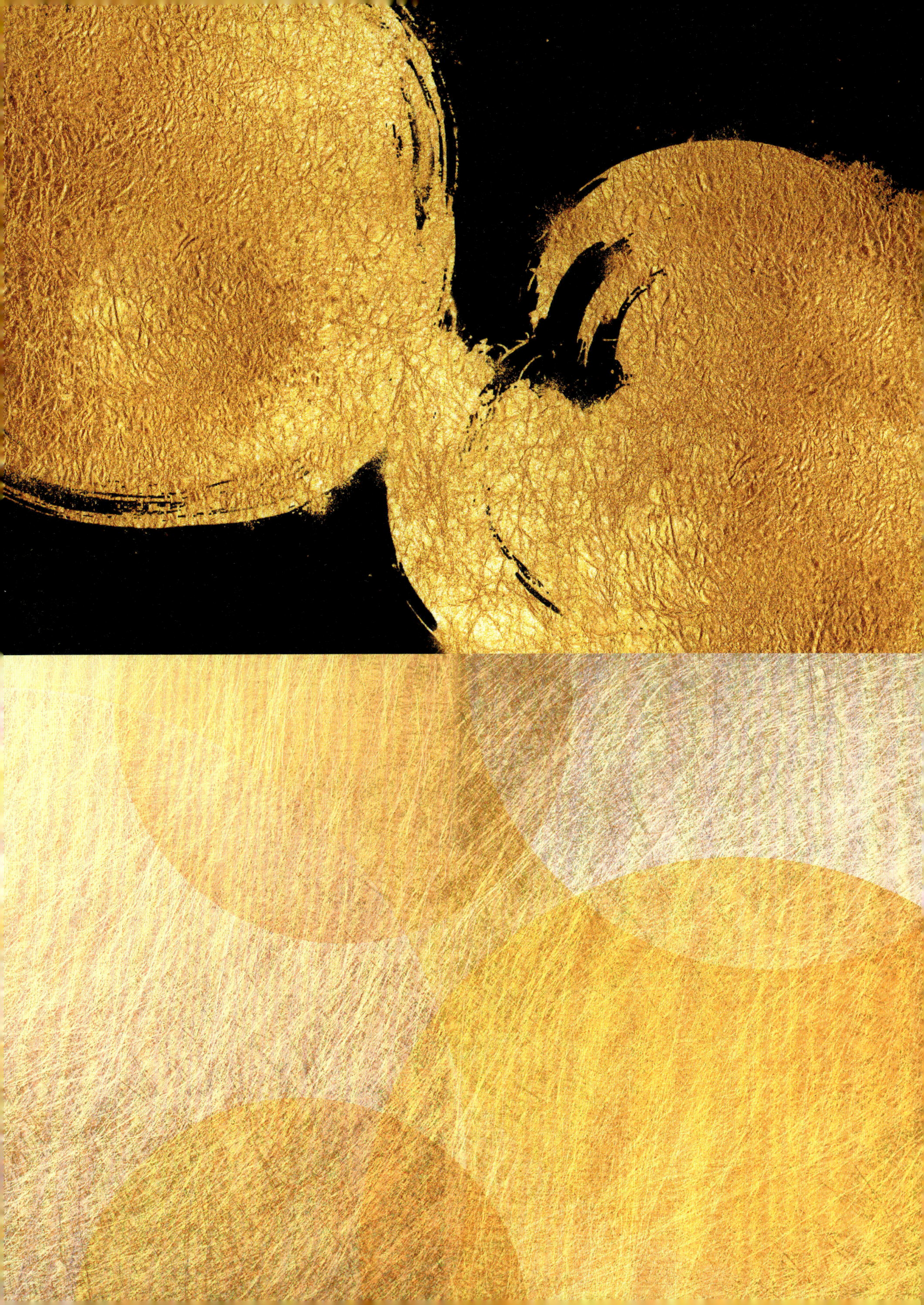

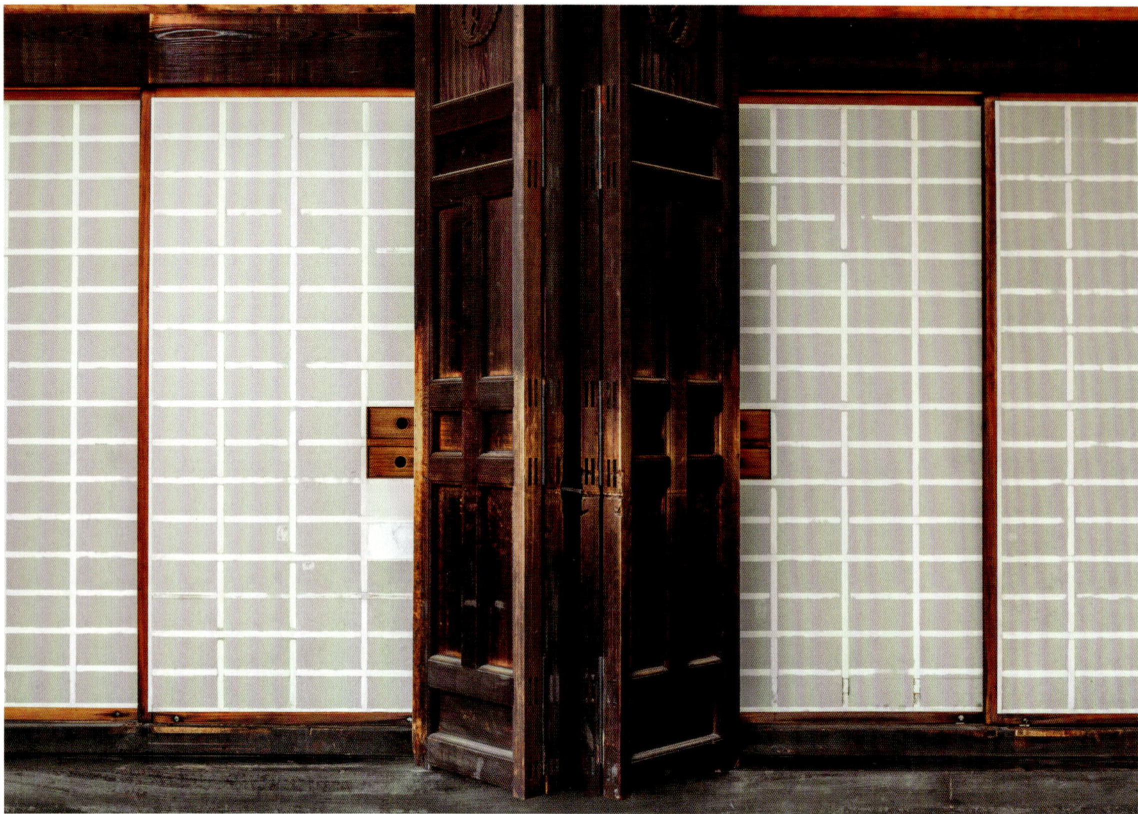

artifacts made of washi that are over 1,200 years old. Even though they're none too clean you can still read the ink lettering on washi paper."

Unlike mass-produced paper, washi paper is traditionally made by hand. Most modern paper is made of wood pulp, but washi is made of the fibers of the inner bark of the *ganpi*, *kozo* and *mitsumata* plants. Kozo, or paper mulberry, is the plant most commonly used. "Washi is usually made in the countryside, with well or river water," says Takagi. "In a year, the kozo grows about six feet [2 meters] tall and it is hard to use at that length, so we bend it in half.

Takamasa Kubo, of Kamisuki no Mura studio in Saitama, says, "We steam the kozo branches so we can strip off the fibrous outer bark easily. Some places then lie the bark out flat, maybe on a rock, to dry. We hang it outside and use this dried-out bark to make the washi. The paper is strong, breathable, and lasts a long time. Production methods differ from region to region. In Gifu Prefecture, for example, they would place the inner bark fibers on a rock, and beat them with a stick to flatten them, although this process is now mechanized. They scoop the fibres up, with a *sugeta* strainer-like tool. The sugeta also takes skill to make, as the gaps can't be too wide or too narrow. Then the paper fibers are dried under the sun."

Kozo washi paper is used for the fixtures of traditional Japanese houses such as the paper screens on sliding doors and windows.

There are three types of washi made from kozo: *sekishubanshi washi* from Shimane Prefecture; *honminoshi* from Gifu Prefecture and *hosokawashi* from Saitama Prefecture. They are all recognized as an Intangible Cultural Heritage by UNESCO.

Above Items that used washi paper include the fixtures of traditional Japanese houses such as the paper screens on sliding doors.
Left Washi is an indispensable part of Japanese everyday life and comes in a wide variety of colors, textures and designs.

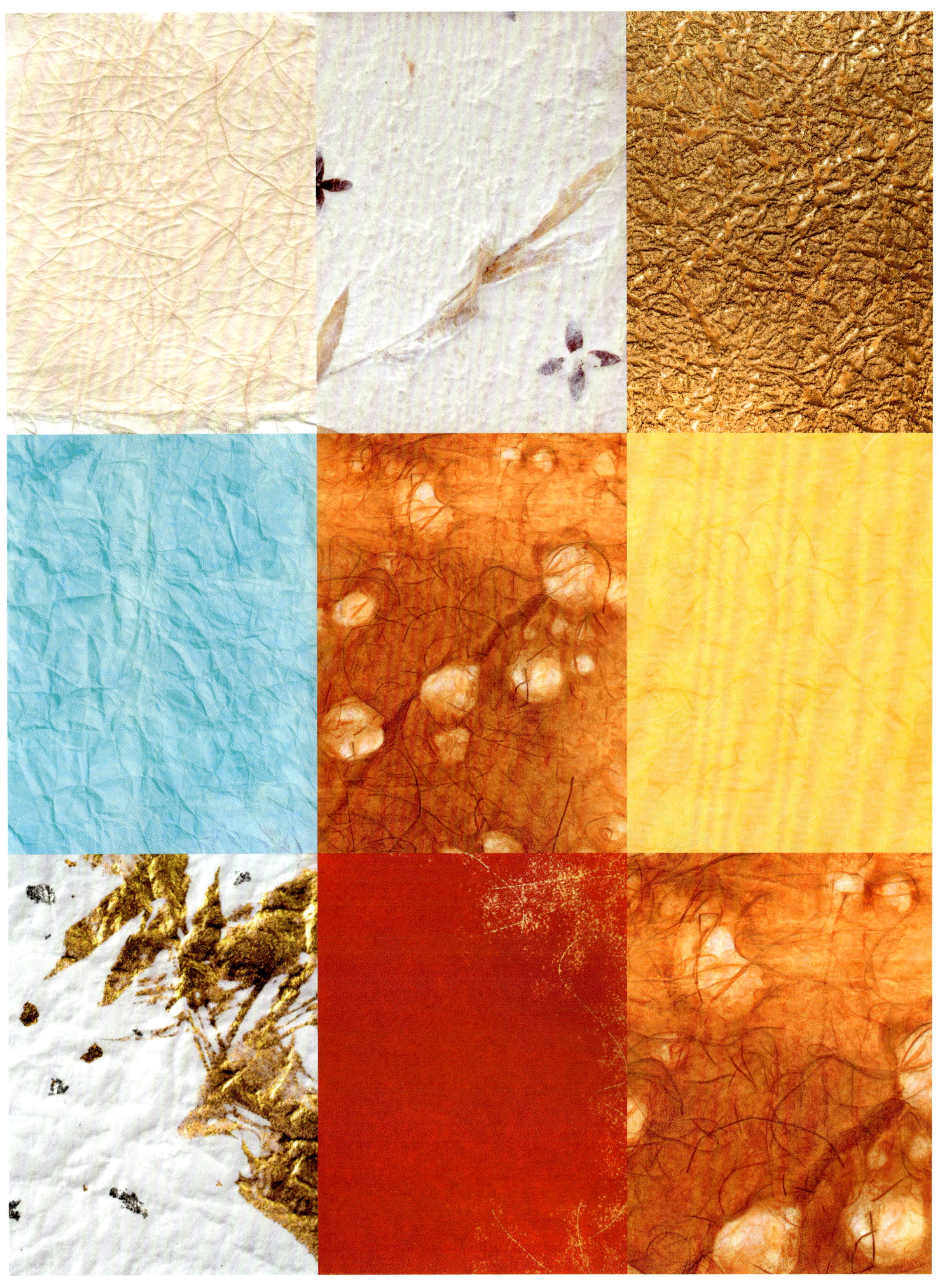

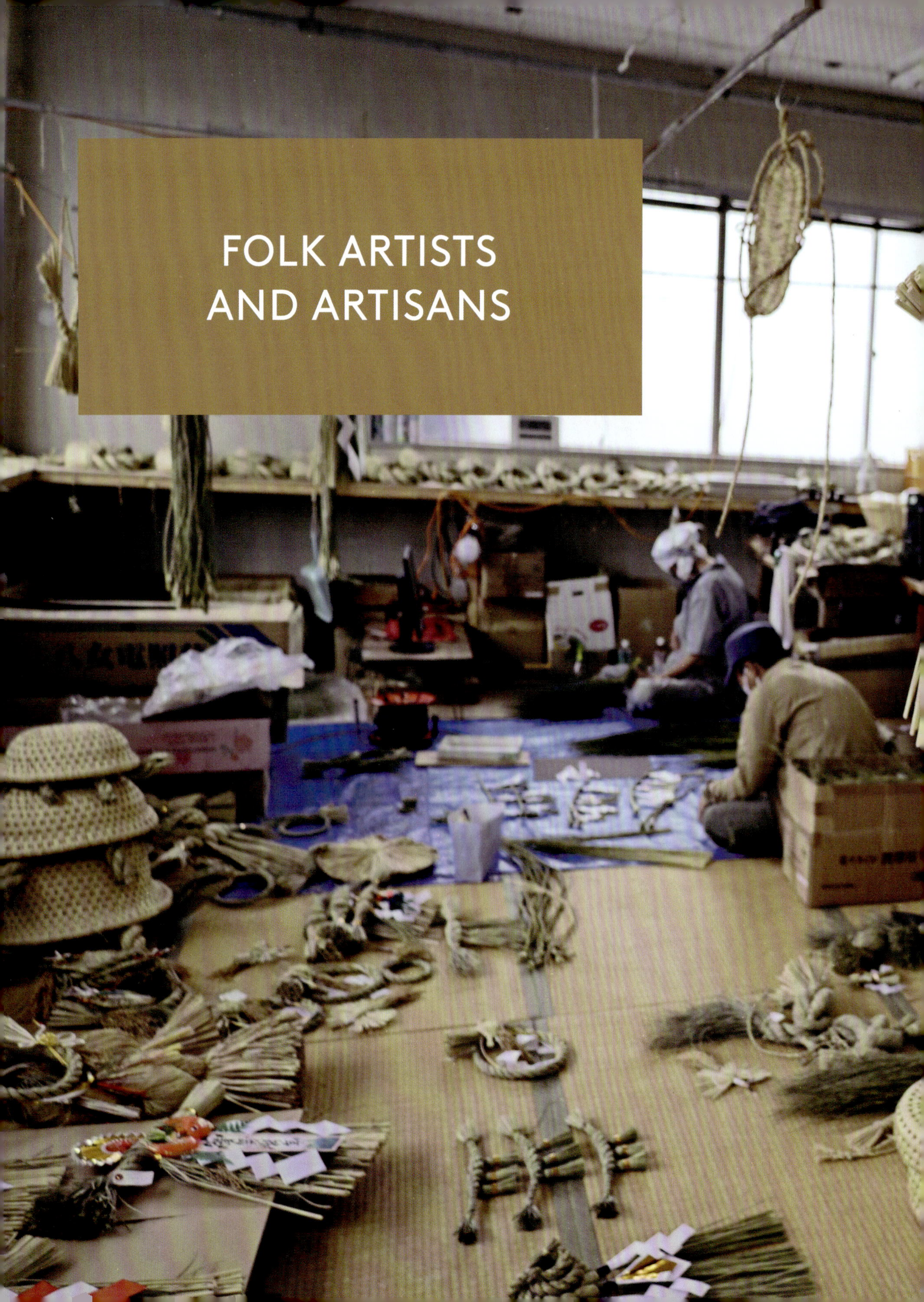

FOLK ARTISTS AND ARTISANS

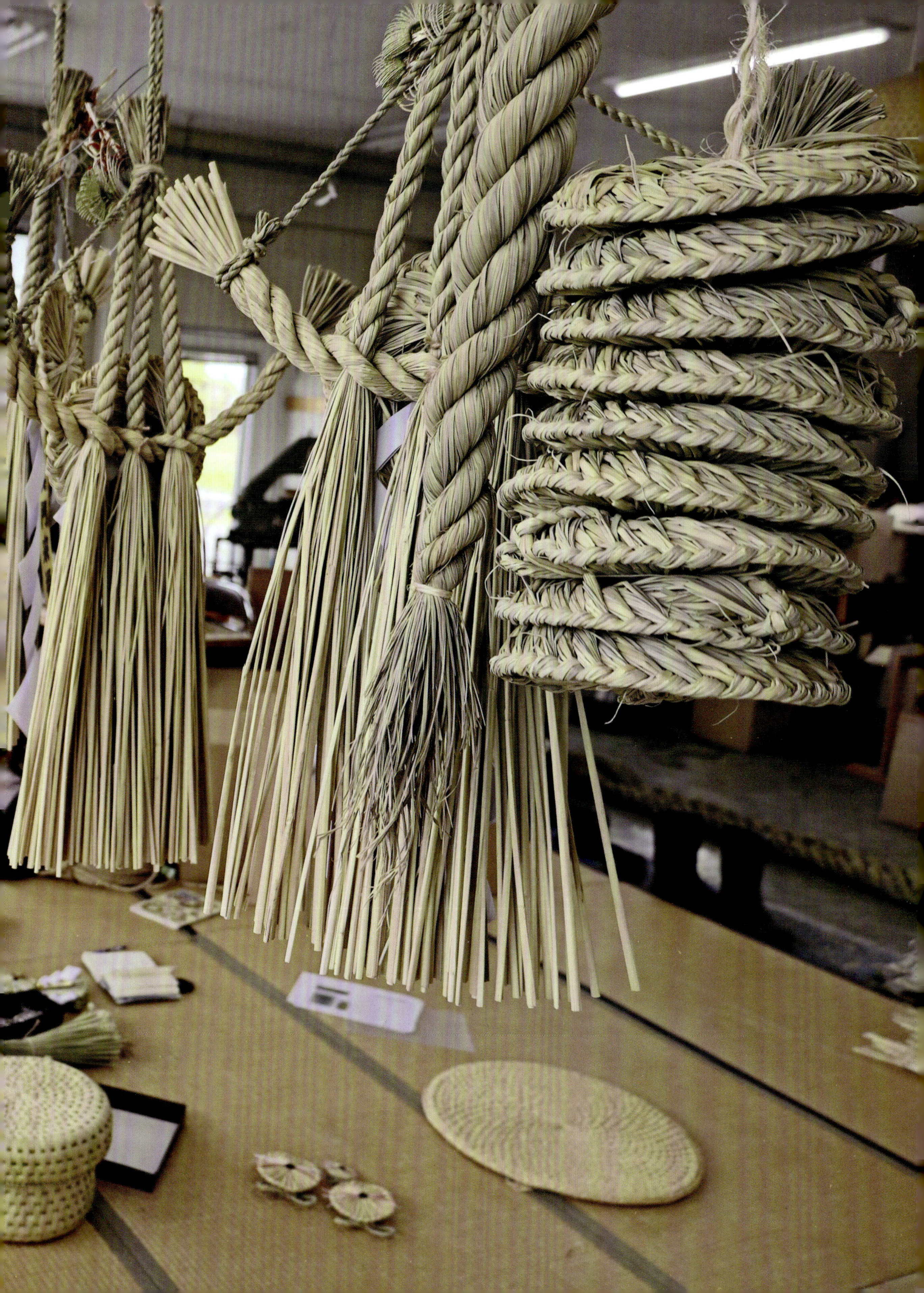

Mieko Taira

A Bashofu Cloth Weaver

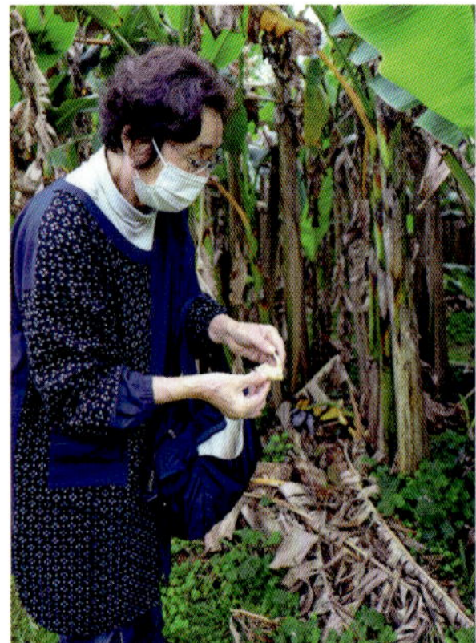
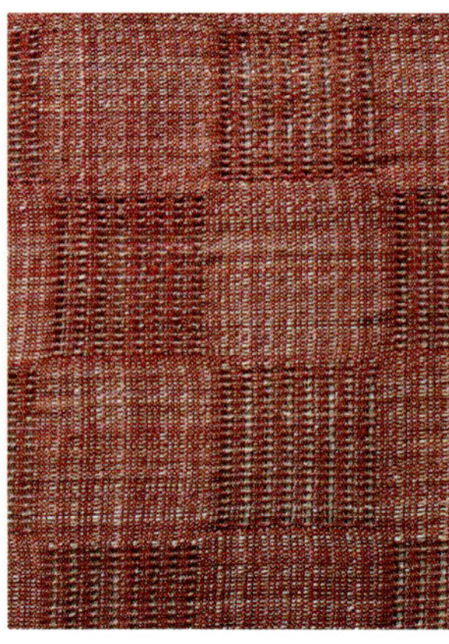
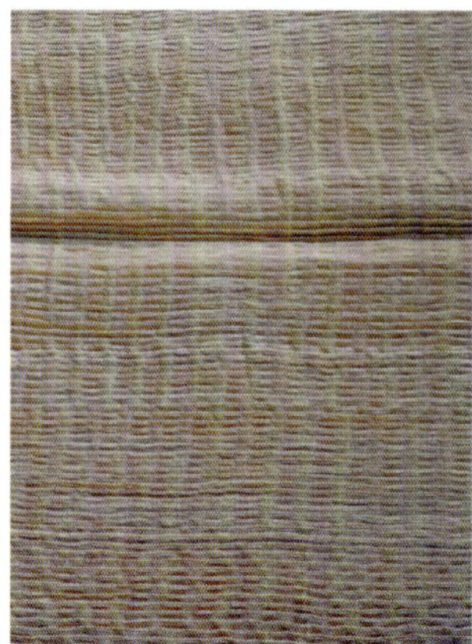

Bashofu is a type of woven fabric made in Okinawa from the fibers of the basho plant, which belongs to the banana family, Musaceae. The fabric produced from basho fibers is extremely light, with a smooth texture. This pleasant tactile sensation and the fact that it doesn't stick to the skin easily makes it ideal for a tropical climate. Bashofu production is extremely labor intensive. Artisans grow and harvest their own basho plants, a process that takes three years and is done entirely by hand, from the planting of the seeds to the spinning of the threads, to the weaving of the cloth. **Mieko Taira** (instagram.com/bashofu.kijoka) first came across bashofu fifty years ago, and now works tirelessly to ensure the craft doesn't go extinct.

Can you tell us a little about the history and characteristics of bashofu cloth?

In feudal times, bashofu was used to make *jinbaori* coats worn by the samurai, and here in Okinawa, it was also used to make garments that were worn by the king. Commoners used it for their clothing as well. Compared to cotton and silk, the cloth is stiff, light and cool and it can be worn all year round. The plant has many uses—its leaves can be used to wrap food for cooking or carrying, and they were also used to line baskets to carry Ryukyu indigo.

In the nineteenth century, cotton became popular for spinning and weaving, and bashofu declined in use because the basho plant takes so long to grow. But as bashofu is our heritage here, we are making every effort to preserve the culture of bashofu cloth.

In 1974, a preservation society was established in order to make sure that the culture of weaving bashofu did not die out, and in the same year bashofu was designated as an Important

This page, top left Mieko Taira inspects one of the basho trees whose fibers are used for bashofu fabric. **Above and facing page** This fabric was originally plain colored or striped. From the late 1800s, however, blurred geometric patterns became popular.

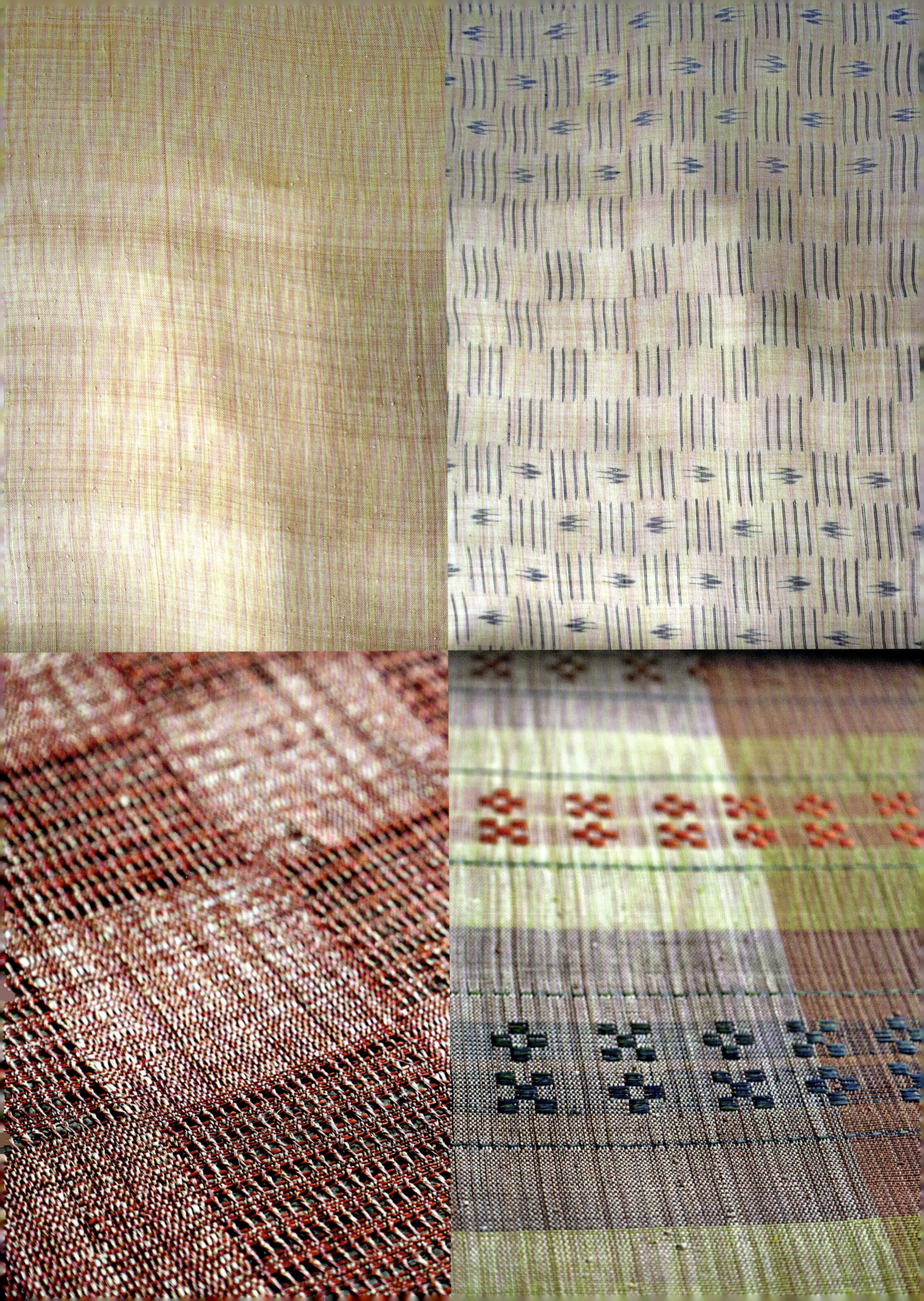

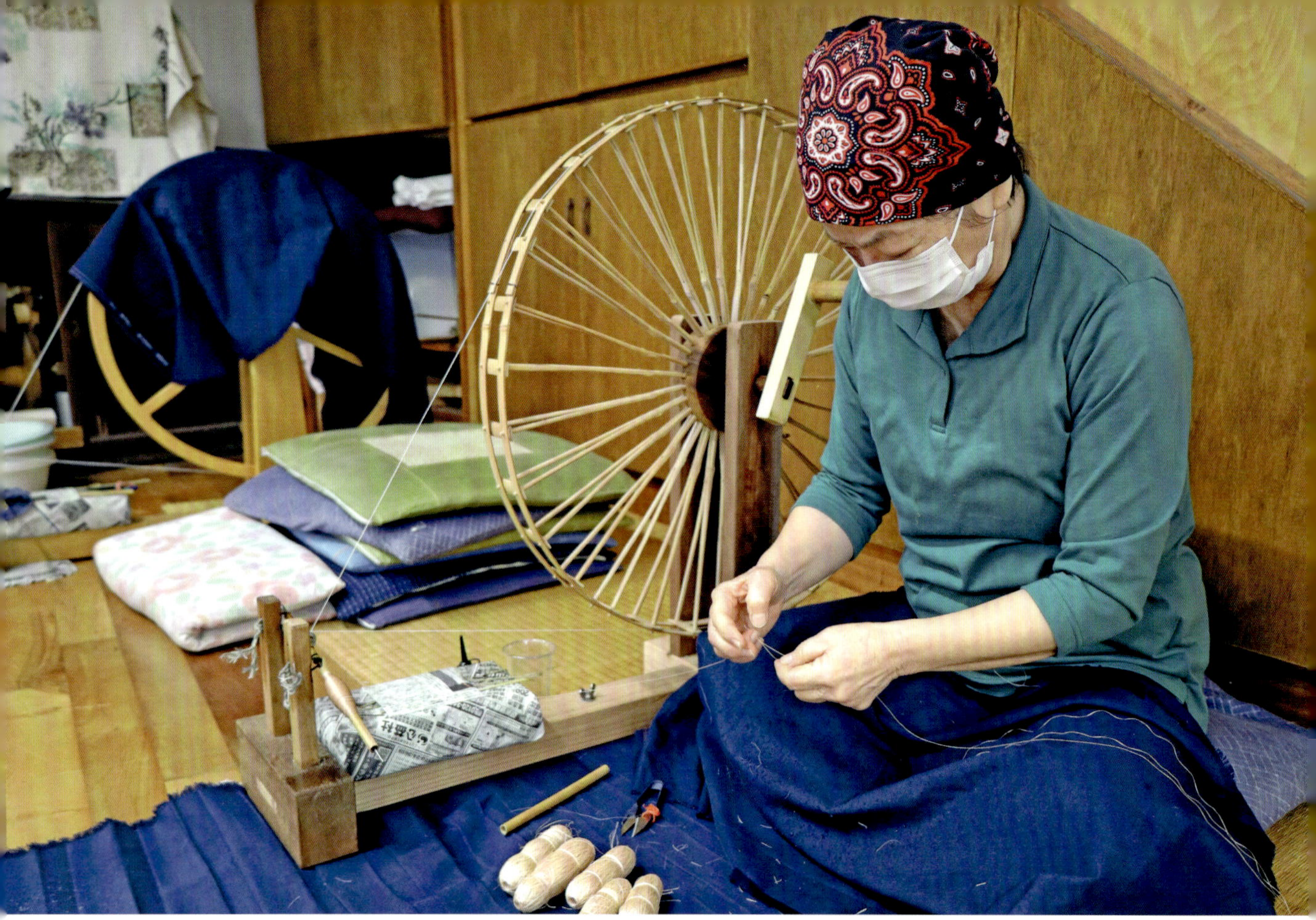

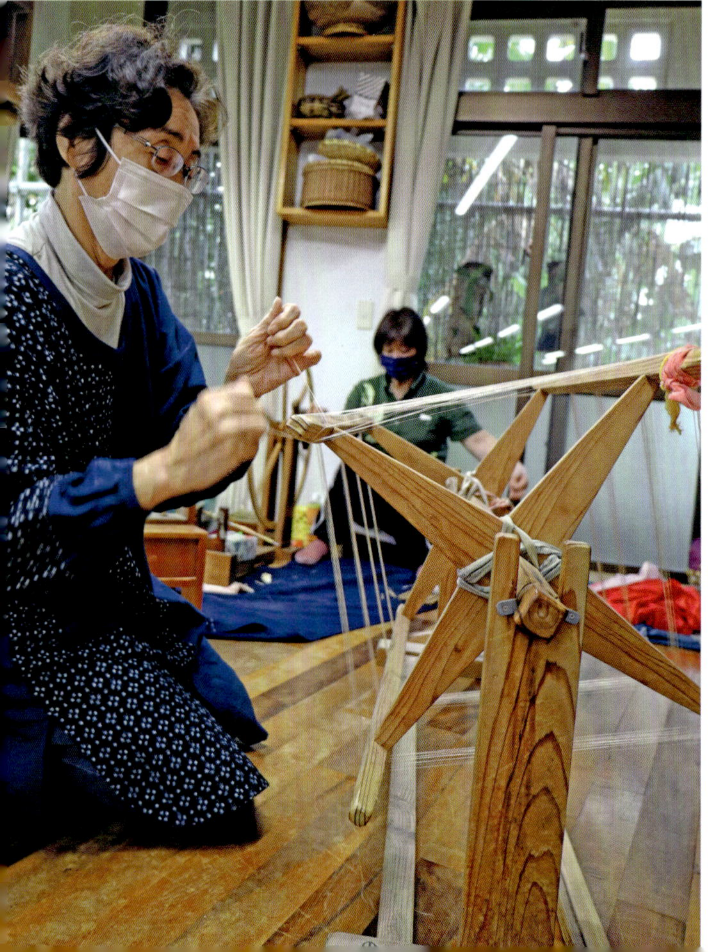

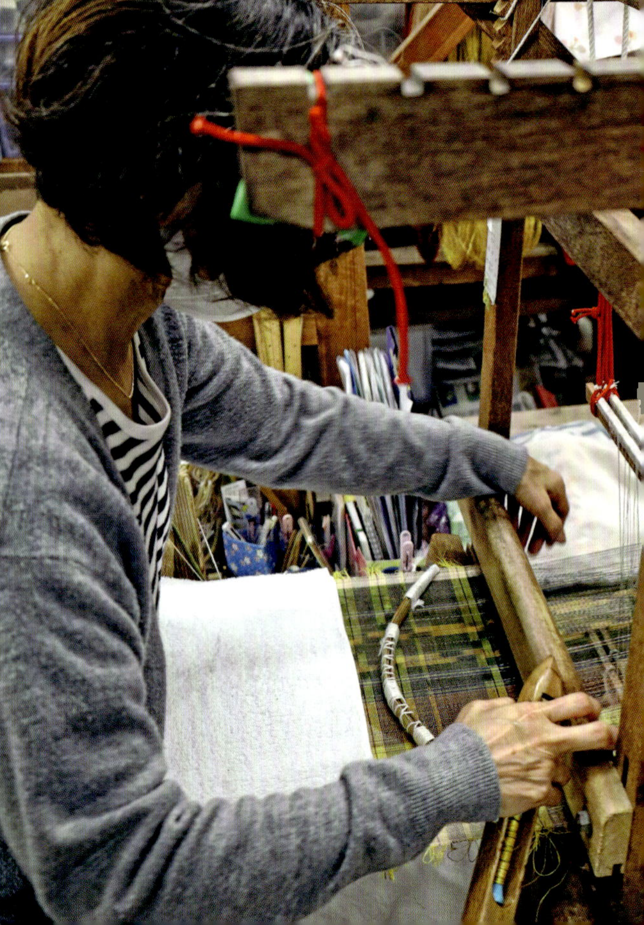

Intangible Cultural Property of Japan. So our preservation society tries to find and cultivate artisans to take over and continue the correct techniques for making this traditional cloth. I feel very strongly that we should preserve this craft and not allow something so beautiful to disappear. It it is really important that we don't let this happen. The plant itself is truly unique, and this in turn makes the fabric itself even more fascinating.

Are there many basho trees in Okinawa?
In the past basho trees were abundant, but over the years they have lost out to other species. Now, because the trees do not grow so easily in the wild, we have to cultivate them. Because Okinawa is known as the home of bashofu cloth, we thought we should at least have some basho plantations.

How many artisans are there?
There are around fifty or sixty of us, but out of those there are only about twenty people who are able to carry out the whole bashofu-making process—from growing the basho crop to making the finished cloth—although we are training other people. Some artisans are just working on the weaving because they are too old to tend to the basho crops. The average age of our bashofu artisans is quite high, because there simply aren't many young people who are interested. We don't have anyone in their twenties and only a few artisans who are in their thirties. The agricultural part is quite hard. It takes around ten years to learn all the necessary skills—and of course you need talent too. The artisans are mostly women—the guys haven't lasted!

What are the characteristics of good bashofu?
Good bashofu cloth is produced from a good quality basho tree. Without that you won't get good thread. The skill and the consistency of the craftsperson is obviously also a very important factor.

Why is it important to stick to natural, handmade processes?
The first time I ever saw bashofu cloth, I was really impressed by the chic monotone shades of the yellow, indigo and brown fabrics. These subdued and beautiful shades are best achieved by hand-dyeing. Obviously hand-dyeing, as well as the time taken to weave the actual basho fibers (it takes an hour to weave 3 grams), is a long process. To make something from machine-woven cloth that is dyed with chemicals is really easy. But you have to ask yourself whether something "easy" to make is "good." I prefer to work using traditional methods.

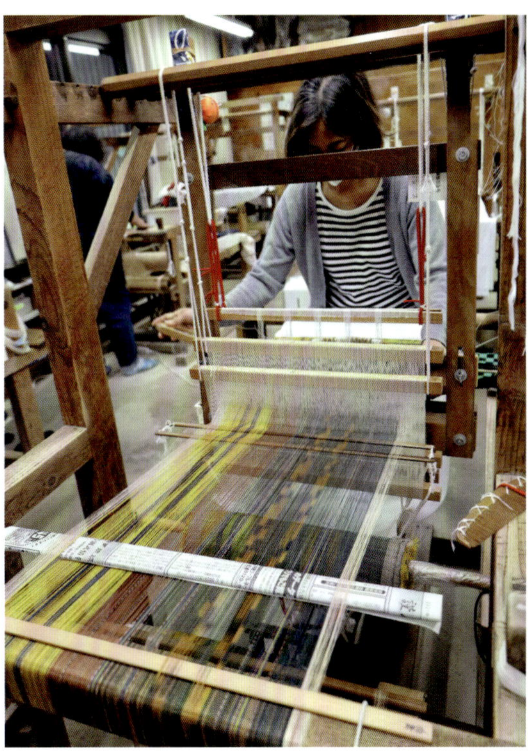

Female artisans at work. The process of making bashofu cloth is laborious and time consuming. Use of the loom results in cloth that is light and doesn't stick to the skin.

Shoko Yamashiro

A Maker of Bingata Resist-Dyed Fabric

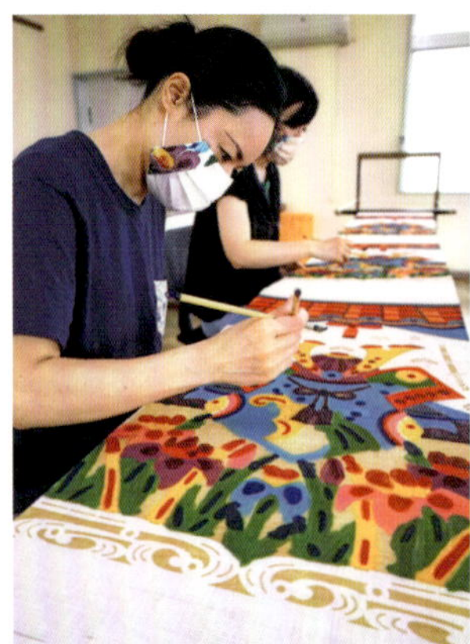

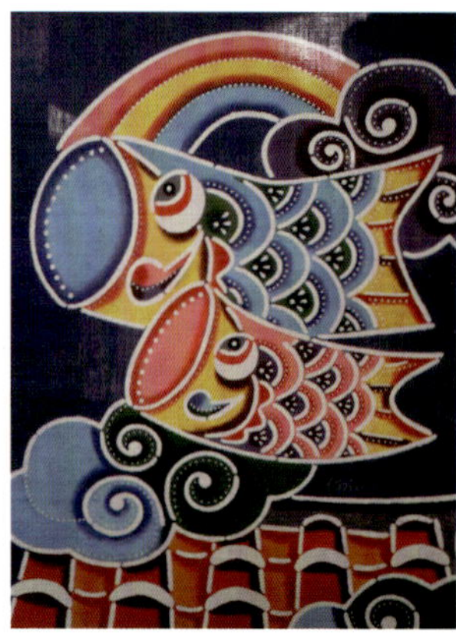

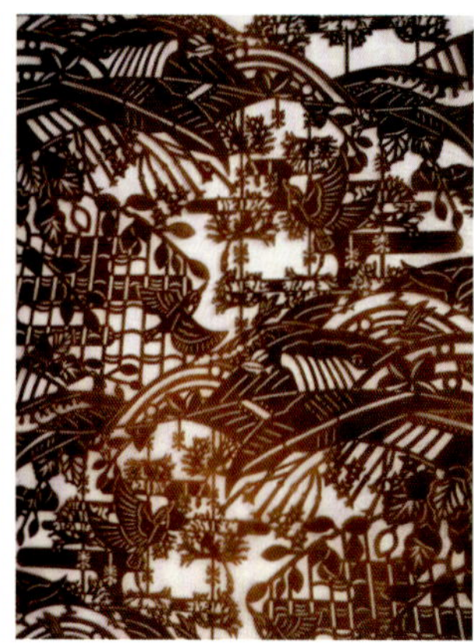

Okinawa bingata is a type of dyeing that is done freehand or with stencils. This dyeing method dates back over five hundred years and was originally used to decorate costumes for local Ryukyu dancers or for the nobility. After World War II, use of bingata-dyed fabric for kimonos spread to commoners as well. Even though bingata uses motifs such as flowing water, irises and birds that are found on other types of textiles, it is easily recognizable for its distinctive colors, such as mustard yellow. Nowadays bingata is mostly used for souvenir items that are embellished with motifs like whale sharks and other Okinawan marine life. **Shoko Yamashiro** of Gusuku Bingata Studio in Okinawa (4-9-1 Maeda, Urasoe; tel: 098-887-3414) tells us more about this vibrant dyeing method.

What are the characteristics of Okinawa bingata?
The characteristics are influenced by the natural environment of Okinawa—the ocean, the bright sky, the really strong sun and the year-round warm weather.

The Okinawan identity is different to the identity of the mainland Japanese. We have a particular brightness that is reflected in the colors of bingata. These bright and vivid colors enrich the heart and soul and have vibrant, healing powers. Bingata's emphasis on natural motifs such as flowers and birds is comforting to the eye.

Bingata seems to use a wide variety of nature-related motifs, especially flowers. Which flowers are commonly used?
Traditionally, when Okinawa was ruled by the imperial court of Japan, bingata motifs were often flowers not found in Okinawa like peonies

Top left Artisans at work at Gusuku Studio.
Top center, top right Bingata designs are incredibly vivid and colorful.
Facing page The strong mustard yellow used in the background of this piece is one of the characteristic colors of bingata.

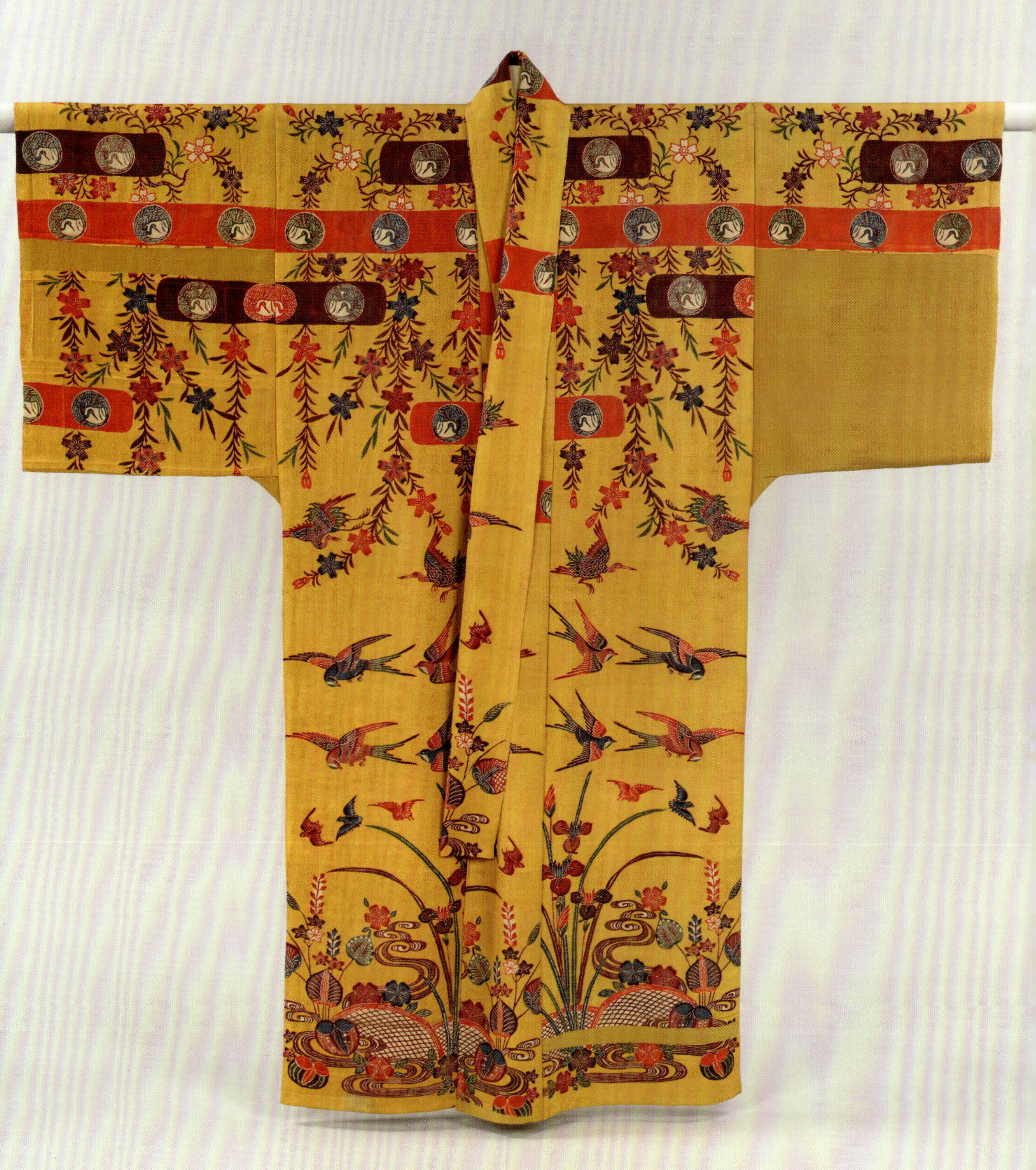

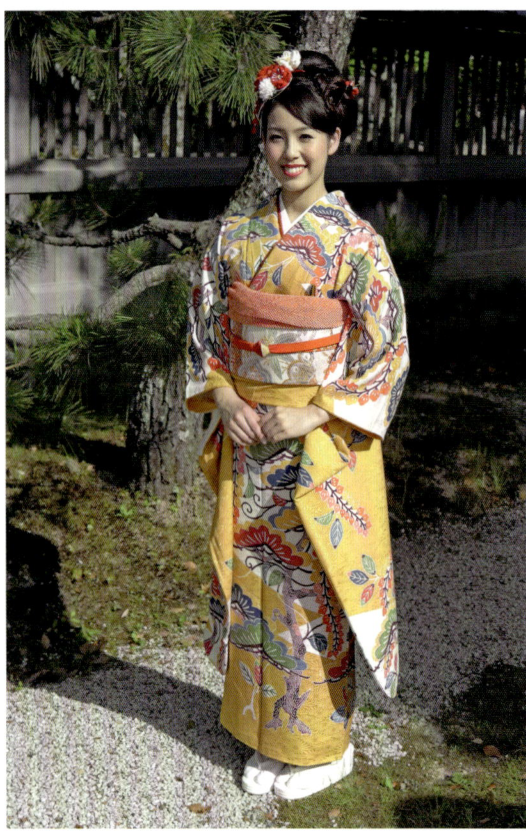

and irises, weeping cherries and chrysanthemums, but these days local flowers are more common, such as hibiscus, shell ginger, Barringtonia, or Queen of the Night cacti.

In the past, bingata was used for costumes for royalty. What do you use it for now?
It's sometimes used for kimonos, and there was a boom in bingata kimonos about thirty years ago. But they are expensive—at least 500,000 yen (US$3,300)—so most people can't afford them, and obviously we couldn't survive if we made only kimonos. So nowadays we make practical, everyday items, like smartphone cases, and kits for crafters who want to practice bingata as a hobby.

Tell us about the bingata dyeing techniques.
There are two techniques—one is freehand and one uses stencils for resist dyeing. To create freehand designs we use a piping bag that you use for whipped cream and we use that to draw freehand. The lines are quite bold. Post–World War II Okinawa had to restart from zero and in those days people would use bullet casing instead of the piping bag we use now. And they would color the cloth by melting down lipstick!

How long does it take to make one bolt of cloth?
It takes two to three months. A lot depends on the weather—if it is too humid, the masking glue doesn't set. The process to make one stencil takes more than a month sometimes. You can't make a mistake; if you do, you need to start all over again, unless you can paste it together somehow. Each aspect of making bingata is fun; it is like a puzzle that gradually becomes complete.

What is bingata to the people of Okinawa?
Do you remember in 2019 when Shuri Castle burnt down? It was like we'd lost part of our soul. Bingata is part of our soul too. It is something we can't lose. If we lost bingata, Okinawa would become a less colorful place.

Above A bingata kimono is beautiful but expensive.
Facing page A selection of bingata designs by Gusuku Bingata Studio.

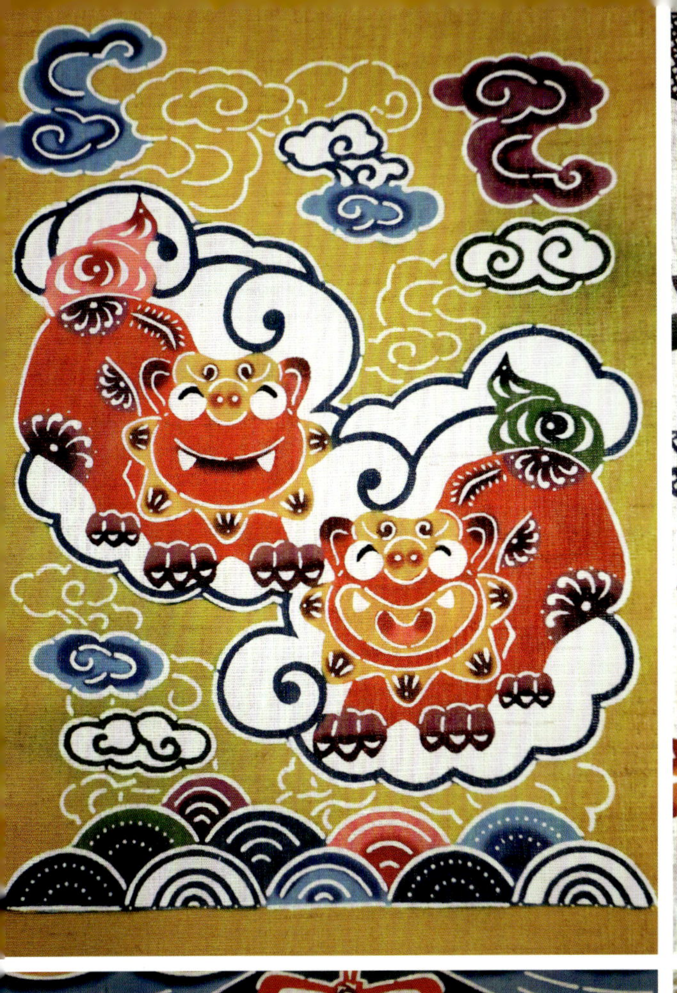

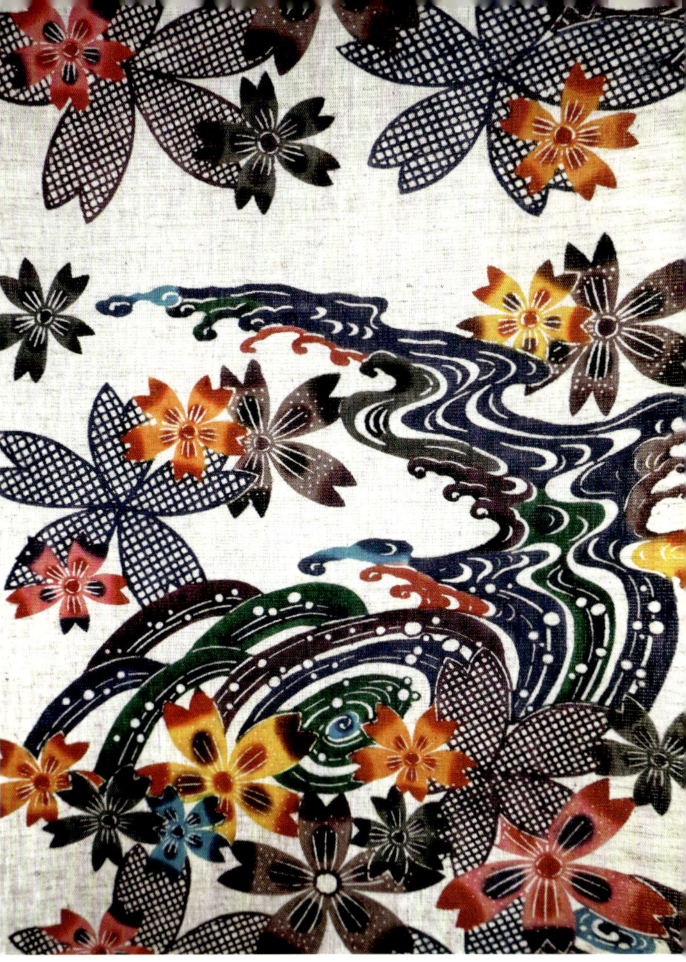

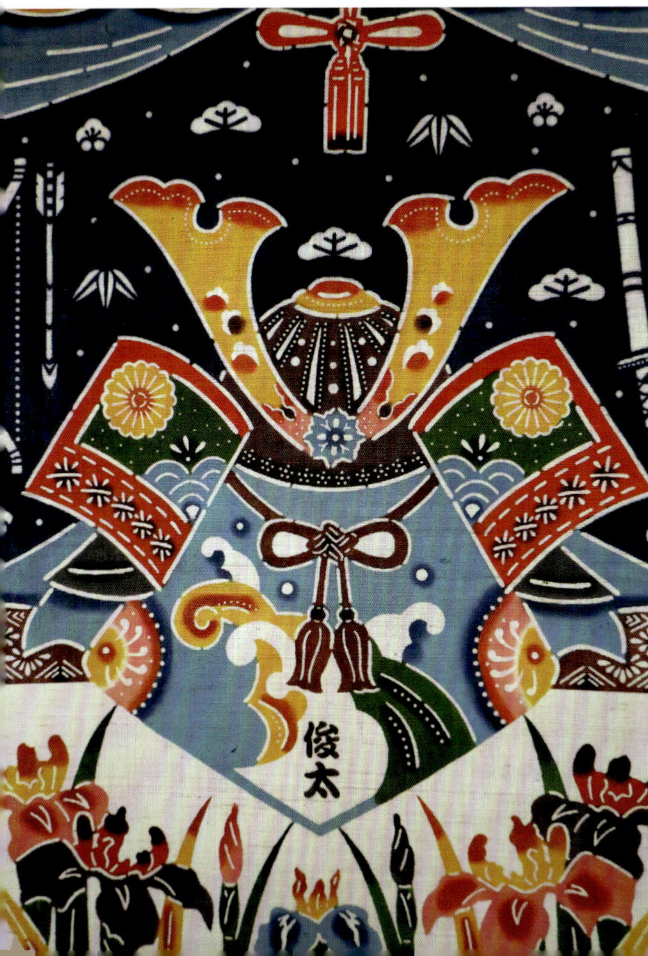
俊太

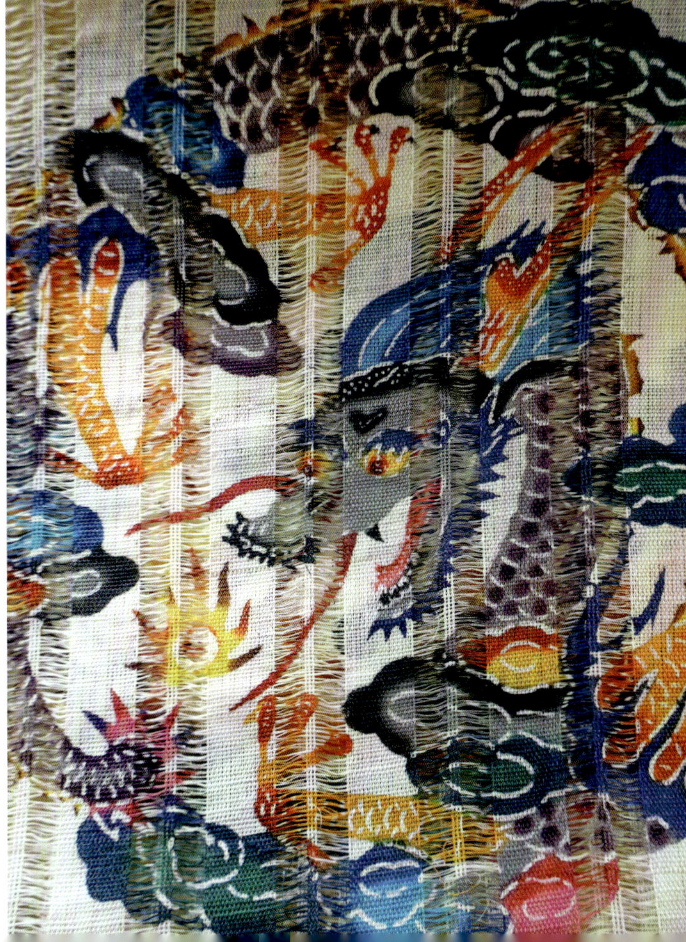

Beverly Maeda

A Hariko Papier-Mâché Artist

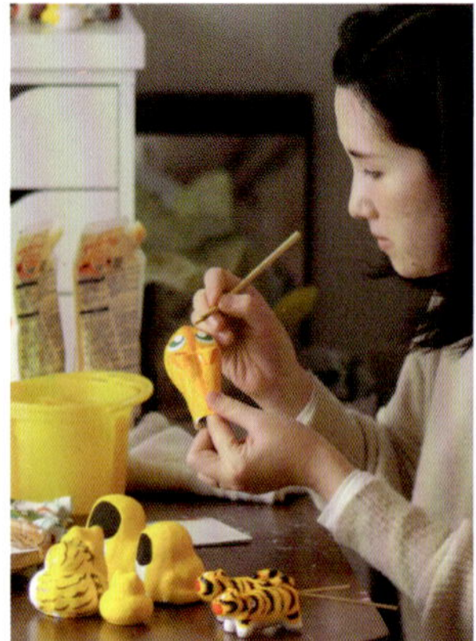

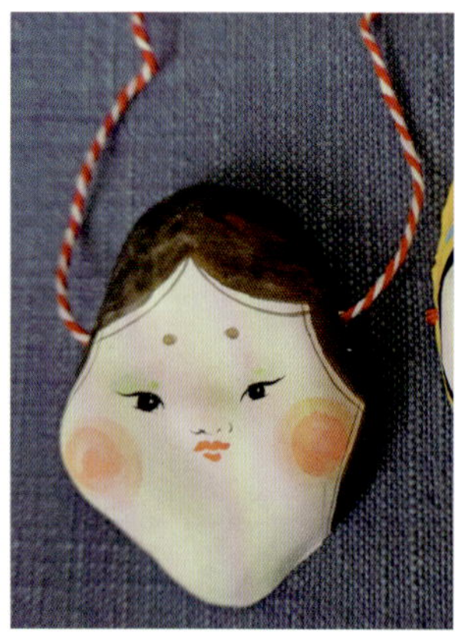

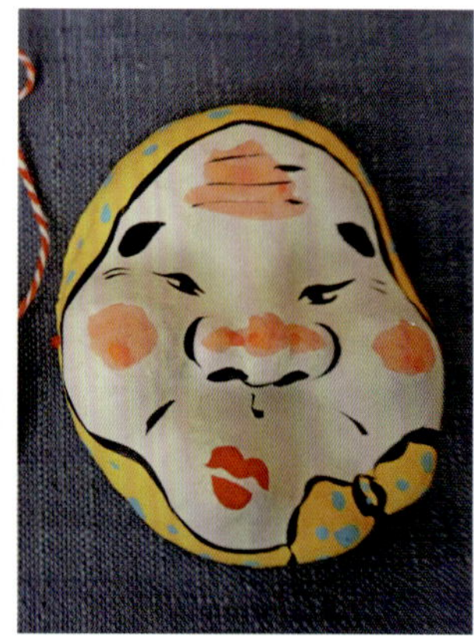

Beverly Maeda (bibariko.jimdofree.com) is an artisan who makes traditional auspicious items using the hariko papier-mâché technique. Trained in oil painting and also with experience of working in the film industry, she represents a new generation of mingei enthusiasts who have different backgrounds to traditional craftspeople. Another unusual aspect of Maeda's background is that she apprenticed under the sculptor Ryo Arai.

Above Beverly Maeda is the best-known papier-mâché folk toy artisan. She creates accessible and pop items in pastel colors.
Right Maeda's maneki-neko cats have a soft, loose aesthetic. She caters to the many females who collect small, cute objects as well as to dedicated collectors of folk toys.

Can you talk us through the production process for hariko items?
If I am making an *inuhariko* papier-mâché puppy, the first step is to create a dog shape from wood or plasticine. Then I paste wet washi paper over it. If you use normal paper it is too stiff and it won't stick. I use a type of washi made especially for hariko called *harikogami*. When it dries, it retains the shape it has been molded around.

How did you first become interested in mingei folk crafts?
I was an art director at a production company and my friend Ryohei Sasatani was researching folklore studies and eroticism. He went around Japan's *hihokan* (sex museums) when he was a student in order to film a documentary and as part of this research he also went to the Otto-boke Museum in Nagano where the work of the folk-craft artist Ranson Miyata is displayed. Miyata was trying to revive an old Japanese craft tradition of making phallus-shaped masks and folk toys. This was twelve years ago and it sparked my interest in mingei as I was curious about eroticism. I also went on a pilgrimage to Iwate Prefecture to see a *konseisama* (phal-lus-shaped fertility god) made of straw. It was

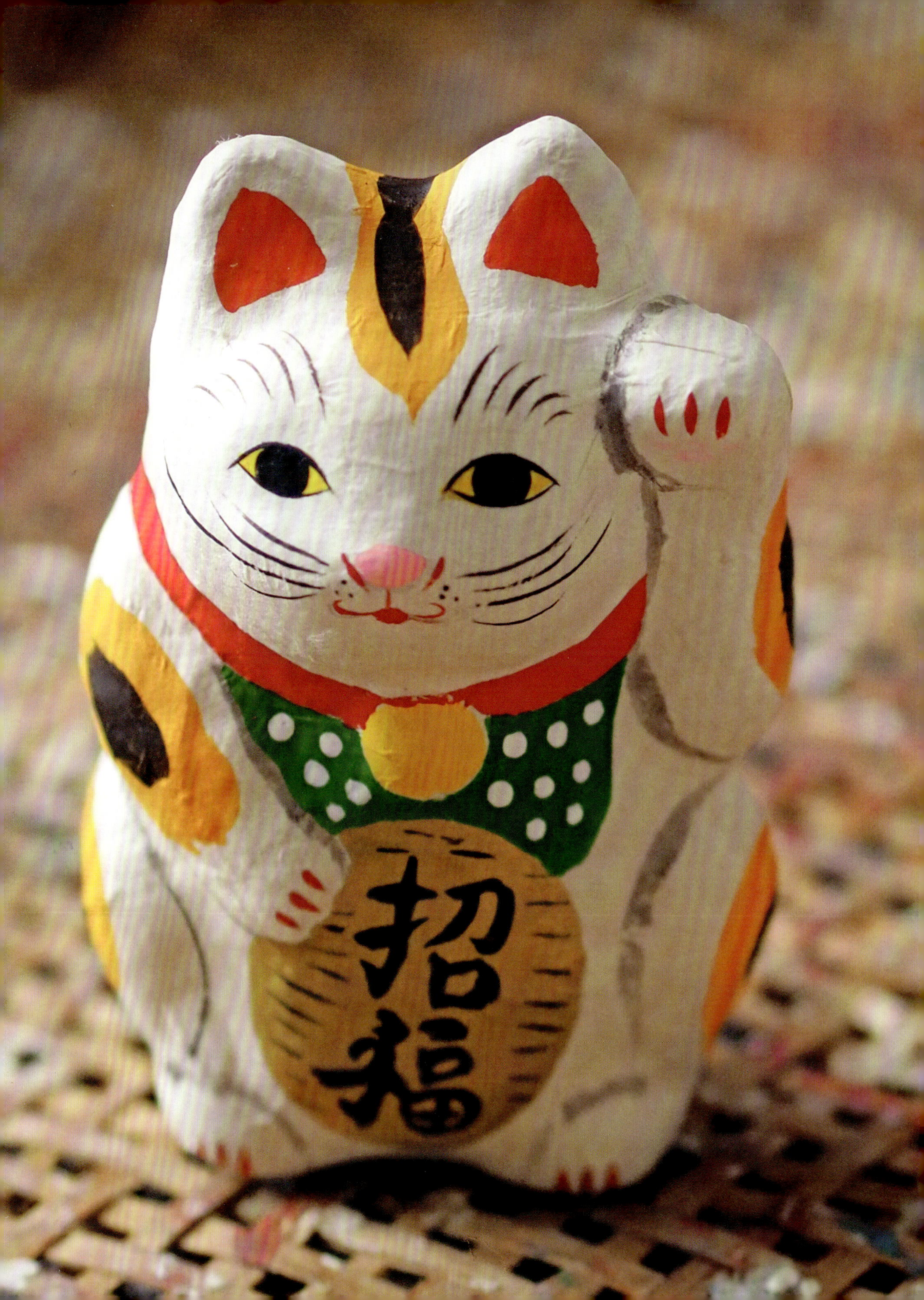
招福

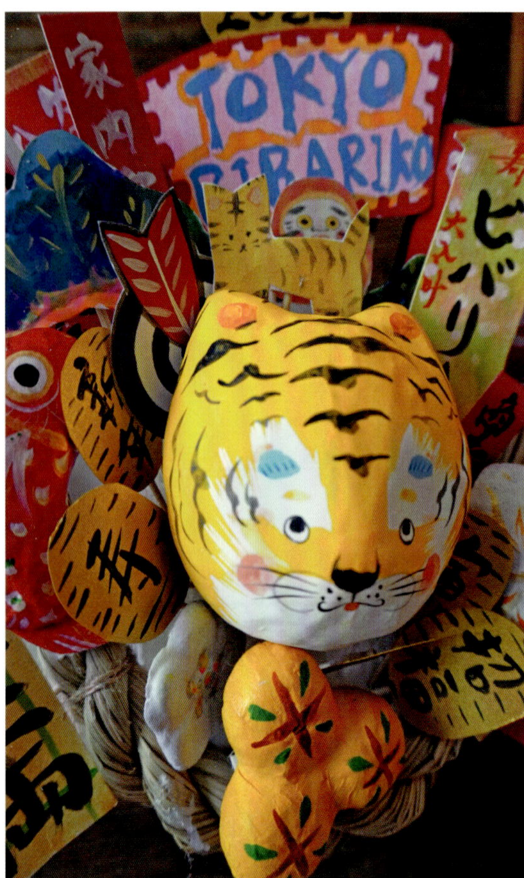

comical and it was also related to sculpture so I thought it was interesting. I became more interested in cute mingei folk toys and started looking around to see what was out there. When I came across hariko with its simple and straightforward technique, I thought it felt really free and fun.

Are there many people from the art world like you who are developing an interest in mingei folk crafts such as hariko?

Yes, I think there are quite a lot of artists and illustrators who are taking an interest in folk crafts. When creators are making things into a 3D format, they are often inspired by hariko figures, which are round and have soft lines. Their smooth surface is quite easy to paint, so if you are an artist making an illustration into a solid form, it's ideal. Lately there's been quite a boom in people starting to make hariko on their own and even selling them. If you check out #hariko on Instagram you'll see what I mean.

You're involved in making a traditional craft, but do you adhere to the traditional belief that hariko are lucky?

I understand that people do have superstitious beliefs about these items, but these are generally related to seasonal traditions. For the Girls' Day festival in March, for example, inuhariko dogs are often displayed to represent a wish that a child grows up happy and healthy. And there are probably people out there who believe strongly in the talismanic qualities of certain folk-craft items. But as for me, I'm not really very superstitious. I just like the shape of hariko, basically!

Tell us about the current interest in mingei items and folk toys as you see it.

After the earthquake and tsunami that took place in Tohoku in 2011, traditional talismanic figures like *okiagari-koboshi* dolls and *akabeko* cows (see page 36) that came from regions that had suffered a lot of damage received a great deal of attention. There was also a revival of interest in simple crafts that risked becoming extinct, such as kokeshi dolls (see page 79) and *tsuchiningyo* clay dolls, and hariko was part of that revival.

There's also a lot of interest in Japan recently in collecting small and cute things, particularly amongst women, and this has also led to an interest in collecting folk toys. Folk toys have been featured in Japanese pop-culture magazines like *Brutus*, and fashionable stores like BEAMS now stock kokeshi dolls and other regional items. Japanese global brand MUJI have been selling folk toy items too.

This page A collection of tiger-themed items Maeda made for the Year of the Tiger.
Facing page A gallery of Beverly Maeda's work.

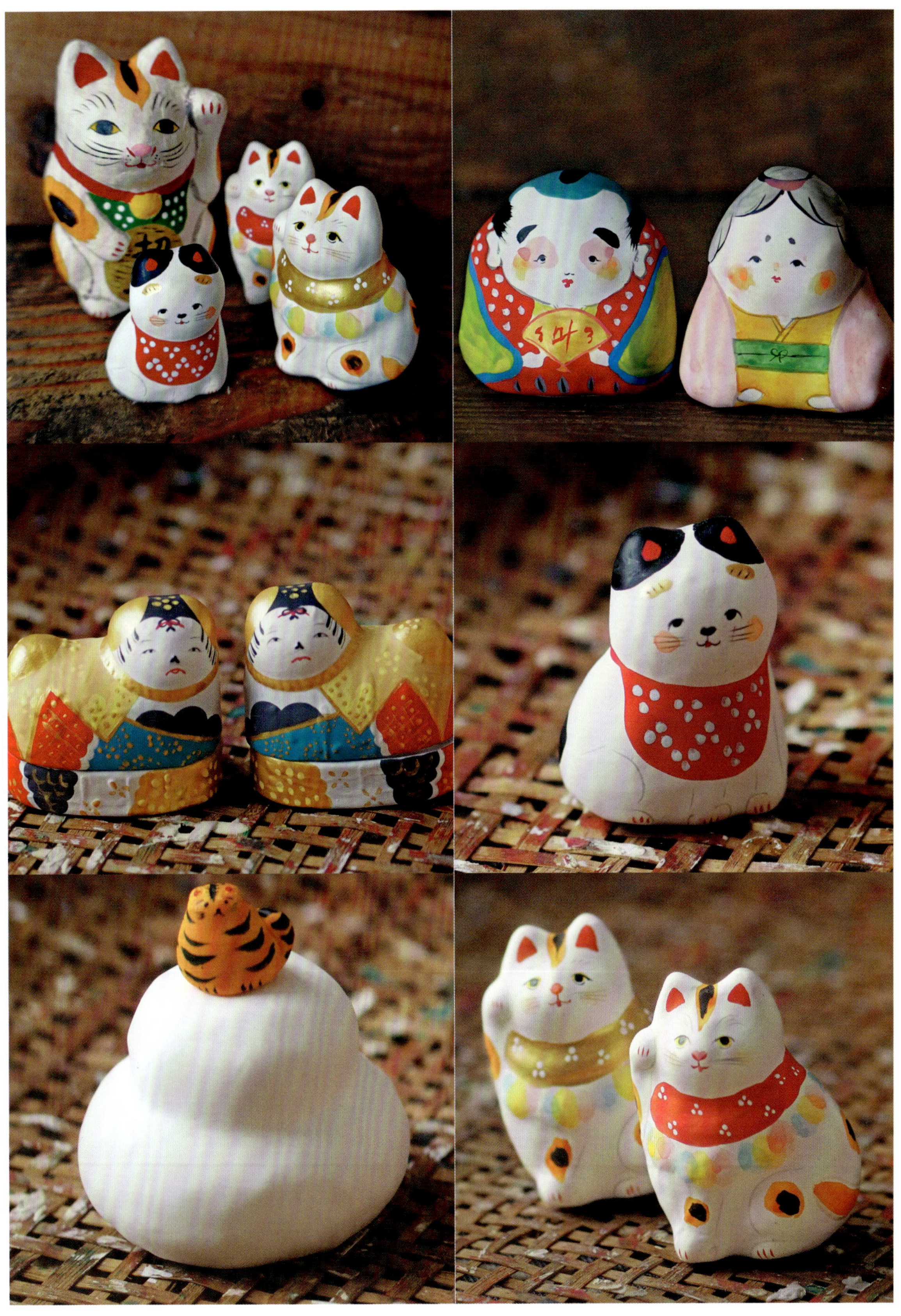

Hiromitsu

A Contemporary Kagura Mask Maker

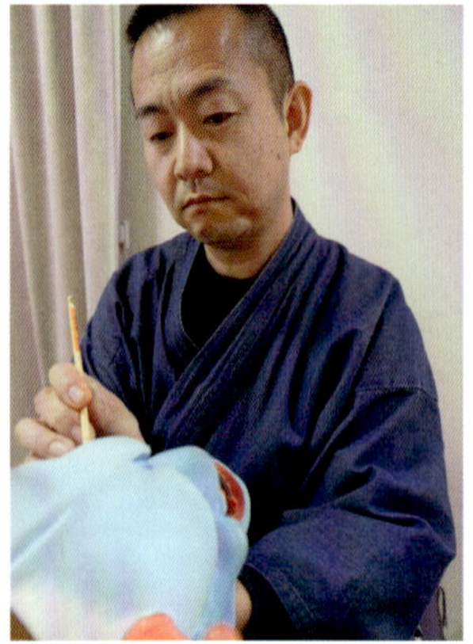
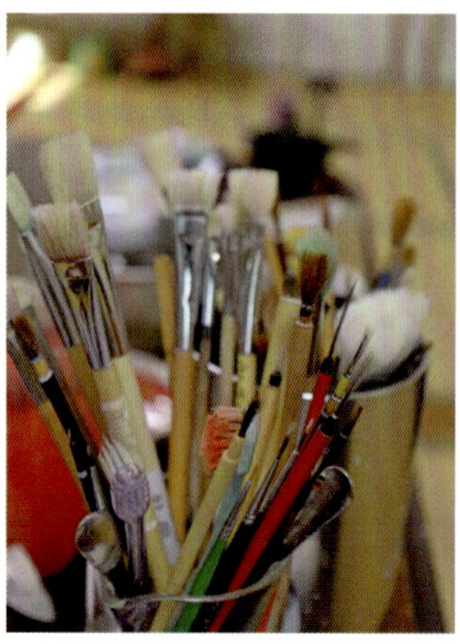
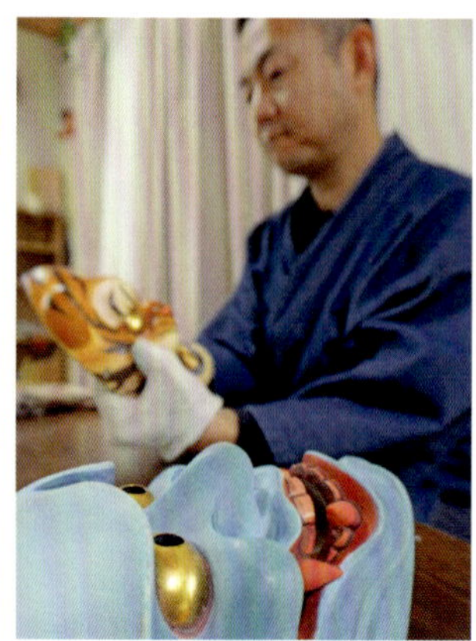

Hiromitsu is a mask artisan working out of his west Tokyo atelier. He has a background in illustration and was also a dancer at traditional Japanese festivals, where he first became familiar with wooden masks. His work is vibrant, contemporary and expressive. Utilizing his prolific Instagram following (@hiromitsu.430), he has a wait list of over two years for his decorative masks, with many overseas customers. Hiromitsu balances traditional techniques and materials with a progressive outlook. He often works with motifs not found in the traditional mask motif lexicon and is also influenced by the works of foreign artists.

Why did you start making masks?
I went to a school for illustration. Originally I wanted to illustrate dinosaurs, insects and animals—I liked drawing grotesque and scary things. But I got a job doing illustrations for children's textbooks which meant I was constantly drawing cute things. Also, when everything went from analog to digital, I couldn't keep up with the changes and I gave up my job as an illustrator.

When I was in my twenties and thirties, I was performing as the comical masked traditional figure known as *hyottoko* at the local festival. The mask I wore for those performances sparked my interest in woodcraft. I started quizzing local woodworkers about tools and techniques for mask making, which led to me becoming an apprentice to a mask maker for two and a half years. I was about thirty at the time. He was elderly, so my apprenticeship finished prematurely but from that point on, I had a lot of connections in the mask-making world.

As well as traditional Noh and kagura masks, Hiromitsu enjoys making yokai masks with strong expressions.

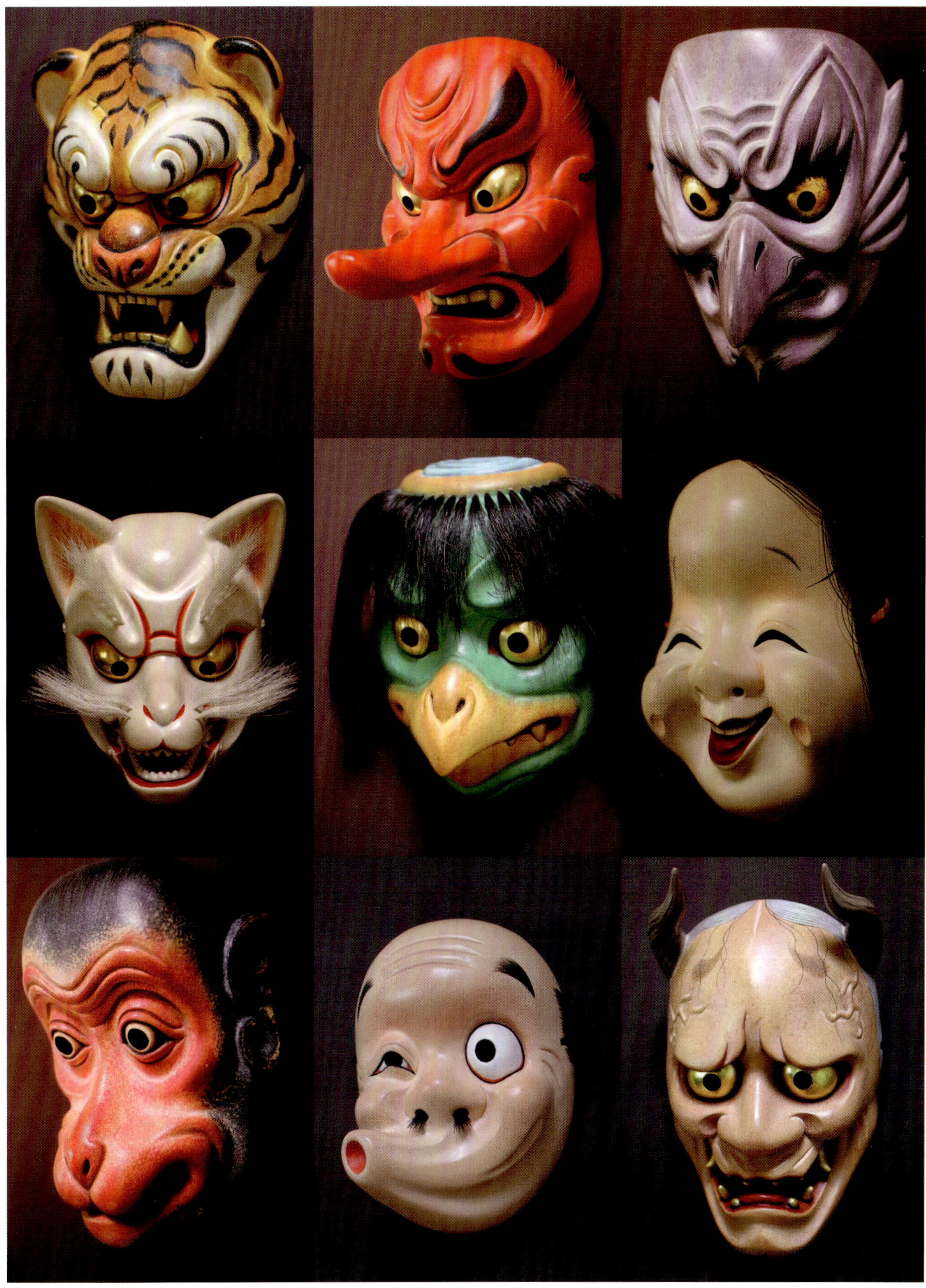

Why are there such a strong mask culture in Japan?
I think its connected to religion. Japan's native religion of Shinto is connected to nature worship—every element of nature is divine and inanimate things are considered to have a soul. For example, lightning is said to occur when the god Kaminari-san is angry. In order to portray the stories of the gods that inhabit these everyday natural elements and occurrences, masks are used. Masks are also worn for traditional *kagura* dance performances, which are a kind of offering to the gods.

What is the appeal of masks made of wood?
Wooden masks have a more artistic quality than masks made of plastic or paper. It is clear that effort has gone in to their production, and this means they are taken seriously by people. The first time a wooden mask was put into my hands, I was aware that it felt notably different from the plastic or paper masks I'd used before, and I was charmed by that.

What was your experience of the process of learning to make masks?
The Setagaya teacher I apprenticed with had a class—nowadays there are large profit-making mask schools, but this teacher was instructing one-to-one and taught me quite well. Usually, in classes for masks for Noh theater, you can't make masks other than Noh masks. There are a lot of rules, and it is quite stiff; you can't even change the shape. You have to copy the traditional Noh masks exactly, using old stencils—they consider it to be the beauty of imitation.

As I am a creator who wants to make masks freely, I was not suited to this way of learning. And the teacher that I apprenticed under let me do what I wanted, so I could make clown masks and things like that.

What kind of masks are you making at the moment?
I'm mostly making contemporary kagura masks for theatrical performances. These masks are of gods as well as *yokai* ghosts such as *tengu* and *kappa*. I also make some masks for Noh theater, but they have to be made in a very rigid style.

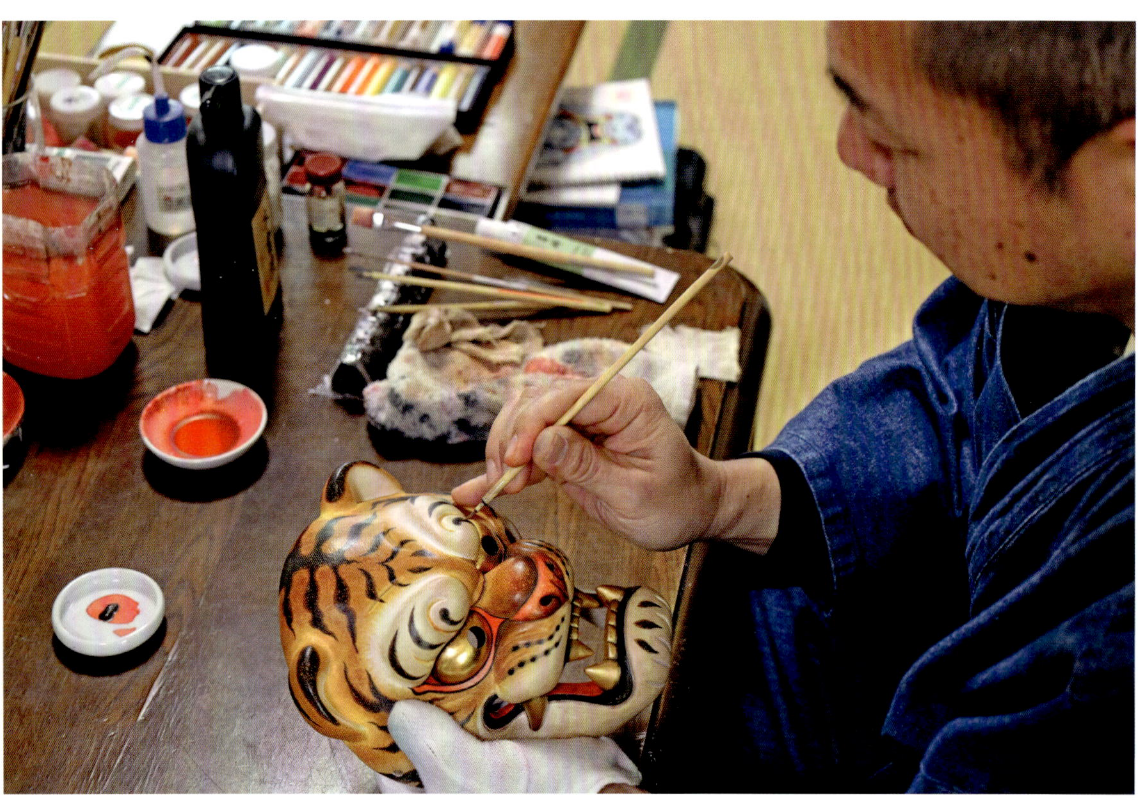

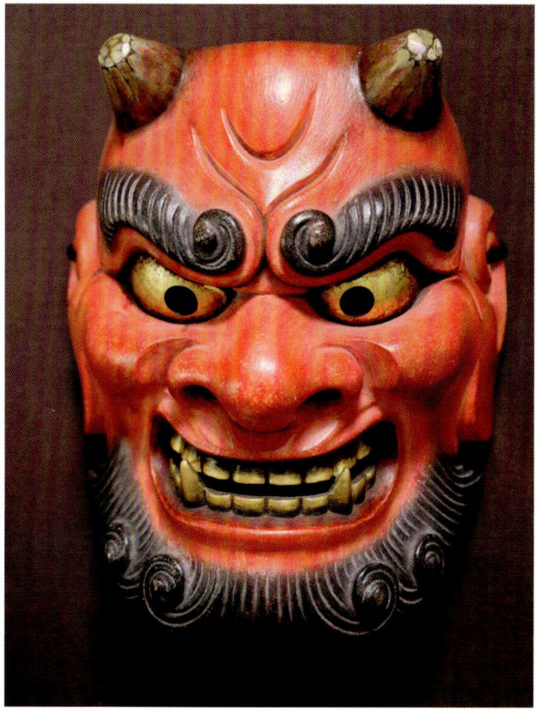

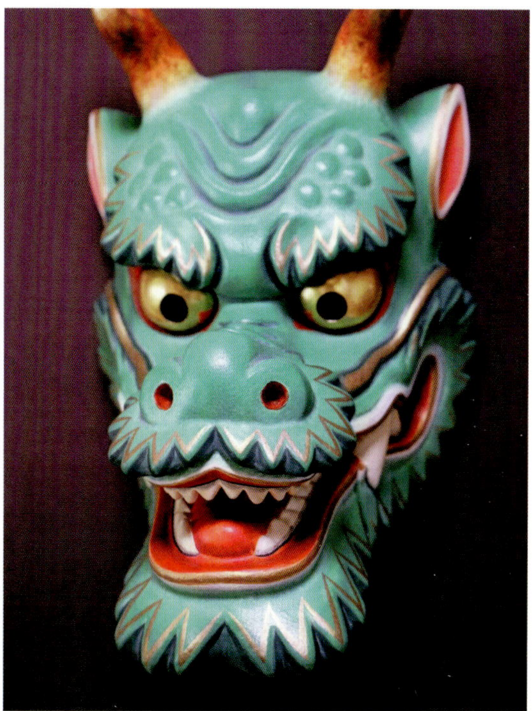

Kagura allows for a more varied artistic expression—sculptors also make them.

Your work is very expressive.
Many of my commissions are for decorative masks that people can display on their wall, so this allows me to make masks with a stronger expression than a Noh mask, for example, which is usually expressionless. I like making yokai masks—they can be scary but they also have a certain charm.

The *hanya* mask used in Noh is that of an angry and jealous woman but within that there is sadness. So the mouth is angry, yet the eyes are sad and according to how the mask is tilted, the face can be that of defeat.

Also, the mask is something that people wear on the face, so I have to decide how much to anthropomorphize it—for example, with a tiger, if I make it "as is," that isn't interesting so I will add manga-like elements.

What kind of wood do you use?
I use paulownia wood, which is used for most kagura masks because it is light, making the masks easy to wear for performances. It's also easy to carve and easy to get hold of.

Noh masks are usually made of *hinoki* cypress. Hinoki is expensive and it is the ultimate material, and the back can be lacquered as well. However, it is difficult to process as it has a lot of oil in it, so it takes two weeks to treat with alcohol, boil and then dry.

Who are your clients?
In Japan, many retirees make masks as they are not dependent on the income, which is small, especially these days when many festivals and even professional actors use paper or mass-produced masks. I'm lucky in that I get many orders from overseas customers, but I can only make two masks a month. Many of my customers have to wait for years.

Facing page "I make a lot of tigers for overseas clients, Tigers are not part of the lexicon of Japanese masks but they are popular abroad."
Above To color his masks, Hiromitsu uses traditional Japanese mineral pigments, the same type as are used in classic Nihonga paintings, He first coats the wood with shell powder and gelatin. He uses *sumi* ink for the black color.

Hiromi Chiba

A Koginzashi Needlework Artist

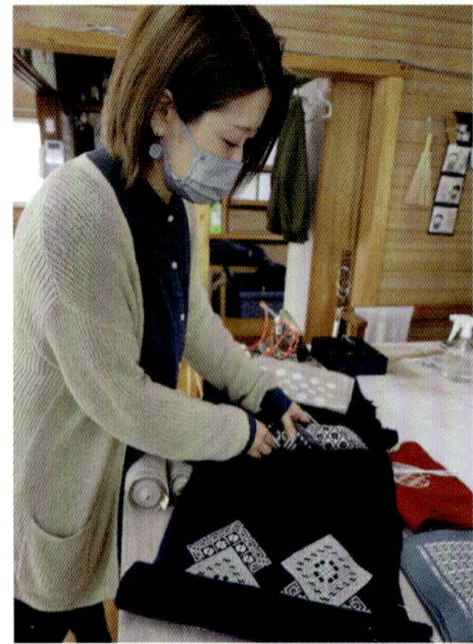
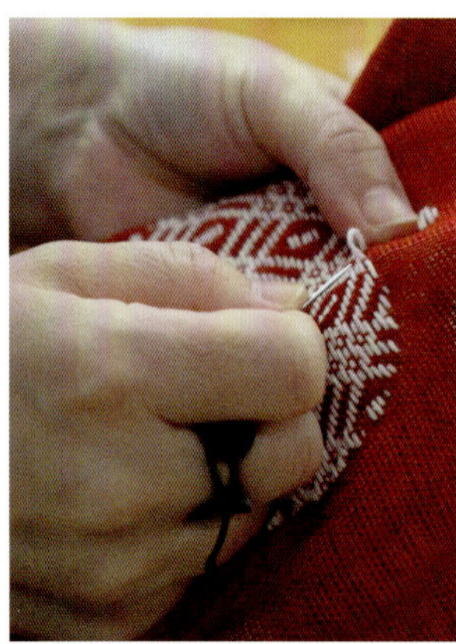
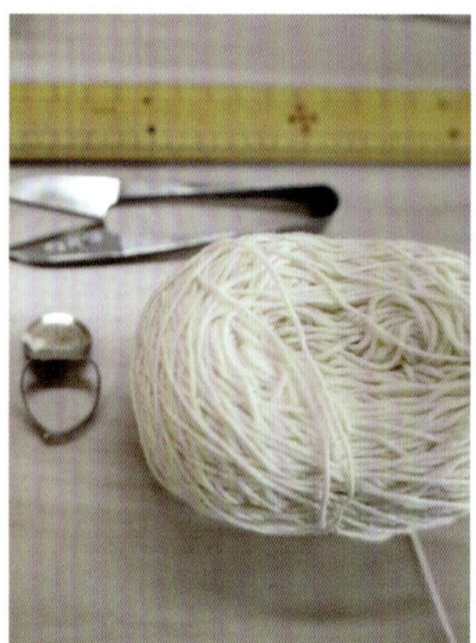

Koginzashi is a type of reinforcement stitching—one of the techniques of sashiko decorative embroidery—that has existed in Japan for hundreds of years. In the Tsugaru area of Aomori Prefecture, clothes were traditionally made from hemp, and koginzashi stitching was used to reinforce the cloth and close up any gaps in the weaving. **Hiromi Chiba** is from the Hirosaki Kogin Institute (61 Zaifu, Hirosaki, Aomori; tel: 0172-32-0595) and explains why koginzashi reinforcement stitching still has perennial appeal.

Tell us about the origins of koginzashi stitching.
Koginzashi stitches weave through the vertical and horizontal threads of loosely woven fabric. The original purpose of sewing in this way was to ensure that woven garments blocked out the cold. But this way of sewing created a particular style of pattern, and gradually the patterns and motifs became as important as the practical reason for sewing in this way.

Is it something only women did?
Yes, traditionally it was women, who would start learning the craft when they were five or six years old. As this is a farming region, women would be expected to work on the farm during the summer months, but during the snowy winters when working on the land was impossible, they would do their needlework.

What are the different types of koginzashi?
There are three main regional types: *nishi kogin*, *higashi kogin*, and *mishima kogin*. Cloth that is

Above Hiromi Chiba at work.
Facing page Bolts of koginzashi cloth in blue and white with incredibly dense patterns.

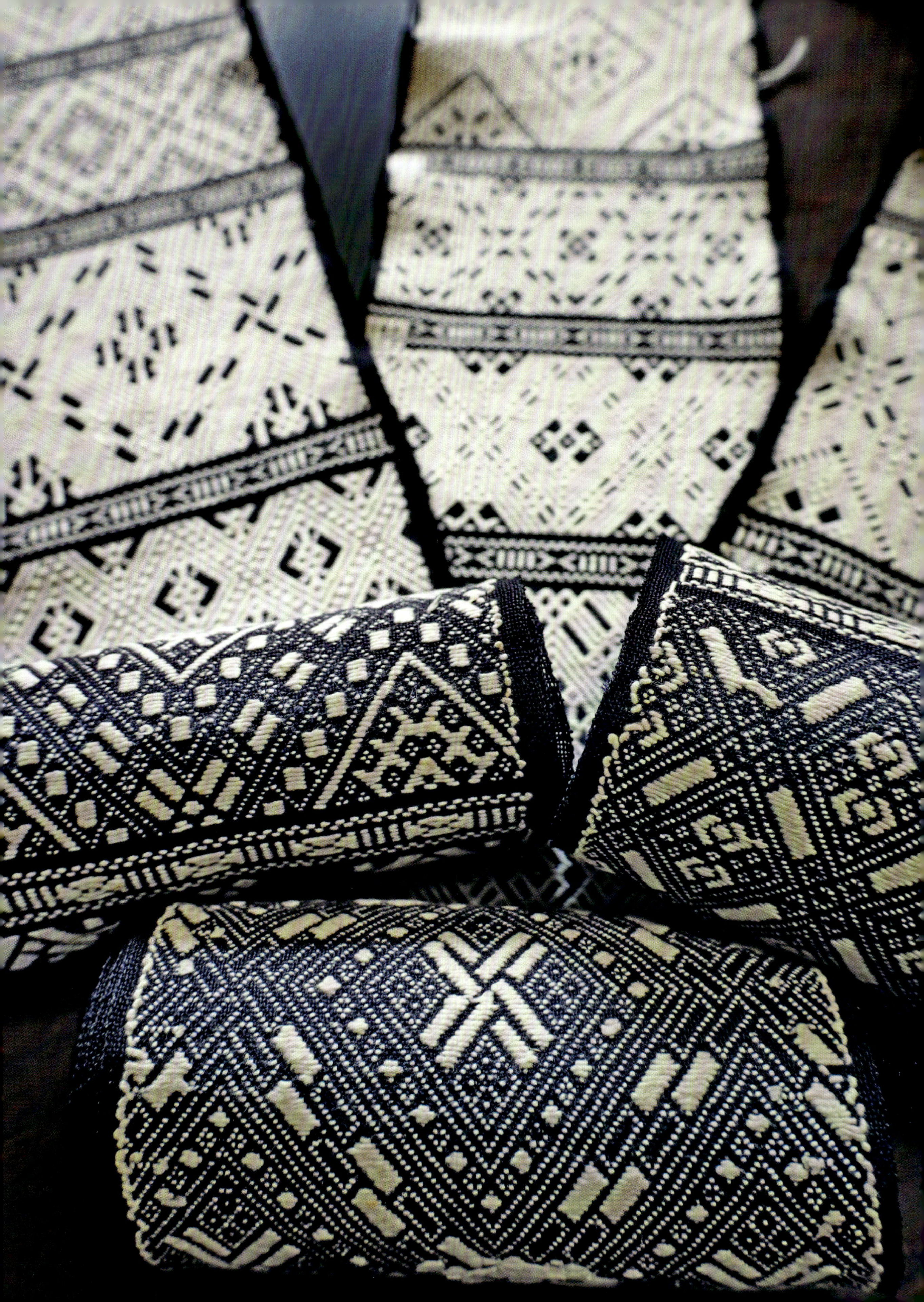

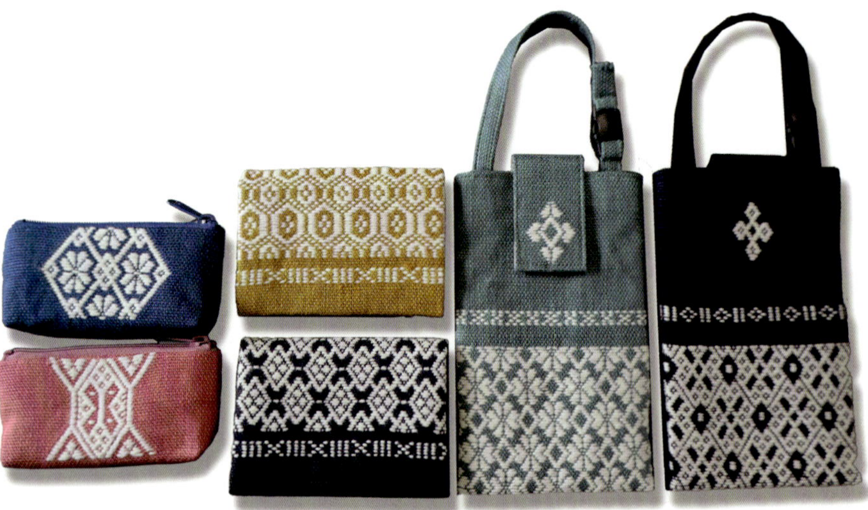

embroidered with higashi kogin has a repetitive pattern. With nishi kogin all the patterns are different and the details are minute. It was said that the women who make it have to be clever, and that if you wanted a clever wife you should try and get one who does nishi kogin!

Mishima kogin's characteristic is that it has a pattern of three stripes. It was also traditionally used for reinforcing the shoulders of garments. In this region, there was a lot of farming work that involved carrying straw, water and rice on the shoulders, which would rub on clothes. If the clothes had an intricate pattern they would be hard to darn, so the mishima pattern has lines only, as the stitches can easily be undone and restitched, or stitched over.

How has koginzashi evolved over the years?
Towards the end of the nineteenth century, Japan started to modernize. A train transport system was developed and goods such as cotton became easy to get hold of, and replaced hemp as clothing material.

As a result the koginzashi culture began to wither. There was a brief surge of renewed interest when the Mingei Movement was established in the 1920s. As there was no longer any need for hemp-woven agricultural clothing, craftspeople began using koginzashi to decorate bags and other accessories.

There are around forty types of motif, which can be combined to create endless different patterns. Some patterns have names and others do not. The names are based on what they look like: *hanako* looks floral; *neko no manage* looks like cats' eyes. Some of the patterns are considered to have talismanic properties—to protect against evil.

It looks like a difficult skill to practice.
Yes, it's easy to make mistakes, and you have to go back and correct them. Now we follow diagrams, but they didn't have those in the olden days. If they made a mistake they would just continue, and in this way new patterns came to be created. If you look closely at the work from over a hundred years ago that we display here at the Kogin Institute, you'll see a lot of mistakes!

Why is it important to keep up these crafts?
To be honest there isn't an actual need, but there are people drawn to the aesthetics of the past who want to perpetuate these things into the future. I understand that. Interest in koginzashi goes up and down through history. Our job at the Kogin Institute is to keep the craft alive.

This page Nowadays koginzashi is used for attractive accessories rather than to reinforce farming clothing.
Facing page, top right A close-up of a koginzashi pattern used on an obi kimono sash.
Facing page, top right and bottom Examples of the mishima pattern, which has three stripes.

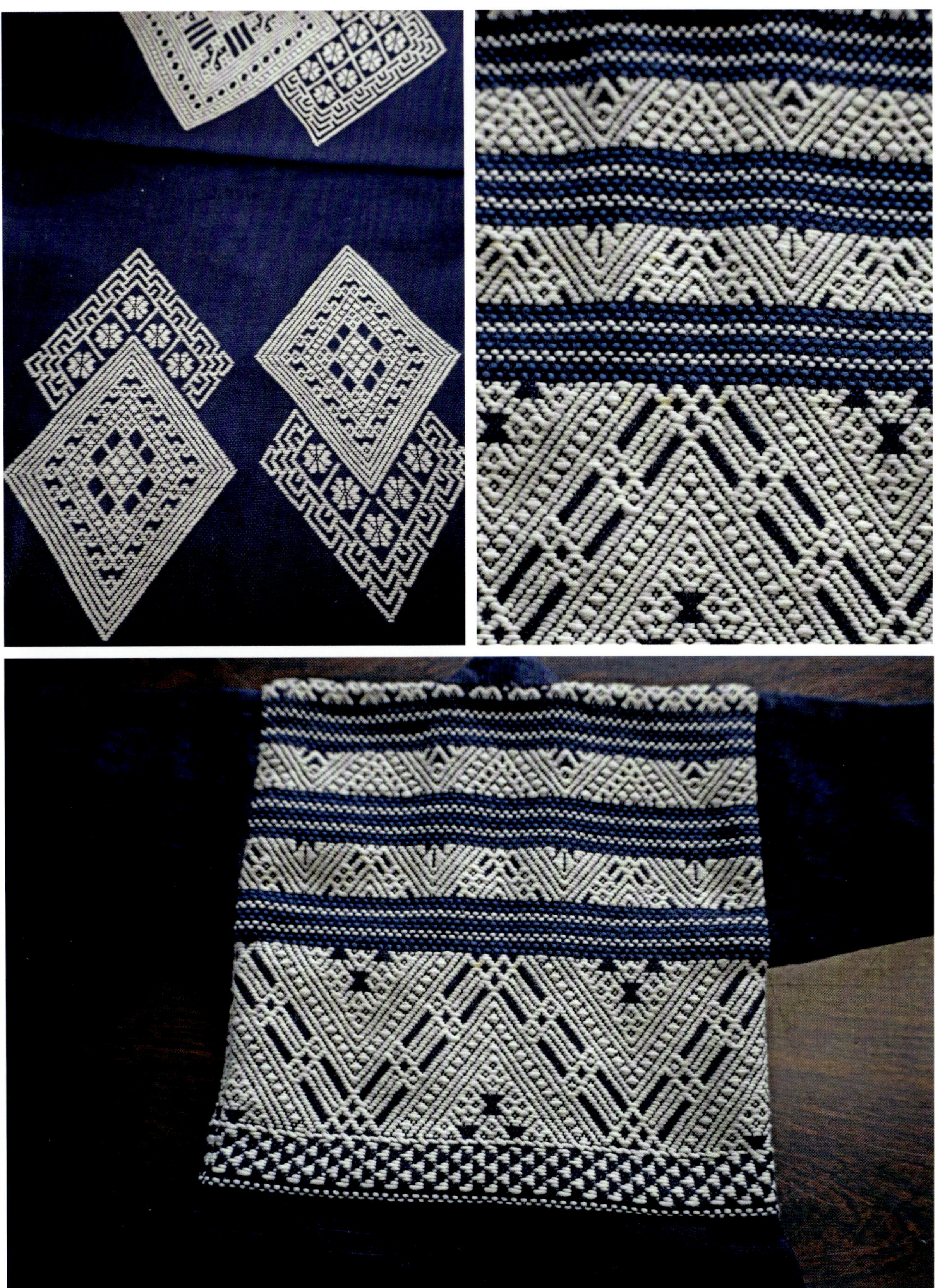

Yasuhiro Koyama

A Sasano Ittobori Wood-Carver

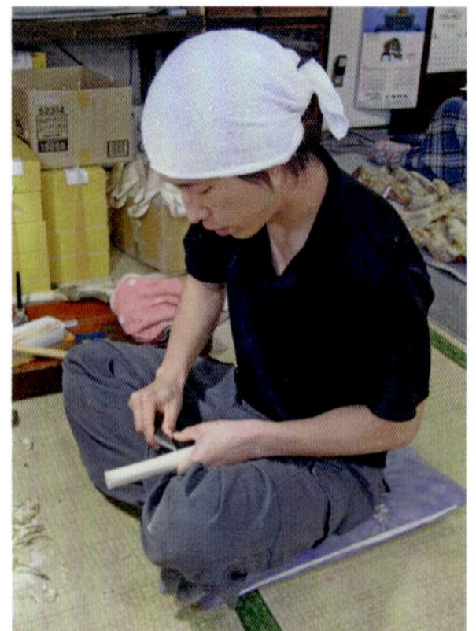

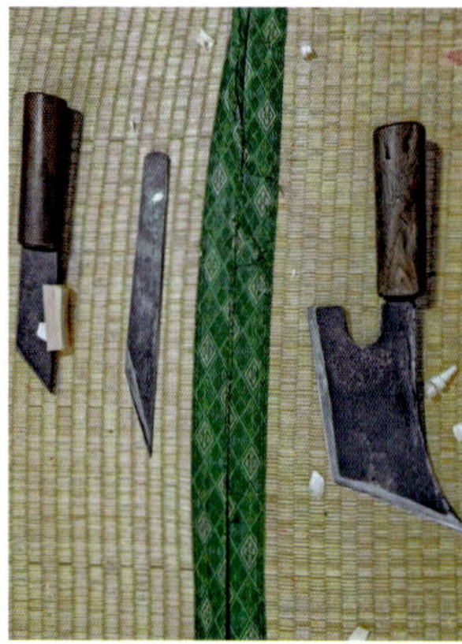

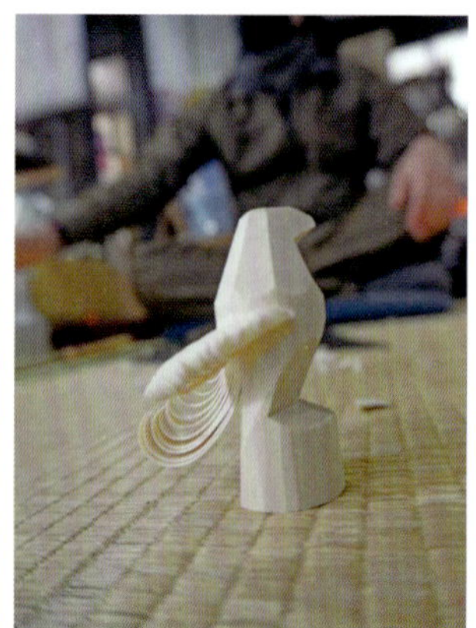

Sasano ittobori, which literally means "one-knife carving," is a woodcraft from Yonezawa in Yamagata Prefecture. The most representative sasano ittobori wood carving is the *otaka poppo*, a talismanic hawk, but artisans also craft other types of animals. The figures are made using the wood of the *koshiabura* tree which is carved with incredible dexterity using a specialized blade. Sasano ittobori has over 1,200 years of history but very few successors remain today. **Yasuhiro Koyama** (Sasano Mingeikan, 5208-2 Sasanohoncho, Yonezawa, Yamagata; tel: 0238-38-4288) is one of them, and is passionate about reviving traditional sasano ittobori figures.

Above At his studio in Yonezawa, Koyama uses a *sarukiri*, a type of blade like the Japanese sword that is made by a blacksmith.
Facing page Hawks are the most common motif in sasano ittobori, but artisans also craft other types of animals, such as these three cats made by Koyama.

Can you give some background to the craft of sasano ittobori?
It's said that sasano ittobori figures first started being made around 1,200 years ago by the indigenous Ainu people of Hokkaido, as talismans that would protect against fire. They were originally in the shape of flowers, and called *sasano bana*.

These days there is a community of around eighteen people in Yonezawa who are said to be sasano ittobori artisans, but the oldest is eighty-five years old and most of the others are seventy to eighty. Including myself, there are probably currently about ten people practicing the craft in earnest. For me, it's my way of earning a living, and I also want to pass the craft on to the next generation.

What exactly is the otaka poppo wood carving and when did you first come across it?
It's a carving of a hawk that was traditionally a folk toy, and these days more likely to be found as a souvenir. It is also regarded as a talisman, with the power to grant protection, as well as prosperity in business.

Although I didn't became a sasano ittobori woodcarver until 2014, I was well-acquainted

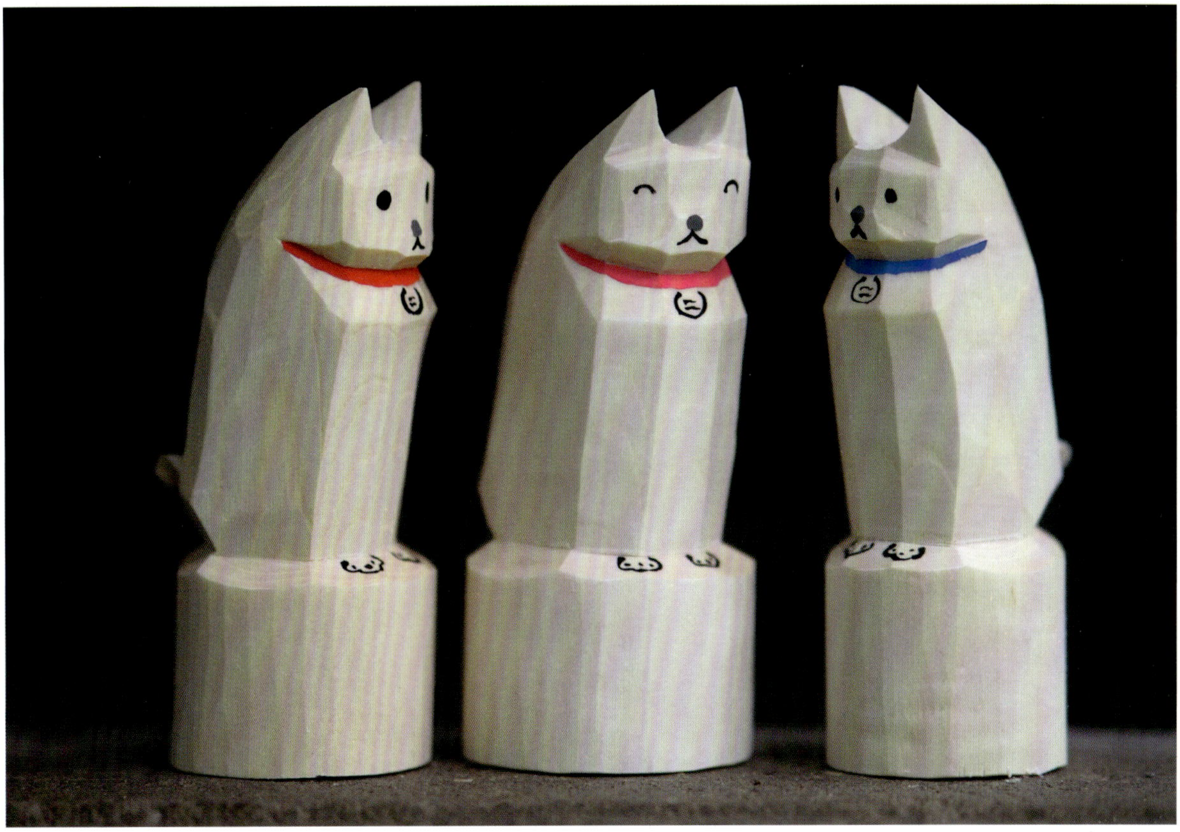

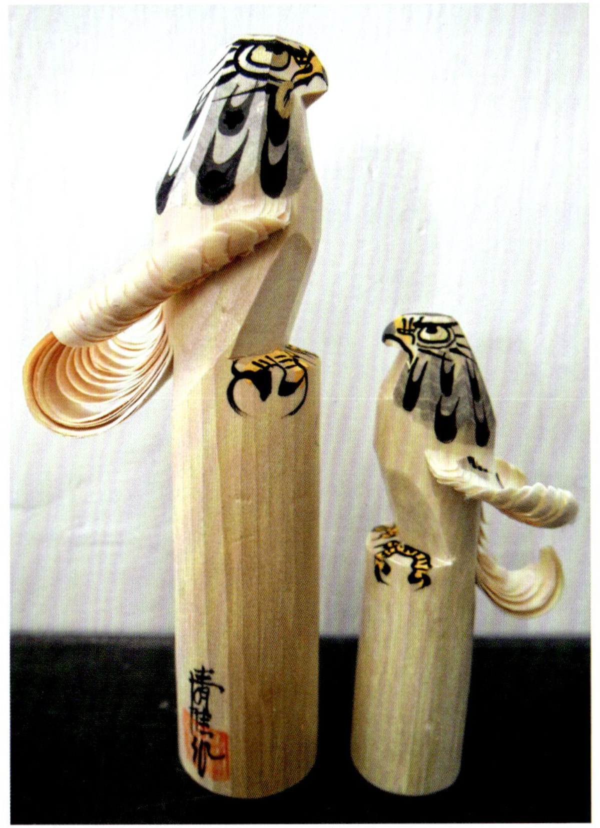

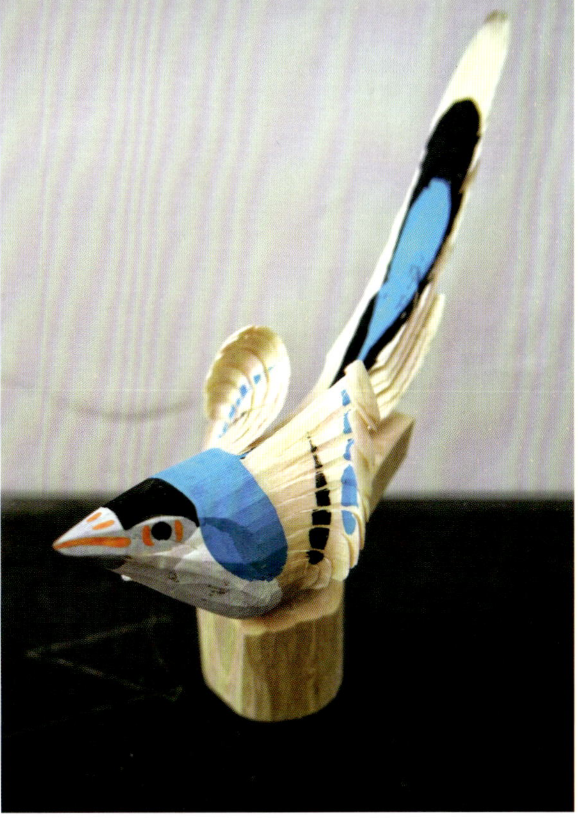

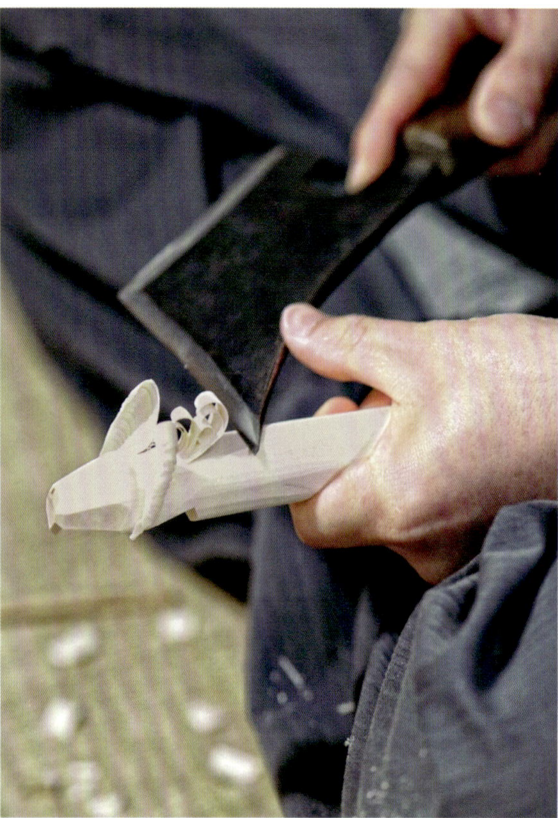

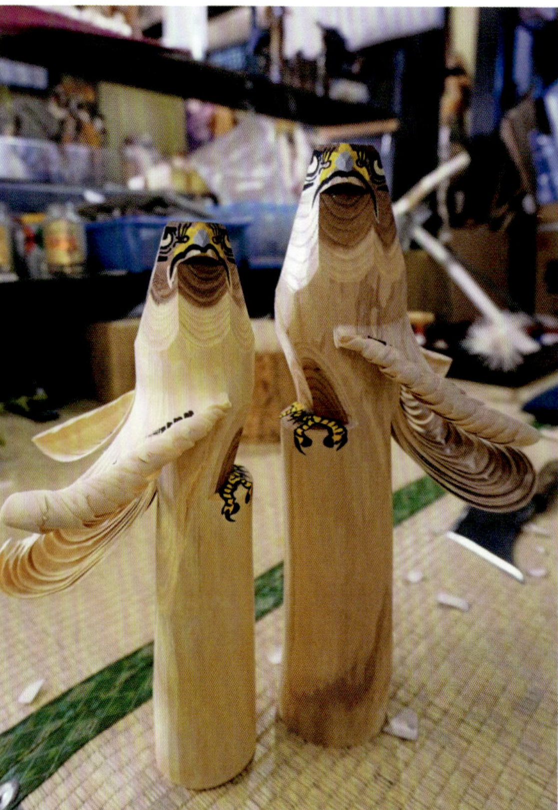

with the otaka poppo hawk figure before then. For the people who live here in Yonezawa they are part of our everyday life. There isn't a single person who isn't familiar with them. Almost all schools, banks and other public spaces are decorated with them, they are on bridge handrails and signboards—you'll see them nearly everywhere you look!

Was it easy to get an apprenticeship to this craft?

It isn't the kind of job where you fill out an application form! You have to approach the master craftsperson directly. I spent a year buildng up a relationship with my teacher before he agreed to take me on.

There are a lot of injuries to the hand caused by accidents with the blade when you're doing a craft like this, so it's a big commitment for both the teacher and the apprentice. I started off practicing the craft two to three times a week. When I sustained the inevitable injuries my teacher just said that suffering wounds is part of the process. But this can be off-putting for many people. Only those who are really passionate about it will continue.

How long does it take for someone to become a skilled artisan?

Traditionally this is a craft that farmers practice in the wintertime, when they can't work in the fields. For a typical farmer working in this way, it might take five or ten years to master the necessary skills. But if it's your main job and you do it every day, then you can learn more quickly. The most important thing to master is the correct shape, and to be able to maintain that same shape every time you carve a particular figure.

What goes through your head when you are involved in the carving process?

Usually I'm not thinking any thoughts. Your psychological condition appears in the work, so if you are in a bad mood you need to try and control it. Being irritated about something might also affect your hand movements, so you could end up having an accident. A calm state of mind is best.

Tell us about the koshiabura wood that the carvings are made from.
We go to the mountains to gather the wood. There are only certain parts of the tree we can use, so we take a chainsaw and cut it ourselves. We can't get the wood all year around, only from November to April, when the weather is really cold. It's a difficult job. The reason we go in winter is that the wood needs to be dried, and if you collect it in summer the wood breaks as you are drying it. In winter, the wood is not sucking up so much water and that is when we cut it. We often run into bears, which can be dangerous, although they don't often come after you—not like wild boars, which will chase and charge, given the chance. I've left tools up the mountain overnight, with the intention of using them the next day, but I learned quickly that the bears are likely to destroy them!

Is it hard to survive as an artisan?
We don't get welfare. I was a regular company employee and then entered this world and the first paycheck I received was for 870 yen (about US$6). The whole of that first year I only made a few hundred dollars.

What is the appeal of being a craftsperson?
If you are a maker of a traditional craft such as sasano ittobori, your skills can't be replaced easily. With assembly-line work, if one person is laid off, another person takes over—lots of jobs are like this. With our craft, it is something that only we can do.

Facing page, left Knife blades used for carving need to be sharpened every day.
Facing page, right The wood used is called koshiabura, which is soft and pliable. There isn't much use for it apart from this craft.
Below A display of sasano ittobori carvings made by Yasuhiro Koyama.

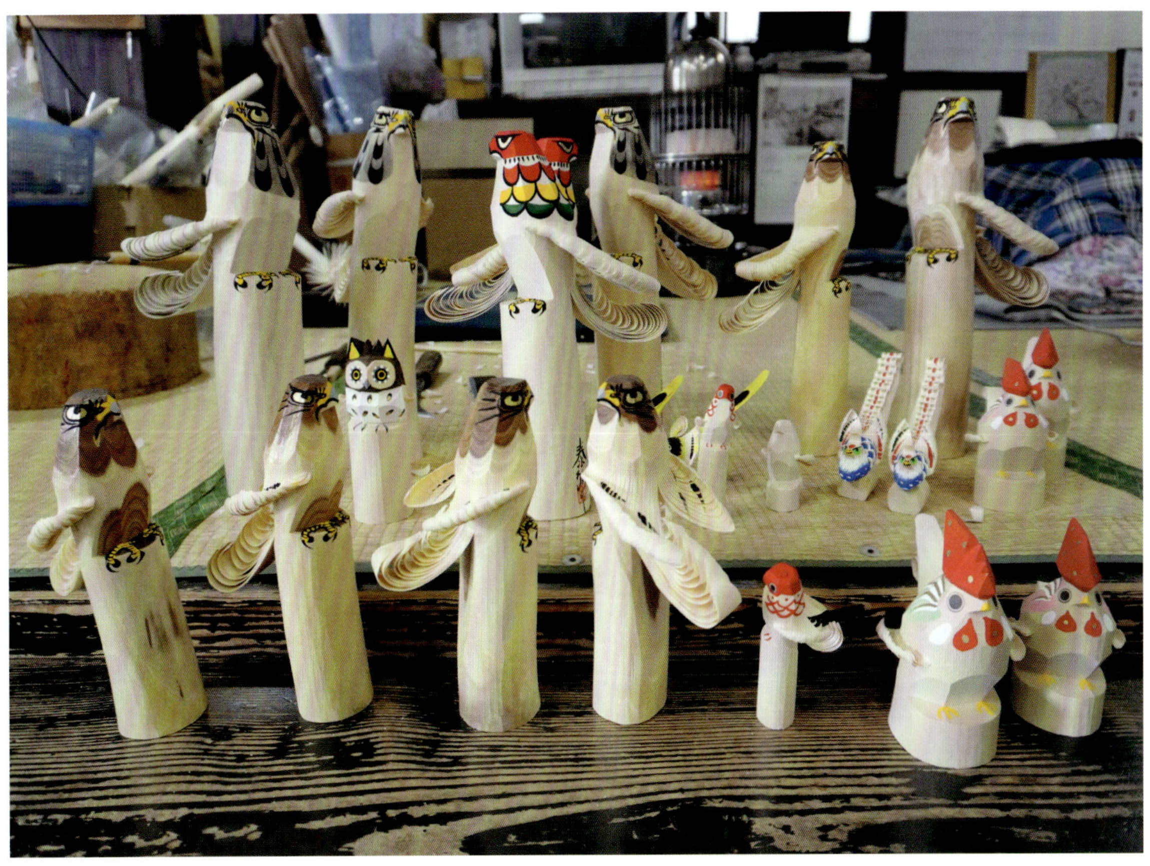

Chihiro Erasmus

A Tamba-Nuno Fabric Weaver

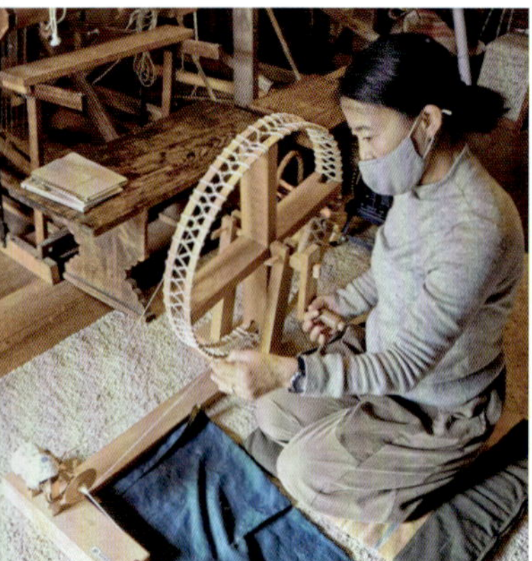

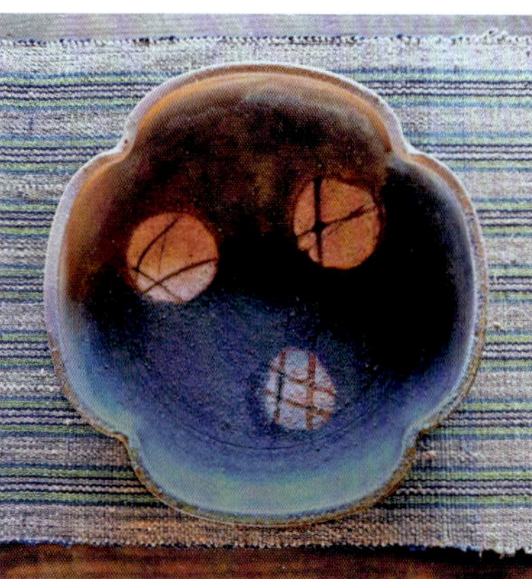

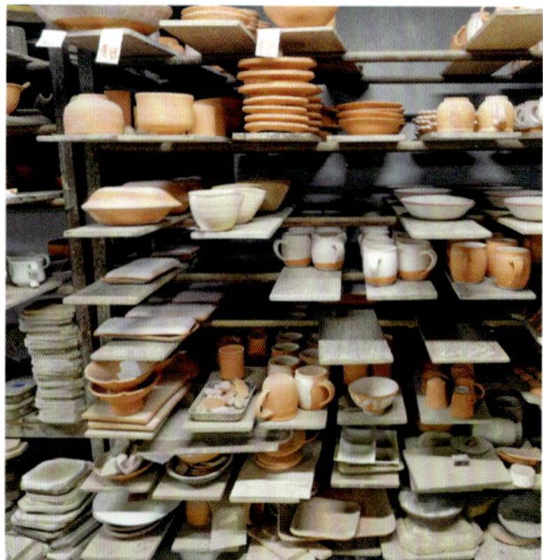

Chihiro Erasmus works at a small studio called Sankara in Tamba, Hyogo Prefecture (491 Kasugacho Kanba) where she weaves Tamba-nuno, a simple type of cotton cloth, often with checkered patterns. The production process involves spinning the cotton to make the thread, which is then colored with plant dyes. The technique took center stage during the Mingei Movement, when its leader Soetsu Yanagi discovered a sample of the then extinct weaving technique at a market and sought to revive the technical skills needed to make it. Erasmus makes not only classic obi kimono sashes but also bags and other small accessories.

Above Erasmus at work in her beautiful studio, where the cloth she makes is paired with pottery and displayed.
Facing page A selection of Tamba nuno cloth, spun and dyed by Chihiro Erasmus.

When did you first come across Tamba-nuno?
I was working in Mitami, Hyogo Prefecture, doing a regular job, when I met my husband. He was a Bizen ware pottery apprentice at the time, about to go independent. I was inspired by seeing him create things and I'd had some previous experience of weaving, with wool. When we moved to Tamba, around 2005, I took Tamba-nuno weaving classes at the Tamba City Nuno Denshokan museum.

What is the appeal of a cotton fabric like Tamba-nuno, compared to wool?
The more that you use cotton, the more it changes—it becomes stronger and softer. In the past, daily items made of cotton took on other forms as they deteriorated; for example they might be recycled as patches for clothing, then that clothing when it fell apart would become tenugui cloths and eventually rags and diapers.

What is the history of Tamba-nuno?
It was historically made in Aogakicho, a district of Tamba, and used to be called *shimanuki* or *saji momen*. It used to be shipped to Kyoto and sold there, but with Japan's industrialization

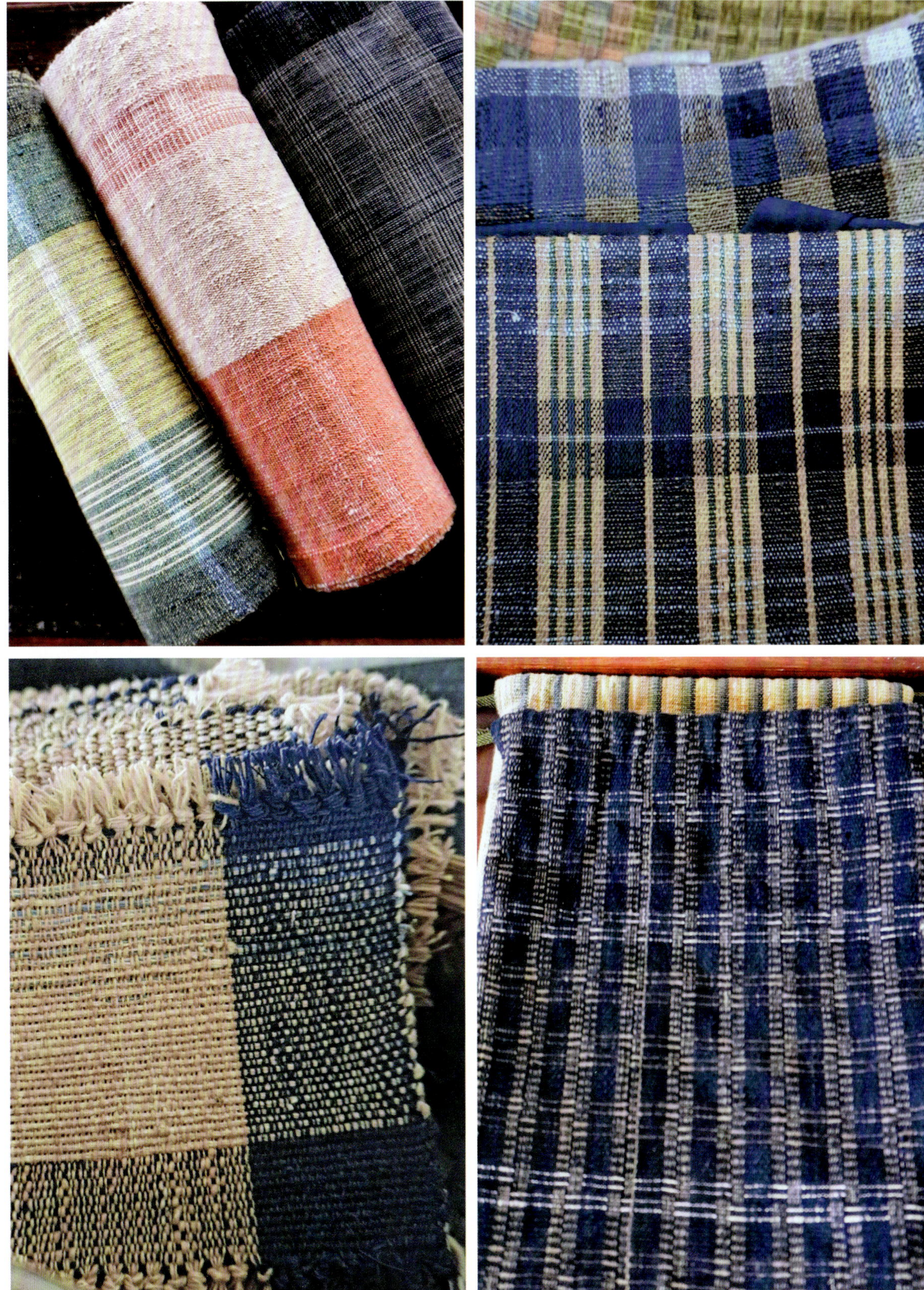

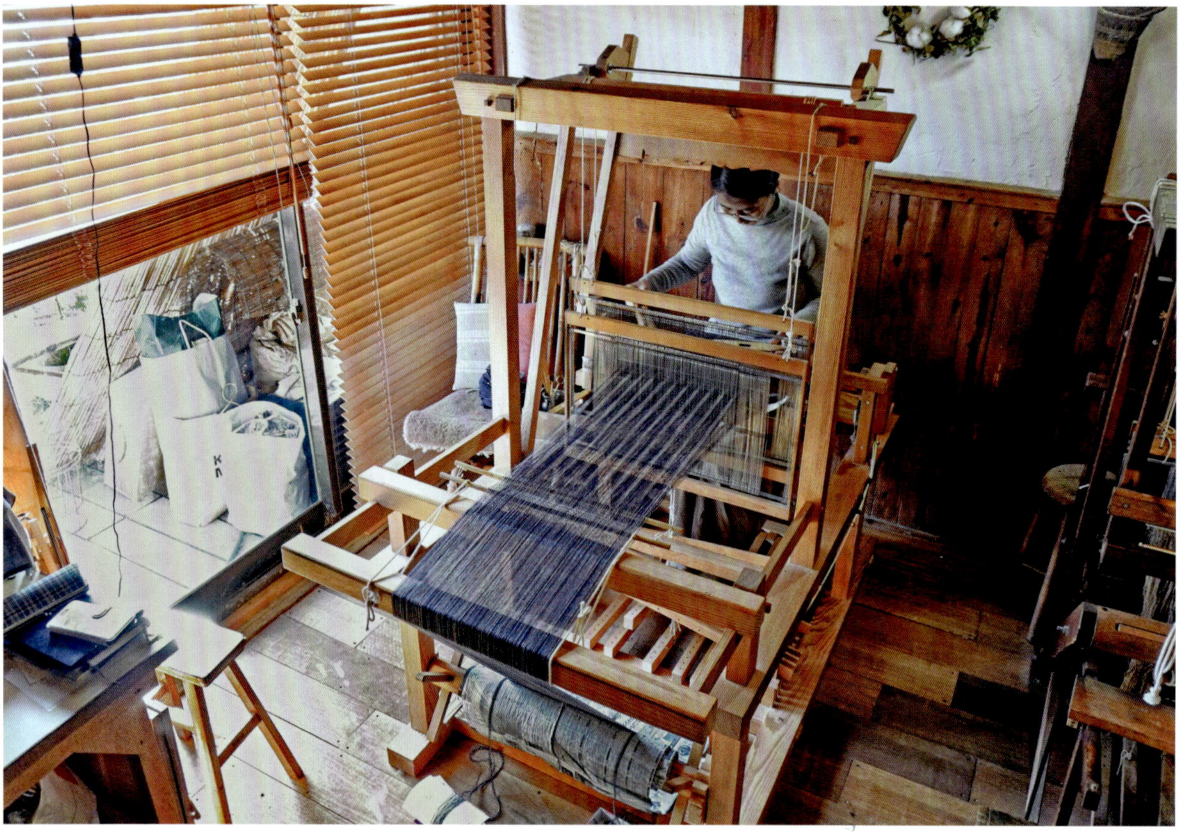

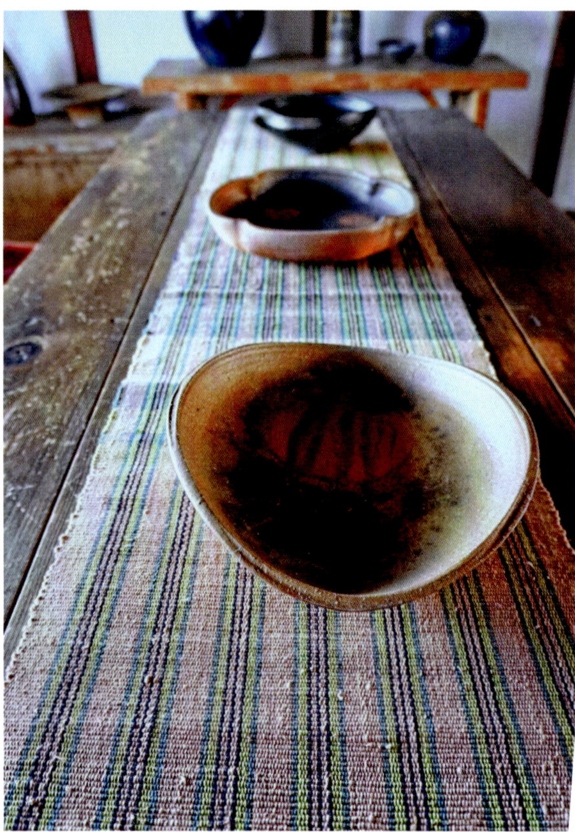

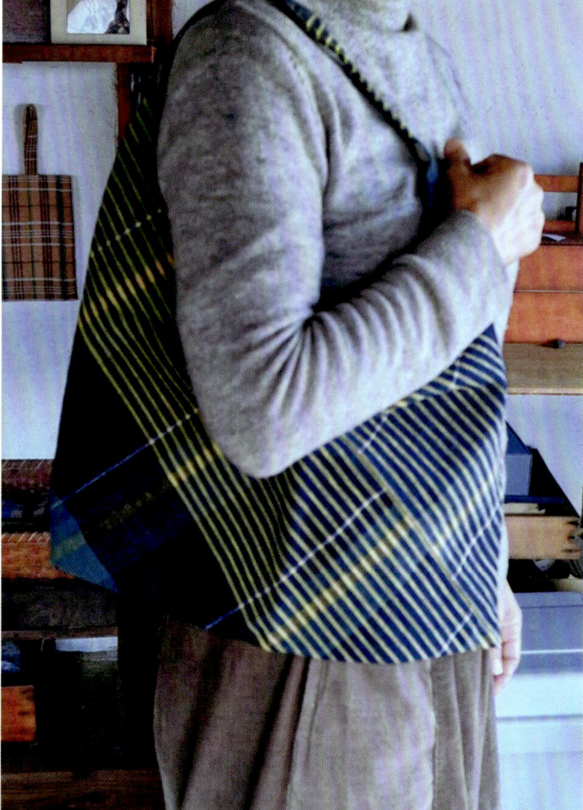

from the end of the nineteenth century onwards, cheap machine-made fabrics became popular, and this led to the disappearance of Tamba-nuno as a craft. But in the 1920s, not long after Soetsu Yanagi established the Mingei Movement, Yanagi came across a small Tamba-nuno cloth at a market in Kyoto and was fascinated by it. A friend of Yanagi's called Rokuro Uemura was interested in reviving the craft of Tamba-nuno, and gathered together a group of like-minded people. They approached the older women of Tamba and asked them to share the techniques for making Tamba-nuno, and in this way, the craft was revived.

Why does Tamba-nuno use plant-based dyes?
During Japan's industrialization from the end of the nineteenth century, chemical dyes started to become widely available. The advantage of chemical dyes is that the color takes easily and they have good staying power. With plant-based dyes, the colors fade quickly, but they also have a softness and naturalness that is very appealing.

Has Tamba-nuno become modernized over the years?
There are no rigid patterns that must be followed, so there's always been a variety of designs and colors. Recent trends include asymmetrical patterns. I like to use shades such as gray or white. But I never use mechanized processes or chemical dyes.

How do you experience the creative process?
It depends on what I'm doing. When I'm spinning, I feel with the fingertips, I listen to the spinning of the wheel. Spinning aligns with the body's rhythm. When I am dyeing I look at the colors, take in the aromas and feel the temperature. So overall, it's a sensory experience.

What do you think folk craft means to Japanese people?
I think it means appreciating the beauty of the simple, handmade items that are used as part of our everyday life. It means taking pleasure in their color, their shape and their practicality. The word "enjoyment" comes to mind. During Covid, I think a lot of people reevaluated their relationship to crafts, realizing that to make an item by hand is one of the most basic aspects of humanity, along with things like growing vegetables and cooking food. No matter how high-tech and mechanized the world becomes, I think that these fundamental things will always be appreciated.

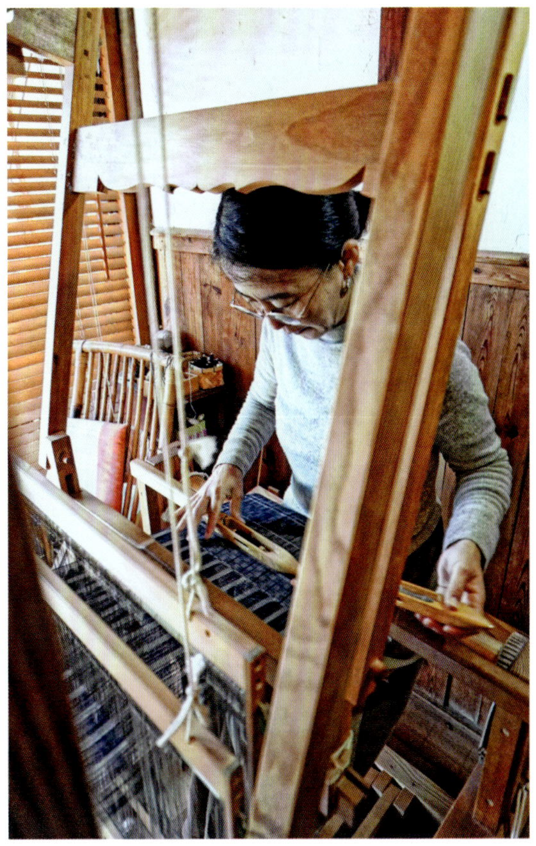

Facing page, top and this page, right Erasmus works the loom. It isn't easy to make a living from tamba fabric and it requires space and tools.
Facing page, bottom Samples of Erasmus' work: a table runner and a bag. Says Erasmus about her inspiration: "I observe nature and I think about color combinations that are beautiful."

Yuki Ogami

A Tambayaki Potter

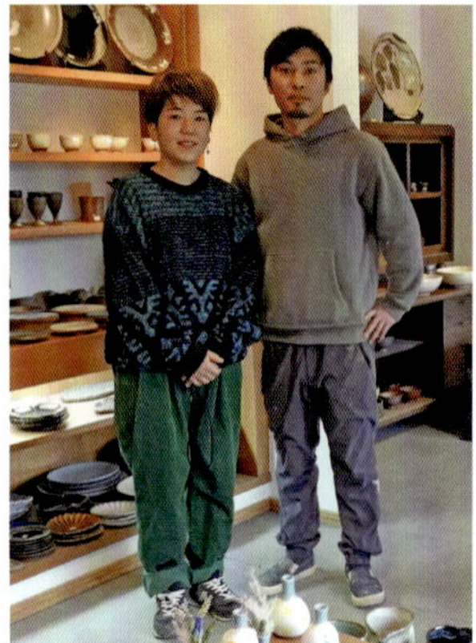
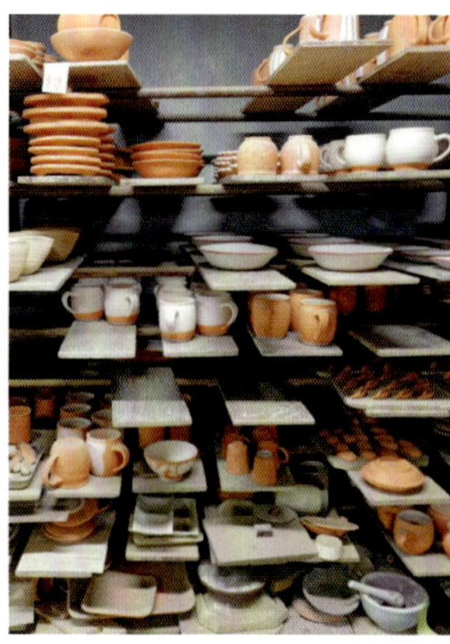
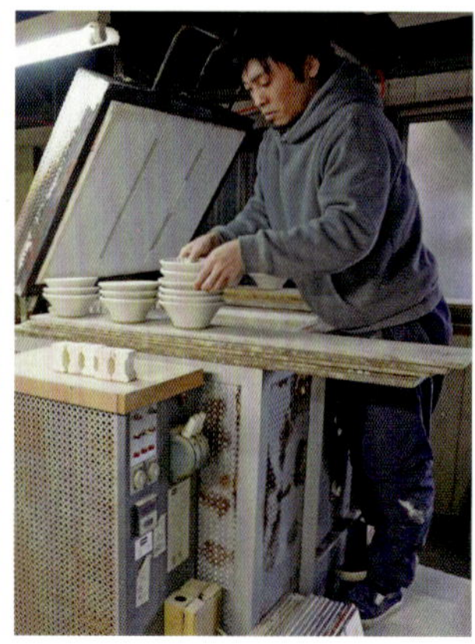

Tambayaki pottery originates in the Tachikui district of Sasayama in Hyogo Prefecture. Tambayaki is one of the six ancient kilns of Japan, with over eight hundred years of history. Traditionally, tambayaki is used to make everyday items such as bowls, pickling jars and hot water bottles. The pottery is colored by the soil of the region, which is brownish with iron from the rice fields and the mountains. It is fired in a climbing kiln, often using pine, the ash of which drifts with the flames and melts on the pots, adding delightful texture to the finished pieces. Shoyogama (8 Kondacho Shimotachikui, Tambasasayama, Hyogo) is the kiln of third-generation artisan **Yuki Ogami**, who brings a fine-art sensibility to his work.

Facing page & above Yuki Ogami works with his wife to display and sell his pottery in a stylish shop, aimed at customers who want to a add a mingei touch to their contemporary lifestyle.

How did you become a potter?
I grew up in this environment and I'd always wanted to become a ceramicist ever since I was a high school student. The impetus for finally becoming a craftsperson was going to the funeral of my grandfather, who was a tambayaki artisan. At the time I was following a science curriculum at high school because I wanted to find a career that would make me rich. But a lot of my grandfather's students came to his funeral and it was then that I truly understood the value of the work he did. I decided to change from science to the arts, and I went on to study visual arts at university.

Is it normal for an artisan to study visual arts at university?
No, it's more usual for an artisan to start by studying economics. My dad went to university first, and after that he went to trade school for a couple of years so that he could learn how to mold the clay and use the lathe. Then he came home and gradually took over the kiln—that is the normal flow for people working in tamba ware. I wanted to approach things differently, and keep my options open, so at university, I studied a range of disciplines, such as pottery, art, design and sculpture.

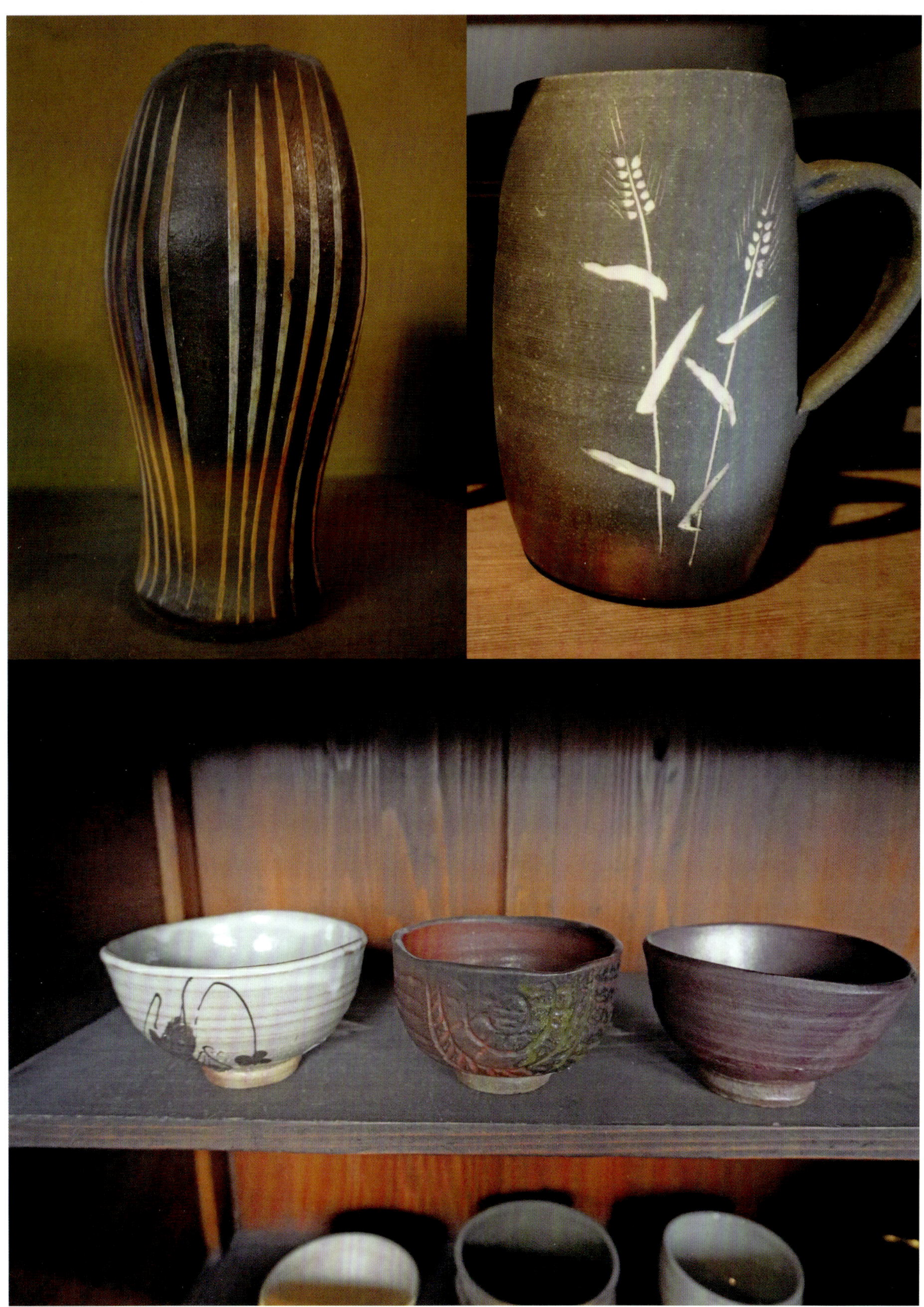

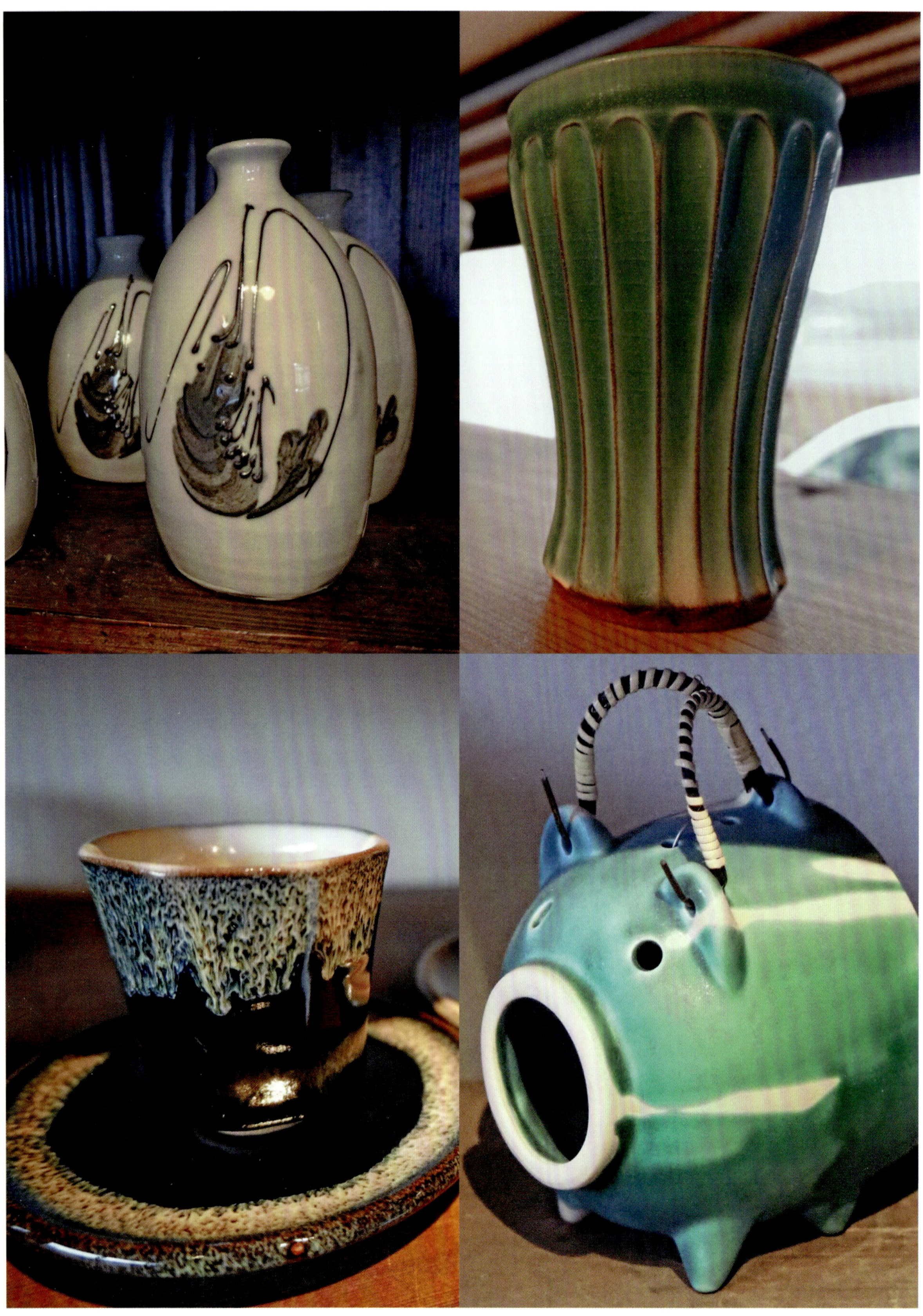

But the psychology of the artist and the artisan is quite different.

Yes, those two psychologies are totally different. I came in to this trade from the art world, thinking about my identity, how I express myself as an artist, the purpose of my existence and why I was working with clay. All questions that don't have an answer. But the regular craftspeople are thinking about practicalities, like, "Let's make these pots lighter."

What's it like being an apprentice?

There was a period in Japan when there were a lot of apprenticeships available for potters in famous pottery towns like Bizen and Seto. But that all changed during Japan's period of economic stagnation that began in the 1990s. That was the end of the apprenticeship boom. When I graduated, I was the only person in my year who managed to get an apprenticeship. I wasn't getting much income so my parents had to support me.

It was a very traditional apprenticeship environment. I was one of two apprentices, the other of whom was senior to me, and he acted as the teacher's assistant. I very rarely had any direct contact with the teacher for those first two years; I spent most of my time cleaning. When the other apprentice graduated, I was able to take his place, but even then you have to "steal" the technique through your own observation—the teacher never explained a single thing.

What do you think of this traditional apprenticeship system?

For me it was fine, but other people might want to be taught more directly. But to be a potter, you have to go out on your own independently, and I think the watching and stealing process is good preparation for that, rather than being formally taught. A traditional apprenticeship teaches you to think independently and how to solve problems.

But along the way did you have doubts?

All the time. I got lost and made mistakes repeatedly. Now that I'm working independently, when I have a problem, I wonder what my teacher would have done, and rather than remember his words, I recall watching him from behind and that enables me to think, "he would have done this."

To work alone as a ceramicist, you need motivation. You need the right psychology, guts and perseverance.

Now artisans have to do marketing and everything else—do you find that difficult?

My brother is in Tokyo and he helps me out with marketing. My friend from Kanazawa University wanted to help with art direction. He is now in Kyoto but he'd come here once a month and he got to know about tambayaki. We also collaborated with a spatial and visual designer who helped us make a studio that people can come and visit.

Once a week, for two to three hours, we have a meeting, and we are always thinking about what will happen to tambayaki in ten or twenty years. Tambayaki has an eight-hundred-year lineage and there are sixty other potters in this area. In the olden days crafts were passed down from family member to family member, but this is no longer the case and we need to be constantly thinking about the best way to ensure that tambayaki continues.

Facing page A selection of tambayaki pottery items ranging from sake jugs to a mosquito-coil holder, The prawn (top left) is a common Tamba motif, and was found on an Edo-period piece. One theory for the popularity of the prawn motif is that it was aspirational to have seafood while drinking in a landlocked region.

Yuji Sakai

A Warazaiku Rice-Straw Artisan

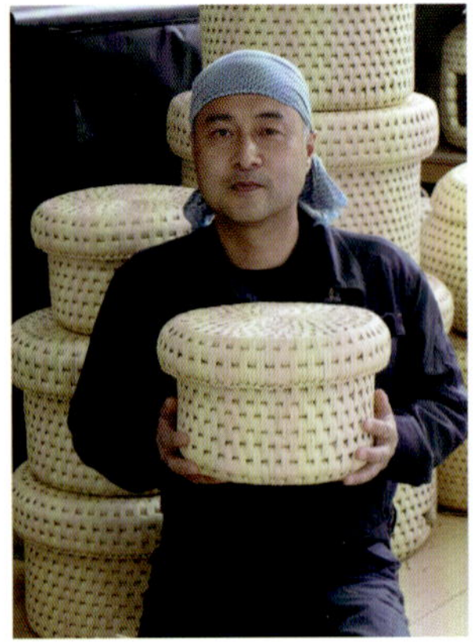
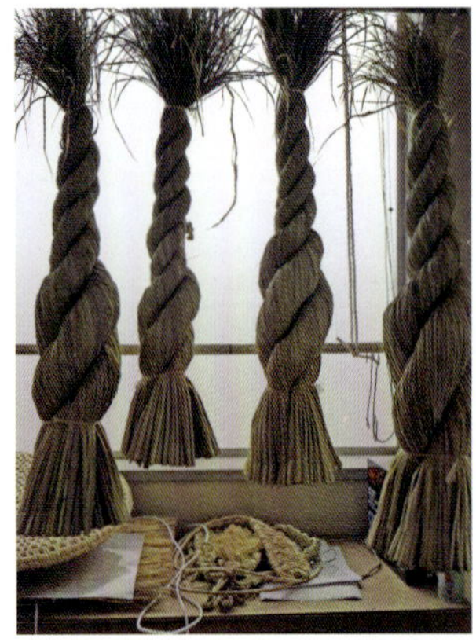
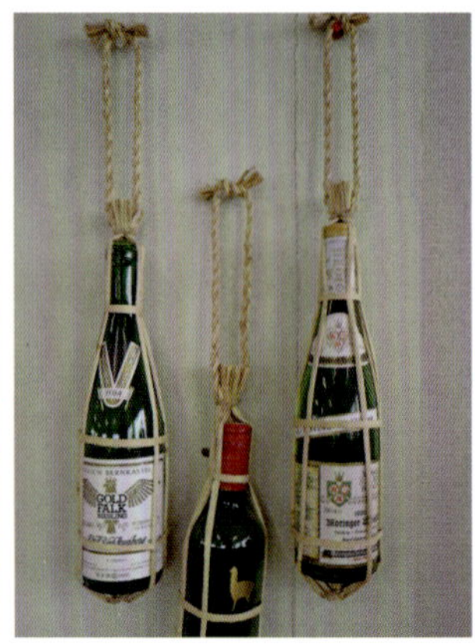

Warazaiku rice-straw artisan **Yuji Sakai** (1482-3 Iijima, Kamiina, Nagano; tel: 0265-95-3315) had an unusual start in the world of mingei. He was working as a butcher and needed a decorative rice bale for an event. They were hard to source and prohibitively expensive and this led to him asking an artisan for an apprenticeship and become a professional warazaiku craftsman. He now has a British apprentice and is proactively working to introduce traditional Japanese straw crafts to a global audience.

Facing page & above A variety of straw items crafted by Yuji Sakai, including his very popular cat basket (this page, top left).

What is warazaiku?
Warazaiku is the craft of making items out of rice straw, traditionally carried out by farmers during the winter season when there is no work in the fields. *Wara*, or rice straw, is versatile and traditionally used for *mino* raincoats and *waraji* straw sandals. It has a lovely aroma, is cool in summer and warm in winter. However, wara is most often used for *shimenawa* ropes that hang at the entrance to Shinto temples, and *shimekazari* New Year's decorations, as well as for the rice bales marking the perimeter of the sumo ring.

Can you tell us about the type of rice straw that is used for warazaiku?
We use rice stalks that are harvested before the rice appears. The rice harvest in Japan is usually in September, but we cut the stalks in July. The color of the straw made from these stalks is really beautiful. Regular straw is brown but this is green and aromatic. We cultivate this straw specifically for use in crafts.

Straw is used in a lot of Japanese religious rituals. Can you talk a little bit about that?
In the native Japanese Shinto religion it is believed that gods reside everywhere, even

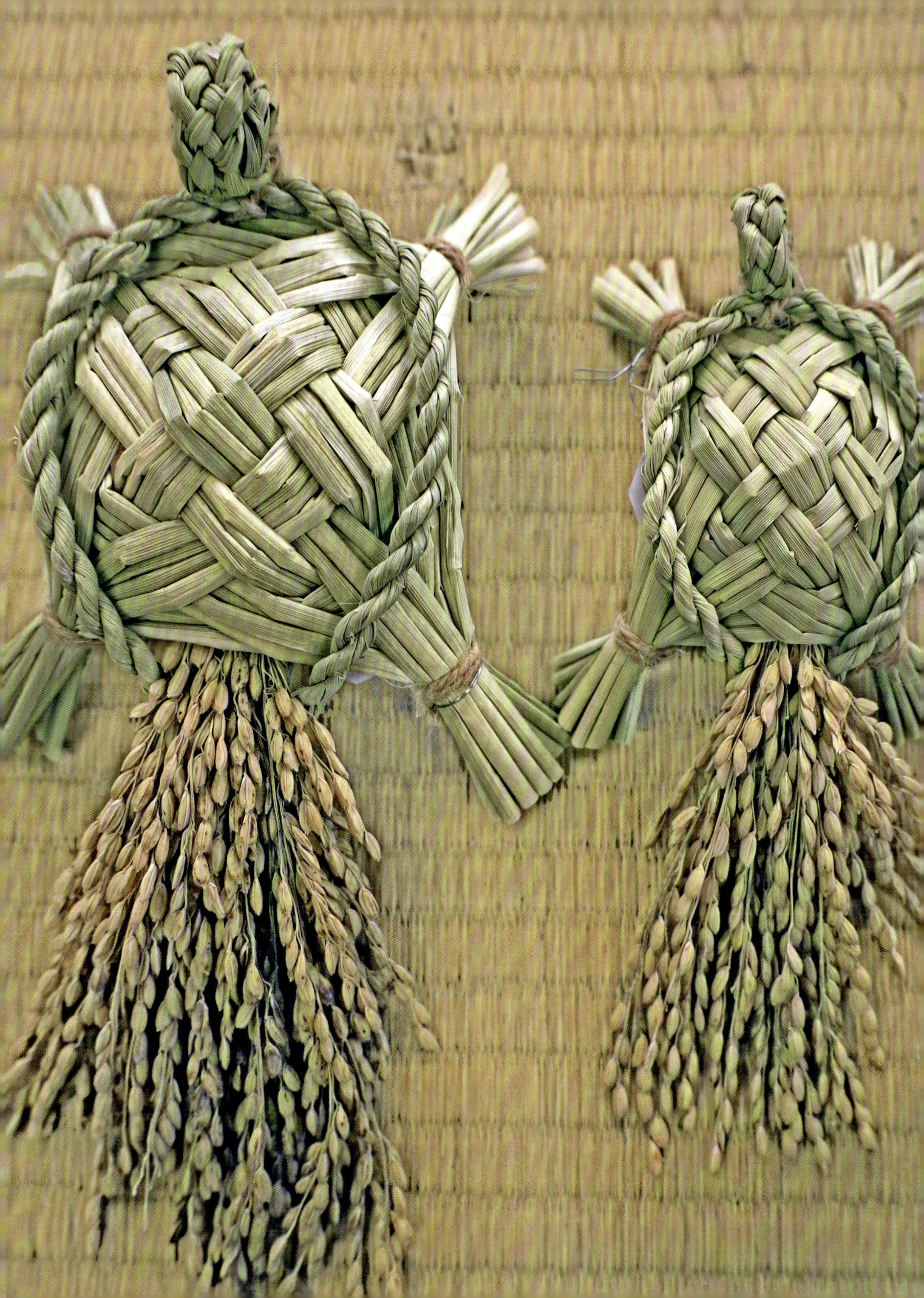

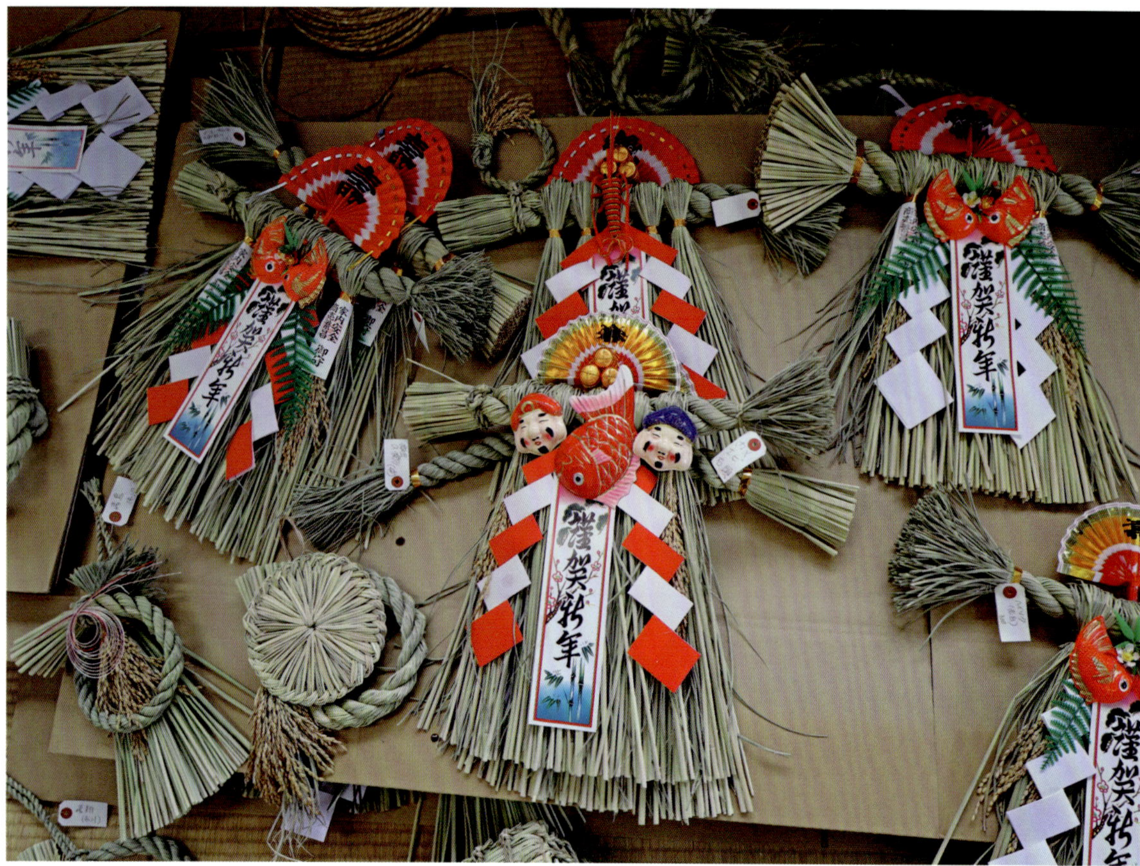

in rice straw. Amulets made of rice straw are thought to be able to beckon the gods. If you go to a Shinto shrine, you'll notice that many of the decorative elements are made of straw.

Rice straw is traditionally used in many Japanese New Year's traditions too.
It is traditional in Japan to adorn the front of houses with straw decorations, as a way of beckoning the gods. It is said that the Japanese Shinto religion has "eight million gods"—it's not an exact number but it demonstrates the traditional belief that there is a god present in almost everything.

You also make contemporary items with cute motifs like cats—are they selling well?
Yes, there's a market for contemporary items among young women in particular. They tend to buy things like cat- or turtle-shaped amulets and talismans. There's also been a recent boom in cat ownership in Japan and our rice-straw cat baskets have attracted a lot of attention in the media.

How is the old craft of warazaiku evolving in contemporary Japan?
Young people aren't that interested in traditional things, in fact people overseas are more interested. But I think that recently there has been a revival of interest in authentic folk crafts. So gradually our sales are going up. Also people aren't eating as much rice in Japan, so there are quite a few open rice fields that we can use to cultivate rice to be used for warazaiku. Perhaps as well as resuscitating an ancient craft, we can also bring about some kind of agricultural revitalization.

This page; facing page top right and bottom right Shimenawa—decorative lengths of rice straw that are used for various rituals in the Shinto religion.
Facing page, top left Turtle-shaped talismans are popular contemporary items among young women.
Facing page, bottom left An artisan works with green rice straw, which has a lovely aroma and color.

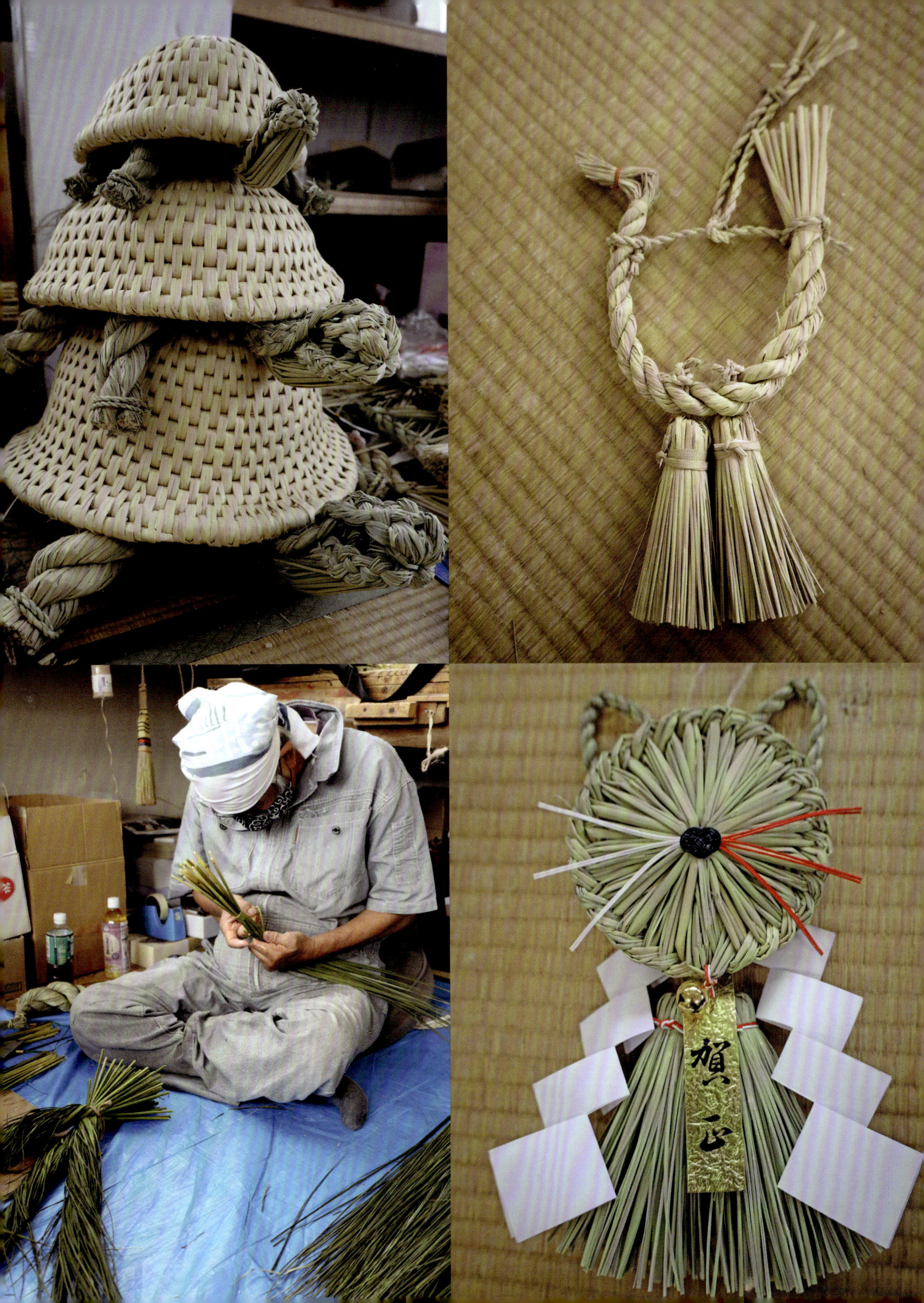
賀正

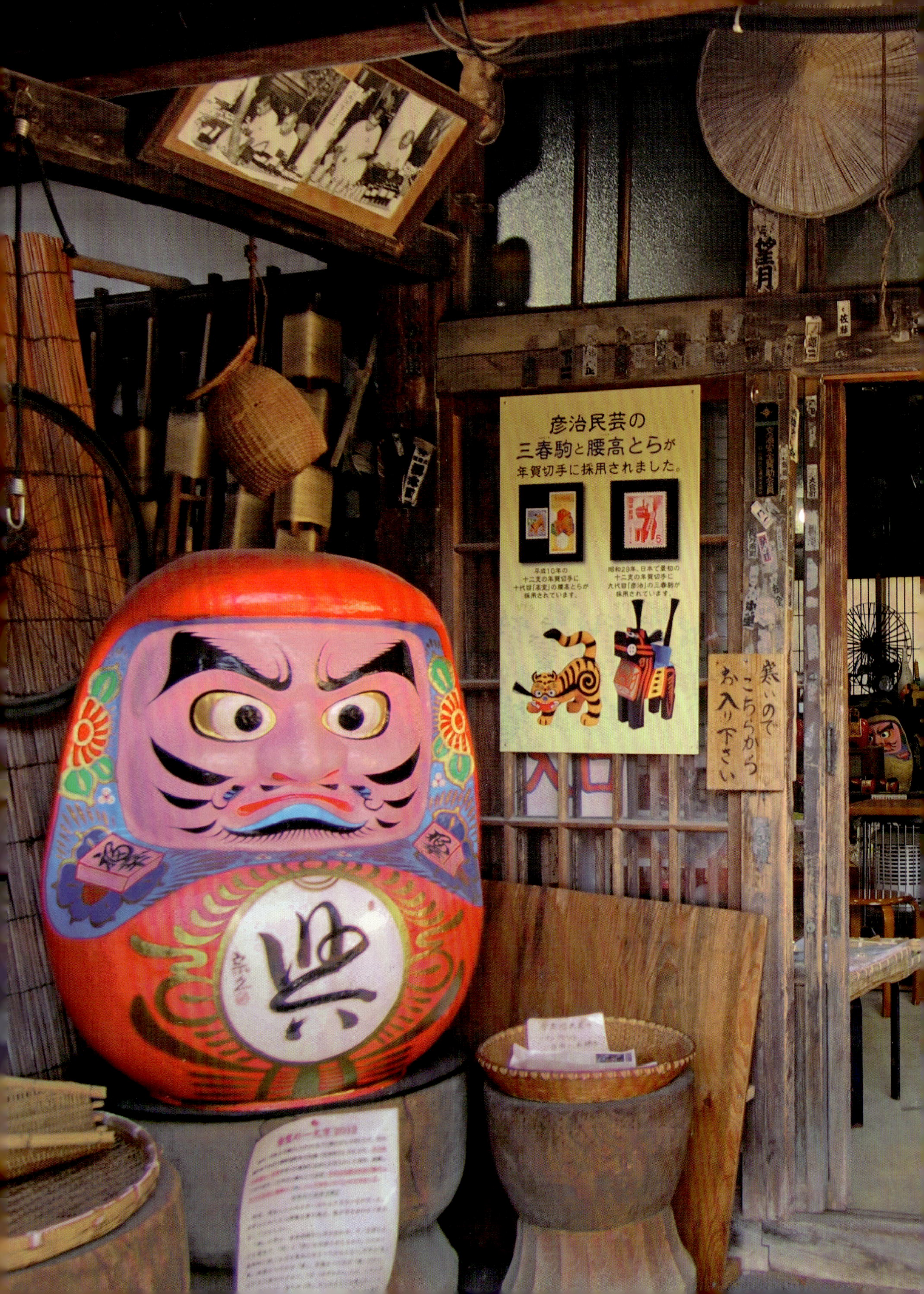
彦治民芸の
三春駒と腰高とらが
年賀切手に採用されました。
寒いので
こちらから
お入り下さい

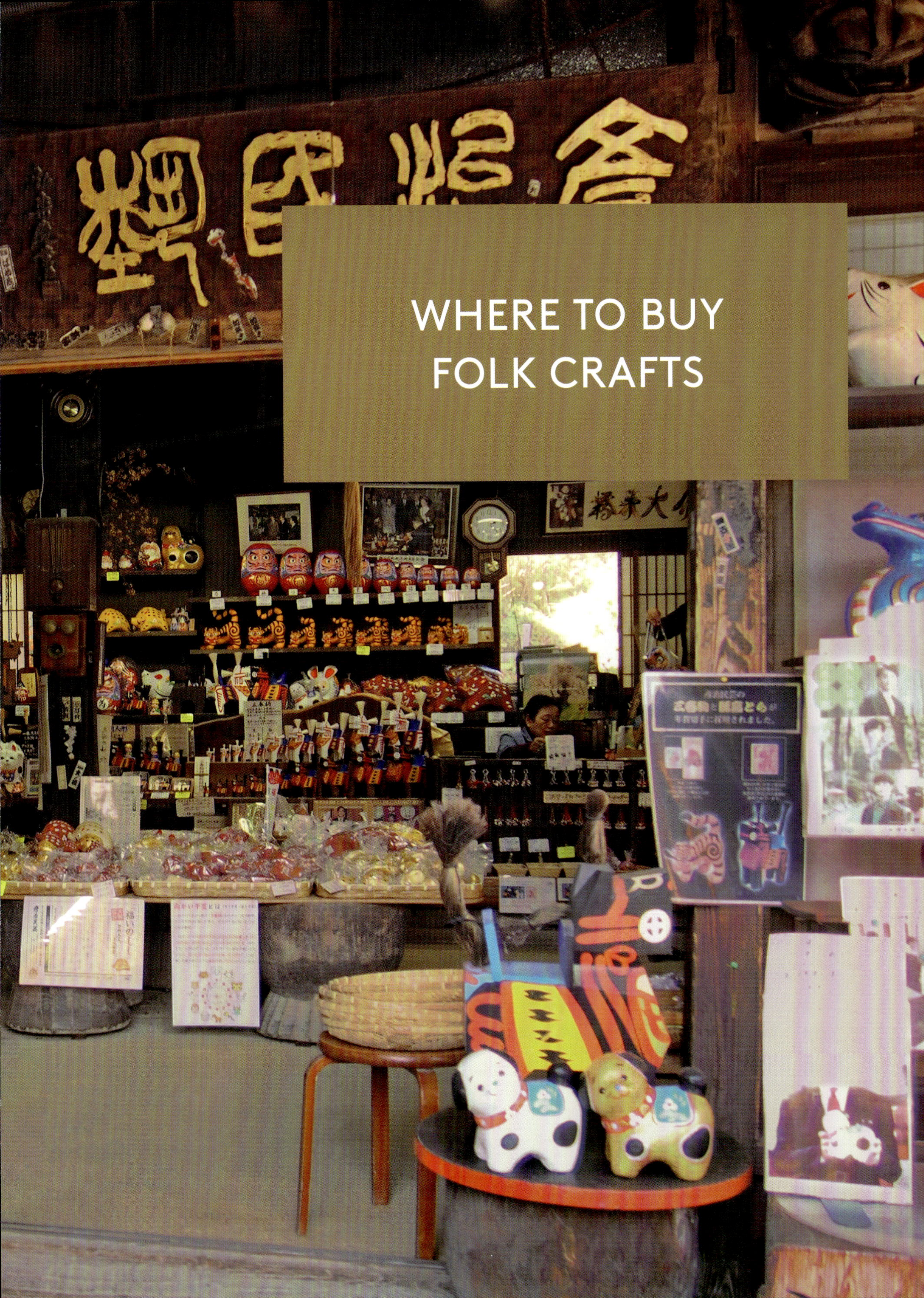

WHERE TO BUY FOLK CRAFTS

There are many ways to experience folk crafts when you are visiting Japan. You can visit a festival devoted to a craft such as a lantern festival (page 49) or a Daruma doll festival (page 53). Or you can go directly to specific artisan studios that accept visitors. At an artisan studio you can see the artisan at work as well as support their livelihood. The atmosphere at these studios is sublime and watching a craftsperson produce an item with their own hands can be an awe-inspiring and meditative experience. Rather than tour aimlessly around Japan, many travelers are discovering the pleasures of themed travel to specific destinations, and "mingei hopping" is one of the ways to enjoy Japan's less visited regions as well as to appreciate the local environment that gave birth to a particular craft. Listed in this section are folk-craft districts where there are a number of mingei-related places to visit. Bear in mind that if you visit a folk-craft museum you may find that the exhibits do not have explanations or artist credits. This is because the ethos of the founders of the Mingei Movement was to highlight the aesthetic value and beauty of folk crafts without context. *When planning to visit any of the places mentioned in this book, remember that many Japanese people do not speak English and it may be a good idea to ask for the help of a native-Japanese speaker when making telephone calls.*

AICHI PREFECTURE

Toyota City Folk Craft Museum (86-100 Haiwa, Hiratobashi, Toyota; tel: 0565-45-4039) is located in a forest next to Hiratobashi Park. There are three themed areas that focus on clothing, food and housing as well as a ceramics museum to commemorate ceramics scholar Shizuo Honda. The museum regularly hosts events and lectures on mingei. Visitors can try their hand at crafts like *shibori* tie-dye and enjoy a cup of matcha green tea in the teahouse.

Akita's Kakunodate Bukeyashi area has old architecture and folk-craft shops.

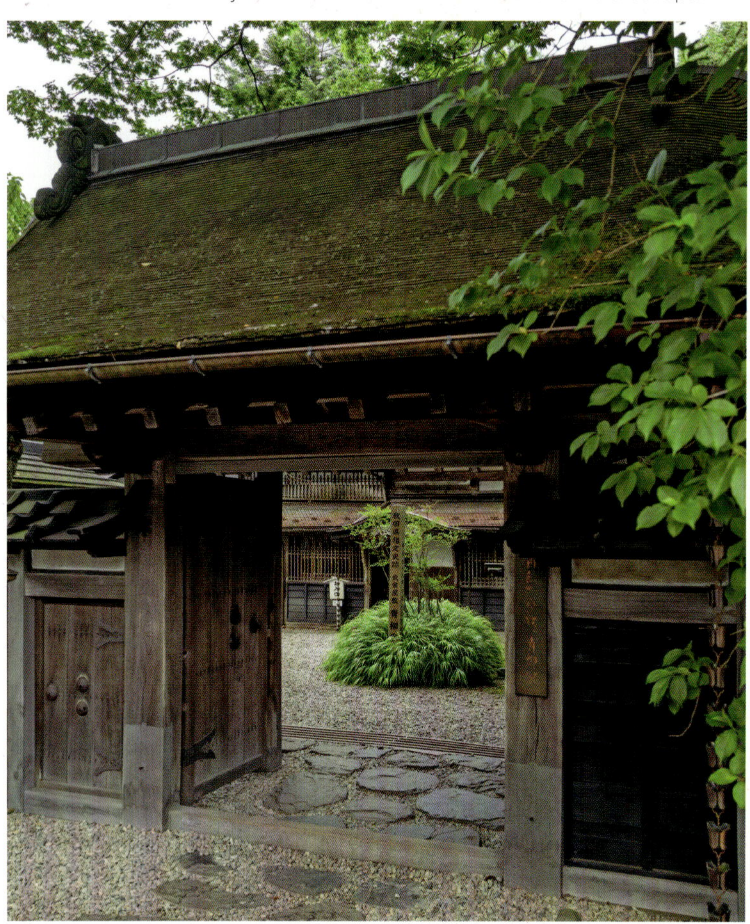

AKITA PREFECTURE

The picturesque Kakunodate Bukeyashiki district in Kakunodate, has well-preserved samurai residences and other traditional architecture. There are several shops selling various types of folk craft. The Kabazaiku Museum (10-1 Kakunodate, Omotemachishimocho, Semboku; tel: 0187-54-1700) has on-site cherry bark artisans, as well as displays related to agricultural tools, talismans and craft items for daily life. The museum shop sells crafts from across Akita Prefecture, such as itayazaiku wickerwork trays, baskets and toy foxes.

The Namahage Museum (Mizukuisawa Kitaurashinzan, Oga; tel: 0185-22-5050) is devoted to a local folkloric demon called the *namahage*. There are dozens of impressive regional masks and costumes from sixty areas in the region. The neighboring Oga Shinzan Folklore Museum is housed in a traditional farmhouse, and a number of traditional crafts

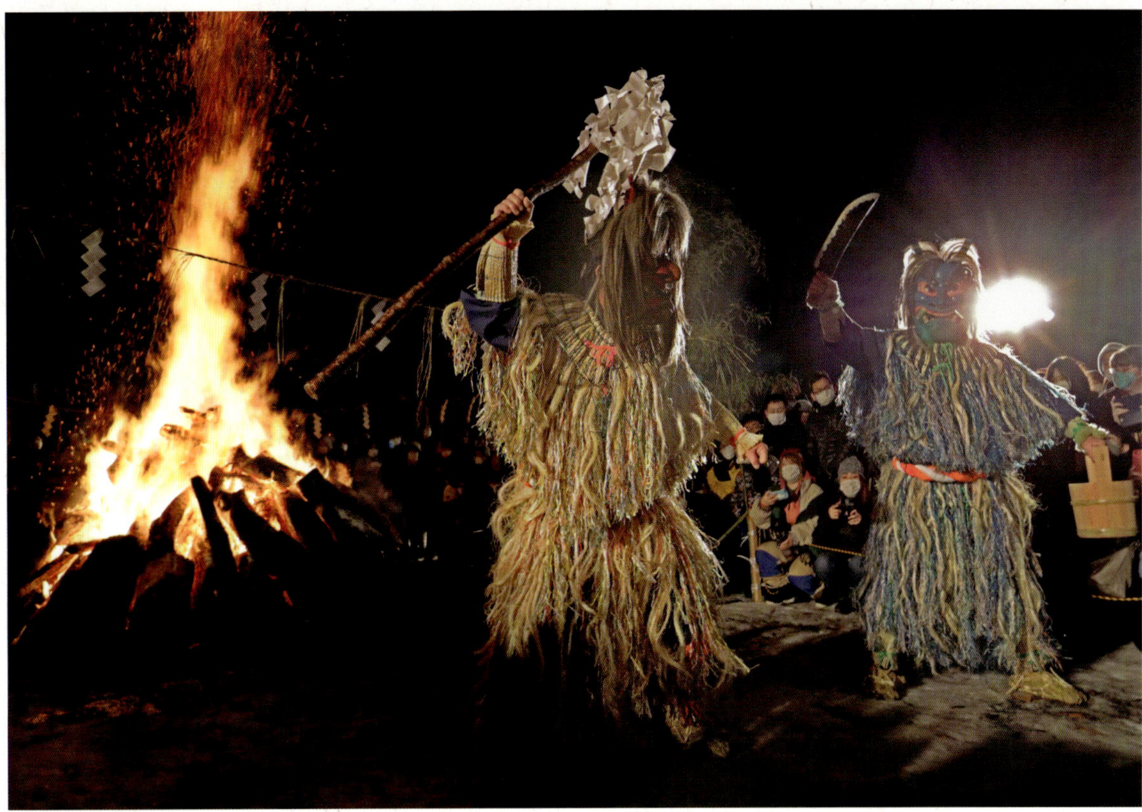

Namahage are local folkloric demons from Akita Prefecture.

are on display, such as *mino* straw raincoats and straw boots.

AOMORI PREFECTURE

One of the names associated with the Mingei Movement, Shiko Munakata (1903–1975), was a woodblock artist born in Aomori Prefecture and supported by Soetsu Yanagi. He is considered to be one of the most important woodblock artists of the twentieth century and his work often features strongly expressive Buddhist imagery. The Shiko Munakata Memorial Museum of Art (2-1-2 Matsubara; tel: 017-777-4567) in Aomori City is devoted to his work.

The Tsugaru Traditional Craft Museum in Kuroishi (65-1 Tomiyama, Fukuro; tel: 0172-59-5300) has a number of artisan studios specializing in various crafts, including lacquerware and kokeshi-shaped lanterns, and is located next to the Tsugaru Kokeshi Museum (72-1 Tomiyama, Fukuro, Kuroishi; tel: 0172-54-8181), one of the best places to source beautiful kokeshi dolls from contemporary artisans.

EHIME PREFECTURE

The Ehime Folk Craft Museum (238-8 Akeyashiki, Saijo; tel: 0897-56-2110), established in 1967, features regional mingei with over two thousand artifacts from the seventeenth century to the present.

FUKUSHIMA PREFECTURE

Dekoyashiki is a village of gorgeous Edo-era folk houses. As well as being a great example of traditional folk architecture, the village specializes in crafting many kinds of folk toy, such as the Miharu horse, Miharu Daruma dolls, masks, and papier-mâché talismans in the shape of zodiac animals. One of the oldest residences, Hikoji (80-1 Tateno, Nishitamachi Takashiba, Koriyama; tel: 024-972-2412) has a kayabuki thatched roof and an interior with thick wooden beams, all constructed without nails. The house is filled with folk toys and is a visual treat.

Daruma Land (30 Yokomachi, Shirakawa; tel: 0248-23-3978) is a fairly new establishment dedicated to Daruma dolls. The main building is a restored folk house and there are on-site artisans at work, many of whom are female. Visitors can observe them as they paint the dolls. The warehouse has hundreds of Daruma for sale in a variety of patterns and colors.

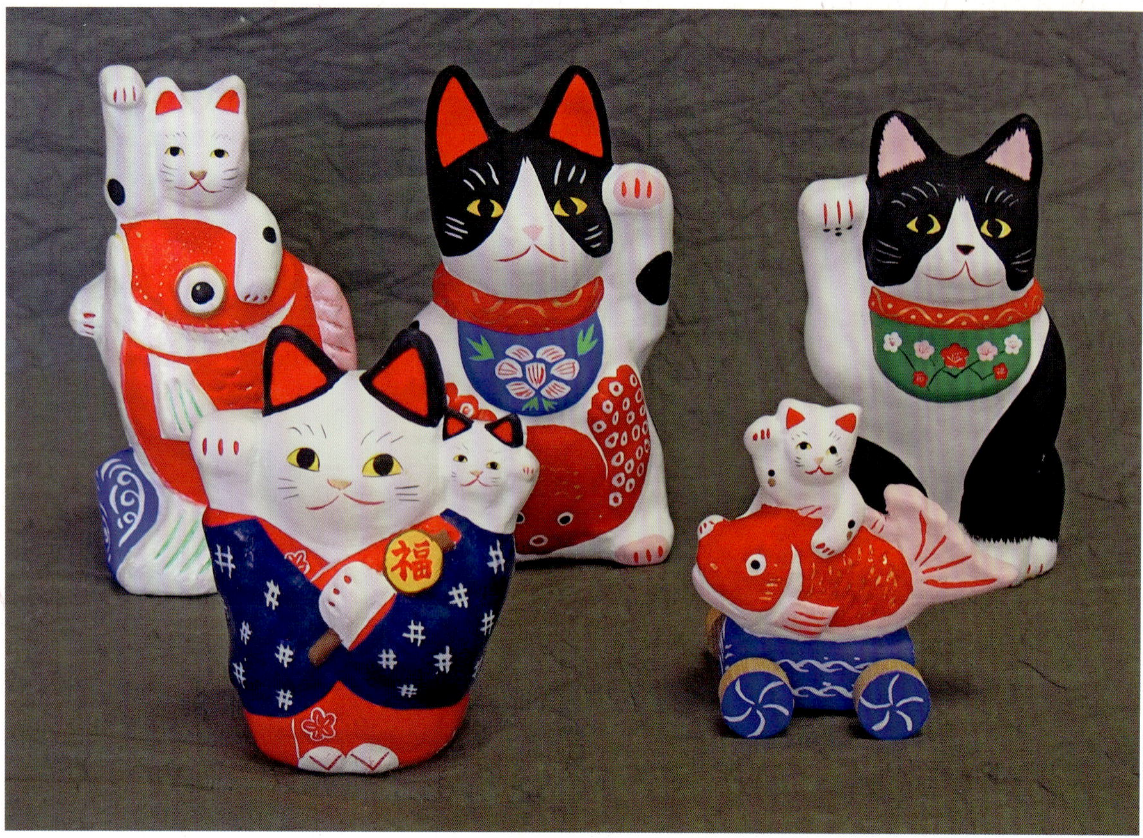

Maneki-neko beckoning cats are a popular souvenir in Japan.

GIFU PREFECTURE

Kusakabe Mingeikan in Takayama (1-55 Oshinmachi; tel: 0577-32-0072) is a showcase of the region's folk craft, housed inside a nineteenth-century merchant house made by local artisans using cypress wood, with 42-foot (13-meter) beams.

Hida Folk Village (1-590 Kamioka-motomachi, Takayama; tel: 0577-33-4711) is a picturesque open-air museum with thirty traditional thatched farmhouses ranging from 100–500 years of age. The museum sits on top of a mountain that overlooks the Takayama Valley. Most of the farmhouses are open to the public, and contain folk items that were used in daily life such as tools for raising silkworms, and weaving looms. Visitors can appreciate the role that traditionally crafted items played in the everyday lives of rural folk while strolling around the grounds. Some of the houses host craft workshops, where visitors can try their hand at straw crafts or lacquerwork, and there is a souvenir shop as well.

HOKKAIDO

Japan's northernmost main island of Hokkaido has a number of museums and other attractions devoted to the culture and crafts of the Ainu indigenous people of northern Japan, who have their own unique culture, customs and beliefs. The Ainu were predominantly hunter-gatherers and held animistic views. Japan colonized their ancestral territories, a process that intensified after the Meiji Revolution of 1868, and resulted in the near extinction of the Ainu people. Attempts have been made to preserve and promote what is left of their culture and crafts.

Sapporo Pirka Kotan (27 Koganeyu, Minami-ku, Sapporo; tel: 011-596-5961) is a small cultural center in Sapporo that exhibits artifacts related to Ainu culture, which visitors are allowed to handle.

The Upopoy National Ainu Museum (2-3 Wakakusacho, Shiraoi; tel: 0144-82-3914) is located in the town of Shiraoi on the south coast of Hokkaido, a one hour drive from Sapporo. The museum has a collection of textiles, talismans, utensils for hunting and cooking, and a vast array of religious items. The museum restaurant serves Ainu food. There is also a park with a number of folk houses, and a concert hall for performances of Ainu dance and traditional instruments. Also south of Sapporo, the Nibutani Ainu Culture Museum (55-55 Nibutani, Biratori, Saru; tel: 01457-2-2892) has over nine hundred folk artifacts including Japan's largest dugout boat.

The resplendent Lake Akan is home to the Ainu Kotan Village (4-7-19 Akancho Akanko Onsen, Kushiro; tel: 0154-67-2727) where you'll find many artisan ateliers specializing in crafts such as woodworking and embroidery. There are a number of Ainu restaurants serving traditional dishes. Visitors can also go to the Lake Akan Ainu Theater (7-84-4 Akanko Onsen, Kushiro) to see ceremonial dances, puppet shows and other performances.

Asahikawa has a number of Ainu-related sites including the Kawamura Kaneto Ainu Memorial Museum (11 Hokumoncho, Asahikawa; tel: 0166-51-2461), and the Asahikawa City Museum, (Kagura 3-7, Asahikawa; tel: 0166-69-2004) which is devoted to the preservation of Ainu artifacts from the Kamikawa district, with over 1000 items in their inventory. Nearby Kamikawa has a number of woodworker artisans who carve bear statues, one of the famous crafts of Hokkaido.

IWATE PREFECTURE

Kogensha (2-18 Zaimokucho, Morioka; tel: 019-622-2894) is a legendary folk-craft store founded by publisher Shiro Oikawa, known for publishing famed magical-realism writer Kenji Miyazawa's *The Restaurant of Many Orders*. Oikawa's company went on to sell mingei, attracting the attention of mingei proponents such as Soetsu Yanagi, Keisuke Serizawa and Shiko Munakata. Visiting the flagship store at the address above is like a pilgrimage of sorts. There are other branches of the Kogensha store in the cities of Morioka and Sendai.

Iwate Prefecture's Tono Valley is a significant region for folklore studies, being home to a number of folktales featuring spirits and ghosts that were collated by folklorist Kunio Yanagita and compiled into his famous book, *The Legends of Tono*. This bucolic valley has a number of traditional farmhouses, and attractions such as the Tono Furusato Village (5-89-1 Kamitsukimoshi, Tsukimoshi, Tono; tel: 0198-64-2300), and the Denshoen historical theme park (6-5-1 Tsuchibuchi, Tsuchibuchi, Tono; tel: 0198-62-8655) which has displays of various folk tools and crafts.

Local museums that also have significant folk culture displays and collections are the Tono Jokamachi Museum (4-6 Chuo-dori, Tono, Iwate; tel: 0198-62-2340), the Tono Monogatari no Yakata Museum (2-11 Chuodori, Tono; tel: 0198-62-7887) and the Tono Municipal Museum (3-9 Higashidate, Tono; tel: 0198-62-2340).

Morioka Handi-Works Square (Oirino-64-102 Tsunagi, Morioka; tel: 0196-89-2201) is a large collection of shops and studios sprawled across expansive grounds, where tourists can also participate in various activities, such as folk-craft workshops. There is also an example of an L-shaped *magariya* folk house (shaped like a L to accommodate built-in stables for horses) and an exhibition of farming implements. Among the artisan studios, there are fabric dyers, folk-toy artisans and bamboo artisans.

The Oni no Yakata Museum in Kitakami (16-131 Wagacho Iwasaki; tel: 0197-73-8488) is devoted to the study of *oni* demons. There are a number of exhibits related to oni in Iwate, across Japan, and abroad, and displays of masks and folk costumes from festivals including Iwate's Onikenbai dance. The museum often gives dance performances and mask-making workshops.

KYOTO

Potter and member of the Mingei Movement Kanjiro Kawai lived in Kyoto for most of his career. His atelier, which he designed himself in 1937, is preserved as the museum Kawai Kanjiro's House (569 Kaneicho, Gojozaka, Higashiyama; tel: 075-561-3585). Here you can see his work, which includes pottery, calligraphy and woodcarving. There is also a climbing kiln in the backyard. The house is a tranquil respite from the tourist-laden streets of Kyoto.

KYUSHU

The Kumamoto Mingei Museum (1-5-2 Tatsuda, Kita-ku; tel: 096-338-7504) is housed in an old brewery building in Kyushu's western city of Kumamoto, and is a repository for the three-thousand-piece collection of Kichinosuke Tonomura who dedicated his life to the mingei philosophy advocated by Soetsu Yanagi. Particularly delightful is the display of handcrafted toys from across the world.

Tonomura was also the founder of the Kurashiki Mingei Museum (see page 155) but recognizing the abundance of folk craft in Kyushu, decided to open a mingei museum in Kumamoto.

Located in a hot-spring resort near the city of Oita, the Kyushu Yufuin Mingei Village (Kawakita,

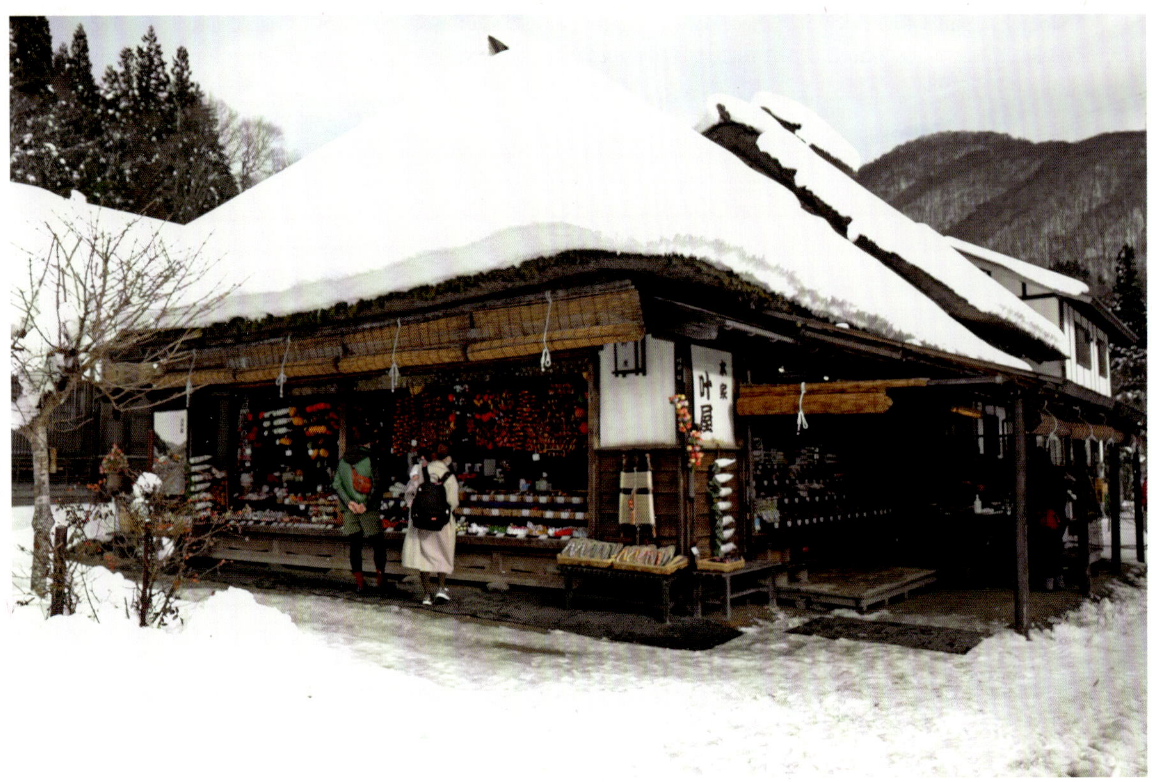

"Mingei-hopping" is a way to appreciate the environment that gave birth to a craft.

Yufu; tel: 0977-84-2021) has displays of many folk crafts from the seventeenth to the nineteenth centuries and holds numerous workshops.

Yamabikoya (2-1-55 Imaizumi, Chuo, Fukuoka; tel: 092-753-9402) is an incredible mingei store that focuses on toys and folk crafts from Kyushu. According to the shop, "Behind the many local toys and folk crafts are the lands, cultures, and makers that nurtured each piece."

MIYAGI PREFECTURE

The Akiu Traditional Craft Village (Uehara 54-20, Akiumachi Yumoto, Taihaku, Sendai) is a cluster of craft studios, including a maker of *tansu* wooden chests, a weave and dye studio and an *umoregi zaiku* bogwood craft studio. There are also three kokeshi ateliers.

Sendai's Serizawa Keisuke Art and Craft Museum (1-8-1 Kunimi, Aoba; tel: 022-717-3318) is located inside the Tohoku Fukushi University and has wide array of the work of Keisuke Serizawa, ranging from textiles to furniture.

Tohoku Standard Market in Sendai city (B1F Parco Sendai, 1-2-3 Aoba; tel: 022-797-8852) is a shop with museum-level curation, showcasing a wide range of exquisite folk toys, crafts, books and high level produce from local purveyors from across Japan's northern Tohoku region. The shop features unique shelving and other interior features by wooden furniture makers Ishinomaki Lab and is a delight to peruse.

NAGANO PREFECTURE

The excellent Matsumoto Mingei Museum (1313-1 Satoyamabe, Matsumoto; tel: 0263-33-1569) was established in 1962 and has around six thousand early-twentieth-century items in its inventory, including mingei from across the world. It is housed inside a folk house featuring *namako* earthen walls, characterized by geometric hashed patterns.

The Tatsue Folk Craft Museum (2030-4 Mochizuki, Saku; tel: 0267-53-0234) commemorates the life of educator, activist and mingei advocate Tatsue Kobayashi and is home to his massive folk-craft collection. There are regular craft exhibits and other events.

OKAYAMA PREFECTURE

Kurashiki is a picturesque town on the Kurashiki River, which is flanked with tile-roofed traditional buildings, white-walled residences and weeping willows. The town is home to the Kurashiki Mingei Museum (1-4-11 Chuo; tel:

086-422-1637), Japan's second mingei museum after the one that was established in 1936 in Tokyo. It has an inventory of around ten thousand artifacts inside an eighteenth-century rice granary.

Also not to be missed is the Folk Toy Museum (1-4-16 Chuo, Kurashiki; tel: 086-422-8058) which has around five thousand charming rural toys, displayed rather chaotically on walls and shelves laden with masks, kites and toys.

The nearby town of Imbe is home to one of Japan's six ancient kilns with approximately a hundred shops and ateliers devoted to Bizen ware pottery, made with clay obtained from the Imbe rice fields. The Bizen Ware Museum (1657-7 Imbe, Bizen; tel: 0869-64-1001), next to the train station, and the Bizen Ware Traditional Industry Hall, attached to the train station, both have a vast collection of pottery as well as shops selling it at affordable prices.

OKINAWA

Japan's southernmost semitropical island chain of Okinawa is also a folk craft hub, known for its exquisite dyed fabrics and pottery. The Okinawa Prefectural and Art Museum (3-1-1 Omoromachi, Naha; tel: 098-941-8200) offers an extensive overview of the unique culture and crafts of the Ryukyu Kingdom (as Okinawa used to be known). Pottery lovers can revel in ceramic delights at the pottery co-op Yachimun no Sato (2653-1 Zakimi, Yomitan, Nadagami; tel: 098-958-4468). There are around seventy studios to visit, as well as impressive climbing kilns. While it is a pleasure to visit at any time, the most popular event is the Pottery Festival held on the third weekend of December.

Tsuboya Yachimun Street in Naha is the 330-year-old center for the local *yachimun* pottery and consists of a delightful alleyway of red-tiled artisan studios and shops. The pottery available to buy is mostly tableware, but there are also thousands of shisa, the lion-dog statue that is Okinawa's icon.

Okinawa is also known for glass crafting, which started in the aftermath of World War II, when locals would craft items from Coke and beer bottles discarded by the US military. There are a number of places specializing in glass crafts, including the Ryukyu Glass Village factory (169 Fukuji, Itoman; tel: 098-997-4784); and Glass House in the Forest (478 Biimata, Nago City; tel: 098-054-2121), home to a collective of professional glass artisans. There are also many independent studios across Okinawa.

One of the best-known Okinawan crafts is bingata resist dyeing (see page 116), with its vivid motifs and bold hues. Gusuku Bingata dyeing studio (4 Chome-9-1 Maeda, Urasoe; tel: 098-887-3414) is well loved by overseas tourists.

OSAKA

The Japan Folk Crafts Museum (10-5 Senribanpakukoen, Suita; tel: 06-6877-1971), whose first director was potter Shoji Hamada, exhibits a wide range of crafts including woodwork, pottery and textiles. In addition to its permanent collection, the museum holds special exhibitions every year in spring

Kokeshi are made in hot-spring villages across Japan.

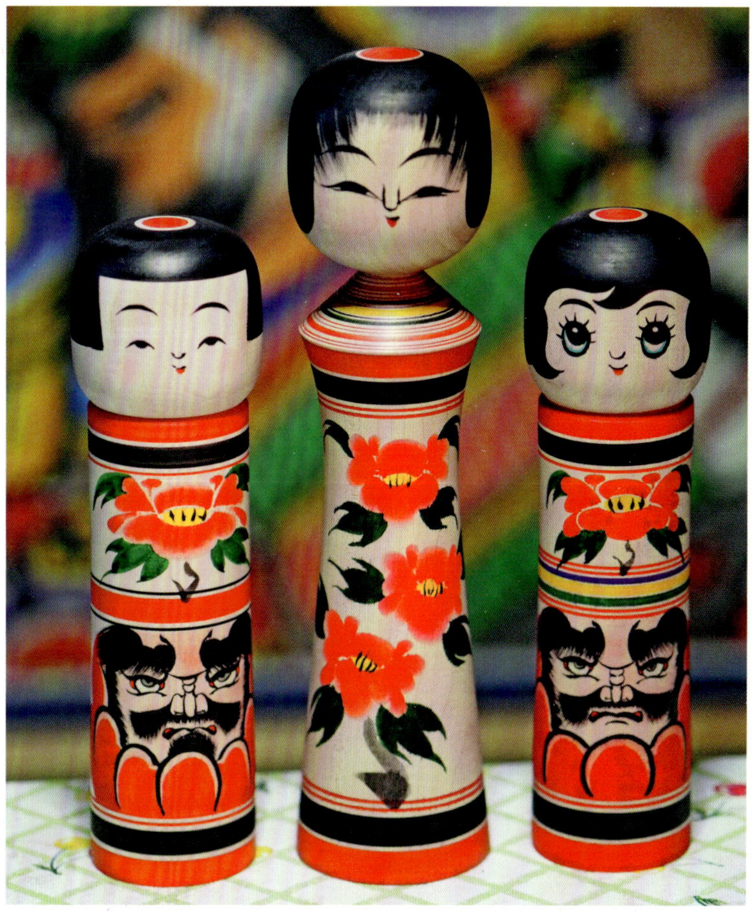

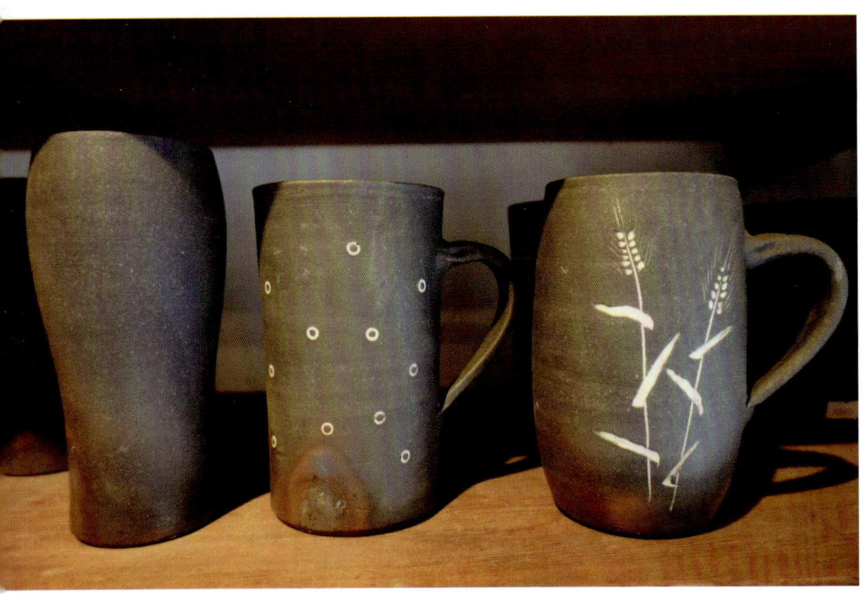

Buying from an artisan studio supports the livelihood of the craftsperson.

and fall. It is located at the site of the 1970 World Expo and was originally one of the pavilions: its aim was to introduce mingei to an international audience. The icon of the site is the Tower of the Sun statue by avant-garde artist Taro Okamoto, standing at 230 feet (70 meters). The piece was inspired by Tohoku folk culture, which Okamoto looked to for a primordial "essence" of Japan.

Located next door to the Folk Crafts Museum is the incredible National Museum of Ethnology (10-1 Senribanpakukoen, Suita; tel: 06-6876-2151). Founded in 1974 and opened to the public in 1977, the museum is a research institute for cultural anthropology and ethnology and houses a prolific collection of over 280,000 artifacts; 70,000 audio visual materials; and 600,000 books. The museum has extensive displays, showcasing crafts, ritual tools, religious and everyday utensils, from Japan and around the world. This museum and the neighboring Folk Crafts Museum will require a full day to explore.

SAITAMA PREFECTURE

Ogawa is the traditional washi paper production hub close to Tokyo, with a paper-making industry that dates back to the eighth century. In 2014, the town received UNESCO Intangible Cultural Heritage Status for preserving the culture of traditional Japanese handmade paper. Kamisuki no Mura (1091 Ogawa, Hiki-gun) is a studio that crafts excellent quality washi paper that they sell at their onsite shop. There are also days where people can take part in paper-making activities.

SHIMANE PREFECTURE

Izumo Folk Craft Museum (628 Shimane, Chiimiyacho, Izumo; tel: 0853-22-6397) is a large folk museum highlighting the folk crafts of Shimane, with exhibits relating to ceramics, *aizome* indigo dyeing, cotton *kasuri* dyeing and weaving, woodwork, and many others. The gates of the museum were built by the master carpenter of the Izumo Taisha Shrine.

The Abe Eishiro Museum (1754 Higashi Iwazaka, Yakumo; tel: 0852-54-1745) was founded in 1983 to commemorate Eishiro Abe, who worked to preserve traditional washi paper-making techniques. This region of Japan was noted for its production of washi paper in the Edo period. There are numerous displays related to paper-making history as well as ceramics and printworks by members of the Mingei Movement such as Bernard Leach and Shiko Munakata.

SHIZUOKA PREFECTURE

Keisuke Serizawa (1895–1984) is one of the central figures of the Mingei Movement, a textile designer designated a Living National Treasure for his *katazome* stencil-dyeing technique. His work is heavily influenced by dyeing techniques used in Okinawa, where he spent time studying. His designs include textiles, paper, and calendar prints as well as book covers. The excellent Shizuoka City Serizawa Keisuke Art Museum (5-10-5 Toro, Suruga-ku, Shizuoka; tel: 054-282-5522) features architecture by Seiichi Shirai (1905–1983) and is located inside Toro Park which is an archeological site from the Yayoi period (c. 300 BCE–c. 250 CE).

TOCHIGI PREFECTURE

The small pottery town of Mashiko was catapulted to fame as a mingei mecca due to the attention its simple pottery with a rural aesthetic received from the Mingei Movement founders. Potter Shoji Hamada established an atelier there which is now the Shoji Hamada Memorial Mashiko Sankokan Museum (3388 Mashiko, Haga; tel: 0285-72-5300). The town has dozens of ceramics shops, and the Mashiko Museum of Ceramic Art (3021

Mashiko, Haga; tel: 0285-72-7555). There are also two major ceramics festivals held in May and November. In addition to pottery-related attractions is the shop Higeta Indigo Dye Studio (1 Jonaizaka, Mashiko, Haga) where vats of blue dye are on display.

Michinoku Mingeiten (130-1 Yumoto; tel: 0287-76-2337), in the town of Nasu, is a folk-craft store housed inside a two-hundred-year-old traditional house. It stocks a wide array of folk toys and crafts such as masks, kites and bamboo items.

The Taima Cannabis Museum (1-5 Takakoku, Nasu; tel: 0287-62-8093) is an excellent small museum and research facility, devoted to traditional Japanese cannabis hemp. Founded in 2001 by cannabis rights activist Junichi Takayasu, the museum archives and displays everything from hemp fibers and thread, to fabrics and other hemp items and artifacts. These vary from traditional items used in Shinto purification rites to contemporary fashion accessories. The museum also houses numerous publications about cannabis hemp, including manga where cannabis motifs are used incidentally. The curators are extremely helpful and there are English explanations on the walls.

TOKYO

The Japan Folk Crafts Museum (4-3-33 Komaba, Meguro-ku; tel: 03-3467-4527) was established and designed by the founder of the Mingei Movement, Soetsu Yanagi in 1936. It took ten years to build and the building itself incorporates elements of folk architecture such as a *nagayamon* farmhouse gate brought from Tochigi, and designated as an Important Cultural Property of Tokyo.

The Yuasa Memorial Museum (3-10-2 Osawa, Mitaka; tel: 0422-33-3340) is inside the International Christian University and was established in 1982. It commemorates Dr. Hachiro Yuasa, the first president of the university and features many artifacts from the university collection. The university also publish their own mingei-related books.

Takumi (2-22-17 Zoshigaya, Toshima-ku; tel: 03-6907-7715) is the Tokyo branch of the Tottori folk art store of the same name (see page 159). It is an important hub for folk-craft distribution and sells a wide range of rural mingei (4-2-8 Ginza, Chuo-ku; tel: 03-3571-2017).

Bingoya (10-6 Wakamatsu, Shinjuku-ku; tel: 03-3202-8778) is one of the best mingei shops in Japan, a five-story emporium with a formidable array of craft from across the country.

Tabineko Zakkaten (2-22-17 Zoshigaya, Toshima-ku: tel; 03-6907-7715) is a cute and charming store selling kokeshi and other crafts and toys.

BEAMS (B1F–5F, 3-32-6 Shinjuku; tel: 03 5368 7300) is a fashionable store that mostly

The Taima Cannabis Museum in Tochigi Prefecture.

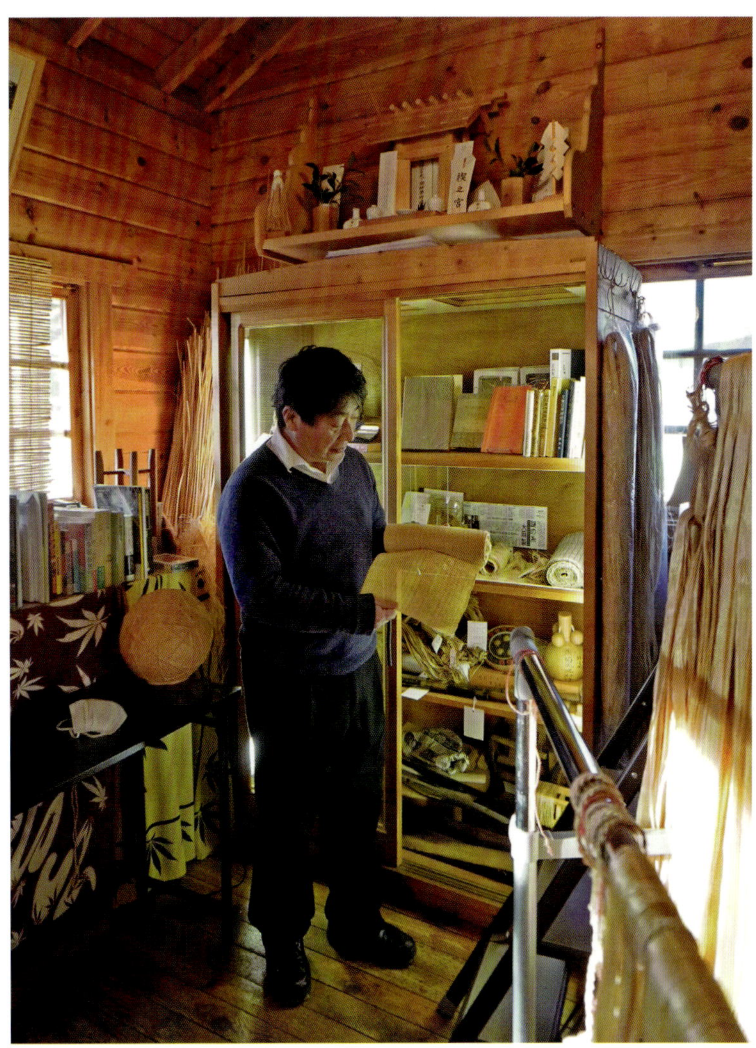

offers casual street fashion for a savvy young clientele, but also sells folk items from craft hubs across Japan. They have two brands, Tokyo Culturart which focuses on artisan-made products that have a street-culture sensibility, and fennica which deals with classic folk craft. This Shinjuku branch of BEAMS has five-stories and a museum.

Mogi Folk Art (3-45-12 Koenji-minami, Suginami-ku; tel: 080-8058-1761) is a shop run by Terry Ellis (see page 26) selling a finely curated array of gorgeous crafts from across Japan.

TonBi Books (204 Fukaiso, 3-49-14 Sumida-ku; tel: 080-4198-0545) sells both books and and a wide array of folk craft, selected by the author of this book. Located in a traditional Tokyo *nagaya* row house, it often holds folk toy pop-up events, such as exhibitions of kokeshi dolls.

TOTTORI PREFECTURE

The Tottori Folk Crafts Museum (651 Sakaemachi, Tottori; tel: 0857-26-2367) was established by local doctor Shoya Yoshida, who promoted folk art in the region and was one of the core members of the Mingei Movement. He also worked directly with artisans, motivating them to make contemporary mingei combining traditional techniques with modern sensibilities. The museum has around five thousand items in its collection. The Takumi Folk Crafts Shop next door is also notable in that it was established in 1932, making it the first shop in Japan to specialize in folk crafts and art.

TOYAMA

The Toyama Folk Craft Village (56-1 Anyobo; tel: 076-433-4109) sits on the bucolic Toyama Plain and features a number of small museums housed in traditional folk dwellings, such as *gassho-zukuri* farmhouses with steeply thatched roofs. The museums include the Folk Art Museum, the Thatched Roof Folk Art Museum, the Museum of Ceramic Art, the Museum of Folklore, the Museum of Medicine Peddlers, the Museum of Archeology as well as a store, the Toyama Clay Doll Studio. Next to the village is the Chokenji Temple with 500 *rakan* Buddhist guardian statues.

Visiting festivals, like the Chagu Chagu Umakko Festival in Iwate Prefecture, is a great way to experience folk crafts.

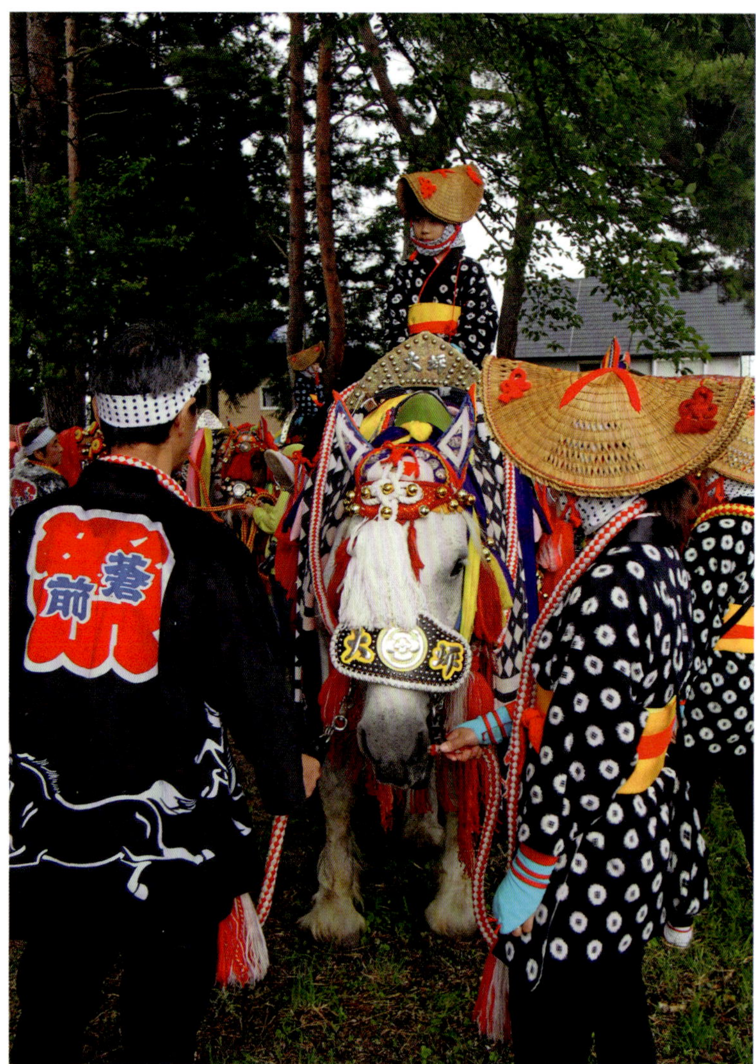

ACKNOWLEDGMENTS

Special thanks to my parents and family. My editor Cathy Layne, and the Tuttle crew for taking on this project. Thank you to my former professor Kim Brandt at Columbia University and the anthropology department at CUHK. Big thank you to everyone who has worked with me, commissioned or supported my mingei-related projects including Ayako Uchino at Sway Gallery London, Sway Gallery Stockholm and Paris, Terry Ellis at Mogi, Emil Pacha Valencia at *Tempura* magazine, Roisin Inglesby at the William Morris Museum, Barbara at Libreria Rotondi, Japan Foundation Rome and Los Angeles, Peter Ryan at AVGVST and Daiwa Foundation London and Kyobashi Edo Grand, the *Japan Times* newspaper, Kyoto Journal, Lonely Planet Tokyo Weekender and Prestel Publishing. Huge thanks to the Taima Cannabis Museum for their help, and to artisans I interviewed multiple times over ten years including Yasuo Okazaki, Naomi Umeki, Yasuhiro Koyama, and the folks at Chugai Toen. Big thanks to photographers Mariella Kai and Julian Krakowiak for joining some of my mingei adventures.

PHOTO CREDITS

Page 23 top, page 54, Julian Krakowiak. Page 40 top right, Met Museum, New York. Page 42 top right and bottom left, Ronin de Goede. Page 64, page 77, Mariella Kai. Page 70 top, page 72 top and bottom left, Japan Cannabis Museum. Page 74, courtesy Ayumu Haitani. Page 81 bottom left, courtesy Hodsdon Kokeshi. Page 88 bottom, Jason Haidar. Page 100, Jerfareza Daviano. Page 108, Antonio Rull.

Dreamstime: page 15; page 36 right; page 94, top left and second from left, bottom; page 95; page 98 top left; page 99.

Pixta: page 49 top center, page 49 bottom; page 57; page 70 bottom; page 71; page 72 bottom right; page 73; page 83; page 87; page 93 top; page 98 bottom; page 150.

Shutterstock: Cover; page 19 right; page 25, top and center; page 36 left; page 37; page 47 bottom right; page 49 top left; page 50, bottom right; page 51; page 52; page 53 top right; page 59; page 62; page 63 top right; page 65 bottom; page 79 bottom; page 93 top right, bottom; page 94, second from right; page 102 bottom right; page 104; page 106 top; page 107; back endpaper.

Wikimedia Commons: page 10; page 11; page 12; page 13; page 14; page 17; page 18; page 19, left; page 25 bottom; page 42, bottom left; page 75, top right; page 91 top left; page 91 top right; page 96 bottom; page 97; page 99 top right; page 106 bottom.

Wikipedia: page 91 top center; page 96 top right.

Books to Span the East and West

Tuttle Publishing was founded in 1832 in the small New England town of Rutland, Vermont [USA]. Our core values remain as strong today as they were then—to publish best-in-class books which bring people together one page at a time. In 1948, we established a publishing outpost in Japan—and Tuttle is now a leader in publishing English-language books about the arts, languages and cultures of Asia. The world has become a much smaller place today and Asia's economic and cultural influence has grown. Yet the need for meaningful dialogue and information about this diverse region has never been greater. Over the past seven decades, Tuttle has published thousands of books on subjects ranging from martial arts and paper crafts to language learning and literature—and our talented authors, illustrators, designers and photographers have won many prestigious awards. We welcome you to explore the wealth of information available on Asia at **www.tuttlepublishing.com.**

Published by Tuttle Publishing, an imprint of Periplus Editions (HK) Ltd.

www.tuttlepublishing.com

ISBN 978-4-8053-1731-0

Distributed by:
North America, Latin America & Europe
Tuttle Publishing
364 Innovation Drive
North Clarendon; VT 05759-9436 U.S.A.
Tel: (802) 773-8930; Fax: (802) 773-6993
info@tuttlepublishing.com; www.tuttlepublishing.com

Japan
Tuttle Publishing
Yaekari Building 3rd Floor
5-4-12 Osaki Shinagawa-ku; Tokyo 141 0032
Tel: (81) 3 5437-0171; Fax: (81) 3 5437-0755
sales@tuttle.co.jp; www.tuttle.co.jp

Asia Pacific
Berkeley Books Pte. Ltd.
3 Kallang Sector, #04-01; Singapore 349278
Tel: (65) 6741-2178; Fax: (65) 6741-2179
inquiries@periplus.com.sg; www.tuttlepublishing.com

Printed in China 2404CM

28 27 26 25 24 10 9 8 7 6 5 4 3 2 1

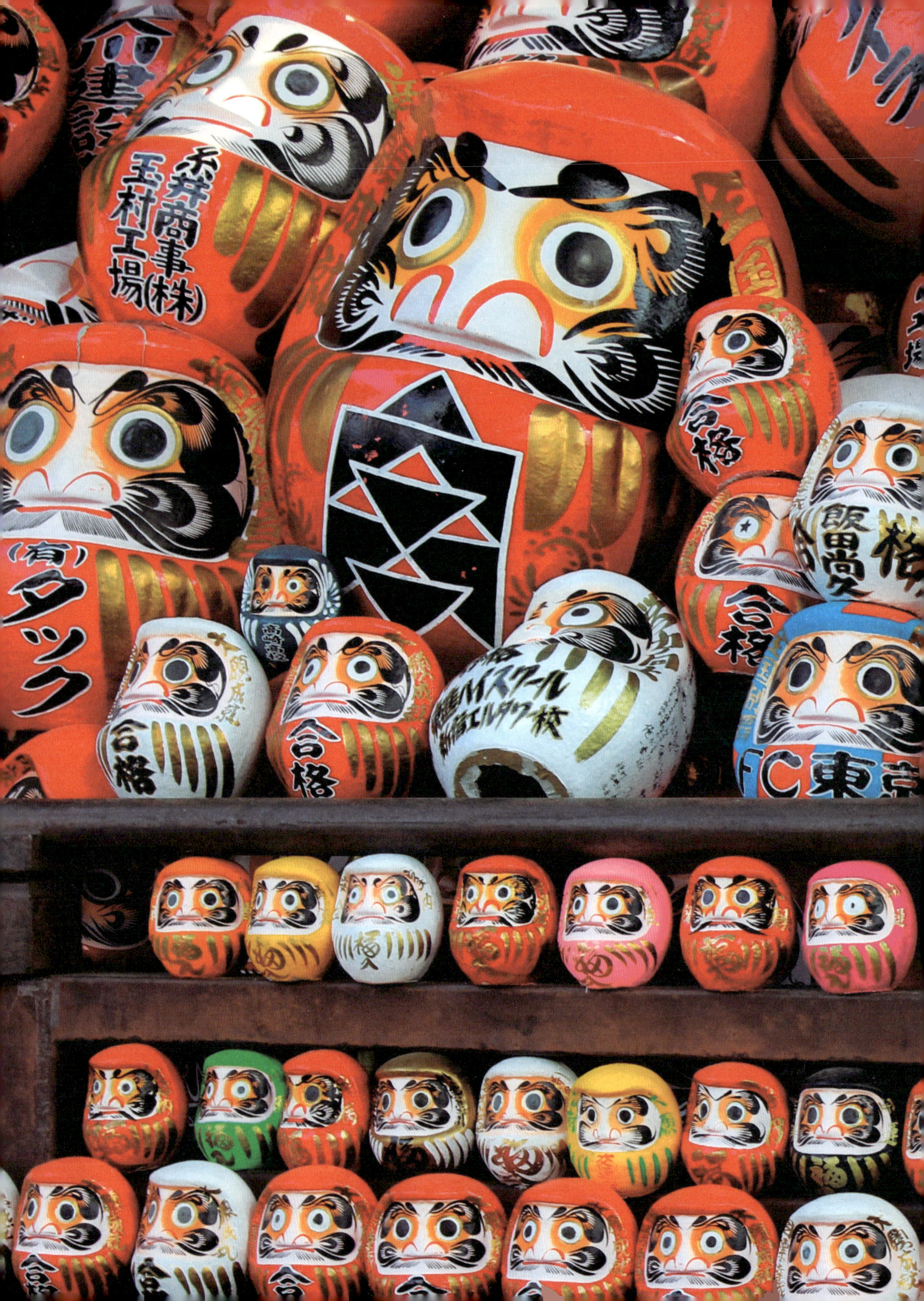
玉村工場
(有)
タック
合格
合格
合格
合格
合格